A Demon's Quest
The Beginning of the End
Volume II

Charles Carfagno Jr.

DEDICATION

To my Mother and Friends.

CONTENTS

CHAPTER 1: REVENGE FOR THE FALLEN (PART I)

The sound of something approaching woke the mighty Konafar. He quickly got up, holding Carnage in his left hand, and hid behind a large tree. He knew that waking his companions would've slowed him down and given away an opportunity to surprise whatever was approaching. He remained relaxed and poised as he peered around the tree, then his eyes widened in delight when he saw Jacko and Delisar escorting several women into the camp.

He loved scaring people, so he darted over, picked up the boarman's head, and returned to his tree, where he waited until they were only a few feet away before tossing the decapitated head in front of them. The head bounced a few times and startled everyone while causing some of the women to gasp in horror.

"Jacko, there's a little gift for you. I think they were the group that was tracking you." Konafar laughed loudly and came out from behind the tree, leering at the women. "Are the women for me?" he said and walked over.

The commotion woke Woo and Mao, who got to their feet. Jacko and Delisar led the women closer to the fire.

"Did you find your friend?" Woo asked.

Jacko shook his head.

Mao noticed the women shaking from the cold and invited them to sit and get warm by the fire. He added more wood to it.

"After they rest for a while, I'll take them back to the town of Wistful. You continue toward Mirkin," Delisar announced.

"How will you find us?" Woo asked.

"I am a tracker and, besides that, the big fellow won't be hard to spot."

"You didn't see me when you entered the camp, did you?" Konafar sneered.

"You mean behind the tree over there, holding your blade with your left hand."

Jacko and Woo chuckled.

"Anyway, I need to buy more arrows and get supplies."

Mao gave the women food and drink, while Delisar and Jacko told them what was happening in Redden. After hearing this, Konafar became enraged and wanted to go back in and deal with the situation. Jacko could see it in his eyes and hear it in his tone that he was serious.

"We would need an army to take the town back," Jacko stated.

"Or some brave men," Konafar replied. "Now tell me again how you made it to the inn."

By the time they finished, the women were warm, fed, and ready to depart. Delisar told the others to leave him signs along the way, so that he could track them. They wished him luck and watched him leave with the women. Konafar stared into the dancing flames, and Woo could tell what he was thinking.

"You need to do this, don't you?"

Konafar nodded and spoke without even looking at him. "I've stayed there before and those people don't deserve this. I have always lived by a code of ethics to assist the needy, and now this is my opportunity to help. I didn't realize how dire the situation was, and I am pained at my ignorance."

"But you might die."

"Maybe, but if I can save the rest of those prisoners, it would be worth it." Konafar stared at Jacko. "Jacko, I'm sorry that I can't come along on your journey."

Jacko looked over at his classmates and said, "Will Master understand if we help him?" Both men nodded. "Then we'd like to join you, Konafar."

Konafar's eyes lit up. "You are brave men indeed, and I like that."

"Do you have a plan?" Mao asked.

"My Order is a few days away. I'm sure my brothers will join me and together we'll make a difference."

"What about Delisar, how will he find us?"

Konafar got up, walked over to a tree, and left a mark with his blade pointing in the direction they would be going. "He'll know now."

Delisar succeeded in delivering the women to town.

After buying two scores of arrows, he went straight to the Magistrate's house to speak with him. At first, the guards denied him access until he pleaded his case and slipped them some gold. He was led to a lavish-looking room, in the far back of the mansion, where he waited for almost an hour before a skinny, middle-aged man entered the room through the double doors. He was still wearing his nightly robes, and his gray hair was all messy. Delisar studied the man as he walked around the desk and sat down directly in front of him, while the Magistrate's guards took up position nearby.

The Magistrate relaxed his posture and spoke. "Delisar, is it? What can I do for you?"

"Do you know what's happening in Redden?"

"I heard they were overrun by a large army, why?"

"Do you know there are still survivors, and they are being tortured and being used to breed?"

"No."

Delisar could tell from his tone and expression that he didn't really care. "Are you going to do anything?"

"There are no plans and, frankly, I care little for those people. If they weren't prepared for an invasion then they deserve whatever happened to them."

"Why so cold?" Delisar demanded.

The Magistrate leaned back in his chair. "Do you live here in Wistful?"

Delisar shook his head no and realized where this conversation was going.

"I'm not sure how you gained an audience with me," the Magistrate looked over at his men in disgust, "so I think that it might be in your best interest to leave."

"Leave, why?"

"Yes, fool, leave. You have no right to be in my presence or have a say about what I should be doing. Guards, remove him from my sight."

The guards closed in.

"Wait a second," Delisar said as he was seized by the guards. "For the love of God, aid those people," he pleaded.

"Remove him."

They pulled him to his feet, while the Magistrate waved his hand as if shooing away an annoying little bug.

"I HOPE YOU ROT," Delisar yelled over his shoulder.

The lead guard ordered the others to stop. "Disrespectful little bastard." He shook his head, curled his fist, and punched Delisar in the stomach hard enough to buckle his knees. Delisar grunted from the blow. "Get him out of here."

The guards dragged him out of the building and threw him down onto the cobblestone street. More guards closed in with weapons drawn and bows notched, warning that any further action would result in his death. Delisar got up, rubbing his stomach. He spat on the ground in disgust and left.

As he walked through the streets, looking at the happy people going about their day, he couldn't figure out why the Magistrate, or anyone else for that matter, wouldn't help Redden. Once or twice, he thought about saying something or even asking them for help but decided against it, because he didn't want to go to jail. He left the town and began his trek toward Mirkin.

Delisar went to the west and, by mid-afternoon, he was unable to find any signs of their passing. He knew something was amiss because there was no way Konafar wouldn't leave a sign, so he decided to backtrack to where he departed from them the night before.

As suspected, the camp was deserted and the campfire had been out since early morning. He searched the area and stumbled upon a tree with two letters SB. *Why would they go to Stonybrook?* He thought, then it dawned on him that Konafar's Order was from there. It still didn't explain why they decided to go there instead of Mirkin. His answer would have to wait until tomorrow because dusk was approaching.

He laid warning traps around the area and built a fire to keep warm. By the time he was through, snow began falling. After eating a quick meal, he wrapped himself in a sheepskin blanket and went to sleep.

Konafar, Jacko, Woo, and Mao arrived in the town of Stonybrook shortly after nightfall. As they walked through the snow-covered streets, the guards nodded toward Konafar's direction, which meant, they knew and respected him.

"Do you know them?" Jacko asked a few minutes later.

"Most of them. I was one of them for many years before taking up my current profession."

"Which is?" Mao asked, beating Jacko to the same question.

"Many things," said Konafar. "I can be a mercenary and represent a certain faction, a bounty hunter tracking down the most dangerous criminals, or even a killer for hire. You see, my Order provides skills that allow me to survive and adapt in this harsh world."

"Very impressive," Woo said. "Your Order is similar to ours."

"How so? Are your students trained to be killers for hire?"

"Not exactly. What I meant was that we learn different skills and techniques."

"I don't see how they're the same but okay." Konafar had to refrain from laughing.

They walked on in silence down several streets and crossed over many others until they arrived at a stone building.

The two-story structure was at least thirty feet wide, had six long windows on the top floor with lit white candles on each of the sills. Trees lined the walkway leading up to the red double doors.

Konafar walked up to the entrance and knocked repeatedly on the door until it was opened by a tall, muscular fellow with a dark brown beard and long, braided hair down his back. He wore chainmail and carried an iniquitous-looking two-headed ax. After seeing Konafar, he smiled.

"Welcome, my friend. It's been a while." They clasped forearms in a welcoming manner. "Are these new recruits?" the man asked, looking past Konafar and directly at the others.

"Are you kidding? Look at them, they're too scrawny, don't you think?" Both men bellowed together.

When they finally stopped laughing, Konafar introduced his comrade as Marik. Marik nodded and Jacko, Mao, and Woo introduced themselves and were led into the building.

Marik walked them down a dimly lit corridor, past many rooms with different items of warfare mounted above the entranceways. There were short swords, daggers, rapiers, spears, and axes. Konafar explained that this was the area for the lower-ranking students and the Order's first line of defense if they ever had a security breach. He also said their motto was simple. If you were inexperienced, or fairly new to the school, then you were the first to die in battle. He chuckled when he saw Mao's expression.

Marik waited until his friend finished having fun before escorting them through a set of doors and down a long hallway. This led them to a massive training area.

Scattered about the room were wooden dummies, deep sand beds, water pools, big rocks of different shapes and sizes, and thick tree trunks planted upright. Marik explained the sand and water pits were used to spar in, because it helped develop power and balance.

Toward the back of the room were four very tall lizardmen holding ten-foot spears. Each wore leather armor on their upper torso, steel shin guards on their legs, and metal helmets that barely covered their heads. Like their aquatic cousins, they had scaly, green and brown skin, and long snouts and tails. However, they were much more intelligent and preferred to walk upright and fight hand-to-hand.

"Lizardmen?" Woo said surprisingly.

"That they are," Marik said.

"How is this possible?" said Mao. "Their kind is too unpredictable."

"I heard of them interacting with some of the other races but never humans," Jacko added.

"About a year ago," Konafar began, "some of our men were exploring the area west of here and stumbled into their domain. The lizardmen didn't take too kindly to our intrusion and attacked. When all was said and done, my kinsmen prevailed and returned to the Order and told our leader Lord Rygare what had happened. Lord Rygare admired their fighting skills and bravery and charged some of our finest warriors to go back into their territory to persuade their king to have an audience with him."

"Why would he do that?" Mao asked.

"Because he's always looking for recruits and saw an opportunity to strengthen our Order and add some new blood, even if it's the cold-blooded kind," Konafar chuckled.

"Konafar, if they are cold-blooded, then how do they function in this region?" Woo asked.

"Good question. It's simple really. They adapt to their surrounding and are able to raise or lower their body temperature."

"So what happened next?" Jacko asked after there was a long

pause.

"We knew it would be hard to get an audience with their king, so my brothers needed to be careful, because they thought we were hostile. Lucky for us, they respect bravery and skills, and after we displayed both, we were granted a meeting. After much negotiating, their king accepted our offer to have a council with our most senior members. The meeting took place at a neutral location, and both parties decided to send forth their toughest warriors and have them fight. The king agreed, if our man defeated theirs, then he'd submit some of their people into our Order. If not…" he paused, "on second thought, you don't want to know."

"Why not?" Mao asked.

"I don't think your stomach can handle it."

"I guess your man won?" Jacko asked.

"He did but would never fight again due to the wounds he suffered."

"Did he kill the lizardman?" Woo asked.

"No. He spared his life, because he knew that it would serve a greater cause if he did. You see, we are a just and thinking Order, not a bunch of hacks."

"Was it worth the risk?" Woo asked.

The big man smiled and said, "Anyone who joins this Order knows the risks and agrees to give up their lives if necessary. They also know that in order for our Order to survive, we have to grow and invite certain races into the fold."

"There will be a great war someday," Marik began, "and we need to be ready if that happens, so that we can rise up and lead the people."

"How do you know that?" Jacko asked.

"Just call it a hunch."

"Was the language barrier difficult to overcome?" Woo asked Konafar.

"At first it was, but we used a series of hand signals to convey all of our messages."

"They're about to begin sparring again," Marik said.

They turned their attention to watch them.

The lizardmen circled each other and suddenly attacked. The awe-inspiring display was vicious with each causing wounds so deep that it would kill an average man. It finally ended when one of the lizardmen lost an arm after a spearhead ripped through his armor, through bone and muscle, and ripped the limb away from his shoulder.

The other lizardmen were assisting the injured warrior when Konafar called one of them by name. The lizardman on the left turned in his direction, nodded its long snout in recognition, and walked over. The lizardman was at least seven feet tall, well built, and looked incredibly strong.

His red eyes appeared to glow whenever the light reflected off of them.

"Konafar, it'sss good to sssee you," the creature said, stopping a few feet away.

"Aye, and you too, my friend. Thessor, how's your kinsman?"

He looked at his wounded companion, then back again. "He livesss." Thessor's forked tongue darted in and out of his mouth after a few spoken words.

"I might need your services." He waited for the lizard to nod. "There's a town nearby that fell a while back, and we might intervene and save some of the prisoners."

"My peoplesss services are always ready."

"Good, I'll stop by after we're finished with our meeting."

Konafar led his guests through a door at the far end of the room and followed the narrow corridor until they came to a set of stairs leading upward. Several flights later, they walked down another long corridor until they entered a rectangular room.

A lone figure dressed in black, with red hair and a full beard, sat at a table writing something on a piece of parchment.

As they were walking toward him, Jacko looked around at the paintings adorning the walls. He was in awe over the incredible colors and the level of detail each picture had. Once they were seated, Konafar introduced his companions.

"Lord Tolar, this is Woo, Mao, and Jacko."

Tolar stopped writing and looked up. "Welcome to the Order of the Dragon. Can I get you something to eat or drink?"

The guests looked at one another before nodding. Lord Tolar clapped his hands and three servants entered.

"Food and ale for our guests," he said, and they left. "Now since that's out of the way, Konafar, what brings you back here? I thought you were on a pilgrimage to see how many wenches you could bed. Did you finish that quest already?"

Konafar chuckled. "Not yet, my lord. I only made it through half of the countryside."

Both men laughed together, bringing smiles to everyone's faces except for Jacko.

"Lord Tolar, there's a serious issue in Redden," Jacko interrupted. The lord's smile faded, and he looked directly at Jacko. "I'm not sure if you're aware, the town had fallen a few months back, and they are torturing the prisoners and using the females to breed."

"Are you sure of this?"

"I saw it firsthand when I went inside looking for my friend."

"Konafar, is that true?"

"I'm afraid it is."

"Lord Tolar, we have to do something," Mao added.

"I agree. These kinds of atrocities can't go on." Tolar paused when the servants ushered in food, ale, and wine.

After they placed it on the table, they were instructed to fetch the map of Redden from their vaults and leave it on the table in the war room.

During their meal, Jacko informed him about the creatures that occupied the town, how he and Delisar infiltrated the town through an underground tunnel, but also that he thought it might have been compromised after they fled. Lord Tolar listened intently without saying a word. By the time Jacko was finished, he had a good idea of what he needed to do but kept it to himself.

When the meal was done, they left the room through a hidden door on their left, down several flights of stairs, until they arrived in front of a massive solid oak door. The two armed guards opened the door and stepped aside.

The war room was big, to say the least. Bracketed torches lined the walls. A wooden chandelier hung above a large, heavy oak table, which could easily accommodate twenty men. Next to the table was a rolling cart with small model buildings and little figurines.

As they drew closer to the table, Jacko recognized the map from his stay in Redden. The cloth diagram stretched the length and was very detailed; from the streets, to the shops and inns, and finally the Magistrate's house.

After they took up position, Konafar walked over to a smaller table on their right, which had goblets filled with wine, and handed one to each of them. Tolar took a long swig and prompted Jacko to tell his tale again. This time, he was to point to each of the locations he'd visited. When he finished, Tolar took another gulp and looked at everyone present and said, "Since the enemy discovered your exit point, then you're probably right in assuming that you can't re-enter the same way again." He rubbed his bearded chin, contemplating.

"We can't enter through the gates either," Woo added.

"You mentioned there are many tunnels, so I suggest you enter through one of the other doors," Tolar said.

"Delisar said they lead to different parts of the town, but he only had the one key," Jacko said.

"If you hire a master thief, then you won't have to worry about the keys. I also think you'll need to create some kind of diversion once you get in. You've already breeched their defensives, so I'm sure they'll step up the patrols in case it happens again."

"We'll need a big one," Woo said.

"Or create several smaller ones," Mao interjected.

"Since we don't have a large army, then Mao's idea is probably the best one," Lord Tolar said.

"How many of our brothers can you spare for this mission?" Konafar asked.

"Right now, there are only about twenty in the school, ten of which must stay here to protect and deal with any situation that might arise. You should go talk to Thessor and find out what he can offer."

"I already said something to him, and he's agreed to help. Do you need me here?"

"No. I'm just going to go over some general things with them."

"I'll go see Thessor now."

When he was out of the room, Lord Tolar looked at the others and said, "He's a good and brave man."

"We can tell," Woo said, speaking for the group.

"Do you think we have a chance to rescue more people?" Mao asked.

"My Order is built for these types of missions, and as long as you stick to the plan, you'll be fine. Konafar will see to it."

They continued talking about basic stuff and the art of warfare until the big man returned an hour later with a broad smile upon his face.

"Well?" Lord Tolar asked as soon as he walked in.

"He's on his way and will return tomorrow." His grin widened.

"Why are you smiling so much?"

"He thinks he'll bring back at least thirty warriors."

"Good, very good."

They spent the next few hours fine-tuning their plan, which was to be carried out as soon as Thessor returned.

Delisar awoke at dawn and was relieved to find that everything was exactly as it was from the night before; the traps were in place, and the fire still burned. He rose, stretched his cramped muscles, doused the fire, and began walking toward Stonybrook.

He preferred traveling off the main road to avoid unnecessary travelers, and, for the most part, it was a good idea until around midday when he detected something tracking him. Whatever it was stayed far enough away and out of sight, which meant it was an intelligent predator. Delisar let the game of cat and mouse go on for another half mile when he decided to run forward thirty yards, make a quick break toward the left until he crossed the main road, then dart back another ten yards to hide inside a dense cluster of bushes. He inched his notched bow through the bushes and watched the road ahead. The forest abruptly went still, and he remained motionless, knowing that whatever was tracking him was about to show itself.

A few minutes later, a dark green head poked its way out of the shrubbery. The scaly, round face and narrow eyes looked right, then left, and began flicking its forked tongue out of its mouth as if tasting the air for its prey.

Delisar was about to release an arrow when the creature suddenly looked directly at him, and they locked gazes, freezing him where he crouched. The beast's eyes pulsated, changed different colors, and brightened, causing Delisar to cower in fear but never diverting his eyes. The beast used its hypnotic weapon for a few more minutes before disengaging its stare and ducking back into the woods.

The trepidation lasted for a few more minutes. After it passed, Delisar slowly backed out of his hiding place and cautiously continued on. He stayed closer to the road and every time riders approached, he hid until they passed, which was strange because he never avoided anything, be it man or beast. Something changed after the encounter with the creature, but he couldn't put his finger on it.

Around midday, Delisar stopped to rest on a fallen tree. He'd just taken out his waterskin when fear overwhelmed him again. It happened so incredibly fast that he got up, grabbed his bow, and crouched down behind a nearby large tree while gripping his weapon with both hands. He was shivering and cowering uncontrollably until he regained enough courage to peer around the tree. He was somewhat relieved to find the forest instead of the creature staring back at him. He sat behind the tree until the fear eventually passed, but then it was replaced with something far worse: nervousness, insecurity, and doubt about his fighting skills. For the first time since he was a child, he was really afraid. Delisar's new feelings caused him to spend the next four hours running and hiding around the area until he became hopelessly lost. By the time the evening hours were ushered in, he felt unskilled, useless, scared, alone, and wished that someone else was with him, so that they could protect him from harm. With the world closing in on him, he found some thick bushes to hide in. With all sense of reasoning gone, he began to cry uncontrollably until fatigue finally overtook him in the late hours of the night and he passed out.

Somewhere deep in the forest, the creature, who changed Delisar, continued searching for him.

Jacko, Konafar, Woo, and Mao met Lord Rygare and Lord Tolar for the early morning meal and discussed the tactical plan once again. *It was simple,* Jacko thought. However, it would require impeccable timing for it to be successful. During the conversation, Jacko tuned out theirs and began wondering who would live and who would die over the next day or two, surely he didn't want to think about it, but he couldn't avoid it either. He also considered if what they were doing was the right thing to do. Could he live with the guilt of leaving helpless people to their deaths? If they succeeded, would he be remembered for doing something great? What if he died and he was forgotten? To live his entire life and it was all for nothing. His thoughts and the conversation were interrupted when the door opened and Thessor walked in.

"Welcome," Lord Rygare said and stood up to greet the lizardman.

"We're prepared and ssset," he replied.

"How many brave warriors?"

"Wesss have twenty ssstrong."

Lord Rygare smiled and said, "Will you be joining us? We have plenty of food." The lizardman nodded, sat down, grabbed one of the roasted fowl carcasses, and began devouring every part of it, from the meat to the tendons and, finally, the bones, as his jaw crunched them into pieces. The loud sound reminded Jacko of someone's arm or leg being snapped in half. Thessor was informed of their plans, in between chomps, and after he finished eating everyone rose and said their goodbyes.

The morning air was sweet and crisp as they stepped out of the building. The sky was clear and the snow from the night before was all but gone.

"Where are your people?" Konafar asked Thessor.

"Theysss waitsss over there," he said, pointing to the outskirts of the town.

Just then, another warrior from Konafar's Order came around from the back of the school and approached the group. He said the rest of the men were getting ready and would be down shortly. Konafar introduced him as Tonles the Mighty, and the first thing you noticed about him was that he was bigger than Konafar, not in height but in girth. He had a barrel chest, thick legs, and arms so muscular they looked like he could rip your head off with a simple tug. His green eyes were slightly slanted, clearly indicating that he was not from around these parts. His dirty blonde hair was braided down his back, and his beard was long, but well groomed. The chainmail he donned was black and slightly rusted and in need of some minor repairs, given that some of the links were separated. The two-headed axe he carried was nasty looking and the round shield draped across his back showed signs of disrepair just like his armor. He was, in a sense, the perfect example of how all true fighters should look and carry themselves.

Jacko gazed at the man and could only imagine what damage he could bestow upon an enemy if provoked.

While they were waiting, Tonles proudly held aloft his deadly weapon and introduced it as the Ripper. Everyone present immediately knew why it was given that name when they saw the jagged edges purposely etched along the blades and the large six-inch spike on top. The warrior then gave his insight into, what he called, the invasion of the town, and what they should do to rescue the townspeople.

His tactical angle was very helpful, Jacko thought.

A short time later, the rest of the men joined the group. Each carried modified weapons, which looked very deadly in their own right, and wore the same armor: black chainmail shirts with thick leather fitted over the top, a steel helmet with a nose guard, and brown leather leggings with boots to match. It was apparent to everyone outside of the Order that you needed to have a dangerous look about you in order to fit in.

The new arrivals introduced themselves. First, there was a young warrior named Ponduit; he was tall—like Konafar but not as muscular—clean-shaven, and kept his long brown hair neatly tied in a ponytail. His weapon of choice was a two-handed, single-headed axe he called Whisper. The weapon got its name after slicing someone's head off, causing the victim's blood to make a whispering sound as it sprayed into the wind.

A husky warrior, with brown hair, that went by the name Krol was next. He proudly swung his War Hammer named Masher in a display of power and said the weapon was named after he hit a short person in the head and crushed his skull into his neck.

He was followed by a muscular fighter with thick, wavy hair named Runit. He introduced his short sword named Vore and said he did so after his son was murdered a few years ago. The men from the Order of the Dragon all stopped what they were doing and bowed their heads in honor of his son.

After they were done paying their respects, a rough-looking man introduced himself as Lud, followed by his long sword named Disemboweled. His broad smile and the way he admired the weapon said it all.

A short, stocky warrior, with blond hair, named Erantel pushed his friend aside and introduced his spear called Reclamation to the group. The steel spear was six feet long with a jagged spearhead on one end and a thick metal cover on the other.

A fighter, introduced as Fleck, by his friend Lud, unsheathed his rapier named Enlightenment and a two-foot main-gauche he called Fate. He said that if people weren't enlightened by his rapier, then they were sure to feel the cold steel of Fate. Konafar laughed.

A tall man named Kildred stepped to the front and introduced his one-handed spiked flail as Equalizer. Awret followed him. He was a bald, mean-looking warrior with a six-foot glaive called Authority. The final two fighters stepped to the front at the same time. The one with the gray short-cropped hair was introduced as Nion, and the weapon he wielded was a morning star called Retaliator. The other man, who went by the name of Stader, was far older than the rest; he was balding, slight of build, and wore a thick mustache. The trident he wielded was called Dissect, and it got its name after he removed the organs from a giant when he pulled the weapon away.

With the introductions out of the way, each man and lizard were handed a mount from one of the aspiring young warriors of the Order.

They left town at mid-morning to rendezvous with Thessor's kin. Along the way, Mao made a comment to Jacko and Woo that he thought it was funny how each man named their weapon and treated it like some sort of pet. Unfortunately, Kildred overheard him, trotted over, and grabbed the reins to his horse, stopping the mare. The warrior demanded an apology for his insults. When Mao saw the anger in his eyes, coupled with his aggressive posture and hand resting on his flail, he promptly did so and added that he wouldn't make fun again. The warrior relaxed a bit, smiled, and laughed loudly. A few seconds later, his brothers joined in on the fun and Mao was left feeling embarrassed, but relieved, after he returned to his position in the rear of the group.

By midday, snow steadily fell and Thessor led the group to an old, dilapidated, abandoned farmhouse with a very large pond in the back. The area was very quiet.

"Thessor, where are your men?" Woo asked after pulling up next to his horse.

"Watchsss, little human," the lizard hissed and pointed to the pond.

"For what?"

Thessor hissed aloud, and twenty lizardmen rose from the murky pond with their weapons drawn and ready for battle. They hissed back in acknowledgement and walked over to greet their commanding officer. Sludge dripped from their leather armor and a smell that no one could describe, followed them.

The group, now numbering thirty-five strong, gave Jacko a sense of confidence that they could succeed in freeing the prisoners, but one pressing matter still bothered him: how were they going to enter the town if Delisar wasn't around? He trotted over to Konafar and expressed his concern regarding the tracker. Konafar was surprised that he hadn't returned and announced to the group that they would stop and look for him once they arrived outside of Redden.

An hour later, they arrived and began searching for signs of Delisar. Tonles touched the wood from the burnt-out fire.

"He was here not more than ten hours ago," he declared.

"Hesss went that way," Thessor said after finding a set of footprints nearby while pointing his clawed hand toward Stonybrook.

"We need this man in order to gain access to the town, so we'd better find him fast," Konafar said and looked skyward, gauging if the weather would turn progressively worse.

It was decided that Mao, Jacko, Tonles, Konafar, Runit, Erantel, Stader, and one of Thessor's best trackers, Kressan, would search for Delisar, while the rest of the group stayed behind in case he returned.

Under the guidance of the lizardman, the search party finally found Delisar. He was unconscious and looked grave. They quickly wrapped his limp form in several blankets and built a fire, hoping that it wasn't too late to save him.

Over the next couple of hours, Delisar stirred many times, drifting in and out of consciousness. They were about to send Kressan back to the others to give them the good news when a tree fell, drawing their attention and causing the horses to stir.

"What do you think it is?" Mao asked.

"It's probably nothing," Stader replied.

Two more trees fell in closer proximity. The men stood up.

"I don't like this," Runit added.

"There's definitely something out there, but what?" Mao asked.

"Only one creature in this area is capable of toppling over a tree."

"And what would that be?"

"A Nocturn," Konafar replied and unsheathed his sword.

Everyone else followed his lead and took out their weapons. More trees fell from the northwestern direction, and the horses tugged and bit down fiercely on their restraints.

"That thing must be huge," Jacko said.

"They can be. Some can grow to the length of ten feet and wide as a man. They're just plain nasty," Tonles said.

"Plus, their bodies are thick as plate, and their jaws are powerful enough to crush steel. Be careful, they have an excellent peripheral vision, so stay in front of the creature," Konafar added.

"I'm pretty sure there's more than one," Erantel said.

"Are we safe in here?" Mao asked.

"No," Tonles said.

"I don't want to be trapped in here." Konafar announced.

"What about Delisar?" Mao asked.

"Leave him," Konafar said and left the large underbrush with the rest following closely behind.

Mao spotted a hollowed-out rock formation. "Would we be safer in there?"

"No. I've seen them tear through rock before, and I really don't think we can make it there in time," Konafar said.

"Then how do we kill it?"

"Go for the underbelly or its eyes."

Another tree fell closer to them, causing the men to spread out. Kressan ran ahead with his sword drawn and shield readied. Then, without warning, an enormous tree fell on top of Stader, killing him instantly.

"Some of you come with me. We'll circle around it," Konafar shouted and ran in the opposite direction from where they thought the creature was.

Runit and Mao followed him.

"See if you can draw him out," Tonles said to Jacko and Erantel and moved some distance away.

"What are you going to do?" Jacko asked.

"Be a target."

Tonles stood poised and ready for the creature and banged Ripper against the shield, trying to get the creature's attention.

Konafar, Mao, and Runit almost ran directly into another Nocturn. Mao had never seen one before, and it was frightening to behold. It was as large as Konafar said and resembled a sleek-looking turtle with legs.

Lucky for them the monster was preoccupied with a squirming deer trapped underneath its claws. The animal thrashed about until the creature opened its maw, exposing rows of sharp teeth, and bit down on its head, removing it in one bone-crushing chomp and swallowing it whole.

Konafar was about to charge ahead when he saw Kressan running directly at the Nocturn and leapt onto its back. The lizardman buried his sword to the hilt into the creature's tough, armored, exterior, causing it to raise up and fall backward onto the lizardman. The Nocturn began rolling to the left, then the right, trying to regain its footing while crushing Kressan in the process. Konafar barked an order to attack and they fell upon it, assaulting its soft underbelly until it lay motionless.

Jacko and Erantel were out of position when the Nocturn charged directly at Tonles. However, it did pass close enough to Erantel, and he jabbed at the creature with Reclamation as it passed. The spear did little to slow or even change its trajectory.

To the onlookers, it appeared that Tonles would be trampled to death, but when the creature was close enough, he dropped his shield, moved to the right, and wrapped his left arm around the creature's neck, holding on for dear life. The creature unexpectedly lifted him off the ground and charged toward a tree. Tonles glanced over his shoulder and, after seeing where he was headed, tried lowering his feet to slow the creature. When that failed, he slammed the butt end of the axe onto the top of its head, but that did little to improve his situation. He thought about releasing his grip but figured he'd be trampled to death, so instead he tilted to one side and hacked at the creature's front paw, almost severing the limb.

The Nocturn slowed and dipped its head low enough to the ground for Tonles to plant his massive legs firmly onto the surface and stop the beast. The creature thrashed its head, trying to fling the pesky human off, but Tonles held firm and delivered a blow right between the creature's shoulders, then he released his hold and gripped his weapon with both hands. As the creature raised its head, Tonles plunged the spiked head of the axe into the monster's throat and shoved the creature over onto its side. The Nocturn twitched until Tonles brought Ripper down upon its neck, then it stopped moving altogether.

A few minutes later, he was joined by Konafar, Mao, and Runit, and they explained what had happened to Kressan. Tonles ordered they bury the crushed and mangled forms of the dead, while Mao was instructed to get Delisar.

Delisar woke to the sound of shouting, fighting, and trees falling. He had no recollection of how he got where he was or who wrapped him in the blankets. He thought about leaving through the opening in the bushes but decided against it and wormed his way out of the rear. Once free, a horse ran past him, nearly scaring him to death. Panic set in which was followed by paranoia. Quickly, he raced around looking for a place to hide and found one deep within a set of shrubbery. After entering, he found a large stick and held it in front for protection. He listened to the outside world in hopes that the battle would end soon.

The fighting lasted many more minutes. After it stopped, he gathered enough courage and began crawling toward the entrance. He felt braver the closer he got until he heard something move just outside and his courage was replaced with fear. He scurried back until he had no other place to go and held the stick defensively in front of his face.

Mao returned to the place they'd left Delisar and was shocked to find him nowhere in sight. While searching the area frantically for signs of the hunter, he heard something moving in the bushes several yards away. He figured or hoped that it was Delisar but stayed guarded and ready with his left arm in front of his right, which was bent at the elbow toward his side.

Cautiously, he moved closer and squatted directly in front of the shrubbery and began shifting his head from side to side, trying to see what was making the noise. Growing up, he was always fearful of the unknown, and this time was no different. Despite being confident in his skills, he was still afraid and knew that if he didn't overcome this affliction, he would fall victim to it someday.

For a brief moment, he thought about getting the others but knew they would never respect him if he did. After moving aside the branches, he entered. The first thing he saw, ten feet away, was something that looked like a boot lying on its side.

It had to be Delisar, he thought and slowly crept closer.

Abruptly, the boot moved frantically back and forth, startling him, and causing him to back up. He waited for it to stop and then pushed his way forward.

After the intruder entered, Delisar waited until he was close enough, then moved his foot back and forth, hoping to scare it away. When he heard it back up, he quickly turned around and tried working his way through the thick bramble exterior and found he couldn't part the branches.

"Delisar, it's me, Mao."

Delisar turned back around with his stick tightly in his grasp and waited. "Stay away from me," he shouted at the stranger.

"Delisar, calm down."

The hunter lunged at him, stick first, trying to ram the makeshift weapon into his throat. Mao moved to the side, grabbed the stick with his left hand, and punched it with his right, splintering the weapon in half. Delisar's eyes widened after he saw his weapon fall apart. He scurried back, begging for his life.

"Delisar!" Mao said firmly.

The hunter tightly closed his eyes, hoping his enemy would go away.

"You're safe. It's me, Mao. I am a friend of Jacko. We met in the town of Wistful."

Delisar paused and looked up at the man as if trying to remember.

"Come with me, we've been searching for you."

At first, he didn't move, but after several minutes of convincing, Delisar finally agreed, and they left the confines of the bushes.

Konafar and the others were approaching as soon as they left the bushes. Upon seeing them, Delisar cowered and fell to the ground.

"What the hell is wrong with him?" Konafar asked no one in particular.

"He looks terrified," Tonles answered.

Konafar knelt in front of him, and Delisar lowered his eyes toward the ground.

"Look at me," Konafar demanded.

Delisar didn't respond.

"LOOK AT ME, DAMN IT."

Reluctantly, Delisar raised his head to meet Konafar's. Konafar grabbed his jaw and stared deeply into his eyes. Suddenly, the fear washed away and Delisar recognized him.

"What happened to you?" Konafar asked.

"I don't know. I can't remember. I'm really scared."

Konafar looked at the others and each one stared back at him blankly, not knowing what to say.

"We need to leave soon," Woo stated.

"We'll protect you, okay?" Konafar said to Delisar. He nodded and was helped up.

Tonles pulled Konafar aside. "What happened to your friend?"

"I don't know. I've never seen him like this."

"Do you think we should take him to Redden?"

"If he doesn't snap out of it by the time we reach Wistful, then we'll get the key and drop him off at the healers."

Konafar and Tonles led the way, followed by Runit, Erantel,

Delisar, Jacko, and Mao guarding the rear. Along the way back, snow began to fall, and Delisar's memory and courage slowly returned. First, he remembered Konafar and their past adventures, then Jacko and his friends, their narrow escape from Redden, his trip to Wistful and the meeting with the Magistrate, and finally, the creature.

"The creature?" he whispered.

Like a piece of the puzzle fitting into place, he realized that's when he started his downward spiral toward terror and trepidation. Whatever that creature did to him, it left him lonely and empty inside. He wondered if it would haunt him the rest of his life. Delisar told the group what had happened to him and the type of creature he encountered. No one seemed to know what it was, not even Konafar or Tonles. Konafar asked him if he needed to stop by Wistful for help, but Delisar said he'd be okay. He went on to tell them about the Magistrate and how he would not help them in their cause.

"WHY NOT!" Konafar snapped.

"Because the fool doesn't feel it's his moral obligation."

"We'll see about that." Konafar made the motion, as if he was about to race off toward the town and deal with him when Tonles moved directly in front of him.

"Don't waste your time, it's pointless."

Konafar grunted in aggravation.

"We'll do this without him and pay him a visit afterward."

"We certainly will."

CHAPTER 2: REVENGE FOR THE FALLEN (PART II)

The sky was growing dark when Konafar and the others entered the camp. Set deeply inside of the forest directly in front of Redden, they were far enough away from the prying eyes of anyone walking the battlements.

Around the fire, Konafar and Tonles told the others from the Order of the Dragon and Thessor what happened while they were looking for Delisar and what befell Stader and Kressan. The men nodded their heads in prayer to honor their brother, while Thessor showed no emotion or said anything.

"I'm sorry about your kinsman," Delisar said to the lizardman. "He was a brave warrior."

"No needsss to sssay sssorry, he'sss protecting our godsss now. I knowsss about that creature yousss sssaid."

"You do?"

"Yesss. Wesss call it Garurtsss. Very dangerous it isss. One look into itsss eyesss and you willsss losss yoursss mind, then it waitsss until you're unable to movesss and killsss you."

"A Garurt. Will I be okay?"

"Yesss you willsss be yourssself sssoon. I must returnsss to my mensss and tellsss them about Kresssan," Thessor said and left.

"It's been a long day and I'm tired," Delisar said and got up.

The rest of the men wrapped furs around their bodies and continued to talk well into the late hours until they fell asleep, leaving the lizardmen to keep watch.

A mild snowstorm, with cold winds blowing from the north, ushered in the morning. The lizardmen seemed more than happy with these conditions, while the shivering men huddled around two separate fires, ate their morning meal, and drank warm ale to help ward off the cold. The only people absent were Krol and Nion, who were tending to the horses, and Pundit, who was off relieving himself.

Around one fire was Erantel, Runit, Lud, Awret, Jacko, Mao, and Woo. They were engaged in conversation about the differences between their Orders.

Konafar, Tonles, Fleck, and Kildred were eating and drinking in silence, for the most part, until Fleck looked over at the lizardmen.

"If they're cold-blooded, then how can they stand this weather better than we can?" he asked.

"I think they can raise their core body temperature. Let's ask them," Kildred said. "Thessor, can you come over here?" The lizardman walked over.

"Yesss, Kildredsss."

"How come you're not cold like us?"

"We cansss adapt to oursss environmentsss. If itsss getsss too coldsss then we cansss raissse our body temperaturesss. Sssame if it'sss too hotsss, we cansss lower itsss."

While he was talking, Tonles was playing with his beard. "Hey, watch this," he said and waited until they looked at him, then wrapped his hand around his long goatee and squeezed it tight. The mini icicles, formed from the condensation, fell away like stalactites do in a cave. He bellowed in delight, and the people around him smiled.

Ponduit finally finished relieving himself, walked over to where Tonles was sitting, and poured himself a mug of warm ale from the steeping kettle. "We should get going soon. There's a big storm coming," he said.

Tonles looked skyward. "We want a big storm, so we can hide in it as we approach the town. You should relax. We have time, eat something."

"I'm not hungry."

Fleck noticed the worried look upon his face. "What troubles you, my friend? I know that look."

"I have a bad feeling about this mission. Something is amiss."

"What do you mean?"

"It's hard to describe. I just have a bad feeling."

"Don't worry, we'll be fine," Tonles said, but his words did little to ease Ponduit's growing fears.

Krol and Nion walked over to Konafar.

"We lost more than half of the horses during the night," Nion said.

Konafar looked up at him. "Lost how?"

"Some died and others ran off."

"That's just great. Thessor," Konafar turned toward the lizardman, "can two of your men watch the horses while we're gone?"

Thessor nodded.

"Listen up, everyone; we need to discuss a few things," Konafar said. When they were ready, he spoke again. "In case you didn't hear, two of Thessor's kin will stay behind to safeguard the horses. The rest of us will follow Delisar to the city's portcullis and enter through the secret doorway. For those who didn't have the pleasure of meeting with Lord Rygare and Lord Tolar before we left, here's our plan: once we enter the town, we'll form three groups. I want Tonles, Mao, Lud, Fleck, Erantel, and Ponduit to be in one; Thessor and his brethren in another and the rest will be with me. We need one group to look for the prisoners and the other two to create the diversions. Who wants to look for the prisoners?"

"I'll go," Tonles said.

"Good. I want to create enough havoc to throw the town into a frenzy. Improvise if you have to but stick together, and don't leave anyone behind. We should be able to sneak past the walls undetected if we wait long enough for the storm. Any questions?"

"Where do you want us to create the diversions?" Lud asked.

"We'll have to figure out where the majority of the enemy is and move in opposite directions."

"What kind of diversions do you want?" Erantel asked.

"What do you think, Ponduit?

"A large fire would be great," Ponduit said.

"We should attack them in order to draw them away from the prisoners. It worked for Jacko and me when we were there before," Delisar added.

"Do we know where the prisoners are?" Krol asked.

"We found them in the inn, so I think that will be a good place to start," Jacko said.

"Do you know how many inns there are?"

"Maybe three. We already cleaned out one, but I'm not sure if they moved people back into the building."

"Does anyone else have any questions or concerns?"

No one responded.

"Good, let's get ready."

During the next hour, the blizzard hit the area, making it very difficult to see ten feet ahead. Realizing it wasn't going to get any better, they wrapped their cloaks tightly around their bodies and covered their faces with cloth so that only their eyes were exposed. The weather was a curse and a blessing on this day. Even though it hindered their progress, they used it to conceal their approach from the creatures standing guard on the battlements and safely passed them by.

By the time they reached the walls, Delisar halted the group and turned to Konafar.

"I will go on from here. Once I open the door, I'll come back," he said and turned away.

Konafar grabbed his arm and said, "Are you sure you're up for this?"

Delisar nodded and left. As he crept along the wall, the snow really hampered his vision, and he almost stumbled upon the two guards stationed near the secret door. He stopped and didn't move a muscle. The guards weren't moving either, making him believe the weather was also masking his presence as well. He notched an arrow, pulled back the bowstring, and lined up his sight. In a fluid motion, he released the arrow at one guard, notched another and fired it at the other guard. The arrows ricocheted off of the guards, flying in different directions as both targets fell, and then a large pit opened beneath Delisar's feet. The last thing he thought about, before plummeting into the darkness, was that he was a fool.

****

"It's taking him too long; something must have happened to him," Nion said to the group. He was holding his morning star anxiously, wanting to get started.

"What do you think?" Konafar said, looking directly at Tonles.

"I agree. We should check."

"Let's go," Konafar said.

Jacko led them toward the secret door. When he reached the huge hole, he stopped.

"The pit wasn't here before," he said, walked to the edge, and peered down along with the others.

"Trapsss," said Thessor, "your friend mussst have fallen. I goesss looksss."

"Thessor, if he's down there, get the key off his body."

Jacko didn't like saying that because of what it implied.

The lizardman nodded and climbed down the dark twenty-foot pit with ease and carefully avoided the rows of spikes when he landed. His eyes adapted quickly to the darkness, and he easily weaved his way through the countless rows of spikes until he found Delisar's twisted and broken form. The hunter's body was outstretched upon several rows of spikes with the most gruesome being the one that ran through his head and held a good portion of his brain as a trophy. The lizardman walked over and searched his lifeless body until he found a ring of keys, then he returned above.

While they were waiting for Thessor, Runit tested the small ledge that ran between the wall and the pit; Tonles, Fleck, and Lud kept watch for guards while the rest kept close to the walls. Thessor returned a short time later from out of the pit and walked straight up to Jacko, handing him the ring of keys.

"I'm sssorry about your friendsss," he said.

Jacko reflected once again on how easy it was to lose your life, noting that one minute you're alive and the next you're not. He was lost in thought when Runit came up to them.

"I believe we can make it across as long as we stay close enough to the wall," he announced.

"Messs and my kin willsss travelsss into the pit and meetsss you over theresss." Thessor pointed and climbed back down along with his brethren.

The rest lined up in a single row, with their backs against the wall, and proceeded carefully with Runit taking the lead. When they were halfway across, Krol slipped on the snow and would've plummeted to his death if not for the quick actions of Kildred, who grabbed him and pulled him back against the wall.

"Be careful," Tonles said.

They slowed their pace while pressing tighter against the wall until they arrived at the far end of the pit. Ponduit saw the two statues on their sides and walked over to study them.

"I think I know what happened to Delisar," he said.

The others joined him.

"The statues were placed on top of pressure plates, and when they were moved it triggered the pit open. He must've thought they were real guards and shot them with arrows."

"I would have made the same mistake," Lud said.

The lizardmen climbed out of the pit.

Jacko walked up to the wall and traced each stone until he found the one he was looking for and pushed it down. A few seconds later, a section of the wall opened and revealed a dark corridor. "Let's go," he said.

They entered the passageway and energized several glow rocks. Jacko pushed down the lever, and the secret door closed. Some of the men began brushing off the snow and rubbing their arms to stay warm.

Konafar looked at each of them and spoke. "I have a sneaky suspicion there will be a lot more traps so stay alert. Ponduit, you're the Order's best at detecting them, so you'll take the lead. Jacko, please tell the men where we're headed."

"I've only been here once, and, with Delisar gone, it might take some time for me to find the correct door. There are many ways to go. What I do know is that the door is made of metal and has an etching of an eagle carved upon the surface. I suggest we split up in teams if I can't remember."

"If we do, how will the rest of us know when someone finds the door?" Awret asked.

"I have something that might help," Tonles said and reached into his pouch, pulling out two wooden figurines. One was a long-toothed weasel, and the other was a serpent with wings. Everyone watched as he placed them on the ground, said a few words, and, on cue, they became live flesh, fur, and scales. The weasel scooted up his leg and rested on his left shoulder, while the serpent flapped its wings and took up position on his right.

"What do they do?" Mao asked.

"The weasel will help detect traps, while the serpent will look for the door." Tonles whispered something to the creatures, and they both left their perches and went down the passageway. Tonles looked over at Konafar. "Don't say anything."

Konafar shook his head in a manner that he wanted his friend to know he shouldn't be playing with items like those. "You know the rules."

"I know."

Jacko led them down several twisting and turning hallways until they caught up to the weasel. The creature was standing there on its hind legs as still as a statue.

"What's it doing?" Ponduit whispered.

"Must be a trap, wait here," Tonles responded, then walked up to the furry rodent, bent down, and spoke to the creature. The weasel made noises back in response, and Tonles stood up. "He says there're gas traps to the north and east. I think we should go west and avoid them altogether."

They agreed and turned westward. Each time the creature found a trap, the men changed their course until they arrived at a tee junction surrounded by traps on both sides.

"Let me have a look," Ponduit said and studied the left side first and then the right. "Jacko, do you remember which way?"

Jacko thought long and hard. "I think left."

"That's what I thought. The type of trap used in that direction is far more complicated than the other one, so it makes sense."

"Cansss you disssarmsss it?" Thessor asked.

"I believe so."

Ponduit stepped gingerly into the passageway and moved his feet in a different manner with each passing step, and carefully avoided certain areas. After he reached the far end, he traced along the wall with his fingertips until he found and disarmed some sort of mechanism with a loud click.

"It's safe," he said, and everyone followed.

They traveled through the endless corridors, finding traps and doors that were barricaded from the inside and inaccessible. When Jacko finally conceded that he no longer knew where he was, they split up. Ponduit showed them how easy it was to spot simple traps and insisted that it was essential to mark the area once they passed through. Once everyone felt comfortable, they parted.

Jacko, Tonles, and Woo found the metal door two hours later, and Tonles sent the winged serpent to retrieve the others.

After everyone caught up, Tonles said a few words to his familiars, and they returned to their wooden form.

"There's been a change of plans," Konafar began. "I want Thessor and his kinsmen to locate the survivors and return so that we can properly plan out the rescue."

"Why the change?" Lud asked.

"We wasted enough time down here, and I don't think we have all that much time left."

"Alright. Ponduit, open the door."

Ponduit turned the key and opened the door slowly. "Too easy," he said.

"How so?" Woo whispered.

"Well, since there were traps throughout the catacombs, and the doors were barricaded, why leave this one alone? Stand back, I'm going in."

Upon entering, nothing happened. Gas didn't fill the room, pits didn't open, or any other type of trap. Ponduit was miffed by this and waved everyone else in.

"This is very strange. Jacko, are you sure they chased you down here?" Konafar asked.

"I don't know about down here."

Ponduit studied the room carefully. When he didn't find anything, he motioned for the lizardmen to proceed up the stairs.

They began ascending the stairs. When the lead lizardman reached the fifth step, the wood splintered, cracked, and his foot fell through, becoming lodged. He grunted and as soon as he pulled his leg free, they heard a loud click.

"GET DOWN!" Ponduit shouted.

For those who weren't quick enough, they were shot with arrows from the spring-loaded mechanism inside of the walls. After the trap was finally exhausted, Nion, Kildred, and Krol, along with five lizardmen, lay dead.

Several others were wounded, including Woo, who had an arrow sticking out of his left arm. Konafar was injured in his thigh, and Runit had a few bolts protruding from his armor, some of which barely penetrated his skin.

Konafar stood up and pulled the arrow free. Blood oozed from the wound and down his leg; it was heavy at first, then in a matter of seconds was reduced to a trickle. He tied a strip of cloth just above the injury and limped gingerly over to Ponduit.

"Check again for traps," he said in disgust after seeing the dead.

"It's not my fault," Ponduit said and did as he was told.

He found another deadly trap near the top step that would have ignited the stairway, along with the entire room, if it had been sprung. He disarmed it, and the lizardmen continued up the stairs.

When they reached the top, they opened the door and entered the room. Inside was empty, except for the cooking pot that was left in the hearth and the small table directly in the center of the room.

They walked into another room with scattered furniture and a front door to the north with two windows on either side. The area reeked of death. From where they stood, one of the lizardmen noticed, and pointed out, that there was something very large outside the windows, blocking his vision from seeing the street beyond. With a nod from Thessor, he went over, looked through the window and reported that there was a giant, holding an enormous spear, sitting in front of the building. He appeared to be sleeping. Because there was no other means of leaving the building, Thessor knew they had no other choice but to dispose of the sentry. He instructed his men to follow his lead, and, slowly, they opened the door. The giant didn't move or stir, and they stepped out onto the porch and surrounded the big creature. On Thessor's mark, they plunged their weapons into his head and back and silently killed the giant. After propping him upright again, they moved on into the night.

The lizardmen ran along the snow-covered streets, avoiding patrols, and assessing the area until they found what they were looking for and returned to the house without incident.

Once inside, they went back downstairs and gave the others their report. They said there were two large groups of humans being held captive in inns to the east and west.

Konafar took on a determined look. "Obviously, we can't save them all, so don't sacrifice yourselves." Konafar looked at them one at a time before continuing. "We should still create diversions to the north and the south in order to draw them away. Once that starts, the rest of us will split up into two groups, storm the buildings, and rescue as many as we can. Ponduit, I'll need you to place a few traps down here to cover our escape. What do you think?"

"I'll set them on the door upstairs and the one we entered through. They won't go off until they are opened again, so we'll close the doors at the last possible second."

Ponduit began scavenging the room for materials.

Konafar continued, "Okay, given our numbers, I want at least six individuals to make up the diversion groups."

Thessor stepped forward and said he and his brethren would create the diversions.

"I'll go with them," Awret said.

"Me too," Runit added.

"You're too wounded and will get in the way," Tonles snapped at him.

"I'll be fine." He hefted his axe to show that he was.

"If he can fight, then we should allow him to go," Konafar said, and the matter was dropped. "Thessor, what kind of distraction are you planning?"

"After wesss lightsss the buildingsss on firesss, wesss willsss attacksss themsss asss they comesss."

"Good. Try to create both diversions at the same time." Let's get going."

Thessor and six lizardmen went north, while Runit, Awret, and four lizardmen went south.

Konafar waited for them to leave before speaking. "We'll wait for them to get into position and then we'll make our move. Tonles, can you use your little trinket again?"

Tonles smiled and put the winged figurine on the ground, recited the same few words as before, and the serpent took shape and hovered in front of his face. It was given instructions and sailed through the door.

Mao walked over to shut the door and his eyes grew wide in fear. He quickly moved away and said, "Did anyone notice the large giant sleeping outside of the building?"

"He'sss not sssleepingsss, he'sss deadsss," a lizardman said.

"Did you kill him?"

"Wesss didsss."

"We didn't even hear you."

"Thatsss becaussse he wasss sssleeping."

To the rear of the room, Konafar pulled Jacko aside. "Are you ready for this?"

Jacko nodded despite being apprehensive, and his stomach, as usual, felt sour like it always did before a fight. "I am. I've always wanted to be a hero and do something like this, and now I'll get my chance." He looked proud. "Are you nervous?"

"It's more of an anxious feeling to get this started. It comes with experience and, in time, you'll feel the same way. Stay close to me. We'll get through this."

"I don't feel brave. I feel scared."

"Bravery is a state of mind and confidence in your skills. To be fearful is also a good emotion. It will keep you sharp and focused. Just make sure you keep it in check and don't let it overwhelm you."

Jacko's opinion of the big fellow changed drastically since they'd met, and he was happy to be in his company and felt inspired.

****

The winged serpent returned a half-hour later. After Tonles was briefed by his pet, and Ponduit had his traps in place, they left the safety of the building and went in different directions. Konafar, Jacko, Woo, and two lizardmen ran west, while Tonles, Mao, Lud, Fleck, Erantel, and Ponduit ran east.

All hell broke loose just before dawn. To the north, Thessor, along with his brethren, lit a few fires and attacked a large patrol party that went to investigate the fires. Their attack left few of them alive.

To the south, Runit set several empty buildings ablaze, and once there was mayhem, ignited more buildings. The somewhat coordinated assaults to the north and south worked perfectly, and as the blazes lit up, smoke filled the town and clouded the morning sky. Most of the guards left the inns that were occupying the prisoners and converged on the locations.

Once they were gone, Konafar and his group stormed the building. The mighty warrior used his shoulder to break through the door, catching the fifteen goatmen by surprise and unprepared. The six closest to the door were easily butchered before they had a chance to draw their weapons, while the others threw aside the tables and chairs, raised their blades and pikes, and charged.

Konafar's affliction, known as wrath, turned him into a fighting machine. He yelled like a deranged madman and attacked them. Two guards on the right lost their heads with one swipe of Carnage, and two others were knocked over and landed hard against the floor, losing their weapons. He hacked them several times each.

Meanwhile, Jacko, Woo, and the two lizardmen engaged the other guards. Despite having a wounded arm, Woo successfully defended himself against multiple spear thrusts. As the last attack sailed past his ducking head, he stepped in and caught the guard right in the solar plexus with an open palm strike. The impact severely shattered his bones and cartilage, crushing his lungs in the process and sending him spiraling to the ground, gasping for air.

On the other side of the room, Jacko's specialized blocking technique not only helped him dodge and evade multiple attacks, but it also allowed him to deflect the spear and slice his adversary's throat with his finger knives. The guard saw something pass by his neck, then felt weak-legged and dropped to his knees. He never realized his artery was severed until blood sprayed out of the wound and darkness clouded his vision.

The two lizardmen fought as a team against the remaining guards with one attacking while the other defended their position. Every time the guards stabbed or thrust at them, the defending lizardman parried the attacks and allowed his partner to vary his attacks with shield bashes and low and high sword swings. They were so good at this fighting style that the guards were eventually overwhelmed and killed.

After the battle, Konafar and Woo rested, while Jacko and the lizardmen searched the establishment.

To the south, a group of the guards, led by three northern giants, arrived just as Runit and the others set their fifth building on fire. When the giants saw them, they hurled their boulders at the warehouse and brought the structure down upon their unsuspecting heads. They ordered the goatmen to move in and capture any of them still alive.

Awret, dazed and bloodied, was getting to his feet, holding on to his six-foot glaive, that he called Authority, as the goatmen came around the bend. He glanced around the wreckage and saw the lizardmen crushed underneath the burning beams. Runit was lying face down, and he wasn't sure if he was alive. There was nowhere left for him to go, so he stiffened his posture.

When the Hurnol creatures saw him, they stopped.

"We have plans for you, human," one of them said.

"Oh, and what will that be?" Awret snidely responded.

"You'll find out soon enough, when you meet the Red Knight."

"The Red Knight? He sounds really scary," he mocked them, holding Authority defensively.

"Capture him. The master wants him alive," the goatman ordered.

"Not today, crossbreed," Awret replied.

Tentatively, the twelve Hurnol began surrounding Awret. Some held nets, while others kept their eight-foot spears poised and ready. Awret knew that there was no way he was going to allow himself to be captured, so he knew that he needed to stay away from the nets. He remained very still until the goatman, directly in front of him, released his net, then he sprang into action.

The warrior, from the Order of the Dragon, raced underneath the net as it sailed over his head, pushed aside a few spears, sliced one of the guards across the throat, stabbed another in the stomach, and smashed a third in the face. By the time the net landed on the ground, Awret killed two more guards and was turned around and ready. The goatmen wailed and set upon him. Awret used Authority to block, deflect, and redirect the slower weapons until he created an opening and sliced a few more guards across their throats. One goatman became so enraged he charged headlong after Awret and was greeted by his heavy glaive as it came down upon his head, splitting it like a melon. The other guards backed up.

"Anyone else want some?" Awret taunted.

The guards knew what waited for them if they ran, so they did the only thing that made sense and attacked. One after the other, they found out the hard way that their skills paled in comparison and were no match for Awret, whose years of training against longer weapons finally paid off. When the last goatman was beheaded, Awret almost collapsed from exhaustion and needed to use the glaive to keep upright.

From a safe distance, the giants enjoyed watching the inferior Hurnol fall before the human, because they viewed them as the lowest form of life and could not care less if they died. When the last of them fell, they approached the human.

Awret was breathing heavy when the ten-foot tall, big-boned giants drew near. Two of the giants, wearing brown furs and boots, cradled boulders under their left arms and carried big hammers in their right. The one in the middle wore black fur and boots and held a thick tree trunk in one hand and a wooden shield in the other. Awret swallowed hard, trying his best not to show fear as the giants stopped directly in front of him. They looked at him as if they were gauging his worth, then the one holding the tree trunk spoke.

"Human, you fight well. However, now your life must come to an end."

Awret was surprised the creature was fluent in his tongue and sounded intelligent instead of dumb like the rest of his kind.

"You should let me go before my men arrive and we end your lives."

"Lies, little man. Do you take me for a fool?" he said, and the giant on his left laughed.

"Yes, little human, do you take us for fools?" the giant on the right repeated.

"I say we rip him apart," the one on the left added.

"Yes rip apart."

"How about this, if I beat you," Awret pointed to the giant on the right, "you let me go, or are you too scared of one little human?" There was a reason why Awret singled out one of the giants. He dealt with them before and knew they respected bravery. If they agreed to his offer, not only would it be a fair fight, but they would keep their word.

Together the giants on the left and the right looked at the one in the middle, waiting for his response.

"You're brave, little man. I'll give you that," the giant said, lowering his tree weapon. He nodded to the giant on the right, who then dropped his boulder and gripped his hammer in both hands.

"Do we have a deal?"

The giant holding the hammer grinned, and the one in the middle, who appeared to be the leader, nodded.

The giant rushed Awret and brought the hammer down with the intent of smashing his head into his shoulders. Awret, bent at the knees, braced his body, and brought Authority up, blocking the attack. The giant brought the weapon back down with even more anger.

When Awret blocked it again, the giant lifted his leg and kicked him in the chest, knocking him back several feet to the ground. In the next instant, the giant charged forward. Awret rolled backward and was up on his feet just in time to block several more attacks before he was grabbed by the giant's big beefy hand and tossed over his shoulder. Awret flew headfirst into the wall of a nearby building and was knocked senseless. The giant paused to admire his work, and his brothers laughed out loud.

"Human, you're no match for my brother," the leader said.

Awret felt like someone dropped a castle down upon his head. He climbed to his feet and picked up his glaive.

"Look, he wants to fight some more," the giant holding the boulder said and then laughed. "It looks like fun, can I try?"

The leader nodded. The giant dropped his boulder, gripped his hammer, and confidently walked over, while his twin walked back to stand by the one in command.

Awret was sore all over. He had a laceration in the back of his head from hitting the wall and felt dizzy from the loss of blood. Nevertheless, he would not give them the satisfaction of giving up. He remained lax, with Authority pointed downward, and waited for the giant.

The giant stopped directly in front of him and said, "Come, human, it's time to die."

Awret didn't move or respond.

"Human, take your death with honor," the giant said.

Awret didn't answer or flinch.

The giant grew agitated and impatient. When he looked back toward his brothers, Awret rushed forward and sliced the giant across the stomach, cutting through his furs and skin quite easily. The giant grunted, turned around, and swung wildly. Awret anticipated his maneuver and ducked under the blow, then jabbed him in the stomach, piercing his abdomen. The giant yelled and grabbed the shaft, preventing him from withdrawing the weapon, then swung his hammer downward. Awret released his hold and moved out of the way just as the hammer slammed into the earth.

The giant moved closer, swinging the hammer with even more resolve. He missed his target's head when Awret fell to the ground and hit the building instead, crumbling the wall and sending debris everywhere. Awret grabbed his booted dagger and lunged upward at the giant, jabbing him between his ribs. The giant's body bent forward and Awret plunged the knife into his neck several times until the big fellow fell to his knees and toppled over.

Awret was in the process of removing Authority from the dead giant, thinking that he'd won his freedom, when a boulder hit him in the chest and pinned him under its weight. The giant who hurled the boulder finally had enough of him and approached.

"Human, this is what you get for killing my brother." His words fell on deaf ears when he discovered the human was already dead.

He was about to leave when he noticed another human stirring underneath the rubble. The giants grabbed him and carried him off to meet the warrior in red plate armor.

To the north, Thessor and his men engaged a group of guards that included giants, Chatar, and pike-wielding Hurnol. They fought them like a unit of possessed warriors. Each time the pike men thrust, they would step back, push aside their weapons, and lunge forward, covering great distance and scoring direct hits.

After the goatmen fell, they attacked and penetrated the boarmen's defenses, killing them while only receiving minor wounds. The giants didn't fare any better, even though they were much more skilled, they were also reckless due to their size.

By the time the battle was through, only one lizardman was dead and another was severely wounded. They were about to leave and cause havoc somewhere else when more troops came at them from all sides. Winded and breathing heavy, Thessor and his brethren hissed in delight when they saw them closing in. It was a battle they knew they wouldn't survive but one they would relish until then.

To the east, Tonles knew it was time to enter the inn after the guards left the building in response to the black smoke billowing into the morning sky from the south.

After entering the inn, they were met by a large group of boarmen poised and ready with long swords, hammers, spiked shields, and wearing studded leather armor. They were bigger and nastier looking than the ones they'd seen walking around town. It was apparent to Tonles that they were anticipating such a rescue attempt.

"What do we have here!" the Chatar in the back said with a snort and chuckle. "Kill them," he commanded.

The first wave of guards, numbering fourteen, engaged the intruders.

Tonles greeted the first two by cleaving them in half and then pummeled two more with the spiked end of his axe, splitting their faces apart.

Lud was next to him. His long sword, Disembowel, lived up to its reputation as it sliced a pair of stomachs open, spilling their contents onto the floor.

Fleck's rapier and dagger technique, along with his footwork, was flawless as he parried a sword attack with the main-gauche and stabbed the guard's throat with Enlightenment. He grinned as his enemy bled out.

Erantel toyed with another pair of boarmen before taking Reclamation and thrusting one end in the throat of one guard, then slamming the butted end into another's chest with enough force to stop his heart.

More guards fell under Ponduit's single-headed axe Whisper and Mao's hard punching technique as he shattered facial bones and crushed ribcages.

Suddenly, more guards came in from the outside. Mao, Ponduit, and Fleck turned around to engage them, while Tonles, Lud, and Erantel continued their onslaught forward.

On two different occasions, Ponduit glanced over and noticed Mao struggling with his attackers and receiving several wounds. He wanted to help, but he was too busy with his own, so he did the next best thing and yelled that Mao needed help.

Mao was bleeding from several areas, and the loss of blood was causing his stamina to falter. Rapidly, he blocked one attack after another until he missed and was struck in the shoulder by a hammer. The impact shattered his collarbone and sent him to the ground, reeling in pain.

Fleck had just killed his foe when he saw Mao fall. He rushed over to help but didn't see another guard closing in on him and was knocked to the ground. The guard was about to bring his sword down upon his head when Fleck suddenly reached up, plunged Enlightenment into his stomach, and killed him where he stood. He was on his feet again just as another Chatar came at him.

Ponduit also saw what happened to Mao, but he was too far away and did the only thing he could. He pummeled the guard's face who stood in front of him, then heaved Whisper at the boarman standing over Mao, hitting him in the head with the axe handle. The guard was furious after being hit. When he turned, searching for the culprit, Mao punched him in the groin, causing him to double over, and clocked him in the side of his head, hitting his temples and killing him instantly. Unfortunately, for Ponduit, his act of selflessness would be his downfall when the Chatar he pummeled sliced him viciously across the stomach and ran him through, piercing his heart.

When Fleck heard his dying cries, he outmaneuvered his opponent while doing a draw cut across his throat with the rapier and then threw Fate, hitting the boarman in his chest as he was removing his weapon from Ponduit's body.

In the front of the room, Tonles, Erantel, and Lud teamed up on the remaining guards and laid them to rest.

Jacko and the two lizardmen searched frantically for survivors and found some chained to the walls in the cellar. The underground room was used as a torture chamber and a morgue.

At the far end, dead bodies were piled up to the ceiling, which angered Jacko beyond words. As they were releasing the prisoners, he noticed their tattered clothes did little to hide the big bruises on their bodies, and their swollen faces bore fresh marks from recent beatings.

Once free, they assisted the prisoners up the stairs. Konafar greeted them, counted twelve men and women, and said to stay close to the group if they wanted to live. He also said they could use help and if anyone had any fighting skills, they should pick up a blade.

A semi-attractive female, with long blond hair and a slender build, stepped forward. She introduced herself as Breen, said she wanted to fight, and asked for a weapon and a change of clothing. Konafar smiled and pointed to the dead guards, indicating for her to go get what she needed.

Two emaciated-looking males followed after her and began

undressing the dead. They said they'd rather die fighting their way out. Konafar admired their bravery.

Woo walked over. "I see guards down the street."

"You just condemned us all to death," a middle-aged man in the back said.

His comment caught Konafar's attention. "How so?"

The man was about to answer when Breen walked over. "Then why don't you go back downstairs, chain yourself to the wall, and wait for them," she said.

The man looked down and didn't respond.

"Are there anymore prisoners?" Jacko asked Breen.

"I'm not sure. After the town was sacked, they split us up."

"All right," Konafar began, "stay close and help those who need assistance. Those who can fight will lead. If we get separated, then continue down the main street until you reach the building with the sleeping giant outside and..."

"Sleeping giant?" someone in the crowd interrupted.

"I mean dead giant. After you enter the building, go downstairs to the lower level and through the door. From there, you'll have to navigate your way through the tunnels until you find the exit. Hopefully, one of us will be alive to escort you to safety."

"Do you have an army waiting?" one of the prisoners asked.

Konafar shook his head, and some of the other prisoners grumbled.

"Then why did you come after us?" another prisoner asked.

"We wanted to help when no one else would do so," Jacko responded proudly.

"We might've been eventually saved by an army."

"Then go downstairs and wait," Konafar snapped at him. He was clearly losing his patience.

"We can't do that. You started this whole mess, now we don't have a choice."

"I'll give you a choice, you ungrateful bastard," Konafar snapped in response, walked over, grabbed him by his torn shirt, and lifted him in the air. "HOW ABOUT I KILL YOU? WE LOST A LOT OF GOOD MEN TRYING TO SAVE YOUR ASS." Konafar shoved him against the wall. "Does anyone else have anything to say? If so, step forward, and I'll gladly answer your questions."

When no one responded, he calmed down. After those who wanted to fight armed themselves and put on what little armor was of worth, they left the building.

At the eastern inn, Tonles and Lud rescued several prisoners from the upper floors, while Erantel and Lud did the same in the basement. After they were gathered in the main room, Fleck addressed them.

"Once we leave here, stay together. If you should get separated, head west and look for the building with the dead giant in front. Enter the basement and wait. We have another group rescuing prisoners as well. If they don't show up after a half-hour, leave through the door and follow the tunnels. Can anyone else defend themselves?"

The group of mostly women looked at each other and, one by one, everyone nodded yes.

An elderly man walked over and picked up a sword. "It's payback time," he said, eyeing the blade.

Tonles smiled at him and said, "It certainly is."

After a few more minutes of preparation, that included the prisoners arming themselves and Fleck helping Mao with a sling for his shoulder, Tonles led them out into the darkness.

****

"Give up, scaly ones," the armored giant said to the lizards.

"Givesss up? Yousss ssshould bow downsss to our sssuperior race," one of the lizards hissed in response.

"You're surrounded and have nowhere to go."

"Yousss will neversss takesss usss."

The giant raised his great sword, indicating to the others to attack.

Instead of waiting for them, the lizardmen, led by Thessor, feinted forward, turned, and attacked the guards toward the rear. The lizardmen took heavy losses as they slashed their way through the giants' ranks. By the time they broke free, only Thessor and one other were left alive.

The giant, angered by the scaly ones, gave chase. Thessor and his companion turned down a few streets and fought guards here and there. By the time they were safe, his kinsman was mortally wounded. Thessor regretted leaving him behind but knew that he couldn't do anything for him. He scaled a nearby building, used the rooftops until he reached the building with the dead giant, then climbed down and entered.

Tonles and the others didn't make it far before they encountered a large group of guards.

"What do we have here?" one of the goatmen said, pointing a crossbow at them.

Tonles looked at his adversaries, hefted his axe, and replied, "Your death!"

He, Lud, Fleck, and Erantel, along with most of the other prisoners led by the old man, rushed the stunned-looking guards. It was a bloodbath as Tonles hacked and chopped all who came in contact with his mighty axe. Fleck parried and sliced many. Lud, working out of a high guard, rained down deathly blows, while Erantel jabbed and thrust his spear into the bellies and throats of the goatmen. The old man managed to eliminate one of the Hurnol before he fell, and the females fought gallantly, slaying a few more. When the battle was through, Tonles and his brothers, along with seven females, stood proud, then ran off until they reached the building now known as the Sleeping Giant.

As soon as Konafar and the others stepped out of the inn, a large group of guards, led by a giant holding a chained war beetle, came upon them from the east. Woo's eyes widened in fear, and he shouted for them to run. The guards heard his warning and fired arrows at them, striking down several prisoners. The giant released the chain and ordered the war beetle to attack. The creature shrieked, snapped its mandibles a few times, and scurried toward the fleeing party.

Konafar guided them down several streets, trying to lose the creature, but it was no use. The bug followed and crashed into several wooden structures with one goal in mind: devour its prey. With the party tiring, and with no hope of outrunning the creature, Breen had an idea, raced over to a building, and told the others to follow her inside. They were almost inside when the beetle came crashing through another building directly behind them, trampled on a few prisoners, and grabbed another one with its mandibles. His dying screams followed Jacko and the others through the room and out the back door.

After the beetle swallowed its meal whole, it followed the fleeing party through the house, bringing the structure down upon its head. When it finally emerged from the rubble, it gave chase and ran into a large pack of goatmen. The beetle mistook them for the enemy and attacked. By the time the giant arrived to restrain the beetle, all the lesser creatures were dead, and the prisoners were nowhere in sight.

The diversion gave Konafar and the others enough time to reach the building with the dead giant.

Once inside, they went down to the cellar.

Konafar realized right away some of their party was missing. "Where's Ponduit? Thessor, where are your men?" He asked.

"Wesss all that'sss leftsss," Thessor hissed, pointing to the two lizardmen next to Jacko.

"Ponduit fell," Tonles stated sadly.

"What about Runit and Awret?"

"We haven't heard from them or the lizardmen," Lud added.

"Let's wait here for them. Jacko, go wait upstairs and bar the door," Konafar said.

Toward the back of the room, the same middle-aged man, who annoyed Konafar, was growing impatient and was talking to another prisoner.

"Now what? Are we just supposed to wait here forever?"

Tonles overheard him, walked over with rage in his eyes, and slapped him in the face. "Open that trap of yours again and you will die." He pointed directly at him, and the man cowered while rubbing his jaw in obvious pain.

Jacko came running down out of breath. "Guards…Lots of guards…and two giants…I think they know we are in here."

They heard someone banging on the door.

"Wesss hasss to goesss," Thessor hissed.

It was obvious they couldn't wait any longer and moved through the door, closing it tightly behind them to set the trap.

A few minutes later, the giants, not knowing there was an escape tunnel below, decided to knock down the building and bury whoever was inside.

Konafar remembered where they were going and led them through the tunnels until they reached the secret door. Jacko pushed the rock and opened it. The morning light poured in from the outside.

"We don't have any cover from the guards above," Breen stated.

"It'sss sssafer in the pitsss," Thessor said.

"He's right," Konafar added.

Everyone agreed and, with the help of Thessor and his brothers, they made it safely down into the pit.

They were near the end of the pit when they heard the front gates opening.

"Now what?" Konafar said.

"I'll goesss takesss a lookssss," Thessor said. He climbed out of the pit and hid behind a nearby tree.

At least twenty guards were coming out of the town and started walking around the area. The lizardman wasn't sure if they were searching for them or if it was their daily routine. When they weren't looking his way, he snuck back down the pit.

"There'sss lotsss of guardsss out theresss," he hissed to the others.

"Can we make it out without them seeing us?" Mao asked.

"I don'tsss think ssso."

"I want everyone to go over there and get ready to climb out and run to the forest," Konafar said to the others.

Jacko could tell he was up to something. "What are we going to do?"

"Give you enough time to escape."

"There has to be another way," Jacko insisted.

"No, there isn't. I'll keep them busy while you escape."

"You're not going without me," Tonles insisted.

"My friend, rage fills me, so let me do this alone."

"And let you have all the fun? I don't think so."

Konafar knew that it was useless to argue with him.

"I'm going too," Fleck said, and Konafar nodded.

"What about me?" Lud asked. "I want to kill some more."

"And me?" Erantel added.

"I need you and Lud to help them get to the forest," Konafar said.

"Isss wantsss to helpsss," Thessor said.

"Help them escape."

Thessor spoke to one of his brothers. "Hesss will helpsss yousss," he said to Konafar.

"You might die," Mao said to Konafar.

Konafar smiled. "We'll see about that. Now get going and wait for us to begin kicking the crap out of them."

They started moving toward the other side when Breen stopped.

"Thank you for everything," she said.

"Thank us later. This is child's play," Tonles responded and began climbing up with Konafar, Fleck, and Thessor's man following close behind him.

Jacko wondered if he would ever see them again.

After they reached the top, they moved behind several trees and took out their weapons. Konafar nodded to the others, and they crept along until they were close enough to the guards and attacked. Without mercy, they began hacking and slashing their way through their ranks.

During the battle, the wrath curse took hold of Konafar and turned him into a fighting machine as he further decimated their numbers. Meanwhile, Tonles was swinging his axe with such velocity that limbs were flying in all directions. Guards tried closing in on Fleck, but they couldn't get close enough, because every time someone tried, he'd parry their weapon with Fate and drive Enlightenment into their throats. Near Tonles, the lizardman was slashing and bashing anyone who came near him.

After they heard the fighting start, Thessor, his kinsman, Jacko, Erantel, Woo, and Lud climbed up and helped the others out of the pit. Mao took the longest because of his shoulder. When everybody was out, they ran for the woods.

With their numbers dwindling, the remaining guards retreated to the town and met their end when two armored giants, carrying great spears, appeared and skewered them with their spears for running away.

Konafar saw the giants, and his bloodlust drove him to attack them. When the first giant saw him running at them, he defended his position and blocked several attacks, then countered with a few of his own.

The other giant was about to jump in when Tonles suddenly appeared and slammed his shoulder into his midsection, knocking him off his feet. Before the giant could get up, Tonles moved behind him, wrapped his left arm under his chin, grabbed his arm with the other hand, and, using his feet for leverage, yanked his head with every ounce of strength he had. The giant struggled and gagged for many minutes until his neck broke.

Several feet away, Konafar and the other giant exchanged wounds, none of which did enough damage to stop the other, until the giant stabbed Konafar in the side, tearing through his armor and biting into his flesh. Konafar remained upright until his foe retracted the weapon, then he fell over, gasping for air and unable to move. The giant was about to stab him again when Fleck suddenly appeared and sliced him across the right wrist, severing a few of his tendons. The giant yelled and swung the spear, hitting him with the shaft in the head, and sending him tumbling away unconscious. The giant turned his attention back to Konafar and was about to kill him when something rammed him from behind, jarring the spear loose from his grip and sending him stumbling toward the pit.

Tonles followed and was about to bring Ripper down on his head, but the giant regained his footing, grabbed his arm, and lifted him in the air. Tonles punched him in the face with his free hand, but, despite dazing the giant, he held firm and grabbed Tonles by the throat and squeezed. Tonles did everything possible to break loose, but it was useless. The giant was too strong, and Tonles soon passed out.

His life would've ended a few seconds later if not for the lizardman jumping onto the giant from behind and digging his claws into his back. The giant couldn't bear the pain any longer. He dropped Tonles and tried grabbing the lizardman instead, but the creature was too fast and worked his way around the front while clawing at the giant's face and tearing into his flesh, drawing huge amounts of blood that dripped into his eyes, blinding him. The giant shrieked as the lizardman continued to claw at his head.

Meanwhile, Konafar climbed to his feet, despite the great amount of pain, and staggered toward the action. When he was close enough, he started running with the intention of driving Carnage into the giant's midsection and ending his life. However, he stumbled and crashed into the giant's legs, knocking him off balance and sending him, the lizardman, and himself into the pit below.

Tonles finally regained consciousness, shortly after they fell over the edge, and got up to see what befell his friend and the lizardman. After he reached the pit, he saw the giant skewed in several places, including his neck, head, and chest. Konafar lay on top of him with a spike poking through his left arm. To their left was the lifeless body of the lizardman. A large spike protruded through his head. Tonles climbed down and went to work on freeing Konafar.

Konafar stirred. "Get my arm off of this thing," he said.

"You're one lucky bastard," said Tonles. "Ready?"

"Make it quick," Konafar said and bit down on his lip.

Tonles grabbed his arm by the forearm and underneath the bicep, then pulled it off the spike in one swift motion. Konafar bit down so hard on his lip, to keep from screaming, he drew blood. After wrapping his arm with a piece of cloth, they retrieved Carnage and climbed out of the pit.

Fleck was on his way over, holding his head. "Let's get out of here," he said.

The guards, watching from above, were terrified of the humans; they didn't do anything but watch them leave.

"We're waiting for them," Jacko said to the prisoners after they were bugging him to leave.

"Your friend is pale and needs a healer, or he's going to die," one of the former prisoners said.

"He'll be fine. If it wasn't for Konafar and the others, he wouldn't even be alive."

Breen touched Mao's head. "Jacko, he has a fever, let me take him and the others to Wistful," Breen offered.

"They're right. He probably has an infection," Lud added.

After realizing he was being selfish, Jacko agreed.

"Let's meet at the Inn of the Slaughtered Fawn tonight," Erantel said.

Jacko nodded and left with the prisoners.

In the distance, Lud saw three humanoid figures approaching. Two of them were assisting the other.

"It's them," he said to the others, and they left their concealment and met them.

The first thing Erantel noticed was the blood dripping down Konafar's leg, then how he was barely able to stand upright. Erantel and Lud relieved Tonles and Fleck of their burden and escorted Konafar back to the fire. Tonles walked over to Thessor and told him what befell of his comrade. The lizardman told him he was at peace and someday he would join him.

Once Konafar was seated by the fire, he was handed a few furs. "Where's everyone else?" he asked.

"They went to Wistful. Mao needed a healer, and the prisoners were eager to have a hot meal and a good night's sleep."

"Good, they deserve it," Konafar said, wincing in pain at the same time. "I'm afraid that I'm in need of a healer as well. Can you help dress my wounds?"

Erantel nodded and helped him remove his armor. His wounds were deep, and it took Erantel a while to dress them properly. When he was finished, Konafar fell asleep within minutes.

"How bad was it?" Tonles asked Erantel as soon as he walked over.

"The one on his side is serious."

"It was from a spear, and the one on the arm was when he fell into the pit."

"Pit?" Lud asked from across the way.

"We fought a couple of giants, and he fell into the pit with one of them."

"Giants? There weren't any present when we left."

"They appeared shortly after we killed the guards. I killed one, and he killed the other. We'll talk later. I'm really tired," Tonles abruptly said, then wrapped himself in furs, sat down next to Konafar, and fell asleep.

Fleck fell asleep as well after he had something to eat.

They waited several hours for them to wake. After they did, they doused the fire, mounted their horses, and rode toward Wistful and the pending storm looming in the distance.

****

When Runit woke, he found himself alone in a poorly lit room and strapped tightly to a table. He struggled against the restraints for several minutes and gave up, because they were too tight. He wondered where everyone was and how he ended up here, but then it came back to him.

He was lighting buildings on fire with Awret and two lizardmen when one of the structures came crashing down on them. Since they weren't with him, he could only imagine the worst had happened. He thought about the others and hoped they were on their way to rescue him, but he knew deep down inside they weren't.

Eventually, he grew weary and fell asleep. In his dreams, he was back at his Order working out with Awret. They were grappling, and after he was pinned, Awret let him get up, then kept punching him in the face. After the third time, his eyes snapped opened, and he was awake again.

The door at the far end opened, closed, and someone began walking toward the table.

"I'm glad you're awake, because I have some questions for you," the person said.

Runit didn't reply.

When he was close enough, he put his hand on Runit's forehead and brought his pale, scarred face into view.

"What is your name?"

Runit didn't answer.

"I'll ask once more. What's your name?"

Runit still didn't answer.

"Okay. Have it your way." His antagonist punched him several times in the face until he broke his nose, then he stopped. "Now will you talk?"

Runit spit at his face.

"Now you pissed me off." The antagonist moved away and returned with a wicked curved dagger. "Every time you don't answer my questions, I will flay you. What is your name?"

Runit did not answer, and his captor took the knife and cut off a good portion of the skin from his left arm. Runit screamed very loud.

"Are you ready to speak?"

Runit nodded.

"Good. Name?"

"My name is Runit."

"Now we're making progress. Glad to meet you, Runit. You may address me as Master or the Red Knight, whichever you prefer. Remember, don't lie to me, do you understand?"

Runit nodded.

"Why did you come to my town?"

"To rescue the prisoners."

"How did you get into my town?"

"We used one of the hidden entrances underneath the town."

"I want the names of the people you came with?"

"I was alone."

"Are you sure you were?" The Red Knight smirked.

"Yes."

The Red Knight chuckled. "I told you not to lie to me." He clapped his hands, the door opened, and someone walked over.

The Red Knight turned away and then back. "I have someone here that I'm sure you'd like to see again," he said and held the head of Awret a few inches in front of his face. "I know you know him." He smiled. "I want the names of the other people you came with."

"You bastard."

"NAMES!" the Red Knight yelled.

Runit stared into his friend's eyes and didn't say another word.

"Have it your way."

The Red Knight took the knife and began flaying another portion of Runit's skin away from his arm. This was too much for him to tolerate, and he passed out. When he finally came to, the Red Knight was still there and was surrounded by a few Chatar creatures holding jars of greenish goo.

"The substance in the jars will prevent you from falling unconscious," the Red Knight said, grinning, then began torturing him again.

Eventually, he got every answer he wanted, including their names, what they looked like, and the Order to which they belonged. After they were finished, they left the room. Runit cursed himself for telling him, but the pain he endured was far too great to resist.

About an hour later, the Red Knight returned. "Runit, I've made a decision."

"Kill me. Please kill me," Runit pleaded.

"That was my original plan, but I have something better in mind for you. Let me show you something."

The Red Knight pulled back his left sleeve and what Runit saw horrified him. The arm was stripped clean of skin, muscle, and tendons, and only bone was left, held together by leather straps.

"What the..."

"I know it looks bad, but really it's amazing work." The Red Knight smiled. "I think that I want you to become my second in command. I'm tired of not having another human around."

"Never. I'll kill you the first chance I get."

"I felt that way about my master, but I changed my mind after he finished his work. Ready?" he said gleefully and picked up the knife again.

The horror that Runit went through that day would have been a nightmare to even the vilest of creatures. His arms and legs were stripped clean of flesh and tendons, and his upper torso was cut repeatedly.

When the Red Knight was through, he returned to his quarters to contemplate more pressing matters. As he walked down the vacant corridor, his echoing footsteps reminded him what his life had become: an empty chasm, which was sad because his fragmented memory told him that he had a much different life. After entering his chambers, he sat down behind his desk and began studying the maps laid before him. He decided to destroy the tunnels underneath the town and send his new understudy after his friends when he was ready.

Over the next few days, his troops laid waste to the buildings that housed the secret entrances. He received word about a group traveling west, fitting the description of Runit's friends, and the Lord of Mind contacted him telepathically. Paven informed his master about the events that took place and how he wanted a second in command. The Lord of the Mind agreed to give him what he wanted and went to work on Runit's mind. Despite the long distance, Repan was still able to shape Runit's mind and turn him into an obedient servant who would go by the name of the Green Knight. How effective, Repan's powers were, from where he was, would be determined over time. Paven was delighted to find out Runit knew his new identity and was ready to kill his former friends. After being outfitted in plate mail with a greenish hue, he was given a small army to lead and left the town.

CHAPTER 3: FOREST OF DESPAIR

It was nearing nightfall when Torhan and Brother Sao came upon a creepy dense forest enshrouded in fog. The wooded area spanned endlessly toward the north and south, so west was the only viable way through.

"Mirkin should be on the other side," Brother Sao stated.

"Have you ever been there before?"

"Once, many years ago, but I don't remember the trees being this thick and impenetrable. Maybe we were further north." Brother Sao stared intently at the old and decaying trees.

Torhan followed his gaze. "Is there something wrong?"

"I'm getting a strange feeling about this place. I don't think it's a good idea to go in."

"I don't have a choice. I have to go. You don't have to," Torhan said and began walking.

Brother Sao reached out, grabbing his shoulder. "You don't understand, there's something evil lurking inside."

"How do you know?"

"I can feel it."

"Are you coming or not?"

"Since I swore an oath to my Order, then I'll go with you," the monk reluctantly said.

"We'll be really careful and mark our way," Torhan said and entered.

It didn't take long before they began to feel like someone or something was watching them. Torhan glanced several times at the scabbard, but since it wasn't glowing, he knew they weren't in immediate danger.

About an hour later, the scabbard began radiating, and Torhan stopped. "We need to change our direction," he said.

"Are we going to be safe?" Brother Sao asked after seeing the scabbard's warning.

"I hope so."

They moved north until the scabbard stopped glowing and then went west again. When the light began fading into darkness, the forest looked even more menacing. The moss-covered trees created an eerie tomb with branches that appeared to sway and dip in their path before them. When they were unable to go further, they found an area inside a cluster of trees and camped.

After lighting a small fire to keep the chill away, they ate and turned in with Torhan taking first watch. He was sitting on an old dead log with his back propped against a tree, staring out into the darkness, thinking about

Jacko and his travels. What he didn't notice was the light mist drifting into their area, causing him to fall asleep.

When morning arrived, Torhan woke from his restful slumber. To him, the forest appeared as it did the day before, but just a little brighter and colder. He was about to say something to the monk when he turned and saw that he was missing. His bedroll was still there, so he knew that he didn't leave. Thinking Brother Sao was relieving himself; Torhan got up and was gathering his blanket when he made an alarming discovery. His backpack was missing, and so were his sword, cloak, and dagger from the scabbard. Everything important was gone including the Ring of Warmth on his finger. He called for the monk. When he didn't answer, he began to worry.

Frantically, he looked around and didn't see footprints or any other traces of intruders. He began walking around looking for him. He started thinking the monk left without telling him, and that made him furious. To leave is one thing, but to take his weapons was unforgivable. What really perplexed him was the scabbard didn't protect him against the actions of the thief, then he remembered something important Molech mentioned about the scabbard. It would only send the dagger to protect the owner if something meant to harm him.

After looking for him unsuccessfully for over an hour, he decided to give up his search and scour the area until he found a strong-looking six-foot branch and tested its potency against a tree. When he was satisfied that it would last, he left and continued west.

A few hours later, Torhan passed a cluster of trees that he thought he saw earlier. He was sure they were the same ones, because they reminded him of the fort his dad built for him as a child. He decided to use an old hunter's trick and mark the area by leaving branches stacked neatly against several trees. Anxiety, or fear of being lost in this hellish place, caused him to sprint ahead. When he came upon the same trees again, he began to panic.

How could this be? he thought and stared at the pile of branches.

He changed directions to the north and again ended up in the same place. His heart sank with dread. He ran toward the east and ended up back in the same spot. He was now wondering if this place was real or just an illusion. He hoped for the latter, because if he was indeed lost, then this would be a fate far worse than death.

The temperature suddenly felt colder. Without his ring or a means to light a fire, he wondered how long he would survive. He began feeling drained, depressed, lost, and uncertain, as he started moving north again.

With nightfall approaching, he had no choice but to stop, and without survival skills, he would certainly have to spend the night awake. He always heard that one could start a fire by hitting two stones against each other or rubbing two sticks together, but when he tried it, he couldn't even produce a single spark. The temperature grew colder as the night got longer, and without the warmth from a fire or his cloak, Torhan shivered uncontrollably. Eventually, his body grew numb, and he began to drift asleep.

Around mid-morning, the mist returned and welcomed him into a deeper sleep.

He awoke at daybreak feeling disorientated and unsure of his surroundings. When he turned his head to the left, he saw a broken staff sticking out of the ground not more than ten feet away. He was sure it was Brother Sao's weapon, and now he knew the monk did not desert him and was most likely taken against his will. *But why didn't they take him the night before? It didn't make sense. For that matter, why was someone or something playing games with him?* He walked west again. After passing the same set of trees that he marked the previous day, he stopped.

"I'm tired of your game, so whoever is out there, show yourself," he shouted. No one responded, so he yelled, "Coward!" to the forest, hoping to entice whoever it was out of hiding.

He was so preoccupied with the forest that he failed to realize the scabbard glowing green, or the needle as it pierced his skin, until he winced in pain. He snapped out of his trance and heard someone rushing toward him from behind. Turning around, he brought the makeshift staff about and deflected a series of sword attacks from a large hybrid creature with the body of a muscular human and the head resembling that of a wolf. The beast wore leather armor over his fur-covered body.

Another creature, similar to the first, emerged directly behind him. Torhan quickly parried three more ferocious attacks and wickedly struck his aggressor several times in various parts of his body, the last of which was on top of his head, knocking him out cold.

Almost instantly, the other creature replaced him, swinging widely and driving Torhan toward the rear until he tripped over a log and fell. The creature was about to deliver a devastating downward blow when Torhan thrust his staff into his exposed belly, causing him to drop his head forward, then he stabbed his throat, knocking the beast backward, reeling in pain.

More creatures emerged from out of the shadows as Torhan quickly scrambled to his feet and frantically ran in the opposite direction. While glancing over his shoulder to see how close they were, he tripped and fell headlong into some bushes bearing sharp penetrating needles that pricked his skin instantly. Within seconds, he became dizzy, and as he tried to rise, he fell back down until, at last, he lay paralyzed and incapable of moving. Black spots danced before his eyes as darkness soon overtook him.

When Torhan woke, he quickly discovered that he was tied to a tree and unable to move or wiggle free from his bonds. Across the way, two rather large individuals, resembling the ones that caught him, were engaged in conversation. They both wore loincloths and leather harnesses around their upper torsos and had hefty battle-axes draped across their backs. The only difference between them was that one had hair on his chin, much like a long beard, and the other had a patch over his right eye. When they noticed he was awake, the one with the eye patch walked over.

"What are you doing in our home, human?" he asked.

"Just passing through."

"Passing through? No one just passes through, so where are you going?" He gazed at him intensely with his good eye.

Torhan thought about lying, but he didn't see how it would hurt telling them some of the truth. "I'm on my way to the town of Mirkin."

"What for?"

"I have personal business to take care of."

The creature got angry and slapped him across the face. The scabbard, hidden beneath the ropes, glowed but not bright enough for anyone to notice.

"I ASKED WHAT FOR?"

"I have a family member who's ill."

"Is that so?" the creature slapped him again, this time harder. "Your friend told us differently."

"The monk? Where is he?" Torhan demanded.

"He's safe for now," the creature with the beard said.

Torhan's interrogator grabbed his face. "I'm going to ask you again. What's the real reason why you're going to Mirkin?"

Torhan wasn't sure if they really had Brother Sao or not, but he couldn't take any chances. "I am going to Mirkin, but it's not for an ailing family member. I need to visit their priest; he's a friend to my family."

"Why?"

"I can't say."

"Din, convince him otherwise," the bearded creature said.

Din unhooked his axe and placed the head of the weapon underneath Torhan's chin. Torhan swallowed hard against the cold steel.

The bearded creature came closer. "Now, human, tell me what business you have with the priest or Din might slip and end your life." His voice was calm yet, by his temperament, Torhan could tell he was growing impatient.

Torhan was left with only two choices. Tell them about Grappin's charge or what Brother Pien wanted him to do. He wasn't sure which story, if any, would save his life, so he decided to leave the monk out of it. "Alright, I'll tell you. Truth is I am going to see Priest Abiathar but not for a friendly visit. I need to disable his protective wards surrounding his church."

"Protective wards? Why would you do that, human?"

"I got mixed up with someone in Redden, and he is forcing me to do this."

"How is he forcing you?"

"I don't think you'll believe me."

"Try me."

Torhan looked at Din, then at the other one. "Tell him to remove his axe from my throat. It's really uncomfortable."

"Din, lower your weapon."

"For your sake, your story better make sense or my axe will find your neck," Din said and removed it.

Torhan told them everything that was in Grappin's note, his memory loss, the items, and the trip to Waisterner to find out about the priest and his wards.

When he finished, the bearded creature spoke. "Human, you tell a wild tale. Do you think you murdered the shop owner and stole his stuff?"

"I don't think so."

"Well, I think you did," Din said.

"Look at the note in my pouch; it has the details."

"If you lost your memories, then how do you know the note is yours? You could've stolen it," Din added.

"He's right, human. I think you're going to Mirkin to kill the priest, and I can't let that happen. You see, he's a friend of ours, and disabling his wards would leave him vulnerable. Din, put an end to his miserable life."

"My pleasure, my lord."

"Don't. Please," Torhan begged.

Din lifted his weapon, and Torhan shut his eyes.

As Din was about to chop off his head, the scabbard glowed so intensely, the bearded creature noticed a light emitting from underneath the rope.

"WAIT!" he shouted.

Din grunted in frustration and lowered his weapon.

Torhan slowly opened his eyes.

"What do we have here?" the bearded creature said, then took out a knife and cut away a few of the ropes, exposing the scabbard. "Where did you get this?"

"I think that's one of the items from Redden."

The bearded creature tried removing the scabbard, but it wouldn't budge, and he wasn't able to cut the string either. "Interesting. How does it come off?"

"I have to take it off for you."

"You'll do that for me later. Where's the letter?"

"It's in my pouch."

He opened the pouched and took the note. "Din, come with me."

They walked away, read the note, and talked for a few minutes before returning.

"I didn't recognize Grappin's name when you said it, but after reading the note, it dawned on me who he is."

"Who is he?" Torhan asked.

"I will tell you in time, human. Do you know what the scabbard does?"

"I do. It warns me of danger by glowing, and if there was a dagger inside, then the weapon would've become enchanted and protected me."

"Correct me if I'm wrong, but didn't you recently encounter strange beings that can manipulate time and even stop it?"

Torhan was really surprised by his statement. "How could you know that?"

"It's a gift my kind possesses. We can detect certain signs left behind by other beings. For instance, the ones you met are known as Chromos Lords, and every time they use their abilities, they leave behind an imprint on just about everything that will last for months. Let me ask you something. After you met them, didn't you wonder why you weren't affected by their powers?"

"I did."

"The ancient relic around your arm protected you. I guess you didn't figure that out, did you?"

"No. Are you going to let me go?"

"After reading the note and finding the scabbard, I know that you're telling the truth."

"I don't understand."

"The scabbard is not from this world and can only be found in the underworld."

"Where?"

"I will explain later."

Din released Torhan from his bonds.

"What are your names?" Torhan asked.

"My name is Lord Sim, and I am the leader over my people. Din is my finest and fiercest warrior."

Din bowed slightly.

"My name is Torhan, and I hail from the town of Wistful."

"I can tell that you're in need of healing, and I'm guessing some food as well," Lord Sim offered.

"That would be nice. Where are my items and, more importantly, my companion, Brother Sao?" Torhan asked candidly.

Lord Sim looked over at Din, and the warrior nodded and left.

"Din will find out how he is and return shortly. For now, come with me."

The forest gradually changed from dismal and lifeless to lively and full of beauty with birds chirping sweetly and trees, with leaves of every color under the rainbow, adorning their branches. Torhan couldn't believe he was in the same place.

Lord Sim noticed his fascination and said, "We keep this area hidden from strangers."

"It's amazing."

"That it is."

Eventually, they passed through another area with a large pond and a twenty-foot high rock wall directly behind it. Torhan paused to enjoy the peaceful sound the water made as it trickled down the rocky surface. He also took pleasure in the beauty of the exotic flowers surrounding the pond. It reminded him of a similar place he'd seen before.

"This is a really nice place," he commented.

"I come here often to think. Shall we continue?" Lord Sim held out his hand in the direction he wanted them to go. Torhan nodded.

They came to a place with a long oak table and chairs running along the sides. Lord Sim seated himself at the far end and asked Torhan to sit next to him on his left. The leader clapped his hands loudly and four of his kind, wearing loincloths, appeared from out of the trees. On large silver platters, they carried various types of foods such as: deer, boar, fowl, and exotic fruits the likes of which Torhan had never seen. After the food was set on the table, more servants appeared, and with them they brought tankards of ale, wine, and one containing strange blue liquid that was placed directly in front of Torhan. After the servants left, Lord Sim raised a tankard of ale and waited for Torhan to do the same.

"To our new friendship," he toasted and together they drank the sweet-tasting brew.

After placing the mug down, Lord Sim said, "The cup with the blue liquid is something very special. Not only will you feel better physically, but it will also help you remember what was lost to you."

Torhan picked up the cup and stared at the contents for several long seconds before throwing caution to the wind and drinking. The liquid tasted bitter as it ran down his throat, and he could feel its healing effects immediately coursing through his body. Within seconds, cuts and bruises began fading and even the scars from his childhood disappeared. He was about to say something when he felt lightheaded and dizzy. It happened so fast, and unexpectedly, that he placed his head into his hands to help deal with the sensation.

What followed next were the memories from Redden. He recalled waiting for Jacko in his room, meeting Molech, the shop owner Tomal, the scabbard, his escape from the guards, his time spent with Grappin, the deals he made with him and Molech, his escape from the town, and finally, the men he had to kill. After the feeling passed, he raised his head.

"Do you remember now?" Lord Sim asked.

"Yes, I remember everything. Thank you."

"I'm glad."

"Lord Sim, I've never heard of you or your people before inhabiting this forest. Have you always lived here?"

Lord Sim sat back, took a deep swig, and began his tale. "The reason is because our people are not from your world, and it was by accident that we even ended up here in the first place."

"What do you mean?"

"A long time ago my world was dying, and, in an effort to preserve our race, the inventor created a one-way device called a portal. We had no idea where we would end up or if we could actually adapt to our new environment. Once the door was opened, the first of the brave ones walked through, and we could tell something was wrong right away after he grabbed his throat and died. The inventor sealed off the entrance and went back to work in his lab until he came up with the idea of expanding the portal into your world. A few days before he was going to test his theories, our world began to disintegrate, so he expanded the portal as far as it could reach into your world and a group of us crossed over. To our surprise, his idea worked, but the size of the portal was limited to this forest," he paused, "so you see, Torhan, we're trapped. We can't go back to our world, and we can't leave this forest."

"What happened to your world?"

"Our world, the portal, and any of our people, who couldn't make it over, were destroyed..." Lord Sim's voice trailed off.

"I'm sorry about your people."

"There wasn't enough time or room in this forest to save them all."

"Did the inventor come through?"

"He did but died shortly thereafter, and with him, any information of how to construct another portal." Lord Sim looked sad.

Torhan changed the subject to something a little more pleasant and kept the conversation light.

After their bellies were full, the leader clapped his hands, and the servants returned, removing the dirty plates and bringing over more wine. They enjoyed another goblet of sweet-tasting nectar.

Lord Sim stared at him. "What do you know about Grappin?" he asked.

"Not much."

"Then how did you come to embark on your quest?"

"It's a long story."

"We have time, so please tell me," Lord Sim said with a strange look upon his face.

Torhan didn't really trust Lord Sim. When he decided to hide the truth from him, he found that he couldn't and told him every little detail. When he was through, Lord Sim smiled.

"I know you wanted to hide certain things from me, but I needed to hear everything that happened to you," he said.

"You drugged me, didn't you?" Torhan leered in disgust.

"Not deliberately. It's one of the side effects of the drink that restored your memory."

"You should have told me before I drank it."

"It really seemed like you wanted your memories back. Am I right?"

"Yes, but you should have allowed me to make that decision." Torhan was upset.

"Fair enough."

Torhan was about to say something more when Din walked over holding a sack.

"I have your belongings," he said and handed him the bag.

Torhan stood up and opened the sack. He was relieved to find all of his items there. "Where's Brother Sao?" he asked Din.

"He's alive but resting from his injuries."

"Injuries? What happened to him?"

"Our people wounded him, while he was being captured. He's still unconscious."

"I want to see him?"

"Tomorrow," Din said and left.

Torhan thought about storming off to find Sao but figured it wouldn't do him any good.

He looked directly at Lord Sim. "Am I prisoner here?" he asked.

"No. You're free to go, but I want you to meet someone before you do."

"Who?"

"After we're finished, I will take you there. Please sit."

Torhan nodded and sat back down. Lord Sim took another swig while looking at Torhan.

"What if I told you that you are a pawn in Grappin's game, and no matter what you do, he will kill you in the end. Will that change your mind about disabling the wards?"

"You don't know that."

"Yes, I do. I've met him before, not by the name of Grappin."

"If you knew, then why did you make me waste my time telling you about him?"

"You humans anger easily, don't you?"

"When you take away our free will, we do."

"I wanted to understand if you were knowingly working with him."

"Tell me what you know about him."

"Grappin isn't just an ordinary person, he's something far more dangerous than anything you'll ever encounter." Lord Sim waited several seconds before continuing. "He's a demon and goes by the name Dybbuk."

"A demon? They don't exist."

"They do and only a few others believe in their existence. I'm afraid your kind's ignorance will be your end." Lord Sim eased back in his chair.

"How did they get here?"

"A long time ago, Dybbuk entered your world through a portal similar to ours," he began, "the location he chose was Mirkin. Can you guess where?"

Torhan shook his head.

"In the cellar of the old temple. Do you know why he'd pick such a place?"

Again, Torhan shook his head.

"So he could murder the priest and assimilate his body and then plot for the day to unleash his hoard from his world."

"Why not just release his kind and overrun the town from the beginning?"

"Demons are very clever, crafty, and do not act hastily in their actions. They'd rather take months, even years, before unleashing their true plan."

Lord Sim waited for Torhan to ask another question. When he didn't, he continued.

"After he assimilated the head priest, he served in that form and began to gain the trust of those around him, but more importantly, the townspeople."

"Didn't anyone suspect anything?" Torhan interrupted.

"Some of the priests did, but when they voiced their concerns, they were met with a stiff punishment by purification, or worse, cast out of the Order. Years later, while Dybbuk was on a pilgrimage, one of the acolytes who thought their leader wasn't who he said he was, used a chant, and it revealed his hidden portal. He reported his findings to another priest and, with the aid of their god, sealed it shut and created wards strong enough to keep Dybbuk from returning to the town. The wards have remained in place for years, and the commands to unlock them were passed down from head priest to head priest. That is why if Priest Abiathar were to fall, then the wards would surely fall as well."

"Why is this town so important to Grappin, I mean Dybbuk?"

"It's not the town, it's the portal. If the wards fail, then he can return and release his horde into your world."

"How do you know all this?"

"Come with me."

They walked deeper into the forest until they came upon a dirt road leading south, and Lord Sim stopped. "If you travel down this path for a while, you'll come to a large pond. In the center of the lake will be an island with a very beautiful tree growing out of it. Go over to the tree and speak with her," he said.

"Speak with her?"

"Yes. You can ask her anything you want and she will provide you with the knowledge you seek, but be warned, choose your questions carefully, because she only has a certain amount of energy, and once it's depleted, she'll fall quietly asleep for a moon's time. Do you understand?"

Torhan nodded.

"Come back this way when you're finished."

Torhan proceeded down the winding path laid before him, never once feeling like he was in any type of danger, nor did the scabbard indicate anything differently. It didn't take long to reach the pond with the small island in the middle and a tree perched on top of it. He heard a unique sound of running water further away that created a very tranquil atmosphere. He scanned the area for anything out of the ordinary, then walked out into the surprisingly warm, waist-high water.

As he cautiously approached the island, he realized that Lord Sim couldn't be more right about the tree. It was simply a thing of beauty; the trunk was the perfect shade of brown, the leaves were the bright color of autumn, and the branches extended and dipped low enough into the water to appear as if they were drinking from the very pond itself.

He climbed onto the island and remained rooted where he was until a female's voice, as lovely as the sound of the wind blowing gently on a spring day, spoke to him.

"Step closer, my child," she said.

Torhan did as he was asked, then stopped and waited, not sure of what to do next.

"Come around to the other side," the gentle voice said.

Torhan walked around the tree and stopped in front of a large, round opening that was dark inside.

"Who are you?" Torhan asked.

"My name is Ailith, and what is your name?"

Perplexed, Torhan could only wonder how the tree could talk without a mouth. "My name is Torhan," he said boldly.

"Glad to meet you, Torhan. What brings you here before me?"

"Lord Sim told me that you might be able to answer some questions I have."

"Lord Sim? I haven't seen him in such a long time." Her voice sounded sad.

"What are you?"

"I was human once, very much like you are, but now I am known as a Tree Spirit."

Once like me? The question reverberated throughout his mind.

"Yes, like you, would you like to know how?"

Torhan thought of Lord Sim's warning about depleting her energy but said yes anyway.

"In a time, not so long ago, I lived in a village toward the west. Even though the name of it now eludes me, I do remember everything about the village. The stone moss-covered homes, the merchant's stores, the smell of fresh-baked bread wafting out of the windows, and, of course, the people, oh yes, the people! How wonderful they were, always helping each other and creating a very peaceful environment. Then one day, everything changed when an elderly man came to stay in our town. At first, everything was fine until a few weeks later people began acting differently. They squabbled with one another for no reason and accused each other of horrendous acts. Their strange attitudes spread like wildfire throughout the village until just about everyone was at each other's throats, and the entire village was in disarray. A small group of us tried to calm the angry people, but it was too late and a riot broke out. For two days, people went on a murderous rampage. When the fighting finally subsided, most of our people were dead, including my husband and children. Shortly after that, I fell into a deep depression and stayed inside my house." Ailith's voice sounded distraught.

"So what happened next?" Torhan sincerely encouraged her to continue.

"A few days later, voices began speaking to me from the shadows. At first, I disregarded them, because I thought I was going crazy from the loss of my family, but when they told me things that only my husband knew, I accepted them as friends. They promised they could lead me back to my family, and I believed them. For several weeks, they were my only friends and kept telling me my family would be with me soon. Then one night, the voices led me to the attic. They told me it was time to see my family, and all I needed to do was slit my throat in order to see them again. As I sat there, contemplating about ending my life, the images of my family began to appear, asking me to join them. I called out to them, but they just kept chanting for me to join them. The chanting continued until I was overwhelmed with guilt and elected to slit my throat. As the blood surged forth from my wound, the images of my family began to grow brighter, and, in that brief moment, I was happy again."

"Did you join your family when you died?"

"NO!" Ailith's voice became bitter and angry. "My spirit lifted out of its mortal shell, and the images were gone. As I hovered above my body, another voice called out to me, not from inside the house, but somewhere outside. I gazed at my lifeless body one last time and floated through the building, following the voice until it led me here to this tree that stands before you. When I arrived, the voice promised me peace, wisdom, insight, and, of course, love the likes of which I'd never experienced before. All I needed to do was enter. Since the death didn't give me release, or my family back, I listened."

"Was the voice right?"

"Yes. We completed each other. I got love and, in return, the tree received companionship."

"I'm glad you finally found what you were looking for."

"Thanks for listening to me. It's been a very long time since I told my story." Ailith's response was a little more upbeat.

"Can you help me?" Torhan asked.

"I'll do my best to answer your questions, but be warned, the information provided could be altered by the path you choose. Please be very direct when asking."

Torhan took his time before asking his first.

"Is Grappin a demon?"

"Yes he is and a very powerful one. His true name is Dybbuk."

"How do you know about him?"

"I'm not permitted to tell you."

"Can you tell me what he wants?"

"He wants to return home but can't as long as the protective barrier is still in place. He also wants to release his minions into your world."

Her answers confirmed what Lord Sim told him already. Torhan paused before asking his next question. "Why was I selected to help him?"

"Because he can't disable the wards himself, and he needed someone who didn't know the truth behind his plan."

"If I don't help him, will he succeed?"

"Eventually, he'll find a way to deactivate them, but it could take a long time."

"Will he let me live if I don't help him?"

"No!" Ailith sternly replied.

"Can I defeat him?"

"With help you can."

"From who?"

"Not who but what."

"I don't understand."

"Demons are immune to mortal weaponry, so you'll need a special weapon called a Bow of Precision and Arrows of Slaying."

"Where can I find the bow and arrows?"

"You cannot find them. You need to make them from the materials located here in this very forest. There are three components total: the first one is the most important; it's a branch from the Aimsaw tree. The tree is located across the shore and is recognized by the large thorns running up and down the length of its bark. One of my vines will serve as the second item, and lastly, the leaves from the fernion plant, which grows next to the Aimsaw tree. The leaves are oblong-shaped with pointy ends. To construct the bow you must first bend the branch into the exact shape of a long composite bow. This will take a great deal of strength and more than one person is needed to perform such a task. Next, the vine must be peeled apart until you reach the center, and there you will find the strongest cord known to exist. Use that for the string, and the bow will be quite powerful and never lose tension. Finally, replace the feathers of the arrows with the leaves. The leaves are special and will enable the arrow to penetrate the demon's defenses and expose him to mortal weapons. Do you have any questions thus far?"

"I don't know how to make a bow, so who is going to help me?"

"Once you gather the items, take them back to Lord Sim and explain to him exactly what I have told you, and he will help you." Ailith's elucidation gave Torhan hope.

"So that's it. All I have to do is shoot him with the arrow?"

"No, there's more. You must provoke the demon into wanting to kill you with intent. Only then will he be at his most vulnerable, and the arrow will penetrate his flesh. Otherwise, it will deflect off his body."

"What happens next?"

"Once the arrow pierces his flesh, the leaves will come to life and feed off his negative energy and inject him with a poison deadly to his kind. Do you understand now?"

Torhan nodded

"Do not despair, Torhan. When the time comes, you'll be brave and your hands steady."

"How do you know?"

"Just like I know how to defeat Dybbuk. I just do. I must rest shortly; my energy drains."

"I have one more question." Torhan pressed, "Where is my friend, Jacko?"

"As we speak, he serves justice for a fallen friend."

"Does he need my help?"

"No! However, you'll need his when…" her voice ceased abruptly.

"When? Ailith. Tell me." Torhan pleaded.

Eventually, he gave up and went to work cutting down one of her vines. He was glad she was asleep, because, to him, it felt like he was removing one of her limbs.

After rolling up the vine, and slinging it over his shoulder, he left the island, went about gathering the rest of the materials needed, then went back to Lord Sim's camp.

When he returned, the first thing he saw was Lord Sim perched atop a big chair with many of his followers sitting on the grass listening to his every word. Din was off to the side.

"It's good to see you again. Did you get all of your questions answered?" Lord Sim blurted out when he was close enough.

"Most of them."

"Good, good. What's the tree branch for?"

"I need it for a bow. She said you could help me construct one."

"We can. We don't have a cord for it though, so you'll need one."

Torhan showed him the vine. "She said you can peel the vine away and use the center as one."

Lord Sim looked over at Din and nodded.

"Consider it done, my lord," Din responded and took the items from Torhan. "The bow will take a couple of hours to make. What will you do for arrows?"

"I'll get some in Mirkin."

"Torhan, would you like some wine?" Lord Sim offered.

"No, thank you. I would like to walk around the forest."

"Very good, enjoy yourself."

Torhan walked through the forest thinking about the days ahead. *What if he was being played by Lord Sim and Ailith as well, and her special bow and arrows were nothing more than ordinary weapons.* He wished there was some way of knowing, because, by the time he'd find out, it would be too late. *But what choice did he really have? If he didn't do as Grappin asked, then he would have to contend with him or his assassin. Maybe he'll just disable the wards and hope that would suffice his obligation to him.* He had a feeling Brother Pien was a man of honor, so hopefully the healer Katara could help him decide what was right. *If only Jacko was on time, then he would've never entered Tomal's store.* His thoughts turned to his friend and what Ailith said about him. *What did she mean when she said he was serving justice for a fallen friend? I wonder who?*

He walked around for another hour before heading back. Din was showing Lord Sim the newly crafted bow and paused when he saw Torhan approaching.

"Is that it?" Torhan excitedly asked.

"This bow is my finest work," Din stated proudly as he presented the weapon. "Use it well and may you strike down your enemies with little effort."

Torhan accepted the weapon, marveled at the workmanship, then tested the bow's tension. "It's amazing. Thank you, Din."

"Was your time in the forest well spent?" Lord Sim asked.

"It was. Thanks for all of your help."

Lord Sim grinned. "Good luck, Torhan from the West, may you live a long time. Din, escort him to the monk."

"If my friend should happen to pass through, please welcome him and let him know where I've gone. His name is Jacko, and he is from the

Order of the Open Palm."

"We will," Lord Sim said.

****

After Din returned, he had a private audience with Lord Sim.

"What do you think about Torhan?" Din asked.

"He should do fine as long as he follows Ailith's instructions."

"And if he fails?"

"Then I fear the worst." He paused. "Dybbuk will return, so we'll need to be ready."

"But we don't have many weapons to stand against him."

"I know."

Torhan and Brother Sao exchanged stories about how each of them was captured. Brother Sao said he was investigating a strange noise when they unexpectedly fell upon him and wounded him pretty seriously. Before they captured him, he was able to lead them away. Torhan told Brother Sao what he experienced and of his time spent with Lord Sim and Ailith. When finished, they traveled west and left the forest.

Once clear of the trees, the town of Mirkin stared back at them. They walked openly onto the plains toward the old city and reached the walled city by nightfall.

Torhan turned to Sao. "Can you stay for a while in town?" he asked.

"No. I must be going."

"Where will you go?"

"I'll make camp for the night and then go to my Order. It's about a half day north from here."

"Do you want me to stay with you tonight?"

"There's no need. I want to meditate and reflect on my brother's passing. Please make sure you keep Katara's identity a secret. You'll like her; she's nice."

"I will, and thanks for your help."

Brother Sao nodded and walked away.

Torhan watched him leave, then turned his attention back toward the closed gates of the city and approached.

When he was fifteen feet away from the doors, a voice shouted from the parapets above.

"I wouldn't take another step if I were you."

Torhan stopped dead in his tracks and looked up in the direction of the voice. He saw a silhouetted figure holding a trained crossbow pointed directly at him.

"Identify yourself or die!"

"My name is Torhan, and I hail from the west."

"What is your purpose, Torhan from the West?" The guard sounded annoyed.

"I've been traveling for weeks, and I'm in need of shelter and food."

"Nobody enters the city after dusk. You'll have to spend the night outside with all the other vermin."

"Please let me in. I am very weary."

"Weary?" another voice said, and the guard turned toward the left. "Look, he's tired, Rin. What are you, a baby?"

The other guard mocked and walked over to stand beside his fellow guard.

"We feel really sorry for you. Now go away and don't return until the morning if you know what's good for you." The tone in the first guard's voice convinced Torhan that he wasn't going to gain access tonight.

As he walked away, he could still hear the guards mocking him about his manhood.

"If I run into those fools again, they'll feel the cold steel of my blade," he said angrily but low enough so that they couldn't hear him.

He walked for another hundred yards and came upon some large boulders which sheltered a small cave with only two entrances. Torhan felt they should provide adequate protection in case the weather grew colder during the night. He'd just lit a small fire, and began eating some fruit, when a figure appeared out of the shadows and entered.

"Can I join you?"

Startled, Torhan looked up and relaxed when he recognized Brother Sao.

"I thought you were leaving?" Torhan asked.

"I was watching you from afar to make sure you were safe. When I saw you leave the city, I decided to join you."

Torhan smiled and offered the monk some food.

It was around midnight when they turned in. Torhan took first watch, because tomorrow night he'd be in a warm bed and Brother Sao wouldn't.

A short time later, his eyes grew weary, and he dozed off without warning.

"It's about time you arrived?"

Torhan snapped awake when he heard the voice.

"If you're going to accept watch, then try not to fall asleep," a masked stranger said and entered.

Torhan recognized him from Grappin's mansion.

"What are you doing here? I still have time," Torhan said and did not let the anger in his voice go unnoticed.

"Let's just say I didn't want you to back out of your agreement with my, I mean, our boss."

"I have no intention of backing out of anything."

"Good. That would be most unwise if you did." The assassin made his statement a verbal threat. "I see you have company, and a monk at that."

"He's an ally." Torhan tensed and was about to grab his weapon, and lunge at the assassin, when Grappin appeared from behind his hired killer.

"I wouldn't do that if I were you," Grappin said.

Torhan relaxed.

"I need you to disable his wards, and I need it done by dusk of the next evening."

"That's not what we agreed upon."

"I know, but things suddenly have changed."

Torhan felt the hairs on his neck stand up as the tension was building. He didn't like what was happening. *If only he had the arrows ready,* he thought.

Just then, Sao stirred awake and was on his feet, with staff in hand, after seeing the two strangers. "Are you alright?" he asked, suspiciously looking at the strangers.

"Stay out of this, monk," the assassin hissed.

"Who are these men?"

Torhan waved his hand to calm Brother Sao and turned back toward Grappin and the hired thug.

"Leave him out of this. He's leaving in the morning."

"That would be wise of him," the assassin added.

"Enough," Grappin told his man and gave him a look of disgust, which the assassin ignored. Turning his attention back to Torhan, he said, "If you do this for me, I'll give you ten-thousand platinum pieces."

Torhan agreed to his offer.

"Good. After tomorrow night, we'll both be happy men," Grappin said.

They were about to leave when Torhan asked, "How did you find me?"

"It wasn't all that hard," the assassin ridiculed, and both men faded into the darkness.

"Who are they?" Brother Sao asked after they were gone.

"The devil and one of his minions, that's all," Torhan responded flatly and remained staring off in their direction. He wondered if the demon noticed the bow or if they knew he passed through the forest.

When morning arrived, they said goodbye and parted. Brother Sao headed westward and Torhan marched toward the town, eagerly wanting to finish his task and be rid of the demon.

Brother Sao had just cleared a large set of rocks when an arrow glanced off his left shoulder. He bent down and rolled away as a second, then a third arrow flew by his head, missing him only by inches. Quickly, he was on his feet again and ran behind a few of the boulders just as several more arrows bounced off the rocks. Now out of danger, he gripped his staff tightly in his hands and shouted in anger, "COWARD!"

"Come on out and meet your death, monk," someone responded, a voice he recognized as the masked assassin from the night before.

"Some assassin you are. You can't even hit your mark."

"That's because I wanted to get your attention before I kill you. Hence, the glancing blow to your shoulder."

"Why are you trying to kill me? You don't even know me."

"Let's just say you insulted me last night, plus, I really hate monks and all that they stand for."

Brother Sao had a good idea where he was hiding and ran out toward him. Within seconds, arrows flew in his direction, which Brother Sao easily deflected with his staff or averted them altogether by moving in a zigzag formation. Meanwhile, when the assassin failed to stop the monk, he threw down his bow in disgust, drew his sword, and came out of hiding.

After Brother Sao was within range, he planted his staff into the ground and propelled his body through the air, kicking the assassin in the chest and sending him stumbling backward. The assassin regained his footing and blocked several pressing attacks from the monk's staff and countered with a series of misdirected attacks, the last of which sliced Sao's arm. Brother Sao spun away, holding his arm as the pain coursed through his extremity. He realized that he was poisoned.

The assassin stopped his assault to enjoy the look of horror creeping on his face, which prompted him to say, "You're finished, monk, but at least you fought well."

Crippling pain suddenly surged from Brother Sao's arm and moved toward his chest. He gritted his teeth, screamed at his adversary, and attacked him with vicious intent. No longer caring for his own safety, he swung the staff repeatedly until he penetrated the assassin's defenses and struck him in several places. The first broke the man's left arm and caused him to drop his sword. The second hit him in the right side of his body and broke several ribs, and the third was a well-placed thrust that hit him directly in the solar plexus, knocking the air from his lungs. The assassin fell to his knees, Sao hit the side of his head, and he fell over on his stomach. The monk delivered a devastating strike across his lower back, then on the back of his head, knocking out the hired killer.

Brother Sao stood over his helpless foe and thought about sparing his life until he felt a sharp stinging pain in the center of his chest the likes of which he'd never felt before. He staggered a few feet backward and started seeing stars dance before his eyes. With one final effort, he brought the weapon downward and blacked out, never knowing if he hit him or not.

It was nightfall when the assassin woke to find the monk's staff only inches from his face. Feeling uncomfortable, he reached over with his good arm and pushed it away. He realized that it would've split his head in two if it had hit him. He followed the weapon's length and saw the owner lying face down dead. The scene brought a smile to his face and a reassurance that he is, and always will be, someone to be reckoned with.

After gloating inwardly, for several minutes, he tried getting up and found his legs wouldn't respond. He tried to move them again but still they wouldn't respond. With his smile fading, he rolled over onto his back, sat up, and tried willing his legs to move. They didn't respond again. Suddenly, a creature howled loud enough to startle him. He anxiously looked around for his sword and couldn't find it. The creature howled again. He grabbed his booted dagger, turned back onto his stomach, and began crawling toward the boulders. Inch by painstaking inch, he pulled his body toward the rocks, then he heard snarling sounds coming from multiple directions. He now realized what his victims must have felt like when he stalked them, and he didn't like it.

Frantically, he clawed ahead until a large creature silently swooped down out of the night and landed on top of a nearby boulder. Bathed in moonlight, he could identify the outline of the creature's girth and its red eyes glaring back at him. The bird creature squawked at him, spread its wings, and took flight. Relieved, he continued his progress toward the rocks. When he was about ten feet away, sharp talons plunged deeply into his back. He screamed as he was lifted high into the air. Before passing out, he came to the realization that he was going to be dinner.

CHAPTER 4: CELTHRIC A BLADE'S QUEST (PART I)

"NO!" Norice screamed, waking himself from his hellish nightmare.

He lay with cold sweat trickling down his face for what seemed like an eternity until his wife, woken by his sounds of distress, spoke.

"What's wrong? Was it those dreams again?"

"Yes, but it was far worse. This time the beast came for you and the children, and I was powerless to stop the fiend." Norice hurriedly got out of bed and headed over to his closet, where he began rifling through his belongings.

"What are you doing?" she asked.

"I have to find a way to stop the madness."

"Don't leave us. It's too dangerous."

Norice ignored her and quickly got dressed, grabbed his hunting dagger, and left the room. He walked down the hallway, to the bedroom of his children, and stopped just short of entering. He stared at their sleeping forms, tucked snuggly under the covers, for a few minutes before saying his silent goodbye. Before turning away, he wiped the tears of sadness from his eyes, then proceeded down the stairs. He'd just grabbed the door handle when his wife appeared from out of their room and said, "Norice, please don't go. I fear that I'll never see you again."

"I have to do this," he responded without turning around. He opened the door and stepped out into the night.

Crying, his wife sank to the floor.

Cool air embraced Norice as he left the house. He was determined to put an end to the nightmares that had been haunting him over the last several months. At first, they were mildly disturbing, but with each passing night, they intensified to the point where he'd hit his wife's face, thinking he was fighting a creature who was about to devour his eldest child. Some of the dreams were the same, while others were totally different, but each one held a connection to the other, and it was on this very night that he finally pieced them all together and knew exactly what he needed to do.

Carefully walking in the snow, with his head down, he avoided the guards patrolling the town and moved swiftly toward the stables. As he came upon the barn, he saw the shadow of someone moving to the rhythm of the lantern's light from within. Being that it was late, whoever was inside would question his sudden appearance, so he carefully crept closer until he saw Tay, the stable boy, cleaning out the stalls. He knew the boy very well and entered the barn.

"Tay?" Norice called out, startling the boy, causing him to drop his pitchfork and turn around.

"Who is it?" the boy nervously asked.

"It's me, Norice. What are you doing here this time of the night?"

The lad relaxed a bit after recognizing Norice and said, "I have to catch up on my duties, because Lord Wellington offered to train me personally as a sentry of the Helix Guard if my duties were finished by morning. He says I have great potential."

"That's great. I'm sure you'll do fine."

Tay picked up the pitchfork and left the stall, approaching Norice. "What are you doing here, sir?" he asked.

"I have a nighttime hunt and need a horse."

"Sorry, but you know I'm under strict orders not to allow any horses out at night, unless Lord Wellington says so." Tay grew suspicious.

"Oh, I see. When should I return?"

"First light, but you still better get permission from him, because the epidemic claimed a few more mares yesterday."

"Thanks, I'll do just that. Have a good night, young Tay."

Norice's eyes narrowed as he turned and walked toward the door. He needed to leave tonight, and there was no way he was going to let a child stand in his way. He exited the barn and hid off to the side. After the boy started working again, he snuck back inside and hid in an empty stall. His original idea was to wait until the boy left before stealing a horse, but his plans took a turn when the mare in the next stall became restless, drawing Tay's attention.

"Who's there?" the boy called.

Norice drew his blade, intending to scare the boy, if need be.

Tay nervously gripped his pitchfork with his trembling hands. "Norice?" he called again. When no one responded, he walked toward the entrance of the barn. Norice watched him as he walked past and stopped in front of the stall next to his.

"Raven, what's wrong, boy?" Tay asked the mare as if the mighty stallion could actually answer. The horse snorted in response and moved around. Tay placed the pitchfork against the stall. "It's okay, boy," he said and took out an apple from a nearby bag.

He was about to feed it to the horse when he noticed the unlatched stall door beside Raven. Immediately, he knew something was wrong, because he always secured them. Tay dropped the apple and started backing away, then realized he didn't grab the pitchfork.

"Who's in the…"

Before he could finish, Norice ran at him, intending to seize the boy, but instead tripped and accidentally stabbed him in the chest. Tay's eyes widened in shock and his legs buckled. Horrified, Norice let go of the weapon and backed away. Tay thrashed about, coughing up blood until he died seconds later. Norice gazed at the boy's lifeless eyes. This innocent boy, no older than his eldest son, was robbed of life, and he was to blame. He stared at the boy for what seemed like an eternity, and was only brought back to reality when he heard people speaking outside.

Norice quickly removed the jutting knife from the boy's chest, grabbed a saddle, and entered Raven's stall. The mare was restless by the sudden entry, but calmed after Norice placed the saddle onto his back and buckled the cinch. Fear and despair welled up inside of Norice, and he knew that if the guards discovered what he had done, they would either throw him in prison, or worse, kill him on the spot. With one last look at the boy's lifeless body, he galloped out of the barn and into the night.

Chief Weis was woken from his deep slumber when a loud knock reverberated on his front door. At first, he didn't react, thinking that the noise was part of his dream, but when the knocking came again, he rose and walked down, telling whoever was knocking to wait. He opened the door to see Norice's wife Tiana. She was dressed in her sleeping gown and crying hysterically.

"What is it, girl?" Weis asked.

"My husband...He's..." she paused.

"What's happened? Is he drunk again?"

She began crying and lunged into his arms. "He's gone."

"What do you mean gone?"

"He just got up and left."

Chief Weis knew she was a bit of a worrier. He pulled her away from his chest and tried his best to calm her. "He's probably gone for a walk to clear his head."

"Not this time. He's been having nightmares and left the house in a panic. I'm afraid he's never coming back."

"Do you want me to look for him?"

She shook her head.

"Okay, wait over there," he said, pointing to one of the chairs in the adjacent room, then walked upstairs to dress.

He returned a few minutes later, dressed in brown leggings, leather boots, a green hemp shirt, and a short sword sheathed to his right side.

"I'll have my men look for him," he said as he reached into his closet and put on a waist-length, sheepskin jerkin. "I think you should go back home and watch the children."

Chief Weis left his house and approached a few of his men walking their patrol route. "Have you seen Norice?"

"He's probably drunk and sleeping it off," one of the men said.

"We need to find him. His wife is worried sick and thinks something will happen to him. Rhanh, you're with me."

About an hour later, a soldier named Timol came running up to the chief. "Sir?"

"What is it?"

"You better come to the barn."

The chief was escorted into the barn and over to where Tay's body was found.

Chief Weis knelt down. "Did you see anything?" he asked his men.

"We came for you as soon as we found him," Timol said.

Chief Weis studied the knife wound. "Did you see Norice?"

"No? Do you think he did this?"

"I'm not sure. Look around for clues, but don't touch anything without telling me." The guard left. "Norice, if you did this, I will personally make you pay," he whispered as he stared at the boy's body.

After they finished their investigation, Weis addressed his men.

"Given the fact that Norice is missing, along with one of our horses, he is our top suspect. Go find that lazy tracker, and tell him he is going to help us."

"What if he refuses?"

"You tell Tranter that if he doesn't help me, then I am going to lock him up. And tell him I mean it this time."

The guard turned to leave.

"Make sure he's sober before he looks at the evidence," Weis added.

Before leaving the barn, Chief Weis told the other men he wanted at least a dozen guards ready to leave in the morning, and not to remove the boy's body or touch anything until Tranter had a chance to look around.

Chief Weis dreaded what he had to do. He needed to tell the boy's parents that their child was murdered, then inform a wife that her husband was accused of it. He'd known Tiana since she was a child, and Norice for several years. Frankly, he liked them both, but justice needed to be served and telling someone their husband was accused of killing a boy wasn't going to be easy.

The couple's house loomed in the distance, and the lantern burned brightly inside, indicating Tiana was still awake. He was only ten feet from the door when it swung open and Tiana stood there, eyes red, and cheeks stained with tears.

"What happened?" she asked after seeing his face and the message his eyes told. "Did you find him?" she pressed.

"Are the kids asleep?" Chief Weis asked.

She nodded.

"Good. Can I come in?"

"Where's Norice?"

"Tiana," he paused, "there's been a murder in the barn tonight, and young Tay was killed."

Her heart sank, and she was afraid to speak.

"We haven't found Norice yet, so we don't know if he was involved."

"He wouldn't do that. He has children of his own," she whispered and began crying anew.

"I'm not saying he did. We'll go looking for him in the morning. And the one who did kill the boy." Weis took her in his arms.

A few seconds later, a voice came from atop the stairs. "Mommy, where's Daddy?"

"Go back to bed," Tiana told him.

The child didn't move. Chief Weis shook his head in sadness.

"I have to leave. If Norice returns, have him see one of my guards right away."

She nodded. He left, and she closed the door.

Chief Weis walked toward Lord Wellington's house to report the news, then he'd have to inform Tay's parents.

The inn still had a few patrons left when Officer Rhanh entered. He looked around and saw Tranter sitting toward the back of the room with his head slumped over the table. Rhanh walked over and called his name sternly. When the tracker didn't answer, he called his name again, louder. Tranter stirred and looked up, squinting at the officer, as if trying to recognize him.

"We need you," Rhanh said. The tracker placed his head back down on the table, obviously ready to pass out again. "Tranter, get up."

"Leave me be, boy."

"Look, you drunk, Chief Weis needs your help."

"Ha. Tell him no."

"He said to tell you if you don't come, then I have the authority to lock your sorry ass up and throw away the key."

The tracker grumbled in disgust and stood up, swaying back and forth. "What's in it for me?"

"You'll have to ask him yourself."

Tranter grinned, took another swig of ale, and then slammed the tankard down on the table. He stumbled over to the barkeep.

"What are you doing?" Rhanh asked.

"I need supplies if I am going to help him," the tracker slurred and laughed loudly, then ordered several wineskins.

They left the inn and made a stop at Tranter's house, where he was allowed to sleep off his inebriated condition until daybreak.

In the early morning hours, Chief Weis was instructing his men when Tranter and Rhanh approached. The tracker swayed slightly to the left, then to the right, causing the chief to roll his eyes in disgust and say, "Do you think you could be sober for at least one day?"

Tranter stopped directly in front of him, pulled out one of his wineskins, and took a long swig. "If I see it correctly, you need me more than I need you."

"Try and sober up before we go," Chief Weis said and started walking away.

"What did you find so far?" Tranter asked.

Weis paused. "Granit will show you the crime scene. I have other things to take care of."

"Come on, I'll show you. It's in the barn," Granit said and led him toward the barn.

On their way, they passed a few guards. One of them looked over. "Look at him, how's he going to track anything? What a drunk. He should climb back inside of a bottle and die." The statement was loud enough for Tranter to overhear.

The tracker stopped and walked over. "I know you weren't talking about me?"

The guard looked at him. "Do you see any other drunks standing around here?"

In the next instance, Tranter had a blade out and pressed against the man's throat, sliding the blade with just enough force against his skin to draw a trickle of blood.

"Now, my friend, you were saying?"

The guard gulped in fear. "I'm sor...sor...sorry," he stuttered.

"Let him go." Granit said.

Tranter glared with deadly eyes at the terrified guard and held the blade there long enough to make a lasting impression, then he pushed him to the ground.

"If you ever address me in a negative manner again, I will kill you," said Tranter, "and that goes for the rest of you as well."

After entering the barn, Tranter and Granit walked over to Tay's body.

"His name is Tay. Norice is the suspect. Now prove your worth and figure out what happened," Granit said and left.

After Tranter finished his investigation, he sought out Chief Weis.

"I don't think Norice killed him intentionally." Tranter said.

"Impossible," Weis responded.

"I'm telling you, that wasn't his original intention. He was most likely trying to take a horse, and the boy was in the wrong place at the wrong time."

"Nonsense, he killed him in cold blood," Chief Weis firmly stated.

"And I am telling you that's not what really happened."

"Show me your findings." Chief Weis stormed off toward the barn with the tracker and a handful of guards in tow.

Tranter led them to the stall at the far end. "The boy was most likely working in this stall when Norice entered the barn and…"

"First off, how do you know that?" Weis interrupted.

"Well, because it's the only one that was cleaned out. Can I continue, or are you going to stop me every time I make a point?"

Weis nodded.

"As I was saying, Tay was working when Norice entered the barn. I'm pretty sure the boy wouldn't allow him to take a horse given the time of night, so I think Norice hid in the stable over there," he pointed, "when Tay wasn't looking." He walked to the stall, across from where the boy's body still lay. "I also believe his intentions were to wait for him to leave and not kill him. I think Tay must've heard him and came over to investigate, and when that happened, Norice had no choice but to kill him."

"How can you be so sure? The boy could have protected himself," one of the guards said.

"Look at him." Tranter waited a few seconds before continuing. "He has one wound to his chest. His hands and arms are free of injuries, so that tells me he was surprised and wasn't ready for the attack. Furthermore, look at the way he is slumped against the stall door."

"So then, what are his motives besides going for a midnight ride?" Chief Weis asked.

"That can only be answered by Norice. We should get going before he gets too far ahead."

Norice rode on through the night at a breakneck pace. He was so focused on his escaping that he almost lost his grip on the horse's reins when Raven slipped on the snow. Blinded by darkness, he could only think about the weapon and stopping the demon who haunted his dreams every time he slept.

It was nearing daybreak when he came upon a small, broken-down wagon. An elderly man, dressed in brown robes and boots, was working on the broken wheel, while a woman dressed in traveling clothes assisted. A teenage girl and two young boys played nearby in the snow. Upon hearing his horse, the woman turned and tried waving him down for assistance, but Norice ignored her gestures and galloped past them for several hundred yards before turning around and riding back.

"He's coming back," the woman said to the elderly man, who stopped what he was doing and stood up.

Norice stopped his horse several yards away.

"Hey there, stranger. Thanks for coming back," the old man said.

Norice looked around before speaking. "Are you having trouble?"

"Yes. This damn wheel finally gave way, and we've been having a hard time repairing it."

Norice dismounted and walked over.

"My name is Rollen. This here is my daughter Girn and over there are her children."

Norice looked over at the children playing in the snow.

"Glad to meet you, my name is Tral. Can I take a look?" Norice asked.

The old man stepped back, welcoming the help.

"My father could fix anything, and he passed his knowledge down to me," Norice said and bent down to check the wheel.

Rollen poked his head beside Norice to show what he found. They continued looking at the axle for several minutes as Norice started plotting his next course of action. He knew that the guards would come looking for him today, and if they encountered this family, they would tell the guards that he'd passed. He couldn't allow them to do that, so he placed his hands on his heart and acted like there was something suddenly wrong with his chest.

"Mister, are you okay?" Rollen asked.

"I'll be fine," Norice said and looked up, then gripped his chest again.

"Tral, please lie down and let my daughter have a look at you. She's a healer," Rollen insisted.

Norice looked up at the old man, while reaching behind his back. "Can you help me up?"

Rollen stood up, while extending his hand to help him to his feet. Norice grasped his hand with his right, then plunged his dagger into Rollen's throat. The old man coughed, choked on his blood, and fell backward. The look in his eyes disturbed Norice, but he knew that he had to kill him.

Girn screamed after seeing what Norice did. He quickly ran over, knocking her to the ground, and stabbed her repeatedly. Her children stopped playing and stared in shock as this person continued to stab their mother.

"I'm sorry, kids, but I had to kill them. Don't worry, you'll be with them again. I promise," Norice yelled over and stood up, covered in blood.

The eldest child told her siblings to run, and then she charged after the murderer with hateful eyes. Meanwhile, the children heeded her advice, while listening to the sound of their sister's dying screams. Once she was dead, Norice gave chase.

A few hours later, Chief Weis and the others came upon the wagon and stopped.

"What happened here?" one of the guards said to the chief.

"I'm not sure," he replied in disbelief, then ordered the men to dismount and investigate.

Tranter pieced the clues together rather quickly and approached Weis.

"It appears our friend might have passed this way and killed the family."

"Are you sure it was him?"

"Pretty sure."

"What do you think happened?" Weis asked.

Tranter walked over to the wagon. "It looks like the wagon was already broken down, and the family was trying to fix it when Norice passed by."

"How do you know that?" Rhanh asked, interrupting the tracker.

"Do I need to explain everything I say?" Tranter's gaze was enough to show he was agitated.

"Rhanh, hold your tongue until he's through. Go on, Tranter," Weis said, and Tranter bent down near the wagon.

"As I was saying, it appears the family hailed the rider down, and he passed them, but then he circled back. The hoof prints are exactly the same ones that passed. The rider dismounted over there," he pointed, "and walked over to the wheel, where he knelt down to surprise and kill the old man with his knife. He killed the woman next and then the children."

"I can't believe he did this. I've known him for a long time and never thought of him a killer," Weis said.

"He's a monster who kills innocent children. We need to find and stop him before he kills again," Tranter added.

"Bury the bodies," Weis ordered his men.

"Chief Weis, we need to catch him now." Weis looked at Tranter. "He can wait. We need to bury these bodies before the animals get to them."

It was around mid-afternoon when Norice's horse was struck by an arrow, which sent Norice flying headlong into the woods. The attack came from a pair of Chatar. They were hiding in thick bushes, waiting to attack anything that passed by. After firing several more arrows in the rider's direction, they left the bushes and gave chase, eager to capture their dinner.

Surprisingly, Norice didn't get hurt after he was thrown from his mount. More arrows sailed past his head, then he scrambled to his feet and ran deeper into the woods, fearing for his life. The cat-and-mouse chase went on for a half-hour and ended when the ground beneath Norice's feet suddenly gave way. He plummeted into the darkness below, bumped his head on the ground, and was rendered unconscious.

Norice dreamt that he was standing in a dense forest with a crackling fire only a few feet away. A thick, leafy canopy blotted out the sun, giving off the appearance that it was twilight. A slight wind suddenly blew from the east and carried the sound of children crying. He listened for what seemed like an eternity, until he heard the distinct voice of his eldest child crying for him. Norice whipped out his hunting blade and ran off in the direction of the cries. He navigated his way through a maze of trees, thick bushes, and across streams, trying desperately to reach his daughter. Just when he thought he was getting closer, her pleas changed direction. Quickly, he followed, running faster than before, until he came upon a large cave with his three children tied to a post near the entrance. Together they turned toward him and pleaded, with tear-streaked eyes, for his help. As Norice stepped closer, an enormous black-horned being, dressed in battle armor and carrying a large pike the size of two men, came lumbering out of the cave on hoofed feet.

Norice recognized the creature from his dreams, and stopped advancing when the fiend hissed at him. The children cried for their father again. Norice looked at their terrified faces and the fresh tears running freely down their cheeks. The creature moved next to his children, and Norice gathered his courage and charged after him. The fiend waited until he was close enough before bringing his mighty weapon about and slicing his eldest child in two at the waist. Norice screamed and plunged his long stiletto several times into the fiend's side, trying desperately to stop the beast. The creature straightened, laughed at his feeble attempt, and brushed the puny mortal aside with a stern backhand. The fiend grabbed his youngest child by the head and ripped it off his shoulders. Norice's heart exploded with sadness as he got up and repeatedly struck the fiend with the dagger. The fiend hissed a horrifying sound of delight before backhanding Norice again, sending him hurtling through the air.

Norice looked up in horror at the fiend, smiling in delight, beside his mutilated children.

"Come, human, it's your turn," the creature said in Norice's tongue and slowly approached him.

A few feet away from Norice, something glistened and caught his attention, causing him to look over. Sticking halfway out of the ground was a glimmering two-handed sword. Something told Norice to grab the weapon, and in one motion, he took hold of the hilt and pulled the weapon free.

Immediately, the sword spoke into his consciousness, "I am Celthric, and I alone can defeat this fiend which haunts you. Allow me to take control."

Norice obeyed his wishes. His arms were moved to the middle guard, as he bravely stood before the demon, poised and ready to strike. Meanwhile, the demon sensed the sword as well and approached the inferior creature that stood before him.

"Know this, mortal. Your kind is doomed, and my brethren will be here soon enough to enslave you all."

The fiend relaxed his guard and invited his opponent to attack.

Norice did just that by charging forward. The melee lasted for several volleys until Norice finally broke through the fiend's guard and pierced his chest. In a final effort, the demon grabbed Norice's head with his massive hand and squeezed. Norice awoke with a startle. The dream felt all too real to him. Despite the horror, he realized that the sword would give him the necessary confidence to defeat the demon, if it was something tangible.

The cavern's damp earth was a welcoming feeling, as reality set in as to where he actually was. His head hurt, along with the rest of his body, as he moved his limbs, one at a time, to make sure nothing was broken. Satisfied, he stood up on shaky legs and checked his body for obvious injuries. When he was through, he lit a glow rock and scanned the area until his eyes adjusted to the darkness, enabling him to identify the outline of the cave. The cold, damp cavern stretched as far as the eye could see, and somewhere up ahead, he heard a constant drip of water reverberating off the walls. A chilly breeze blew from the north and spurred him to wrap his worn, and now tattered, cloak tightly around his body.

Gazing skyward at the opening, he realized two things: it was dusk, and his only chance of escape would have to be by other means than the hole he fell through. Without something hanging down from the hole, there was no way he was going to leave the way he'd come. After taking out his knife, he began walking.

Chief Weis, and the rest of the men from the town of Solarce, found Norice's horse shortly before nightfall. Tranter examined the scene and figured out what occurred, then he found the hiding place the boarmen used to launch their deadly attack. Following this path, Tranter led the men until they reached the hole.

"What do you think?" Chief Weis asked Tranter, after he studied the hole.

"It looks like the ground gave way beneath his feet, and he fell in."

"Do you think we should go after him?" Granit asked the chief.

"I'm not giving up until we either take him back alive or find his body. I need four, or five, volunteers to go below and search for him. Who wants to go?"

Granit, Rhanh, Timol, and two others raised their hands.

"Good. I also want someone to stay with the horse while everyone else comes with me," Chief Weis said and left with the others following close behind.

Rhanh dropped a torch into the hole to gauge its depths. He grabbed a fifty-foot length of rope, secured it around a tree, and dropped the other end into the hole. Afterward, the men descended below.

Norice's glow rock eventually diminished and went out. He was left alone in the darkness with only the wall to use for guidance. He began to feel hopelessly lost in the cavern until he saw a faint glow of a torch emitting from behind. He had a feeling that whoever was following him wasn't friendly, so he moved along the wall until he found a niche large enough to conceal him.

It didn't take long for his pursuers to pass his hiding spot. Once they did, he recognized their uniforms. He knew now they were from Solarce. He figured they must've left rope hanging, in case they didn't find a way out and decided to go back to where he fell. Stumbling through the darkness, he reached the hole and was delighted when he saw a rope dangling from the entrance above. He listened for voices, and when he didn't hear any, he climbed up.

He was halfway to the top when someone said, "Did you find him?"

Norice replied that he'd be right up. He pulled his knife, clenched it between his teeth, and continued to climb. As he neared the top, a face suddenly emerged, along with a hand, reaching down to assist him. He realized the individual couldn't see his face and was grasping blindly to assist.

Holding the rope with his left, he grabbed the knife with his right hand and said, "A little lower."

The guard reached down further. When he was close enough, Norice plunged the weapon into his throat. The guard fell away, choking on his blood for a few seconds, before dying. Norice finished climbing out of the hole. Realizing he was alone, he cut the rope, so no one could follow him up, and then he put on the guard's gambeson, took his sword, and proceeded to kill all of the horses, except for one. Adding insult to injury, Norice took their supplies and left.

About an hour later, Granit and the four men emerged from the cave. They approached Chief Weis and the others.

"Did you find him?" Tranter asked them.

Granit nodded.

"You must have missed him, because we didn't see him come out."

"Now what?" Timol asked.

"Go back in and check again," Chief Weis ordered.

Tranter's face turned white. "Damn him!" he exclaimed, then ran where they left the horse.

"Wait here until we come back," Weis said and followed the tracker.

When they arrived at the top of the hill, they saw the body near the hole, the cut rope, and the dead horses.

"How far ahead is he?" Weis asked.

Tranter bent down and checked the dead man. "No more than a half-hour."

Weis counted the dead nags. "That bastard killed all the horses except for one."

"We'll have to get more if we want to have any chance of catching him."

"There's a town a few miles away. We'll get them there."

"He's becoming a real pain in the ass," Tranter stated.

Disgusted, Chief Weis gathered the men and left the area.

By midnight, Norice arrived at a small deserted and dilapidated town. He was really tired, so he knew that he was going to spend the night. After surveying the area for any signs of danger, he proceeded down the snow-covered road while remaining vigilant as he passed the buildings.

When he was halfway down the road, one building, in particular, caught his attention, and he stopped directly in front of it. The sign, cracked and hanging by one fastener, read "Trint's Supplies." Norice felt compelled to enter. He ruffled through the horse's knapsack until he found a glow rock. He activated the little device and dismounted. He withdrew his sword, looked around once more, and walked up to the door. He was about to enter the building when he felt someone, or something, watching him. The intense feelings caused him to turn around and stand ready. For several long minutes, he remained poised, and when nothing presented itself, he walked into the store.

From across the street, an angry entity watched the mortal enter the store. It wanted to destroy him, but cursed the living instead, because he had no means. Its loathing gave way to prospect and thoughts of opportunity that maybe It could use him as a host and leave this retched place of loneliness. The entity knew It would have to be careful given Its other failed attempts. It now desired to remember Its past, but found it couldn't. It grew angry again and followed the mortal inside.

Norice found the room in complete disarray. On either side, broken tables and chairs littered the floor along with torn parchments, shattered jars and glass containers. To the far end of the room, a counter stared back at him, and slightly to the right of that, stairs leading upward. As Norice moved toward the counter, he once again felt the same presence. This time, it felt very close and directly behind him. Without pausing, he whipped his body around as he swung the blade. To his surprise, there was nothing there. He remained poised for an opponent that never appeared and waited until the sensation passed before moving to the counter.

Behind the counter, he saw the skeletal remains of a humanoid dressed in a torn black shirt and leggings with arrows lodged in between its ribcage. A rusty saber was still gripped tightly in its bony left hand and a dagger in its right. There was nothing of value, Norice decided, and proceeded up the creaky stairs.

After reaching the top landing, he saw three closed doors down the hallway. One on his left, another on the right, and double doors at the far end. He listened carefully for anything out of the ordinary, then he quietly approached the door on the left, pressed his ear against the wood, and listened. Beyond the door, nothing stirred, prompting him to open it and hold the glow rock higher in the air. The room was empty except for a broken-down bed and a fireplace with a few scorched logs. He was about to enter when a chill unexpectedly raced up and down his spine, making the hairs on the back of his neck stand on end. Quickly turning around, Norice was greeted by an empty hallway. He was positive more than ever that something was following him even though he couldn't see it.

He called out to the empty space, "Whoever is here, I mean you no harm and will be gone by morning. Please leave me be."

He felt foolish talking to an empty hallway, but his mother always said that if you ever felt like someone was watching you, then most likely it was a restless spirit that refused to leave their place of death. She also said that if you tell them your intentions, it should be enough to ward off any harm. The eerie feelings lingered for a few more minutes before dissipating. He silently thanked his mother for her advice and walked over to the room on the right.

This room was in even worse shape than the last. The bed and dresser were smashed to pieces. There was a skeleton inside of the fireplace and another in the corner with a spear wedged inside of the stomach cavity.

Norice moved on to the last room. After listening to the silence, he opened the door. To his surprise, the room was tidy, and the furniture was in perfect condition. In the center was a small round table with chairs. Off to his left was a bed big enough to sleep several people comfortably. Beside the bed was a dresser and nightstand, and opposite of the bed was a fireplace with logs placed into a bucket. A lone window to the right provided very little lighting throughout the room. He walked over to the fireplace, added a few logs and tinder, grabbed two pieces of flint and struck them together until sparks ignited the tinder.

After the logs caught fire, Norice removed his gambeson and climbed into the bed. The warmth from the fire and the comfortable bed allowed him to fall asleep within minutes.

Norice's dreams began peacefully. He was at home with Tiana and the kids, and they were sitting around the hearth singing songs. They were halfway through their third song when they heard a knock on the front door, prompting his eldest child to get up and answer it. A cloaked figure, dressed in black, quickly stepped inside. He was a tall, thin, young man with a scar running down his left cheek and wore his long, dark hair tied neatly into a ponytail. The man walked over, sat down beside Norice, and introduced himself as Celthric. Norice spoke with him, and Celthric told him of things to come, and how he must travel north to an ancient battlefield. There, they will meet, and together they will face his fears and save his family. The conversation lasted until the loud sound of trees being knocked down, or thrown, erupted from somewhere outside. Norice knew who was coming and began to panic. Celthric reiterated what he needed to do. Norice got up and moved toward the door just as something crashed into the house.

Norice awoke with his arms and legs flailing. It took him several seconds to calm himself and realize that he was only dreaming. He listened to the darkness and then reached for the dagger under the pillow and pulled the weapon close to his chest. He looked at the fireplace and noticed the fire was reduced to embers, prompting him to leave the warmth of the covers, walk over, and place two more logs onto the dying fire. He stoked the embers until the wood ignited, then returned to the bed and began thinking about his dreams. They were beginning to feel more real every time he slept. He was so afraid, not only for himself, but for his family as well, and it made him sick knowing that they could get hurt. What did his dreams mean? Who was Celthric? Was he a god, a demon, a part of his consciousness, a figment of his imagination, or was he going insane? His thoughts shifted to the family he murdered, how he killed innocent people for his own selfish reasons.

Deep down, he knew that he'd have to atone for his actions, but he hoped to save his family before that day came. The warmth and crackling of the fire brought a sense of peace to him. Soon, his mind drifted to another time and place, and his eyes began to flutter until he was overwhelmed and fell asleep.

From the other side of the room, the Presence lost Its opportunity to enter the mortal's dreams when he awoke abruptly. It was busy thinking about the mortal's free will and cursed him for the lost chance. Its anger gave way to calmness when the mortal fell asleep again, and it entered his dreams shortly thereafter.

Norice was dreaming that he was standing on a bloody battlefield with dead bodies stretching as far as the eye could see. He recognized some of the dead as Tay, the stable boy; Rollen and his family; and Chief Weis with his wife and children. He began walking east, through the dead, when a voice called to him from the west.

"Norice, come to me," the voice said.

Norice stopped abruptly, turned around, and began walking west. The voice guided him until he came upon a clean-shaven, gray-haired old man wearing black robes.

"Who are you?" Norice asked, standing before him.

The old man smiled and said, "I am Celthric."

"Why are you old this time?"

"I can be many things." Celthric shifted to the appearance of a child, then a sword, and back to the old man.

"Are you a god?" Norice asked.

"No, I am here to guide you to me. There is a great evil afoot, and it hunts for you and your family."

"Why me?"

"You're special."

"In what way?" Norice asked, even though he was afraid of the answer.

"The fruit of your loins holds the key to mankind and his salvation, and they must be kept alive."

"Which one?"

"I do not know." Celthric shifted his stance and suddenly turned his head toward the north.

Norice followed his gaze. "What is it?" he asked.

"Another Presence is here?"

"The fiend?"

"No, something real, and very dark, and not part of this dream."

"Where?" Norice anxiously asked, looking around frantically.

"There," Celthric pointed, "follow me."

From further away, the Presence studied them. It knew the old man was not part of the dream, and when they began walking toward It, the Presence read Norice's mind and left the dream before they arrived.

The old man suddenly stopped and said, "It's gone. The intruder has left."

"Where did it come from?"

"I don't know." Celthric turned and faced him. "You have to be careful and trust only me. Do you understand?"

Norice nodded, then a low rumbling echoed beyond the battlefield. "The demon comes for you. Go, I will protect you," the old man said and ran off in the direction of the noise.

Norice watched him until he was gone from his sight.

The Presence gazed upon the sleeping human after leaving his thoughts. It wondered why the being named Celthric was in his dreams, and what purpose was he trying to accomplish. The Presence did not sense another entity nearby, so It would have to be very careful when dealing with Celthric, because if he could influence Norice from where he was, then he must be very powerful indeed. The Presence, if anything, was clever, and this other entity would not deter It from Its ultimate goal: to leave this place and eventually the world. The Presence mulled over the information It acquired from Norice, and with more resolve, It carefully plotted Its next course of action as he stirred awake.

Norice awoke from his dreams drenched in sweat. The fire blazed brightly, and it was still dark outside. He figured dawn would be approaching soon, and he needed to leave the town before his pursuers found him. It wouldn't take them long to get new horses and track him here, and he wanted to stay far ahead of them. He thought about his dream and what it meant, then he felt something, or someone, in the room. He quickly grabbed the dagger and got up.

"Who is it? I know someone is here."

Despite Its ability to cloak, the Presence was detected and now had to put Its plan into action. It stepped forward.

"Norice." It paused. "I am Celthric."

Norice studied the shadowy being for a few minutes, trying to gauge whether the poor lighting shrouded it in darkness or if that was the being's natural form.

"What? How did you find me?"

"You led me here." The Presence could tell by his tone that Norice was being cautious, and It needed to be careful.

"How do I know that it's truly you?" Norice was growing nervous.

The Presence felt his anxiety and quickly scanned his thoughts and memories and gathered information before speaking. "I have shown you many things thus far, and I can save you from the mortals that follow you now."

"You told me to find you, so why do you appear to me now?"

"I fear the men that follow you will capture you."

"I'm not sure that I believe you," Norice said, then grabbed his sword and pointed the blade at the Presence.

"Norice, let me prove to you that I am Celthric."

"And how are you going to do that?"

"By telling you about your dreams and what they really mean."

Interested, Norice lowered his weapon and agreed. The Presence told him exactly what he wanted to hear. When It was finished, Norice wholeheartedly believed that It was Celthric.

"So what are you?" Norice asked. He was no longer able to keep that burning question at bay.

"I am an entity that is trapped between the planes of existence."

"How did you become trapped?"

The Presence quickly came up with a story. "In my previous life, I was a bad person. I robbed and stole and even murdered people. One day, I broke into a monastery, intending on robbing the place, when their head priest confronted me and left me no other option than to fight him. During our long battle, he bestowed a curse of separation upon me that would eventually divide my soul from my body. For many years, I searched for an answer to my curse and discovered that the only way was for me to save another human from damnation."

"But why me?"

"Because the demon who hunts you will steal not only your soul but the souls of your family if you should fail. Remember, one of your children is slated to save all of mankind."

Hearing those words sent chills up and down Norice's spine. "What's needed of me?"

The Presence delayed his answer long enough to allow the mortal to feel the weight of his response. "We need to meld in order for us to continue."

"What do you mean, meld?"

"By bonding together, you will gain power, insight, and the knowledge to survive this ordeal."

"For how long?"

"Once the quest is completed, we will separate, and we'll both finally know peace. You and your family will be saved, and I will be allowed to leave this world and find eternal rest." The Presence let his words rest for a few seconds before continuing, "You've trusted me thus far. Allow us to be one, and together we will be triumphant."

Norice was scared, and the Presence felt his fear.

"If you don't allow me to help you, then the dark one will eventually find and destroy you and your family."

Norice's shoulders slumped forward as he thought about the offer and what he already did. He finally conceded to his fate, allowing the Presence to guide him to the bed.

"Sleep. When you wake, you will be a new man," the entity said.

Norice closed his eyes. After he fell asleep, the Presence entered his body.

Norice dreamt that he was walking in an open field with an old man close by his side. The surrounding forest was ablaze, and the sky was filled with ash and soot. The old man unexpectedly stopped and turned toward him.

"This is the future of mankind if we do not stop this demon," the Presence said after reading his companion's thoughts, then selected information that Norice could relate to Celthric.

Before Norice could respond, a young woman emerged through the fire and walked straight to them.

"Who are you?" she asked, looking straight at the Presence.

"I am Celthric."

The girl smiled. "You lie, impostor," she said and morphed into a doppelganger of the old man. "Norice, listen to me, this creature doesn't belong here."

Norice looked at the old man to his right and then back at the other. He was confused and didn't know who or what to believe.

"What are you?" the Presence asked Celthric.

"That is none of your business."

"You're going to ruin everything," the Presence hissed. "I need to leave this town, and Norice is going to help me."

Norice shrunk down, becoming terrified.

"Maybe we can help each other, then?" Celthric offered the Presence.

"And why should I help you? If you took control over him first, would you have helped me?"

"You don't understand. I am something totally different than you."

"How so?" the Presence curiously asked.

"You will need to find me in order to discover my true power."

"I'll ask again, what are you?"

Celthric stared at the entity. "I can offer you a small glimpse of my true nature, then you can decide."

The Presence mulled over his offer. "Okay. Reveal your inner thoughts to me and I will decide."

Celthric smiled inwardly. "Look into my eyes and understand." Celthric opened up a very secret and secluded part of his mind, and what the Presence saw pleased It immensely.

"I understand now," the Presence began, "we will find you." The Presence turned to Norice. "Norice, you will be safe here within your dreams. I will protect you and find Celthric, and together we will end your nightmares."

The dream's landscape changed. They were standing in a meadow with a nearby stream. Norice saw his wife and kids happily playing in the water. They were having so much fun. Norice no longer felt terrified. Smiling, he looked over at them. "I haven't felt like this in a long time."

"Enjoy yourself. We will fix everything," Celthric said and looked at him, then at the Presence.

"I think I will stay here for a while," Norice said and ran off to join his family.

"You are indeed powerful," the Presence said to Celthric.

"We will rule the world someday. Just remember to go north until you come to an ancient battlefield with the dead littering the ground. Look for me in the hands of my former owner and all will be revealed to you."

"You're an object, then?"

Celthric faded from the dream.

The Presence was delighted with the outcome and woke the host up. Chief Weis, Tranter, and the others left the small town of Yoken shortly before dawn. During their stay, Tranter drank himself senseless with the guards, while Chief Weis, Rhanh, and Timol spoke with several of the townspeople. One, in particular, was an old timer named Rian. He was a cartographer and tracker by trade who lived in the area for a very long time, so he knew the land. Rian gave them a map and advised them to stay clear of several locations, especially an evil place called the Circle of Demise. He also noted that the man they were following most likely would've stopped at the deserted town of Sinual.

With the snow falling heavily, they rode southeast and arrived at the town of Sinual by midday. Just like Rian said, the town was indeed deserted. They easily spotted the fresh tracks, leading away from Trint's Supplies, and stopped in front of them. Tranter dismounted and analyzed the hoof prints.

"Well?" Chief Weis asked impatiently.

"I'd say he's about a day ahead of us. We should look inside."

"Why? He's gone," Rhanh said.

"Don't you people know anything?" Tranter said in disgust and walked into the store.

Chief Weis gave his guard a look that caused him to hold his tongue in check. The tracker returned a short time later and mounted his horse as he carried their stolen supplies.

"Did you find anything?" Chief Weis asked once Tranter was situated in the saddle.

"He forgot to leave with our bags, so he's low on food."

"So, who cares," Rhanh commented.

Tranter sighed. "Chief Weis, I'm getting sick and tired of your men questioning everything I say or do. Please explain to that idiot why my findings were important."

Rhanh reached for his sword, and, in the next instance, Chief Weis had his blade out, pointing at the man. "I'm only going to say this once, so listen up. Tranter is vital to this mission, and if anyone questions his process in a demeaning way again, you will have to answer to me. Am I clear?" After his men nodded in turn, Weis sheathed his weapon and continued, "Now, that piece of information is important, because if Norice runs out of food, he'll be forced to stop somewhere since he isn't a hunter by trade."

"Knowing our prey is vital to our success," Tranter added. He took out the map and began studying it.

"Did you find anything in the building that would indicate where he is going?" Granit asked.

"Nothing." Tranter looked directly at Chief Weis. "When you spoke to his wife, did she know anything?"

"She said he was having nightmares."

Tranter looked at the map for a few minutes before nudging his horse northward.

The Presence and his host rode north for the next two days. On several occasions, It pondered about giving up the quest for finding Celthric, but something kept It focused on the task, and so, they rode on until Norice swayed atop his mount and eventually fell off due to exhaustion. At first, the Presence didn't comprehend what had happened to him because It needed neither sleep, food, nor water, then It remembered that humans required such necessities in order to survive. It willed his host to crawl over to a nearby stream and drink from the cool water, then gorge on berries from a bush a few feet away.

After Norice regained some of his strength, the Presence had him tether the horse to a tree and climb inside a few bushes to sleep. While he did so, the Presence found itself standing on a battlefield. It knew right away It was in Norice's dreams. In the distance, the entity saw an elderly figure, dressed in gray robes and holding a walking stick. To Its left, It saw Norice playing with his children. The old man beckoned the entity forward, and It complied. Celthric watched and waited to speak until the shadowy Presence was standing before him.

"He seems very happy, doesn't he?"

"What are you?" the Presence asked.

"I am a being like you."

"No, you're not. I sense something else, something darker."

Celthric grinned. "All will be revealed in due time. I need you to understand that Norice is important and without him, this journey would not even be possible."

"How so?"

"I am not permitted to reveal anything to you until the right time."

"What about me? Aren't I just as important?"

"What about you? You're only here because you forced your will upon him."

"What if I decide to give up your quest if you don't tell me everything?"

"You can try, but you won't be able to. I can sense that you crave salvation and purpose as well as he does."

The Presence knew Celthric was right. "How much further until we meet you?"

"Another day or so, but be very careful. The men who pursue him are relentless and won't stop until either he is captured or killed."

"I am skilled in the art of battle and will not let that happen."

"Good. I want you to ponder this. Once we are joined together, you will be invincible and nothing, and I mean nothing, will stand in our way. Go talk to Norice and reassure him that we will prevail, and he will be safe." Celthric looked over at him. He was playing a game of chase with his kids. "I guess he already feels safe."

"I guess he does," the Presence said and walked away.

Celthric stared at Norice. "Very soon, my precious little toy, very soon," he whispered, then disappeared from the dream.

When Norice woke from his dreams, so did the entity. The Presence thought about Celthric. Something was amiss, and no matter how hard It thought, It couldn't figure out why. Maybe it was the way he was always present in his dreams or how he figured out Its own desires.

Using Norice's voice, the Presence spoke softly. "Celthric, you think that you're smarter than me? Think again."

The entity willed Norice to his feet, left the safety of the bushes, mounted the horse, and left.

Chief Weis and the others rode hard through the night in order to gain ground on Norice. By dawn, they arrived at the killer's makeshift camp. Tranter determined that he was only a half-day ahead of them. Chief Weis looked at each of his tired men and could see fatigue etched upon their faces.

"We'll ride for a few more hours and rest," he stated.

"But we should have him by nightfall if we don't," Tranter interjected.

"Good point, but if my men are tired, how effective will they be?"

"He's just one man."

"Keep moving, I'll decide later," Chief Weis said, nudging his mount forward.

They ultimately followed Tranter's advice, but failed to find Norice, and made camp as nightfall approached.

Meanwhile, a few miles away, the Presence came upon a small camp with two armored men sitting by a fire with bowls in their hands. The entity saw their horses tethered to a nearby tree and recognized the insignia on their saddles. They were from the Order of the Blessed, which he knew was a good omen if he played his cards right. By their creed, they helped distressed individuals if deemed worthy. The entity grinned and put Its plan into motion. It took out the knife and cut Norice's body in several different places before stumbling into their camp.

When the knights saw the stranger stumble into their camp, they stood up immediately, weapons in hand.

"What do you want, stranger?" the man with the long unkempt hair, on his left, asked.

The entity fell to his knees, breathing heavy. "I've been on the...run for...days."

"Why, what happened?"

"Brigands. They attacked my village and are still chasing me."

The knight on the right gazed at Norice, trying to gauge if he was telling the truth. He also noted that he was only carrying a dagger.

"Please help me!" the Presence pleaded.

"Where are they now?" the man on the right asked.

Norice looked around nervously. "I'm not sure. The last time I saw them, it was early today."

"Do you know how many there are?"

"At least ten."

"Well, you're safe here, so sit by our fire and rest."

The entity sat near the fire. The knights did as well.

After they were situated, the knight with the long unkempt hair spoke, "My name is Hrist, and this is Prol. We are knights from the Order of the Blessed."

"Glad to meet you. My name is Norice."

Hrist handed him a bowl of hot stew, and the entity began eating.

"So, Norice, tell us what happened," Prol said.

The entity told them an elaborate tale of how his town of Solarce was attacked by a bunch of brigands led by a man named Weis. It also mentioned that Its family was murdered, held prisoner for days, and eventually escaped and was now trying to reach Stonybrook for help.

Prol waited for him to finish before speaking, "Norice, after you leave, we'll keep an eye out for them and stop them from finding you if we have to."

"You would do that for me?"

"Yes. Our Order lends support whenever it's needed," Hrist added.

The Presence smiled inwardly. "But what if there are too many?"

"We are highly trained and can deal with them." Prol took hold of his two-handed axe and smiled at Norice.

"How can I ever repay you?"

"Next time you travel to a town, please give a small donation to our Order and make sure you tell them of our deeds."

They talked for a while longer before the Presence turned in for the evening. The knights went about placing small warning traps in case unwanted people or animals showed up unexpectedly. By morning, the Presence thanked his hosts and bade them farewell.

It was around midday when Chief Weis and the others came across the knights' deserted camp. Tranter dismounted, took two steps forward, and stopped dead in his tracks.

"What is it?" Weis asked him.

The tracker held up his hand and remained motionless while studying the area intently. Impatient, one of the guards dismounted and walked past the tracker. Tranter made an attempt to stop him, but he was too late, and everyone watched in horror as a row of two-foot long spikes sprung up from the ground and into his stomach. The man choked on his blood and died. Chief Weis dismounted and rushed over. Tranter anticipated his actions and stopped him before he made the mistake of rushing into another trap.

"It's too late for him," Tranter said.

Several arrows were fired from their flank, killing two more men. Rhanh galloped off toward the direction of the attack and was immediately hit in the throat by a well-placed arrow. The guard tumbled from his horse. The rest of the men dismounted and took shelter behind a few trees. Tranter and Weis squatted low to the ground just as another arrow flew by their heads. The tracker recognized the holy symbol etched on the arrow's shaft.

"Why would Knights of the Blessed attack us?!" he said.

"What?"

"The arrow carries their makings."

"They are mistaking us for someone else," Chief Weis said.

Another arrow whizzed by his head, missing him by a few inches.

"KNIGHTS OF THE BLESSED, WE ARE NOT HERE AS ENEMIES," Tranter shouted. "AND WE MEAN YOU NO HARM."

A few seconds later, someone answered, "Throw down your weapons and come out."

Weis looked over at Tranter, who nodded, removed his weapons, and stood with his hands held high.

"Tell the others to do the same, or we will kill you."

Weis and the other guards did as ordered. Two armored men, one with a large axe and another with his bow pointed at Tranter, came out of hiding.

"Who are you?" the knight with the axe asked Weis.

"We are a search party hunting down a known criminal."

"I didn't ask what your purpose was, I asked you for your name."

"My name is Chief Weis."

"Weis. You must be the leader of them."

"And you, tracker. What is your name?" the bowman asked.

"My name is Tranter."

"What is the name of the one you hunt?"

"We are looking for a killer who goes by the name of Norice."

Granit was seething with hatred as he began reaching for his hidden dagger while plotting exactly what he would do to the knight holding the axe. The scene played out in his mind how he would enjoy running the dagger across his throat and watch his blood ooze out of the wound until he choked to death. The knights did not notice his arm inching closer toward the blade. Just as he was wrapping his fingers securely around the grip, one of the other guards lunged toward the bowman, who fired out of instinct, shooting him through his throat, then reloaded quicker than humanly possible.

Weis quickly shouted for the rest of his men not to move. Granit moved his hand away from the blade, suddenly fearing that his own plan would end in failure as well.

"Does anyone else want to die?" the bowman asked, pointing his weapon at Weis' head. "Good, I didn't think so." He continued, "Now, what did this Norice character do?"

"He is wanted for several heinous crimes, including the murder of a young stable boy named Tay," Weis answered.

"Is that so? We met him a few hours ago, and he says that you and your men ransacked his town, killed his family, and are chasing him."

"That's a lie," Granit interjected.

"Well it looks like you have your version, and we have ours," the knight with the axe said, holding his weapon menacingly.

"I thought your Order wasn't supposed to pass judgment hastily?" Tranter asked.

"Fair enough. How about you tell us everything, then we'll decide whether to let you live, send you back from where you came from, or allow you to pass."

Chief Weis told the knights everything from the beginning, and when he was finished, the knight with the axe spoke, "The man we met last night does not appear to be the man you're looking for, so we'd like you to turn around and leave."

"We're not leaving," Chief Weis firmly stated.

"Then you will die," the bowman said, pulling back his bowstring.

"You men have no honor," Granit added.

The situation was about to come to a head when Tranter spoke up, "All we want to do is take him back and have him stand trial, not kill him."

The knights looked at each other, contemplating the tracker's words, then back at Tranter.

"That will be acceptable only if you allow us to come along," the bowman said.

"Fine, but if he refuses to be captured, I will take matters into my own hands. He needs to pay for his crimes, one way or another," Weis said to the knights.

He was about to pick up his weapon when the knight with the axe stepped closer. "And if you're lying?"

Weis grinned. "You may have my head. Now what are your names?"

"My name is Prol," he lowered his axe, "my brother is Hrist."

Hrist nodded and slung his bow over his left shoulder. Chief Weis picked up his weapon and began walking toward his horse.

"Chief Weis," said Hrist, "if we are wrong, we will make amends for our own actions."

"You are wrong, so start by helping my men bury the dead," Weis coldly said.

CHAPTER 5: DEMONS RUNNING WILD

Except for a few guards and merchants, Torhan's arrival in town went virtually unnoticed. He was a little hungry and in need of supplies, so he stopped a young lad passing by.

"Excuse me; do you know where I can find an armory and the best food in town?" Torhan asked.

The boy reminded Torhan of himself when he was an adolescent.

"Well…" the boy began as he rubbed his chin, thinking. "There are two armories in town. Killington is over there," he pointed west, "and Wakefield is down there." He pointed south. "If you want quality weapons and great service, go to Killington. If you are looking for a bargain then Wakefield is your better bet." The boy suddenly looked around, then back at Torhan. "As far as the best food in town, go up that road." He pointed north to a street that was slightly to the left. "You'll run into the Inn of the Wolf. The stew is the best in the land." The lad looked around nervously.

Torhan reached into his pouch to grab a coin. When he looked up again, the boy was gone. *Odd,* he thought.

While debating where he should go, his stomach grumbled loud enough to convince him he was hungrier than he thought, so he walked toward the inn.

Along the way, he passed various establishments, including the Mayor's house, Valor's Potions, Mintor's Melody Store, and several outside merchants selling their wares, such as clothes, perfumes, cheeses, and crockery.

When he finally arrived at the Inn of the Wolf, he was taken aback by the pungent fragrances wafting out of the place and recognized them as roasted wild boar, chicken, and berry pie. His mouth watered in anticipation, and he quickly succumbed to the aroma and entered the building.

The inn was crowded with merchants, warriors, priests, and a few other common people as they enjoyed their midday meal. He paused long enough to find the only available table. He walked to where it was located in the far corner and sat down.

A few minutes later, a very attractive serving wench, wearing a tattered dress, walked over.

"What can I get you, my lord?" she asked, brushing aside her long, blonde, curly locks that clung to her face.

"What are your specials?" he kept his eyes on hers in order to restrain himself from staring at her well-endowed cleavage.

"Well, we have two specials today: wild boar stew and greens, and roasted fowl with potatoes."

Torhan's mouth salivated with anticipation, as it often did, and he ordered both dishes, because he couldn't make up his mind.

"Would you like some ale, my lord?"

"Indeed, I would," Torhan responded eagerly.

"Excellent, sire, I'll be right back with your brew," she said and walked away.

Torhan couldn't help but stare at her lithe, delightful body as it swayed back and forth until she was through the kitchen door.

As he waited, he took notice of the patrons who were seated all around him. One table, in particular, caught his attention. There were three gentlemen dressed in black robes sitting quietly. Each prominently displayed a religious symbol of some sort and carried very strange-looking maces with long, sharp spikes. He thought it was odd that holy men would be carrying those types of weapons. He tried to get a momentary glimpse of their features, but it was impossible, because the cowl to their robes was covering their faces.

Just then, the serving wench arrived with his order and placed it down.

"Here you go, my lord," she said.

"Can I ask you something?"

"Sure, what is it?"

"Those men in black robes, who are they?"

She looked around and saw the table Torhan inquired about. "Those men belong to the religious order of the Temple of the Wind."

"Why do they carry spiked weapons?"

"Priest Abiathar demands that they do so for protection."

"Protection from what?" Torhan pressed.

"From the demon whom we don't dare to mention his name."

"A demon?" Torhan paused.

"A long time ago, a demon tried to enslave our town, and if it wasn't for Priest Abiathar, he would've succeeded, and we would all be imprisoned."

"How did he stop him?"

"I was told Priest Abiathar used his book of magic to banish the demon to another plane."

"Is that so?"

"Yes. Everyone loves and respects him for saving us. He's our guardian," she stated with glee in her eyes. "I have to go back to work. Is there anything else, my lord?"

"Not right now, thanks."

Torhan ate his meal reflecting on what the serving wench said about the priest. Lord Sim and Ailith told him one version, Grappin another, and hers; it was certainly going to be tough figuring out whose story was right. He was halfway through dinner when the innkeeper made an announcement.

"Attention, everyone!" he bellowed. "Priest Abiathar's sermon will begin shortly. The inn will be closed during this time. Please leave."

At once, the three cloaked figures simultaneously rose and left the building. They were followed by the remainder of the patrons.

Bells chimed seconds later and Torhan stood up, took one last swig of his beverage, grabbed the chicken leg, and left a hefty tip for the serving girl. He walked out the door to join the ever growing masses. He followed the townspeople toward the enormous temple several streets away, and noted people of all ages walking with a purpose. Some spoke in hushed tones, while others gleefully talked about the priest like he was the second coming of a god. Overall, they appeared to be enthralled with him, which added to the mystery of who he was.

Once they arrived, the people filed into the building, while Torhan stopped directly in front and stared up in awe. The structure was easily forty feet high, carved out of granite, with columns made of dark marble supporting the copper-shingled roof. The doors were made of thick iron. He waited until most of the people were inside before entering.

The inside of the cathedral was just as elaborate as the outside. Rows of dark wood pews lined both sides of the aisle and ended at a platform stage with a large gold altar set upon it. Tapestries decorated the walls, elegant-looking curtains sealed off the windows, and brass chandeliers dangled from the ceiling.

Acolytes wearing black robes quickly escorted people to the pews with Torhan being led to the far left side of the room and seated next to an elderly couple. After everyone was seated, the doors to the entrance were closed with a loud thud, silencing the chattering voices of the people. It was so quiet that everyone in the church heard a coin hit the floor near the front.

A few minutes later, a door behind the altar opened and in stepped a tall, husky middle-aged man wearing blue vestments. Hanging loosely around his large belly was a strand of autumn-colored beads. The priest wore his gray hair in a ponytail and his salt and pepper beard braided down past his chin. When he was positioned in front of the pulpit, he spoke.

"Welcome, my children," he began, "we are gathered here today to thank our god, Hecadoth, for the protection he has bestowed upon our town, and for providing the abundance of food for our tables." He proclaimed as he raised his arms high in the air, "Let us bow our heads and thank him with the chant of salvation."

At once, everybody bowed their heads and repeated the priest's words.

"Oh mighty Hecadoth, You have given us salvation and protection from all that is evil. Please continue to shine Your love upon us and deliver us to Your kingdom."

Torhan had never witnessed any kind of holy services before and couldn't comprehend how dedicated these individuals were. After they finished reciting the chant two more times, the priest addressed them again.

"My children," he said and lowered his arms, "it wasn't long ago that Hecadoth provided me the power and strength to exile the demon named Dybbuk and to protect our home from his return. Last night, the Almighty spoke to me in a dream saying the foul beast has broken free of my spells and will be returning to enslave us all. To me, this is—"

"What will we do?" a patron cried out, interrupting him.

"Help us, Priest Abiathar," another worshipper pleaded.

Priest Abiathar held up his hands to stifle the crowd. "My children, Hecadoth has given me the necessary steps to overcome the beast and banish him once more." The priest paused for effect. "As I speak, Dybbuk gathers a force to invade our home, and we must repel him at all costs. The first thing we must do is arm ourselves. I want every man, woman, and child to become proficient with a weapon, whether it be a sword, spear, dagger, or even a sharp pointy stick."

"Priest Abiathar, do we know when they'll attack?" someone near him asked.

"No, but it will be soon."

"We don't have any weapons that will hurt him?"

"I was given knowledge to construct new weapons of power that will banish him and his horde and burn them in eternal damnation forever."

The crowd stirred. "How is he able to return? You said he couldn't," a young man near the stage shouted.

Some of the other people voiced their concerns as well.

"He has grown stronger, but our god has said for us not to worry. We will prevail."

The crowd continued to stir and talk over each other.

"FEAR NOT, MY CHILDREN, WE SHALL OVERCOME THIS OBSTACLE," Priest Abiathar shouted. The crowd went still. "I have already crafted one of my special maces. It is designed to send evil back to hell. Would you like a demonstration?"

"Yes," someone shouted, followed by many others.

Priest Abiathar smiled and called forth one of his acolytes. The servant walked over and presented a dark black mace. Torhan noticed that it was similar to the ones the other followers from the inn were carrying. The priest moved from behind the altar and accepted the unholy-looking weapon.

"Bring me some deviants," he commanded.

Two of his servants disappeared into the back and brought forth a couple of dirty-looking men who could have passed for thieves.

"Now watch me send them into oblivion."

The men were shoved forward. When they were within striking distance, the priest unleashed his assault with amazing speed and accuracy, hitting one, then the other. Both men cried out and were engulfed in gray smoke. When the thick smoke dissipated, they were gone. The crowd, amazed by what had happened, cheered and clapped their hands in delight.

The priest smiled. "When we meet Dybbuk again, our new weapons will send him to the abyss." More cheers erupted. "My children, to be protected against him you must receive my protection and have your sins purged from your body. Now who among you will step forward and accept my anointment?"

"Pick me," a man, not more than ten feet away from Torhan, shouted.

"No, me," a woman, halfway up front to his left, said.

Soon, people were in a frenzy, each one wanted to be the one selected.

"My children," Abiathar responded in a joyful voice, "Hecadoth would be very pleased with each of you. I will now contact our god for the selection."

The townspeople quieted down as the priest began to chant softly at first, then louder with each passing minute. Suddenly, he stopped.

"Hecadoth chooses Jonah." Jonah stood up. "Come forth and you will be rewarded with eternal salvation."

"Thank you, my lord," Jonah said in a calm voice, kissed his wife, and walked up to the front of the stage.

Two acolytes stepped in front of him, assisted with the removal of his red woolen shirt, and gave him something to drink.

"Come forth and lay your weary body upon the altar of new life, my son," Abiathar commanded.

Jonah did as he was told. After he lay prone, Priest Abiathar reached into his robes and extracted a snake-shaped blade.

"Hecadoth blesses you, my son." The priest lifted the weapon high above his head and chanted.

The crowd shouted joyfully in response to his words. Torhan thought about intervening but decided not to. The priest brought the dagger down into Jonah's sternum and worked the blade up and down his body with such precision that Jonah didn't squirm or make a sound.

Minutes later, the priest removed the blade, reached into the opening, and pulled out a black organ.

"This was the sin growing inside of Jonah's body." He held it in the air. "Jonah, you have been cleansed. Go with my acolytes and become one with us."

The bloodied Jonah rose to his feet and was helped off the stage.

"My children, Jonah is now blessed."

The crowd cheered as he was led away to the back room. More people began calling out to be next.

The priest quieted them down. "I can only bless an individual once a day," he said and began preaching the final part of his sermon, which lasted a few more hours.

When Priest Abiathar was finished, he told his followers to go forth, spread the word, and practice with weapons.

After they were filing out of the church, Torhan approached the cleric, who was in the process of walking toward the back of the room.

"Priest Abiathar, can you spare a moment of your time?" Torhan asked.

The priest paused and turned around. "Ah, yes, the person whom I've never seen before. Please step closer, my child."

As he did, Torhan noticed the outline of two trapdoors on the stage.

"Now, what can I do for you?" Abiathar asked.

Torhan quickly adverted eyes back to him before the priest discovered what he was looking at. "I have some questions about your sermon."

"Go ahead, my son."

"The demon Dybbuk, what can you tell me about him?"

Priest Abiathar smiled. "Why do you want to know?"

"In case I come across him in my travels."

"His story would take some time, so I will give you the shortened version. Dybbuk entered our town a few years ago and wanted to enslave every man, woman, and child. At that time, we had no defenses against such a foe, so I made the ultimate sacrifice and made a pact with my god to save the town. He responded by granting me adequate power to banish this demon. He also offered the town further protection if we were willing to make a sacrifice every month for five years."

Torhan didn't like what he was hearing. "What sort of a sacrifice, a person or an animal?"

"What do you think I am a killer?" His tone had a bite to it. "Every month someone must offer up their soul to him."

"What do you mean?"

"Like Jonah did. They must offer up their undying loyalty to him. Only then will he bless them and deliver skills to me."

"I see. What sort of a power does he grant you?"

The priest grinned. "Let's just say it's of the divine right. You won't be able to understand, so that is all I am going to say."

One of Abiathar's acolytes entered from the backroom, walked up to the priest, whispered something in his ear, and left.

"I apologize, but I must be going. Why don't you come back tonight, and we'll talk some more?"

Torhan nodded.

"What's your name?"

"Torhan."

"It was really nice meeting you, Torhan," the priest said and left.

There was something odd about this whole setup, but Torhan couldn't put his finger on it. He pondered several things as he left the temple. First, there was his power to stop Dybbuk or keep him at bay. Second, there was the strange sacrifice the people had to make to his god—from what he knew only evil gods required such an act. Then, there was the illusion of the thieves disappearing, when, in fact, they must have fallen through the trapdoors. Maybe in time the truth would reveal itself.

Torhan decided to pay Killington's armory a visit and arrived a short time later. The two-story stone building with two windows on each floor was set back off the main road. The path leading up to the building was clean and well kept with an abundance of pretty flowers and shrubs leading up to the door, which proudly displayed a flowered wreath. The building reminded him of a cottage he always dreamed about and wanted to live in when he was old and gray. Smiling, he entered.

Inside, various types of armor and weapons were on display, while a lone figure worked behind the counter in the back. Torhan took his time looking at the items and one piece of armor, in particular, caught his eye. It was from the chainmail family and had a combination of black and gold links interwoven in a diagonal pattern. The matching chainmail coif was on another stand next to it. He'd never seen such an unusual piece before and knew immediately he wanted it.

"That's a good choice," the clerk said and approached.

"What's it made of?" Torhan asked without taking his eyes off the item.

"A new material called titanium. It's supposed to be the strongest material known to man. A blacksmith named Yarn crafted this suit. If you're interested, and have a few minutes, I'll show just how impenetrable the material is."

"I'm very interested." Torhan turned around and faced a short, stocky, balding fellow.

"Good! By the way, I am Killington, and you are?" He extended his forearm.

"My name is Torhan." Torhan reached out and both men clasped forearms.

"Glad to meet you, Torhan." Killington turned his head back

toward the storeroom. "Mekel, come out."

"Coming!" a loud voice answered.

"While we're waiting for my son, take a look around and let me know if anything else catches your fancy."

"I'll do that."

Torhan was just about to walk away when Mekel appeared. He was a tall, strapping, young man, not more than twenty, with a physique that looked like he could crush a giant.

"Yes, father?" Mekel asked.

"This gentleman would like to see how strong this piece of armor is." Killington pointed to the display.

"Right away," he said and removed the armor from the dummy, then walked toward the back of the store, grabbing a regular chainmail shirt off another table on his way out.

"Give him a couple of minutes," Killington said and left.

Torhan wandered around the store until Killington returned and asked him to come with him through the back. They took a flight of stairs down into a large training area enclosed by a fence with no roof. There were weapons, armor, practice dummies, straw hay bales, and wooden poles, all of which were used for testing Killington's wares.

Mekel had just finished taking weapons out and walked over carrying the chainmail. "Father, we are ready."

"Now give our guest a demonstration," Killington said.

"Sir, what's your name?" Mekel asked.

"My name is Torhan."

"It's nice to meet you. Here, catch!" Mekel threw him a silver chainmail shirt. "Try to pull the armor apart," he said.

Torhan did as he was asked. Even with the gauntlets providing additional strength, he was still unable to rip the links apart.

"Now give it back to me," Mekel said.

Torhan handed it to him and Mekel grabbed it by the ends and proceeded to pull the armor apart with ease. Torhan had never seen such a feat of strength before. Mekel dropped the useless armor to the ground and took hold of the titanium shirt. He pulled the armor in opposite directions, but the links didn't budge. Torhan was a bit suspicious and thought it could be a game they were playing just to sell it to him.

Mekel saw the look on his face. "Take hold of one end, and I'll take hold of the other," he said.

Torhan did as he was asked and braced his footing firmly.

"Ready?" Mekel said, and Torhan nodded.

Together they tugged and neither man, nor armor, gave way until Mekel pulled the armor free from Torhan's hands. Mekel held forth the armor to show him that the links were still fastened tightly and handed it to him.

"Impressive," Torhan finally said after he inspected the armor.

"We're not done yet," Killington added, "Mekel, show him just how protective this armor is."

Mekel grabbed the armor, walked to the far end of the area, dressed a dummy in the chainmail, and came back.

"Torhan," Killington began, "here are some arrows. Feel free to shoot as many as you like into the dummy."

Torhan released his bow from across his back and notched an arrow. After looking at the owner for his approval, he began firing them at the armor. Upon impact, they fell away helplessly.

"Are you impressed?" Killington asked.

"Very," Torhan responded.

Killington nodded to Mekel, and he walked over to the dummy and placed the armor on his body. "I'm ready, father."

"Go hit him with your sword," Killington said.

Torhan looked at him like he was crazy. Killington encouraged him with several nods, and Torhan obliged by unsheathing his weapon.

"Torhan, use this one instead," Killington said and offered him a long sword. "I don't want you to ruin your blade."

Torhan took the weapon, tested the weapon for strength, and ran his hand across the blade, feeling the sharpness. Satisfied, he walked over to Mekel.

"Are you ready?" Torhan asked.

Mekel nodded, and Torhan began slashing and stabbing the armor. The big fellow neither flinched nor made any attempt to move away. When Torhan was finished, Mekel took the armor off, and, to Torhan's surprise, there wasn't a scratch or nick on him.

"How much?" Torhan said in amazement.

"Let's go inside and make a deal," Killington said gleefully.

While Mekel was getting them refreshments in the cellar, Killington and Torhan sat in the backroom.

"Torhan, you're not from around here are you?" Killington asked.

"Is it that obvious?"

"It's your accent, where are you from?"

"I'm from a town just southwest of here called Wistful, have you heard of it?"

"I have but never met anyone from there before. So what brings you to Mirkin?"

"Why are you asking?"

"A man would have to be either foolish or brave to travel through the forest just west of here."

Torhan was growing uncomfortable with his questioning and

placed both arms on the wooden table to help hide his discomfort.

"What I meant was if you're capable of making the trek alone, then you must have some real fighting skills."

"And your point?" Torhan said flatly.

"I have a proposition that might be worth your time. The blacksmith Yarn has a hidden mine somewhere toward the north. I would like you to locate it for me."

"Why?" Torhan detected a hint of jealously and greed in his tone.

"Because if I could get my hands on the precious metal, then I can craft armor on my own and offer a wider variety of items for a fraction of the cost."

Before Torhan could respond, Mekel walked in carrying a canister, filled their goblets to the brim with ale, and sat them down in front of the two men. Torhan nodded in appreciation and drank the smooth tasting liquid, which soothed his parched throat. After he finished, he asked for a refill without hesitation, and Mekel poured him some more.

"So what do you want me to do?"

"Travel north to Yarn's establishment and find out the location of the mineshaft. If you do this for me, and bring back proof, I'll sell you the armor for the same price I paid for it, which was two thousand gold pieces."

"How much are you selling it for?"

"Fifteen thousand gold pieces."

"Let me think about it. I have to go." Torhan took another swig and stood up.

"Torhan, you're not going to find armor of this quality for that price."

Torhan smiled. "It seems like you need me more than I need the armor." He took a step.

"Okay, how about we make a deal, then?" Killington replied out of desperation.

Torhan was leery about making deals, especially after the most recent one, but it never hurt to listen.

"What's the deal?" he asked.

"Get me what I need, and I'll give you the armor and make you an item of your choice."

"Sounds fair, but I'll need a couple of things first."

"What are they?" Killington's eyes lit up.

"I require one of your strongest daggers, preferably silver; a score of arrows; and the whereabouts of a girl priest named Katara."

"Katara? Why do you want to see her?"

"That's my business. Do we have a deal?"

Now it was Killington's turn to hesitate, and after weighing his desires for the mineral, he agreed and asked his son to go get the items.

"What do you know about her?" Torhan asked.

"She's one of the town's healers."

"Is that it?"

"She did study with Priest Abiathar before they had a falling out."

"Do you know why?"

"No one does, so you'll have to ask her. Her cottage is in the western part of town. It has a wooden sign above the door displaying a pair of hands in a healing manner on top of someone's chest. My son will take you there when you're ready."

Mekel returned and handed Torhan the quiver full of arrows and the silver dagger, which he placed in the scabbard. Torhan went about replacing the feathers of some of the arrows with the leaves from the forest, while Killington and his son watched in bewilderment but didn't bother asking him what he was doing. When he finished, Torhan had five demon-slaying arrows and placed them back into the quiver.

"I'll bring you back the information you asked for as soon as I take care of some business. Mekel, are you ready?" he asked the fellow.

Mekel nodded and they left.

Along the way to Katara's cottage, Mekel expressed an interest that someday he would like to leave Mirkin and go on an exciting quest. With Brother Sao gone, Torhan decided to ask if he wanted to join him.

"Mekel, how would you feel about accompanying me when I leave?"

"Where are you going?"

"In a couple of days, I will be traveling northwest to a town called Snowdrift. There's a little girl who has fallen into a deep sleep, and I need to find out why. They say an ancient item called REM can awaken her, but no one knows where it is hidden."

"Sounds interesting."

"I'll give you fifty gold pieces a day, and we'll split any treasure that we find."

"Let me think…"

Torhan's eyes were fixed forward. When Mekel didn't finish his sentence, Torhan turned and saw him enshrouded in the same grayish hue he experienced back in the cave. The grayness was coming at him from all directions until it engulfed him.

"Chromos Lords!" he gasped, stiffened his body, and didn't move a muscle.

The scabbard began glowing right away, faintly at first, then stronger the longer he remained motionless. Suddenly, two cloaked figures, at each end of the street, emerged from out of the shadows and began killing everyone in their path. Torhan looked at Mekel, then at the street to his left.

There were just too many, and there was no way to save Mekel, he thought and ran down the alleyway.

Before he could reach the far end, another Chromos Lord stepped directly in front of him and sliced a few frozen people in between them. Torhan knew there was no escaping him and unsheathed his blade.

"Give it to me," the Chromos Lord spoke in an eerie tone as he killed another hapless victim frozen in time.

"Give you what?" Torhan responded.

The Chromos Lord ignored his question and inched his way closer. "Give me that trinket, human," he sneered. "You should not be able to resist our powers," he hissed.

As Torhan moved backward, the Chromos Lord suddenly lunged forward with lighting speed, catching him off guard, and slashing him across the stomach. The ferocious strike happened so fast the scabbard didn't react until the maneuver was completed, and when it was, the silver dagger left its home and became frozen in time. Torhan stumbled into a wall, looked down, and saw the chain links split apart and colored crimson with his blood. The Chromos Lord rushed forward to end his life but was careless and didn't anticipate Torhan sidestepping the attack while thrusting his sword forward. As a result, the keeper of time ran himself through and died after coughing up some blood. Along with his death, time resumed in the alley, his snake-shaped sword turned to dust, and Torhan's silver dagger stabbed him in the head a few times before returning to the sheath. Screams of horror erupted from the nearby alleyways. Torhan removed his sword from the dead man's stomach and was about to leave when he heard someone shout from behind.

"Hey, you, stop!"

Guards poured in from both ends and closed in rapidly.

"You're under arrest," one of them said.

"For what?" Torhan snapped back.

"For the death of that man," he pointed to the body at Torhan's feet, "as well as all of those innocent people just a street away."

"I didn't do it. This man and his friends did," Torhan pleaded.

"You can tell it to the magistrate."

Several of the guards produced chains, of various lengths, and closed in.

The scabbard glowed dark green, and the dagger launched itself and attacked the guards. Some of the guards fearfully backed away, while others did their best to parry the weapon.

Torhan's options were limited, either fight his way out this mess or end up in jail. With no intention of the latter, he decided to attack the smaller lot of guards and escape. Despite being the much more skillful fighter, he was overwhelmed because of the number of guards and received many cuts across his arms and legs.

After the third guard fell, a burly giant of a man lowered his shoulder and rammed him from behind, sending him flying into the wall ten feet away. The impact left Torhan dazed and confused.

One of the other guards gave chase, wanting to end his life. He was about to succeed when the scabbard, sensing that its master was in danger, commanded the dagger to strike down the assailant, which it did when the blade ripped through his throat.

The other guards closed in to avenge their fallen brother and were immediately met by the dagger, which kept them at bay long enough for Torhan to regain his footing and his senses. He was about to run in the other direction when the giant guard saw the dagger fighting three others. The giant pushed through them, grabbed Torhan, hoisted him high into the air, and slammed him down onto the ground like a rag doll, knocking the wind out of his body. In response, the dagger flew toward the husky guard, but it was intercepted by another guard, who parried the weapon several times before it found its mark and struck him in the head, becoming lodged in his skull. The big guard quickly grabbed Torhan's right arm, placed one knee on his neck, and extended the limb, snapping it in two. Torhan winced in pain.

"I'll snap your neck next, unless you recall your weapon," the guard commanded.

The dagger began working its way out of the dead man's head. Torhan, realizing the dagger would never reach him in time, conceded. "Have your men stop their...aggression toward me and let...go of my arm," he said through gritted teeth.

The guard ordered his men to stand down and did as he was told. After the dagger wiggled free, it returned to the scabbard, but the sheath remained glowing green due to the hostility of the men around him.

"We need to disarm you. Will the dagger attack my men if they do?" the big guard asked Torhan.

"As long as you don't hurt me."

He nodded to another guard who walked over, removed Torhan's weapons and placed them in a sack, then bounded the prisoner in chains.

"Captain, what about the scabbard?" he asked.

"Leave it. Take him to the healer for mending and then throw him in jail," the captain ordered and left.

When he was gone, one of the other guards stood over Torhan and produced a small club.

"This is for my friend who you killed," he said and cracked Torhan over his head, knocking him out cold.

The man smiled, not knowing it would be his last, as the scabbard commanded the dagger to defend its master. In the next instant, the dagger came to life, stabbed through the sack until it was free, and attacked the guard. The others, knowing better than to help, watched helplessly until their comrade lay dead. They carefully removed the dagger from the scabbard and placed it into a metal coffer, this time locking the lid in place. They were careful not to hurt Torhan as they carried him away.

Katara had just finished her dinner when she heard a loud knock on her door.

"Who is it?" she said from the eating area.

"OPEN UP!" someone shouted back at her.

Katara made haste to the door and asked again, "Who knocks this time of the evening?"

"If you don't open up the door, we'll break it in."

Katara hesitated, then did as she was told. As soon as the door was opened, guards pushed their way past her, carrying an unconscious person in chains.

"What is the meaning of this?" she demanded.

"Mend this fool," the guard said and threw the unconscious body on the ground and unchained him.

"What's wrong with him?" Katara asked.

"Broken arm, ribs, and a rather large gash across his head," the snickering guard boasted.

"On whose orders?" Katara was clearly not amused by his comments.

"Captain Strom's, that's whose orders!" the guard said and slapped her hard across the face, snapping Katara's head to the side and causing her eyes to water. "And make it quick, we'll be outside."

The guard stormed out of her house with the rest of his men following closely behind.

Katara was seething and about to grab her mace, run outside, and bludgeon the guard to death when the prisoner stirred. She regained her composure and helped the semi-conscious man over to her mending table.

"Where am I?" he asked weakly.

"My name is Katara, and you're in my home for healing."

"What happened?"

"I'm guessing that you ended up doing something that the guards didn't care for."

Before Torhan could say anything further, he lost consciousness abruptly and Katara went to work on his battered body. First, she applied her secret ointments all over his wounds and then placed his arm into a sling. During the procedure, Torhan mumbled information about Grappin and Priest Abiathar, causing her to stop more than once to listen. She didn't know what to make of this information and wished he would wake up and explain it to her.

"Hurry up!" the guard shouted from outside.

She tried to wake him, but it was useless. His head wound must have been far worse than she anticipated. She began searching him for any relevant information that might tell her who he was or what he was doing in Mirkin. Her search turned up two notes that were tucked away within his armor. Just then, the guards entered her house, and she quickly hid them.

"We have to go, witch," the antagonistic guard snapped. Some of the other guards brushed past her and chained Torhan again.

"Be careful, his wounds need healing," she warned.

"Be careful! Do you know what he's done?" the guard barked at her. "Don't guess, I'll tell you. He killed over a dozen citizens. I wish we could serve justice right now," he said and hoisted him over his shoulder, gave her an angry look, and left.

Katara poured some tea, sat down, and placed both letters in front of her on the table. The first one was marked with her name, which she thought was odd that a stranger carrying a note addressed to her would end up in her house. The other one had what she thought was the stranger's name. She broke the waxed seal of the one addressed to her and read the note:

Katara,

If you're reading this note then it means the stranger named Torhan made it to Mirkin safely. He told me that he wanted an audience with Priest Abiathar but wouldn't say why. I have a sneaky suspicion his intentions are far greater and deadlier to our cause, so try to uncover why he is there. If he jeopardizes your mission, stop him. We are counting on you.

Regards,
Brother Pien

She picked up the other note, carefully unfolded the parchment, and read it several times.

When she was through, she realized that she had more questions than answers, *Was Torhan an assassin sent here to eliminate Priest Abiathar or is he a puppet for this person named Grappin? Grappin mentioned there are wards in Mirkin, but where are they? I never sensed them in all my time here. If Grappin did indeed have a guardian, then he must be a high priest of some sort, but why would a high priest command the death of another priest, unless he was evil?*

Katara knew what she had to do, so she finished her tea, walked into her bedroom, removed her diary from the locked chest, and penned one final entry into her journal. After she was through, she hid the untitled book somewhere deep inside of the chest and locked it. With that taken care of, she slipped into her perfectly fitted chainmail, secured her sling and father's oak mace on her side, and wrapped a dark-colored cloak around her body, using the hood to cover her head and conceal her identity. She extinguished the candles and left her home.

Her first order of business was to find out where the wards were and the best place to start was around the temple. Taking a deep breath, she reached into her pouch, grabbed her lucky trinket, and turned the rock several times in her hand. It was a ritual she did before every mission to gather her courage. When she felt at peace, she started her trek down the dark street.

The guards arrived at the three-story jail, shoved Torhan through the doors, and pushed him up the stairs to the second floor. After opening the door to the corridor, the guards ushered him down the hallway until they reached the far end. Torhan noticed the other cells were empty.

"This is your new home," one of the guards said, laughing.

Several guards pointed loaded crossbows directly at his head, while another unfastened his chains and roughly jostled him into the cell, slamming the wooden door shut behind him. Another guard stuck his face right in front of the square hole with the tiny bars and told him to enjoy his stay, then he led the rest away.

When they were gone, Torhan surveyed his room for a way to escape. He checked the floorboards, the door, and the tiny window that allowed a small amount of light to filter into the room. All of which didn't yield any hope of escape. Sometime later, he gave up and lay down on the creaky wooden bed in the corner. Despite being uncomfortable, he fell asleep within minutes.

When he woke up, he was first disoriented and nervous, because he didn't know where he was, but moments later, his memories returned, and he calmed down. He lay there thinking about his predicament and cursed himself, as this was the second time he'd been accused of a crime.

A few moments later, the door down the hallway opened, and someone came lumbering toward his direction. Torhan sat up just as a guard appeared at the cell door.

He looked through the window. "Hey, dirt, by tomorrow the magistrate will either lock you up for a very long time or have you hanged, drawn, and quartered. I prefer the latter of the two." He opened the small feeding door. "Here's your food," he said and pushed the tray of food into his cell. The tray landed onto the floor, spilling its contents. He closed the little door and left laughing as he walked away. Torhan wanted so bad to get his hands around his arrogant neck and choke the life out of him.

A few hours later, the door down the hallway opened again and Torhan quickly sat down in the back of the cell with his head between his knees. The guard opened his cell door.

"Hey, scum, what are you still doing awake?" he said.

Torhan looked up, didn't answer, and put his head back down. When the guard failed to get a reaction out of him, he became enraged.

"HEY, SCUM!" he shouted.

Torhan continued to ignore him, not bothering to raise his head in acknowledgement. He knew the guard was losing his patience.

"If you don't answer me, I'm going to…" the guard's voice went silent.

Torhan looked up and saw him frozen in time and the cell area entrenched in grayness. A bearded, cloaked figure materialized from out of the shadows, took hold of the guard's head with both hands, and with one quick jerk snapped his neck around. Torhan rose to his feet, watching in horror at the brutality of his actions. The Chromos Lord dissipated the grayness and stepped into the room.

"Let me introduce myself," he began, "my name is Yourie, and I belong to a special race of creatures called the Chromos Lords, or as some have labeled us, Shadow Warriors." Yourie stepped a little closer and continued. "Our race has studied the gradual effects of time, and now we are able to bend and, as you have already discovered, manipulate time itself. We mean you no harm, so please tell me your name."

"So you mean me no harm, huh? Then why did one of your friends try to kill me?"

"I'm sure it was a misunderstanding."

"Misunderstanding? I'm locked up here because of this misunderstanding." Torhan was growing angry. "How did you find me?"

"It wasn't hard after the guards seized you."

"What do you want with me?"

Yourie smiled. "Just an answer to the obvious question."

"Which is?"

"How are you able to resist our powers?"

Torhan knew that as long as he kept it to himself, he was safe. "Wouldn't you like to know?" he calmly said.

"We would, because only demons can resist our powers, and I know you are not one in disguise."

The Chromos Lord slid back his cloak so that Torhan could get a glimpse of the pair of short swords strapped to the sides of his body. The scabbard remained silent during their exchange of words, so he knew, for the moment, he wasn't in danger.

"You never did tell me your name," Yourie pressed.

"My name is not important."

"Come to think of it, you're right. I don't need to know your name. So after you tell me how you're able to resist our powers, I'll be on my way." Yourie grinned and slid his right hand over the hilt of the sword on his left.

Torhan's scabbard started glowing. "It appears you're lying to me, so let's drop the charade," he challenged.

"That's interesting, why does your scabbard glow?"

"It warns me when someone wants to harm me."

"And why does it do that now? I mean you no harm," Yourie said sarcastically.

Torhan was trapped with nowhere to go and no weapons for protection.

"I'll ask you one more time. How are you able to resist my powers?" The Chromos Lord was clearly agitated.

"I don't know how I am able to resist them, so I can't help you."

"I have a strange feeling that scabbard might have something to do with it, so why don't you remove it and let's see if you still can resist my powers." The Chromos Lord's eyes started glowing red. "We can do this the easy way or the hard wa…"

Yourie was in midsentence when suddenly his eyes went wide with sheer terror as a dagger was pushed through his throat. He gargled on his last words incoherently and slumped to the ground dead.

"I guess it's the hard way." The humorous statement came from a man dressed in black leather with his face covered in soot. "What? You don't recognize me?"

Torhan shook his head.

"I guess you wouldn't with my face covered the way it is." He wiped the blade on the dead man's cloak, sheathed the weapon, and removed some of the soot away.

Torhan finally recognized him. "Molech," he exclaimed, feeling somewhat relieved to see him.

"In the flesh, my friend." He bowed slightly as if they were introduced for the first time. "So this is where you've been hiding?" He straightened and looked around the cell.

"I wish I was."

"Well, it doesn't appear you'll be living up to your part of the bargain, does it?" he said in a sly voice.

"Not from in here I can't."

"What did you do? You don't look the type to commit a crime to warrant your arrest, but then again."

Torhan didn't like what he was implying. "Let's just say I was in the wrong place at the wrong time."

"Again?" He chuckled. "If I allow you to escape will you still be going to Snowdrift? Because if not, I'll lock the door and leave." Before Torhan could respond, he continued, "And I'm sure the guards won't take too kindly to the bodies in your cell."

"I'll need my weapons first."

"Do you mean these?" Molech reached outside of the cell, produced a sack, and handed it to him.

Torhan opened the bag and started equipping himself with his wares. "I need one more day in this town first. Is there any chance that I won't be accused of the deaths of these men?" He asked even though he knew the answer.

"I don't think so. You're getting quite a good reputation, wouldn't you say?"

Torhan frowned.

Molech reached out and grasped his broken arm. "Allow me," he said.

Torhan nodded.

Molech applied a strange-looking salve to it. "It should mend your arm; give it a few minutes before moving it."

Torhan felt a strange sensation race up his arm. "What is it?"

"Don't ask."

"How do I get out of here?"

"The passage has already been cleared for you." Molech smiled sinisterly.

Torhan searched the sack again. "I guess you didn't see the gem or the rest of my coins, did you?"

When there was no reply, he looked up, and to his surprise, the thief was gone.

After his arm felt normal, he left the cell and cautiously descended the stairs. He soon discovered what Molech meant when he said the passage was already cleared. There must have been a dozen or so guards all of which were slashed or stabbed to death. He thought briefly about searching them for coin but opted to leave instead, not wanting to risk being caught.

Katara arrived at the temple just as nightfall descended upon the town. She spoke several low to mid-level chants, and when they failed to detect the wards, she used the one that was taught to her by a powerful priest. She was halfway through when a very faint glow began to appear around the building. She was surprised to see wards of this magnitude and stopped chanting. The ward's glow dissipated, and she began chanting again. By the time she finished, the initial wards were wrapped within other wards creating a circumference that stretched too far for the eye to see.

What could Abiathar be afraid of that he needed to create powerful wards? I'd never imagined he had such power or maybe… someone helped him? she thought.

She followed the wards from end-to-end and realized the entire town was one big giant maze of them, the last of which ending at the entrance to the city. Quickly, she traversed her way back to the temple and went around the back. With the help of the small footholds in the stone, she climbed over the ten-foot high stone wall and ran to the side of the building and up the stairs. She tested the door and found it locked.

Gazing to her left, she saw a large window with a ledge wide enough to give her ample footing. She climbed onto the small wall surrounding the top of the stairs, took a deep breath, and jumped for the ledge, grabbing hold of the windowsill. She swayed a few times, then pulled herself up. Once situated, she knew the darkness behind her would shroud her presence, so she took her time as she peered through the beveled window.

Inside the backroom, a short, stocky, robed figure was in the process of lighting the candles. Once he was finished, he barred the doors leading to the main service room and left through the doors in the back.

Katara waited a few minutes before trying to open the windows. To her disappointment, they were locked. She was about to break the glass and drop down into the room when six acolytes entered carrying an unconscious half-dressed man. They placed him onto the large oblong table in the center of the room, bound his arms and legs, placed a gag into his mouth, and surrounded him. After uttering a few muffled words, the acolytes lowered their hoods and produced long knives. She thought about intervening but decided that uncovering the greater plan was priority. She watched as the acolytes chanted something in unison and one-by-one plunged their daggers into the man's stomach. As soon as the first blade bit into his flesh, he began thrashing about. His horrified screams were muffled by the gag and glass as they continued to stab and slice their victim until his stomach laid opened and he stopped moving. The acolytes reached into his cavity and began removing his organs one at a time. His still beating heart was first to be placed on the table, it was followed by his lungs, liver, intestines, and kidneys. After that, each servant grabbed an organ, held it high into the air, said a few words, and began consuming it.

The ghastly scene made Katara turn away and almost retch up her dinner. After she regained her composure, she looked back into the room just as one of the acolytes walked over and opened the door to the cellar.

A few seconds later a strange-looking black imp hobbled into the room and over to the table. The creature began consuming the man's flesh until it morphed into an exact replica of him. The scene, coupled with her nausea, was too much for her. When Katara turned away, she lost her balance and fell off the ledge, banging her head on the ground when she landed.

After Torhan left the jail, he was determined to disable the wards and disappear from the city by morning, so he made haste toward the temple. Given the time of evening, it was easy for him to avoid the guards who patrolled the streets. However, after he arrived, his first obstacle laid before him in the form of two armed priests standing by the door. He had an idea as to how he was going to gain an audience with the priest and moved rather quickly toward the doors. The priests stepped forward and blocked his way.

"The temple is closed," one of them said.

"I need to see Priest Abiathar. It's important."

The guard moved his cape aside so that Torhan could see his spiked mace hanging from his belt.

"The temple is closed for the evening," the other guard said. His tone was firm and authoritative.

"You don't understand, I need to see him because he's in grave danger." Torhan pleaded to emphasize just how dire the situation was.

The guards looked at him suspiciously.

"You should leave." The guard gripped his mace in a threatening gesture.

"Please, I need to see him. I just uncovered a plot to kill him. You have to do something besides stand here."

"We are more than capable of guarding him."

"You don't get it. He will be dead by morning, and you'll be to blame."

"Look, fool, we are not waking his holiness for you or anyone else." The guard looked in disgust at Torhan.

"There's an assassin in the area that wants him dead," Torhan said.

Both guards looked at him, then at each other.

"What's your name?" the guard on the right asked.

"My name is Torhan."

"Wait here." The guard opened the door and slipped inside.

"You had better be telling us the truth," the other warned.

A few minutes later, Priest Abiathar emerged with the guard right behind him.

"What's the meaning of this intrusion?" he asked, looking directly at Torhan.

"You're in grave danger, and me standing here puts us both at risk. Can I come in and talk to you?"

"You're the person I met earlier, aren't you?" Torhan nodded. "If you leave your weapons here with my acolytes, you may enter."

Torhan agreed and was led down a series of corridors until they arrived at a set of double doors with four acolytes guarding the entrance. They stepped aside when they saw Priest Abiathar and closed the doors once he and Torhan were inside. Torhan was asked to sit at the table in the far back so that they could talk privately.

Once seated, Priest Abiathar spoke, "Now, young man, what's this about?"

Torhan spoke directly. "There is a person named Grappin who wants you dead."

"I've never heard of anyone by that name before, so why would he want me dead?"

"He says you killed his family."

"Let me ask you something. How did you acquire such information?"

Before he could answer, the door burst opened and three armed and very dangerous looking men entered the room. Abiathar quickly held his hand up, halting their progress.

"News travels fast about the possibility of an assassin. So let me ask you and don't lie to me. Are you the assassin?"

The guards drew their maces.

"Not anymore."

"Not anymore?"

The guards were about to pounce on him when the priest held up his hand again.

"Please explain yourself."

Torhan told him the events that happened in Mirkin and how he felt that he was framed and forced into his current situation. When he mentioned the forest and Lord Sim's people, Priest Abiathar's eyes lit up and he interrupted him.

"Ah, Lord Sim, now that is someone I do know. Go on, my son."

Torhan continued. As he mentioned the Tree Spirit, Ailith, and how she revealed Grappin's true nature, Abiathar murmured her name.

"Do you know her?" Torhan asked.

"I've heard of her." He paused. "Tell me about what she meant by true nature?"

"She said Grappin was a demon."

"Did she now?"

"Yes, and I have no intention of helping him."

"Then let me ask you something. What do you hope to accomplish by telling me all this information?"

"I think he has you all wrong and wanted me to murder an innocent man. I can't do that."

The priest grinned. "If he is a demon, you do know what will happen if you don't fulfill his wishes, don't you?" Abiathar paused. "Wouldn't it be easier to kill me?"

"It would, but I can't."

"Interesting predicament, don't you think? So again, I'll ask, what is your plan, to hide in here and hope he grows weary and leaves? Or…wait…I have a better idea, I could disable the wards, and together we can kill him," the priest leaned back and said almost jokingly.

"If I told you that I have an item that could expose him to mortal weapons, could I stay here for the night?"

Priest Abiathar looked surprised for the first time. "You can, but first, tell me what you have."

"I need my items, and I'll show you."

Priest Abiathar nodded to his guard, who left and returned a few minutes later with his wares. Torhan got up, under their watchful eye, grabbed the quiver of arrows, and removed one. He then offered it to Abiathar, and just as he was about to grab the shaft, he pulled his hand back suddenly.

"What's wrong?" Torhan asked.

"I almost forgot; it's against my order to touch projectile weapons."

Torhan could tell it was something more by the expression on his face.

"If you have a weapon to deal with him, then why are you here?" Abiathar asked bluntly, his demeanor quickly changing.

"Like I said, I'm here to warn you that Grappin is trying to kill you, and I may not be the only one he sent."

"What do you mean?"

"He has a couple of trained assassins working with him."

"I'm in no danger from him or any other person. My God has bestowed in me the adequate power to keep demons at bay or destroy them if I like. And my men are quite capable of handling anyone else he might be traveling with." He paused and shifted his body, "Plus, my men are immune to demons."

"Immune? So that's why he needs me to dispose of you, because he cannot get close enough to do it himself," Torhan said, realizing why he was here to do Dybbuk's dirty work.

The priest grinned. "No, he can't, and even if he did penetrate my defenses, he will fail."

"May I have sanctuary for the night?"

"Yes, but you must stay in your room. Do you understand?"

Torhan nodded.

"I have to go. One of my acolytes will take you to your room."

Torhan waited a couple of hours before attempting to leave his room. When he opened his door, he found the hallway empty. He was prepared to do whatever was necessary if he encountered any resistance. He gathered his items and left.

He was halfway down the hall when an acolyte came running toward him. At first, he thought maybe he was going to send him back to his room, but, by the look on his face, he knew differently.

"You need to come quickly. Priest Abiathar needs you."

Torhan followed him downstairs to the basement. When he arrived, he saw Abiathar talking to several guards. Torhan knew something was wrong by the way he was speaking with them. After the priest finished addressing his men, he walked over.

"It appears you weren't lying after all. Someone is trying to deactivate some of my wards. My acolytes are checking them as we speak," Abiathar said.

"I'm here to help anyway I can."

"Good."

A few minutes later, another acolyte came running into the room and whispered something into the priest's ear.

Priest Abiathar looked at Torhan and said, "Several of our key wards have been breached."

"Did any of your men see who did it?" Torhan asked.

"No, but I'm guessing we'll find out soon enough. Come with me."

Torhan was led to the main room, where he saw acolytes barricading the vestibule doors and Priest Abiathar's most trusted guards preparing for a fight. The doors separating the area were next to be sealed, then a handful of guards lined up in front of them.

They were the first line of defense, Torhan thought.

When they were finished, acolytes stood ready in the center of the room with their maces and slings loaded with strange-looking red stones.

Abiathar led Torhan behind the altar. "I sure hope that weapon of yours works," he said.

Torhan hoped for the same as he silently notched a Demon Slaying arrow.

Outside, something that sounded like a battering ram crashed into the front doors, time and time again, until they gave way. The sound of a fight ensued, which was followed by horrifying screams confirming Abiathar and Torhan's worst fears.

The priest gave the order for his men to stand ready. After the screams died away, a loud thud pounded against the inner doors. Several acolytes threw their bodies against them for additional support, but Torhan knew it was useless. The doors were struck again. This time, the frame began to crack and give way. Torhan trained the bow at the door and told Abiathar to stay behind him for protection.

After the fifth time, someone shouted on the other side, **"RAUM, COME OUT!"**

To Torhan, the voice sounded like Grappin's but somehow different, deeper, and more sinister.

"Who's Raum?" Torhan asked the priest without taking his eyes away from the door.

"I don't know," he quickly answered.

Torhan pulled the bowstring back further.

"STEADY!" the priest shouted to everyone.

The thick doors were struck again, causing dust to fall from the ceiling and the hinges to rattle. After two more times, the doors began to buckle.

Torhan remembered the Ailith's words and went over them again in his mind:

For the arrow to work, Dybbuk needs to become enraged with you, and then you should be able to draw enough of his negative energy to activate the leaves' power, thus breaking his invulnerability to mortal weapons.

The doors were hit again, and they finally shattered. A creature standing nearly eight feet tall with scaly, dark skin; large protruding teeth; and claws the size of daggers stared back at them. Grappin's humanoid remains hung loosely on his form.

The demon must have been hiding inside of Grappin all along and ripped through his outer shell, Torhan thought.

The demon roared and began his violent assault on the two closest guards, ripping through their armor with one swipe of his left claw, then cutting them in half with the other.

The guards released their slings and pelted him with the red stones, but he paid them little mind as they bounced off his thick skin. Dybbuk turned his attention toward the altar. When he saw Torhan pointing his bow in his direction, he became enraged at his betrayal and proceeded toward the religious platform. Along the way, he engaged the remaining guards.

Torhan's scabbard glowed intensely, and, just as he was about to release the arrow, his silver dagger left the scabbard and flew behind him. His instincts kicked in, and he rolled away, then turned around to witness Abiathar swatting at the dagger.

Torhan thought for a brief moment that the dagger made a rare mistake until the illusion began to disintegrate before his eyes. While defending against the weapon, Abiathar's body was sliced, cut, and flayed to the point where Torhan could see scaly, red skin underneath. The priest, or whatever it was, continued to swat at the knife until he snatched it out of the air and flung it into a nearby pew, where it became lodged down to the hilt.

The creature looked directly at Dybbuk and began ripping apart Abiathar's tattered skin like the outer shell of a piece of fruit, revealing a large head with short horns, sharp claws, similar to Dybbuk's, and a ridged tail. The demon straightened his body to a height of nine feet tall and thrashed his crimson tail back and forth ever so slightly.

Torhan's dagger revealed who his true enemy was, and he fired the bow at the demon formally disguised as Priest Abiathar. The arrow scored a direct hit to his head but bounced away helplessly. He quickly notched another.

The demon turned his attention and anger toward the pathetic human who dared to attack him like a coward. He roared and began moving toward him with hatred. Torhan waited for his intensity to build before firing another shot. This time, the arrow broke through his defenses and pierced the demon's shoulder, causing him to lose his balance and fall backward, screaming in pain.

In the next instant, more hideous screams erupted from the front of the church. Torhan turned around and witnessed the other acolytes shred their outer skins as they were entering from the basement. The smaller demons flung themselves at Dybbuk. They were no match for him as they were viciously sliced apart one after the other until they were all dead. He then turned his gaze on Torhan. Fearful, Torhan notched another arrow and pointed it directly at him, but the demon ignored his gesture and looked past him.

"RAUM!" he shouted.

Torhan didn't notice the red demon standing directly behind him until it was too late. He was struck in the shoulder with a tremendous backhand that sent him flying through the air and slamming hard against the wall, knocking him senseless.

The demon Raum called for the other in a challenging tone. Eyes glowing, Dybbuk stared at his nemesis for only a moment before leaping through the air and landing on top of him. The demons fell backward onto the ground and began rolling around until Raum was hoisted high into the air and thrown against the wall. The intense impact shook the foundation of the cathedral and broke Raum's right arm and some of the bones along his back.

Dybbuk smiled as he watched his foe rise to his feet and struggle to straighten his crooked form. Seeing the arrow, still protruding from the ugly wound in Raum's shoulder, broadened Dybbuk's smile further knowing that Raum was exposed to his environment. Dybbuk knew he never experienced pain of this magnitude before, especially in the place known as the Other.

Raum followed the other's gaze and grabbed the shaft. Instantly, the arrow turned searing red hot and started burning away his flesh until the pain was unbearable and he released it.

Dybbuk snickered. "Well it appears you're finished, my old friend," he said.

Raum quickly surmised that this battle would end with his death if he wasn't smart enough to outwit Dybbuk, so he held up his good arm, dropped down to his left knee, and pleaded, "Please let me live."

Dybbuk approached his former comrade. "Would you be so kind?" he hissed.

"Let me live, and I'll go home and never return. You can rule this world, and the Overlord will be proud of you."

"You and your bitch have caused me great suffering and almost succeeded in turning my pawn against me. Death is your only release,"

Dybbuk said and moved closer.

Raum waited until he was close enough before acting. In one fluid motion, he moved his good arm behind his back, unhooked the flail strapped across his back, and swung the spiked ball at Dybbuk's head.

At the very last second, Dybbuk raised his right arm and blocked the attack, but, in doing so, caused the chain to wrap around his forearm and drive the spikes into his flesh. Raum then jerked the weapon to his left, knocking Dybbuk off balance while freeing the weapon and giving himself enough time to get to his hoofed feet.

In the next instant, Raum swung his deadly weapon with accuracy, hitting Dybbuk in the right shoulder, then left leg, and, finally, his ribs, tearing flesh and sending the demon stumbling backward. Raum pressed his assault with the intention of missing easy targets and drawing Dybbuk's defenses away from his true mark, his head. The attack was so fast that it would be nothing more than a blur to the human eye.

Meanwhile, Dybbuk's years of experience told him exactly what he was doing. When he invited his nemesis to swing for his head, he quickly dashed out of harm's way, causing the heavy spiked ball to slam into the marble floor, cracking the green and blue limestone, sending bits and pieces in all directions. As Dybbuk was closing the distance on his foe, Raum pulled the weapon upward, hitting Dybbuk's right leg with the shaft part of his weapon, knocking him to the ground.

When Torhan finally regained his wits, he looked over at the demons battling, saw that Raum was winning, and realized that if he didn't do something to change the outcome, he would die.

Frantically, he looked around until he spotted his bow and quiver not more than a few feet away. As he crawled to retrieve the weapon, his movements didn't go unnoticed by Raum, who disengaged his fight and lumbered over. The scabbard glowed in response and commanded the dagger to protect its master, which it did by moving frantically back and forth until it wiggled free from the pew and attacked the advancing demon.

Raum noticed something coming at him out of the corner of his eye. As he was turning his head, he was stabbed in the right eye, blinding him and stopping him dead in his tracks, wailing in pain. The dagger swiftly withdrew, along with his eye, from the socket and stabbed and sliced him repeatedly in the body, neck, and head. Raum dropped his weapon and tried to grab the dagger, but his injured eye hampered his perception, and he was quickly becoming a gory mess as blood ran down his red, scaly skin.

Torhan notched an arrow, pulled back the bowstring with all of his enhanced might, and fired.

Raum never saw the arrow, but felt its impact for only a brief second, as it pierced his good eye and punctured his brain, causing the demon to stagger backward, then fall forward dead.

Dybbuk was on his feet again and limped over toward Torhan.

"Torhan, you have fought very well," he began, "and more importantly, fulfilled your obligation. You may keep the scabbard as my..."

"Was I just a pawn in your game?" Torhan interrupted him.

The demon smiled as best as he could. "We are all pawns, are we not?"

"How so?"

"For starters, how did you acquire the leaves fastened to the shaft of the arrows and know what to do with them?"

It was no use in hiding the information from him, Torhan thought. "A Tree Spirit named Ailith told me all about you and how to break your immunity to mortal weapons."

"Ailith? She's a Tree Spirit? So that's what happened to her," Dybbuk laughed.

"Happened to her? What do you mean?" Torhan was puzzled.

"Where did you meet her?" The demon's eyes narrowed.

"On my way here I traveled through the Harazon Forest and met a creature named Lord Sim. He introduced me to her."

"Lord Sim? He's with her as well." The demon snickered. "This is indeed getting good. I bet they crafted some wild tale about me, didn't they, and how I did them wrong?

"They did tell me a lot about you."

"Not that I need to explain, but would you like to hear the truth about her?"

Intrigued, Torhan nodded.

"Before she became the so-called Tree Spirit, Ailith was a demon much like me and my former associate." He looked over at Raum and then back. "It all began in our home world when the Overlord granted her the right to serve with me and take control of your world, which was an honor given the fact he never allowed females to have such privileges. For the most part, we worked well together and things were progressing, until one day, an attempt was made on my life by Lord Sim's people, and I found out she was behind it. I've known her for a long time, and I can tell you this, she did not come up with this idea on her own. So when I confronted her, she denied this, of course, until I showed her the heads of those responsible, and I had no choice but to torture and kill her for her treacherous plot. I'll give her credit, she never revealed her accomplice."

"Did you ever find out who that was?"

"Not directly, but I have a good idea it was Raum."

"How?"

"Because he suddenly arrived into your world unannounced and tried to kill me a few moons later."

"So Raum tried killing you?"

"He did, but that's a long story, and I don't have time."

"Are you sure he was here for revenge?"

"Call it a demon's intuition, because no one from my world enters yours without the Overlord's consent, and he didn't prove it to me."

"What's going to happen to Ailith?"

"She will atone for her actions, and I promise you this, she will not exist anymore." His voice sounded gleeful as his eyes glowed red with hatred.

"I have a question for you. How did you know that I wasn't going to shoot you?" Torhan asked, snapping the demon out of his vengeful trance.

"I didn't, nor did I detect the arrow's true nature until the shaft burned Raum's hand as he tried to remove it."

"I think Raum knew something was different about the arrow, because he had a chance to touch it before the fight but didn't."

"Maybe, but I'm also guessing he didn't know about the scabbard's abilities either, because, if he had, he would've taken action against you sooner. Too bad for him." Dybbuk snickered.

"So giving me the scabbard was a part of your plan as well?"

"I gave you the relic so that the odds were stacked in your favor. I couldn't take a chance on you dying along the way."

"How was he able to hurt you, aren't you immune to mortal weapons?"

"The flail he used was from my world, not yours. It's useless to mortals and will turn to dust if they choose to wield it."

"Did you kill Tomal?"

"Did I? No. I had one of my men do that for me, because you would have never agreed to help me then, right?"

"Who was it, the assassin?" Torhan snapped.

"It might have been," Dybbuk replied coldly.

"Where is he now? I want to confront him."

"Who, the assassin?"

"Yes, the assassin," Torhan demanded.

"I am unable to accommodate your request, because he met with an accident this morning. You see, he didn't take too kindly to your monk friend and wanted to kill him, so I left him to his own contrivance. It turned out your friend was more than a match for him, but unfortunately, he died as well."

Torhan felt responsible for Brother Sao's death, and Dybbuk saw the look upon his face.

"Don't mourn him, he served a definite purpose."

"How so?"

"Well, my assassin also had an issue with you, and he was going to kill you as soon as you left the town."

Torhan's heart sank at the probability. Just then, Dybbuk heard what sounded like troops approaching the cathedral, but they were still far enough away.

"Like I said before, we are all pawns in someone's plot." The demon rubbed his arm. "I must be going now. I have my own affairs to contend with in my world. Plus, guards are coming, and I'm in no shape to fight. I advise you to do the same."

Torhan was about to turn away.

"I'll take that quiver of yours," Dybbuk said.

"For what?"

"I can't have you armed with a weapon that you could use against me. Plus, there are no more demons in your world."

Torhan hesitantly handed it to him and slung the bow over his shoulder.

"Torhan, if you make it back to Redden, you're entitled to anything within my house. I have no need for such trinkets anymore."

Torhan nodded and left through the side door.

Dybbuk looked at Raum and then at the carnage he was leaving behind. He knew his time in the place known as the Other was wasted, and he'd have to make amends with the Overlord. He took a deep breath, limped toward the backroom, and entered the cellar stairs just as the guards came through the church's vestibule. When he reached the bottom floor, he opened the portal with a wave of his hand, stepped through, and sealed the entrance from the other side.

Outside, Torhan hurried down the stairs three at a time until he reached the landing and quickly sprinted through the cemetery toward the western wall. He was halfway across when he heard someone shout that there was someone in the cemetery.

He paused and saw guards climbing up the fence. He knew that if he got caught this time, there wouldn't be a trial or someone to save him. Fearful, he ran on. When the first of the guards landed on the ground, he shot his crossbows and missed Torhan. In response to the attack, Torhan's scabbard glowed and sent the dagger to engage the man. As more men climbed over the fence, the back door to the church suddenly slammed opened. Torhan glanced over his shoulder and saw his worst nightmare. It was that bullish captain of the guard, who captured him earlier. Even though it was dark, he could see his delightful grin.

"Hold your fire," he shouted, "this one is all mine!"

The big man was agile enough to jump over the railing, land on the ground, and burst into a full run while releasing his cudgel from his back. Torhan ran harder, and when he reached the wall, he frantically looked for a way to climb over it.

"You're a dead man," the captain shouted.

Torhan grabbed the rough edges of the stones and pulled himself up but lost his grip and slid back down. After his second failed attempt, the scabbard sensed the captain's intentions and commanded the dagger to fly from across the grounds to engage him. The other guards ran over to join their captain. Torhan tried again to climb the wall. After he slid back down, he conceded that he would have to fight his way out and turned around, unsheathing his sword.

The captain successfully deflected the weapon with the cudgel, then timed his strike perfectly, and whacked the blade, sending it spiraling into a nearby tree, where it became lodged and couldn't release itself.

Torhan swallowed hard as the giant of a man smiled in anticipation and slowly walked over savoring the coming battle. Torhan readied his stance, then something brushed against his back. He turned around and saw a rope hanging down in front of the wall. He didn't care if it was intended for him or not, he grabbed the rope and began climbing. When the captain saw him climbing toward freedom, he raced over, jumped up, grabbed the ledge with his left hand, and began pulling his bulky form up. Both men reached the top at the same time.

"Trying to escape? Not this time," the guard said.

Torhan carefully backed away as he closed in.

Down below in the cemetery, the other guards pooled around the wall to watch their commander fight, while on the other side of the wall, a lone figure came out of seclusion, swinging a sling above her head. She took aim and hurled the rock at the captain, hitting him in the side of the head and dazing him. He began teetering to the side and dropped to his knee for support. Torhan seized the moment and pushed him over the side, where he landed on several of his men.

"Jump down," a female voice shouted from below.

Torhan jumped down. When he tried pulling the rope up, he was met with resistance. He knew what that meant, so he cut the rope and heard someone fall with a thud. He turned and saw a raven-haired figure emerge from the shadows holding a sling. Torhan recognized her as the healer.

"Follow me, we have to go," she said.

They ran through the streets, toward her house, and made it there without any confrontation. Once inside, she barred the door behind them and frantically collected anything of importance that they would need during their travels.

A few minutes later, they heard footfalls and voices approaching her house, which was followed by someone pounding on the door.

"Open up or we'll break down the door, witch," someone shouted.

Katara grabbed Torhan's hand and pulled him toward the backroom. She opened the window and moved to the corner of the room.

Outside, the guards began kicking in the door.

"Time to go," she said.

Torhan looked through the window. "We're never going to get away."

Ignoring him, she moved the table aside and pulled the rug back just enough to reveal a trapdoor underneath. She opened it, grabbed him by the arm, and practically shoved him down the stairs. She followed him, lowered the trapdoor, slid the latch into place, and ordered him to move.

They traversed the stairs quickly, then went through another door.

"Where does this lead?" Torhan asked.

"Out of the town," she said and handed him a glow rock. "Activate it."

While he was doing so, Katara closed and locked the door and led him down the tunnel.

After the guards finally broke the door down, they raced through the tiny house looking for the criminals. When they reached the backroom and saw the window open, they naturally assumed that the duo climbed through and left. Two guards stayed behind to look for clues while waiting to see if they would return.

One of the guards noticed the carpet was moved recently and pulled back the rug, discovering the trapdoor.

"What do we have here?" he said, tried lifting the door, and couldn't. "It's locked from the other side."

"Smash it in," the other said.

Together they pounded on the door until it cracked and splintered apart, allowing them to descend. They came to the other locked door. The guard who found the trapdoor was an expert locksmith and took out his tools.

"This won't take long," he said and went to work on the lock.

The tunnel ended in a circular room with different shaped logs scattered about and another passageway at the far end. A backpack sat neatly beside the exit, which Torhan figured was left there in case of an emergency.

Katara instructed Torhan to gather the other logs, while she rolled the largest one toward the center of the room. When she was finished, they placed the remaining branches on the side of the larger log as if they were arms and legs. After that, Katara knelt down in front of the wood and began chanting in a language Torhan did not understand and could only surmise was ancient in origin.

Eventually, the wood began vibrating and moving around until the thick branches inched their way closer toward the center log and attached themselves to it and each other, creating a wooden figure complete with a head, torso, and bendable arms and legs. The wooden figure came to life and opened its mouth, revealing rows of sharp teeth, then its eyelids parted and two large, round eyes appeared.

Her chant intensified, and the creature began rolling around until it stood up. Katara stopped her chanting, stood, and instructed her animated sentinel to guard the room and kill anything that entered. The timber warrior began moving slowly toward the entrance and stopped when it was less than a foot away from where they entered.

"That should hold them long enough for us to escape," she said.

Torhan was about to ask her how she created this creature, but she just waved him off.

"Another time, right now we have to go," she said, picked up the backpack, and ran down the tunnel.

"Got it," the guard said after he heard the faint click of the locking mechanism.

"Captain Strom will be proud of us when we bring them back," the other added.

They drew their swords and ran off in pursuit of their quarry.

After moving through the semi-darkness of the chasm for several minutes, they entered a circular room and failed to see the guardian until it was too late. They were both struck by its wooden arms and sent flying backward. The sentry lumbered toward them, maw snapping in anticipation, when it saw them staggering to their feet.

One of the men gained enough of his senses to attack, but his sword did absolutely nothing against the bark. The six-foot wooden protector swung one of its limbs and ripped his head clean from his shoulders, leaving his body standing where it was for several long seconds, spewing blood from the stump, before falling over.

Stricken with fear, the other man remained motionless as the guardian slid its limbs under his armpits and hoisted him into the air kicking and screaming. The wooden man opened its mouth, shoved his head in, and, with one powerful chomp, severed his head at the neck. With the threat neutralized, it returned to its post and waited for more intruders.

The passageway eventually ended at a closed wooden door. Katara took out a strange-looking key and unlocked the door.

Smiling, she said, "We're free."

However, when she turned the knob and pushed on the door, it wouldn't budge. She tried again, and the door wouldn't give way. "It must be jammed on the other side," she said.

"Can I try?" Torhan offered, and Katara stepped aside.

After placing both hands squarely on the wood, he pushed. At first, it wouldn't budge, then the bracers sensed he needed more strength and glowed a bluish hue, which was followed by a strange sensation coursing up and down his arms. Torhan's physical strength increased to the point where he felt powerful. Grunting, he pushed harder, and the wood moaned and began to creak. Dust fell from the ceiling. Wood began splintering, and, with a mighty shove, the door tore from the hinges and slammed to the earth. Torhan looked over and smiled at Katara. She smiled back.

"Where did you get the gauntlets?"

"I found them in a cave."

"Do you have an extra set?"

Torhan grinned and left the tunnel, walking out into the emerging sunlight. Once they were outside, they found a large enough boulder to cover the doorway, then they walked westward.

A few hours later, they came upon a cluster of trees and decided to rest for a while. Torhan quickly lit a small fire, while Katara placed a blanket on the ground, so they could sit in comfort and eat.

She opened the backpack. "We have cheese, crusty bread, and rotten fruit, or rotten fruit, crusty bread, and cheese," she joked.

"I'll take the second option without the fruit."

Katara smiled and placed the small block of cheese alongside the loaf of bread, then divided it into four portions. Torhan sat down and together they ate.

During the meal, Katara noticed Torhan had something on his mind.

"What are you thinking about?" she asked and took a bite of bread.

"How did you animate the wooden guard?"

Katara finished what was in her mouth before responding. "It's a little hard to explain, so I'll do my best." She took a gulp of water from the waterskin and continued. "The wooden guard is called a Tirip and…"

"Tirip?" Torhan interrupted.

"That's what they're called. I guess you've never heard of them, have you?"

Torhan shook his head.

"Tirips are spirits from another plane of existence, and if you have the right chant, you can summon them to inhabit a particular host and do your bidding until they expire."

"Expire. What do you mean?"

"There are two ways. When their physical host is destroyed or after two weeks. Both will send them back to their dimension."

"I'm guessing there are more than one Tirip?"

"From what I've been told, there are seven: Vacuum, Stone, Fire, Metal, Wood, Water, and Air. Each one has their own strengths and weaknesses, and some can defeat others. For instance, Wood Tirips can defeat Water Tirips, but not the Fire Tirips, unless they are larger than the Water Tirips."

"How so?"

"The Fire Tirips cause the water to evaporate quickly. Pretty simple, huh?"

"I'm guessing fire is a good way to get rid of the Wooden Tirips, but the Water Tirips sound really hard to destroy, unless you have some sort of fire weapon."

"That's not necessarily true. Water Tirips will become weaker when they start to dry up or stray too far from their water source. When that happens, they will expire. Plus, if you can trap them in a deep ditch, they won't be able to get out."

"That's good to know. How do you defeat the ones created out of air?"

"The Air Tirips are quite deadly, but there are a couple of tricks. You need to lead them away from where they were created or find a way to contain them."

"How do you conjure them?'

"You saw how I did the Wood Tirip. Air, you need an open space, and water, you need a pond. The bigger the mass of water, the stronger the Tirip will be, and the farther it can travel.

"It's really important to keep in mind that Tirips, no matter what form they appear in, will take on the caster's alignment, so if a wicked person summons one, then the Tirip will be evil."

"Can you summon all types of Tirips?"

"No. My Order can only summon Wood, Air, and Water. The others are evil in nature."

"But you said they take on the same alignment as the caster."

"I did, but the ones that are evil by nature are really hard to convert."

"Who can conjure the other four?"

"Demons and high priests, who deal in the dark arts, can summon all seven," she said flatly.

"I've seen a Stone one before."

"Stone? Is that what Grappin had, a Stone guardian?"

"How did you know about him?"

"While I was healing you, I found a note addressed to you from him." She reached into her tunic and handed him back the note. "So who is he?"

He accepted the parchment. "He's someone I met while I was in Redden."

"Is he a priest?"

"No. He's something far worse," he paused. "He's a demon, and his true name is Dybbuk."

"A demon? How did you get involved with a demon?"

"A few weeks ago, I was staying in Redden, waiting for my friend Jacko to arrive. While I was waiting for him one night, I decided to go out for a walk and found an equipment store to occupy my time. While I was there, I met someone named Molech, who told me about his friend Tomal's store and how he had some of the finest items in the region. With nothing else to do, I went there, and he was right, his items were of remarkable quality. He also had some interesting ones as well. Have you ever heard of a Ring of Warmth?"

"Like the name says, they're supposed to keep you warm, right?"

"They sure do." He showed it to her. "Try it on."

She did and immediately felt the warming effect course up her left hand, arm, and entire body.

"This feels nice," she said and handed it back to him.

"What else did you buy?"

"I really wanted the scabbard I'm wearing on my arm, but it was overpriced, so I went back to my room and slept."

"You said it was overpriced, did you steal it?" she interrupted.

"No, but when I woke the next day, it was in my room."

"How did it get there?"

"Someone planted it there."

"I'm guessing it was Molech."

"I'm not sure."

"What's so special about the scabbard?"

"It's magical by nature, and the minute someone wants to harm me, it warns me by glowing green."

"Really. Maybe I'll hit you with my mace and see if it glows." she smirked.

"Now's the time to try, because once I place a dagger in the scabbard, it becomes enchanted and will fight anyone who wants to harm me directly," he said, smiling.

"I know you're kidding."

"I'll show you once I get another one."

"So what happened after you found the scabbard?"

"I went back to the store and found out Tomal was murdered, and some of his items were stolen. I didn't know what to do, so I panicked and went back to my room. It didn't take long for guards to show up at the inn and start questioning people."

"What did they ask you?"

"They never got the chance, because while I was hiding in my room, a masked stranger appeared on my balcony, told me someone wanted to meet me, and offered to help me escape. I knew that it would be really hard to explain the scabbard to the guards, so I followed him, and he led me to Grappin's mansion."

"Very convenient, don't you think? You were told to go to Tomal's store the night before, the shop owner turns up dead the next day, and you end up with a very expensive item in your room. And on top of that, a masked stranger appears just in time to save you from getting questioned or possibly thrown in jail."

"Looking back, it sure was, but I was scared and wasn't thinking clearly."

"So, who was the masked stranger, Molech?"

"He never revealed his identity, plus, he was taller."

"What happened when you met Grappin?"

"When I met him, I still wasn't sure why I was brought there until he accused me of stealing the scabbard and killing Tomal. My first mistake was denying I had the item, because he found out real quick that I had it under my tunic."

"How?"

"Like I said, the minute someone wants to bring harm to me, it glows green, so he had one of his henchmen become aggressive toward me, and it glowed. After that, he was convinced I stole it."

"Did you try to tell him you didn't?"

"I did, but it was useless. What would you have done?"

"Instead of hiding in my room, I would've looked for clues. Who told you about Tomal and his stuff missing?"

"I ran into Molech near his store."

"I guess I should have known. Continue."

"Grappin gave me a couple of choices. I could either fight my way out of the room, which he knew I wouldn't be able to do, or repay the debt by going to Mirkin and disabling Priest Abiathar's wards."

"What reason did he give you?"

"He said he committed some horrific acts against his family and wanted revenge."

"Did you believe him?"

"Not really."

"So just like that you were going to come here and disable the wards? Did you even know what they are used for?"

"I didn't have a clue at the time, and I think he knew that."

"So why did you agree?"

"Because I was trapped. It was either help him or die."

"Trapped?" Katara angrily said. "No one is trapped."

"Not without proof I wasn't," he firmly said.

"You should have gone to the authorities in the first place, and maybe you wouldn't have been in this mess."

"And how do you think that would have played out? I was one of the last people to see him alive, and I had the scabbard in my possession, which, by the way, wasn't even for sale," Torhan fired back at her.

Katara was about to say something more on the matter but held her tongue.

"What if I refused his offer and died that day? Don't you think Grappin would've done the same thing to another person? Let me tell you something. Just because I agreed to disable the wards doesn't mean I would've done it. Even though my life was on the line, I would have talked to Priest Abiathar first and made my own decision."

Katara could tell he was really upset. "I apologize for jumping to conclusions."

Torhan nodded in acknowledgement.

"When did you find out Grappin was a demon?"

"On my way here I passed through the Harazon Forest and was captured by a being named Lord Sim and his people."

"Never heard of him. How did you get free?"

"He was about to kill me when he saw the scabbard glowing green and wanted to know where I got it, which led to a series of questions with him explaining that Grappin was a demon. I didn't believe him until he introduced me to a Tree Spirit named Ailith and she—"

"A what?" Katara quickly interrupted.

"A Tree Spirit, but in reality, she's a demon too."

"A demon? How did you find that out?"

"Be patient, I'm getting there. When I met Ailith, she confirmed that Grappin was a demon, and I would die even if I helped him deactivate the wards."

"Now I know why you were conflicted."

"She did tell me there was a way to expose him to mortal weapons."

"How?"

"I needed to construct the bow I'm carrying and create special arrows by replacing the feathers with certain leaves found only in their forest."

"Did it work?"

"It did but not on him."

"I don't understand?" Katara looked puzzled.

"I used it on Priest Abiathar, who turned out to be a demon after he tried to attack me in the temple."

"It doesn't surprise me after what I saw in the church before I helped you escape from there."

"What did you see?"

"I'll tell you after you're done."

Torhan told her about the encounter with the Chromos Lords; Molech helping him escape from jail; the epic battle between the demons, and how he contributed to the ending of Raum's life; what Dybbuk was planning to do with Ailith, and his departure from their world. He also mentioned what Dybbuk said about Brother Sao and how sorry he was.

"I have a question," she began. "If Priest Abiathar was killed by Dybbuk, and he is going to kill Ailith, then who is going to get rid of Grappin?"

"Maybe he'll leave."

"Torhan, demons are manipulative, cunning, selfish, and, more importantly, evil. We, as a race, cannot allow them to exist in our world, because they will enslave us all. You should have killed him when you had the chance." She didn't wait for him to reply and continued her rant. "There's a reason why they entered our world in the first place, and I don't think it is just to say hi and leave peacefully."

Torhan knew she was right.

"Do you have any more arrows?"

"No. Dybbuk took them with him."

"Why did he take them?"

"He was afraid I would use them on him if he ever returned."

"What part of the forest did you find these magical leaves?"

"They grow from a plant called fernion near where I met Ailith, but like I said, you'll need to use my bow or construct a new one just like it."

"I'll let my Order know about them. Hopefully, they can make something useful out of the leaves." She grew calm again "On the other hand, maybe we'll hire you to be our champion demon slayer." She chuckled. "I'll need to report everything to my Order, including their names. Grappin was Dybbuk, Abiathar was Raum, and was Ailith her real name?"

"Dybbuk never mentioned any other name than Ailith when he referenced her."

"So is your debt paid?"

"Dybbuk said so." Torhan looked disappointed.

"Look, don't blame yourself. Dybbuk and Ailith manipulated you into doing their bidding. Just learn from your mistakes. Okay?"

He nodded. "Why did you help me escape?"

"Let me explain why I was in Mirkin in the first place. Brother Pien sent me there to practice with his friend Priest Abiathar, then one day he changed, and he decided he couldn't teach me anymore. After that, Brother Pien instructed me to observe his strange behavior. So when you showed up for healing, I found the notes and read both. Brother Pien wanted me to discover why you were in Mirkin and had an interest in Abiathar, and the one Grappin wrote you spoke of wards. After the guards took you away, I decided to go to the church and find out about the wards and what the good priest had been up to. However, what I found was the most gruesome ritual I'd ever seen."

She paused, reflecting on what she saw, then she continued, "Some of his acolytes tied a man to an altar, gutted him, and removed his innards.

Once they did, a hideous creature hobbled up to the table, ate some of his organs, and transformed into an exact copy of the man. I'm not sure, but I think the creature was some sort of a changeling or demon. The procedure horrified and sickened my stomach to the point that I lost my footing and fell to the ground and hit my head. When I came to, guards and acolytes were everywhere outside of the cemetery, so I left. While I was escaping over the wall, I heard shouting and violence erupting inside of the church. I waited on top of the wall to see what would happen next, and then you opened the back door. I was about to call out your name when the guards spotted you, so I jumped down on the other side, waited until you were close enough, and threw over the rope."

"I forgot to thank you for saving me."

"I have a feeling it won't be the last." She smirked and stood up. "We should get going," she said and began folding the blanket. "By the way, how did you get past Grappin's stone guardian?"

"He gave me a command that allowed me to do so. Do all Tirips have secret commands?"

"It all depends. If you conjure up a very powerful one, like the stone guardian, then you would be wise to tell it a word or phrase so that it would become disabled or allow you to pass." Katara put the blanket into the backpack.

"Do you want to come with me?" Torhan asked.

"Where are you going?"

"Molech asked me to help his niece, Sybil. She lives in the town of Snowdrift."

"Help her how?"

"She fell into a deep sleep, and he wants me to find a way to wake her."

"How do you get involved with these people?"

"He offered me a lot of money. And before you ask, I do not think he knew Grappin."

"If I come along, what's in it for me?"

"I'll cut you in for a third."

"I need to stop by my Order eventually, but it can wait as long as I send word." She adjusted her cloak. "You're offering me a third? How about half?"

Torhan smiled. "Only if you can prove your worth."

"Then you should give me all of it." She laughed, and Torhan couldn't help but laugh along with her.

They traveled northwest through a wooded area and a few miles above the Harazon Forest. Along the way, they told each other about their families, friends, and background in their respective fields of study.

By nightfall, they decided to make camp. A light snow was already falling, and the temperature was growing cold. Torhan gathered wood to build a fire, while Katara hung a thick sheet of water resistant cloth in between two trees to create a makeshift tent. While they were eating, Torhan noticed his companion shivering, so he handed her the Ring of Warmth and told her to wear it.

"What about you, won't you be cold?" she asked.

"Don't worry about me; I'll be fine," he said, drawing his cloak tightly around his body.

They talked a little while longer before turning in.

Chapter 6: The Trial

Dybbuk passed through the portal that separated his kingdom from the one known as the Other. As he limped down the dirt-covered trail, in his full fiendish form, he watched the female demons fill the charcoal-colored sky, flying around, eagerly searching for food. He grinned inwardly, because he was finally home, and it felt right.

Three years to the day, it'd been, since he'd taken the assignment, a failed one that tested his patience time and time again with the deceitful ones. He thought about Ailith and Raum. It still puzzled him as to why they both turned on him. First, it was Ailith, then Raum. His only conclusion was that they wanted to move up in rank, but that didn't make much sense either, because Ailith was ranked so much lower than he was. Could Raum have persuaded her to help him? If so, what could she gain? He turned his attention back to the road ahead.

The trek took nearly a half day to reach his sanctuary. For the first time since the building was completed, some several hundred years ago, he adored his imposing structure as he neared. The keep rose two hundred feet skyward and was fabricated from colandoorian, the sheerest, blackest stone in the plane.

When his sentries saw their master approaching, they waited until he was close enough and lowered the drawbridge, so that he could cross the churning, boiling, red waters of the moat.

Dybbuk halted just before the black gated entry. "No one is permitted to enter on this night," he said with a stern voice.

The lesser demons acknowledged his command in unison and elevated the iron gateway.

Dybbuk proceeded through the elaborate entryway and down the hallway until he entered the eating area. To the far right, he saw at least a dozen impish demons preparing food for their master and three more setting the massive table to his left. His imp in charge was about to say something to him, but Dybbuk waved him off and walked through the steel doorway at the far end of the room.

He descended the winding stairs until he entered a large dimly lit room, which mysteriously got brighter the further in he went. The room that once served as a torture chamber was now used to house some of the sweetest nectar throughout his realm. As tempting as it was to grab a bottle from one of the shelves and drink its contents, Dybbuk ignored it, walked to the end of the room, and stood directly at the center of the wall. Before him was the escape door leading to the outside. It was hidden from sight and guarded by a powerful ward that disintegrated anyone who uttered the secret words incorrectly. While checking the strength of his trap, he suddenly sensed his most loyal servant. He turned around and called for him.

"Darkener, come here."

A few seconds later, a large four-legged beast with reddish-brown skin, sharp claws, long horns, and an elongated snout with charcoal-colored eyes, emerged from the darkness.

Its sudden appearance, even though sensed, surprised its master. Dybbuk bent his eight-foot frame, ever so slightly, and rubbed the animal's muzzle.

"I have a task for you, my pet." He paused. "There's a portal in the north that I want you to go through. It will take you to the place known as the Other. I want you to journey southwest and enter the dense forest and kill anything walking upright." He paused again. "I also want you to find something in hiding. Do you understand?"

Dybbuk waited for his pet to acknowledge his order, which he did by retracting his jaw and revealing row upon row of razor-sharp teeth, then he emitted a low growl to the enjoyment of his master's pointed ears.

"Good, good." He walked over to a small hanging cabinet, dispelled the ward, and opened the glass door.

Inside were many labeled vials that contained the essence of every demon in service to the Overlord. They were given to demons of fifth ranking, or less, as a precaution in case someone decided to overthrow the Overlord and go into hiding. He swore an oath never to use them for his own purposes, and now he was going to break his promise and hunt down a traitor. His need for revenge far outweighed his pledge to the Overlord, and it was a risk he was willing to take.

He searched through them one at a time until he found one, in particular, and called his pet. Darkener trudged over, and the demon knelt down before him and opened the bottle.

"I want you to find the owner of this scent and eradicate her."

Dybbuk placed the bottle under his snout, so that he could inhale its contents. The beast inhaled and growled.

"Do not leave the forest until I return. Do you understand?"

His pet's eyes turned blood red, and he snarled in gratification. Dybbuk rose, said a few words, and disabled the ward guarding the hidden door. Next, he waved his hand and a low rumble of stone moving upon stone opened the secret doorway.

"Go now and do as I instructed."

Darkener bellowed in delight and ran through the doorway. Dybbuk watched his pet run until he disappeared from view, then he passed his hand in front of the opening, causing the door to slide back into place. He recited another chant to safeguard the area and went upstairs.

After emerging from the dungeon, he sat down at his table and clapped his hands, indicating he was ready to be fed. Servants of various shapes and sizes nearly tripped over one another in haste as they carefully placed food and drink in front of their master.

For the next two hours, he gorged and drank in delight, never once taking a break or even glancing up from his plate. After he had his fill, he rose from the chair, wiped his fanged mouth, and headed over toward the staircase at the far end. He was about to ascend the stairs, leading to his private chamber, when one of his minions came rushing over.

"Master?" the demon said, panting.

"What is it, whelp?" Dybbuk firmly said without even turning.

"My lord, one of the Overlord's messengers has arrived."

"Invite him in, and tell him that I'll be down as soon as I indulge myself in the pleasures."

"Yes, my lord," the scrawny servant replied, bowed, and left.

Dybbuk walked several flights of stairs until he reached the top landing with the closed door. Posted outside were two guards he called the Elite Ones. Personally trained by his hand, they were bred for one purpose, and one purpose only, and that was to protect their master or die doing so. He paid them little mind and motioned a few symbols in the air to deactivate the wards guarding the entry. Once they finished dissipating, he opened the door and stepped into the hallway beyond.

"No one is to enter, not even the Overlord himself," he said, closed the door behind him, and reactivated the wards.

The long hallway led to a large square room with the mummified corpses of his most challenging foes. Four in total, and each was erected as if they were frozen in a time of their demise. Each form told a different tale of how they perished and the unspeakable horror they endured by his hands.

There was Anzu the Troubled, with his head placed neatly by his feet; Sron the Mighty, with his arms and legs twisted behind him; Eligos the Slayer, with his body cut in half; and finally, his toughest and deadliest opposition to date, Orias the Influential. Not only was Orias proficient with his tongue in the art of persuasion, but his fighting skills were superior to his own. Now, the former advisor to the Overlord was kneeling before him, holding his intestines from his gutted stomach. Dybbuk had him posed that way because his death was so rewarding. It also reminded him that not even the Overlord thought he had a chance to defeat him.

Dybbuk thought about them for a few minutes longer, then walked into the main room and out onto the terrace. The view was spectacular and overlooked his domain. He shrieked a sinister cry, and within minutes, three winged demons landed beside him. They were the most beautiful of his pride.

"Come," he commanded, and they eagerly followed him into his bedroom to mend his injuries and satisfy his hunger.

"Will he be down soon?" an irritated Grasant asked.

"My lord hasn't been home in a long time," the servant began. "He is satisfying his hunger for the pleasures. Even you can comprehend that, Grasant." The servant placed the tray of food and wine down in front of the guest.

"Very well. Just remember I am here on behalf of the Overlord," Grasant said, making it known he was offended.

The servant left the room, and the Overlord's messenger set about eating.

Several hours later, Dybbuk emerged into the dining area, and upon seeing him, Grasant stood up and bowed to the mighty demon, who was fourth in command throughout the plane.

"What brings you here, Grasant?" Dybbuk said to the most useless messenger he'd ever laid eyes upon.

Grasant smiled. "The Overlord would like to have a meeting with you."

"So soon? I just arrived."

"He knows that but wanted to speak with you while everything is still fresh in your mind."

"Tell him that I'll meet with him tonight after I first tend to some pressing matters."

"Very well." Grasant bowed in acceptance.

Dybbuk turned.

"One more thing, Lord Dybbuk."

"What is it?" he responded, trying his best to veil his annoyance.

"The master sensed that Ailith and Raum have ceased to exist, and he'd like to know why."

Dybbuk did not respond and left the room.

It was nearing twilight when Dybbuk left the confines of his keep. His path to the Overlord's domain was a direct route through the dry wasteland and was guided by the orange moon, which turned the sky cerise in color. Despite his rather large build, he moved quickly and tirelessly over the shifting terrain.

Eventually, he crested over a hill, and the Overlord's fortress came into view. The obsidian structure was at least twice the size of his keep. Scores of guards walked around the perimeter and hovering high above the structure were many female demons flying erratically. The cool wind licking at his face brought back memories of the first rebellion many centuries ago.

The uprising began in the west where a demon named Kappas decided it was time for a new and younger breed of demon to lead them into the future. He convinced many of their kind that his cause was just, and they agreed to join his ranks if he led the rebellion against current Overlord Uvall.

The deadly confrontation began when Kappas marched a legion of demons against Uvall's stronghold. Uvall and his protectors, led by a powerful demon named Bathin, fought bravely against the rebellious demons and continued to do so even after the fortress was breached. With their numbers dwindling, Bathin sensed the end was near and convinced Uvall, who was mortally wounded, to escape through a hidden passage into the Timinom Mountains. Those that remained behind sealed off the pass and held the masses at bay for a full day before falling. With the battle at an end, and the Overlord sent scurrying away from his castle, Kappas deemed them traitors and sentenced them to live out the rest of their days in hiding. The punishment meant Uvall could not regain his title, and his band of protectors would never return.

In the third moon of exile, Uvall finally succumbed to his wounds, leaving Bathin and the others in a most dire of situations. Without him, they would never rise up and retake what was rightfully his, and they couldn't return home because death was what awaited them. They were also low on food, and with winter upon them, it meant a season filled with the harshest conditions.

Bathin took control of the situation and went off in search of shelter and food, knowing that, without both, they would perish. He came upon an abandoned cave and, deep within the bowels, found water and a peculiar fungus that would provide nourishment for many moons to come.

Delighted with his discovery, he was about to return to the others when he stumbled upon a corpse holding a staff with strange carvings on the wood. He studied ancient lore throughout his life, and, after deciphering most of the symbols, he realized that he'd found the lost relic called the Staff of Influence. Further translating explained exactly how to employ the weapon. After showing the others the staff and displaying the power it possessed, they pledged their loyalty to him. It would take Bathin a few years to master the staff's power. When he did, he started what would be known as The Battle of Subjugation.

After leaving the safety of the mountains, he recruited many demons by tongue. Those he couldn't sway, he had only to use the staff, and they pledged their loyalty without question. With the backing of many high-ranking demons, Bathin led an attack on Kappas and his horde of the most vicious and lethal Superior Drones in their realm. Due to their lower intelligence, the drones were no match for the staff's power and were easily persuaded to change their allegiance or perish. With his numbers swelling, it didn't take Bathin long to overthrow the newly appointed Overlord and his highest ranking demons.

After they were imprisoned, he became the new ruler of their kingdom and sent Kappas and his accomplices to trial. Kappas never had a chance at a fair hearing, because the judges were appointed and influenced by Bathin, and they were found guilty.

For their punishment, Bathin had their limbs removed and their torsos left hanging high above the castle walls where they could swing back and forth every time a strong wind blew. Servants kept them alive for Bathin's entertainment. After a hundred and fifty years, he grew tired of their pleas for death, and gladly accommodated their request piece by piece.

Dybbuk turned his attention toward the long drawbridge leading up to the castle and the many guards stationed along the length. He found it excessive for the Overlord to have so many guards, but maybe things changed since he'd been gone.

As he began crossing over, he felt heat radiating from the fiery water below, and it made him think of how hot it would be to humans, and how long it would take them to dissolve. He found it amusing, because the water was just a warm bath to his kind. He was halfway across the span when a pair of purple-skinned drone guards broke ranks and barred his passage.

"What do you want?" the drone on the right said after Dybbuk stopped.

"The Overlord sent for me," he replied.

Simultaneously, both drones looked at each other as if they needed to agree upon what he was saying. Dybbuk knew they were quite stupid, but what they lacked in intelligence they made up for in size, strength, and obedience. In a sense, they were the perfect guards; they never asked questions or disobeyed orders. A few seconds later, they turned their attention back to him.

"State your intention and your title."

"I am Dybbuk, fourth in command, and my purpose is meant for the Overlord's ears only."

The guard on the left rumbled in annoyance. His initial temptation was to squash the visitor, as it was all too enticing, but, like a switch in his little mind, the Overlord's order was remembered:

Attack only if assaulted or if the Overlord's life was threatened.

A third drone now approached. This one was much larger and darker in color than the others were. When he was close enough, the set of guards parted and allowed him to stand before Dybbuk. Dybbuk recognized his status immediately. He was a Superior Drone, a personal protector to the Overlord and handler of the inferior drones.

One time, he had the privilege of seeing this powerful being in a tournament facing off against twenty other lesser drones. In a matter of minutes, he'd ripped them apart. The Superior Drones were the most feared throughout the plane, and were smarter than the ones they handled, but they lacked leadership and, for that reason, could never rule.

Towering practically three feet taller than Dybbuk, the creature stared down at him. "What are you doing here?" he bellowed at him.

"I am Dybbuk, fourth in command. The Overlord has sent for me, so please allow me through."

Dybbuk knew his ranking meant nothing to this drone. In his eyes, the Superior Drones were second only to the Overlord himself. For several tense minutes, neither the drones nor Dybbuk moved. When the precious time was right, the Superior Drone told him to wait where he was and walked back toward the castle.

A few minutes later, Dybbuk heard commotion coming from behind, which made him turn around. Another Superior Drone approached him and stopped in front of him.

"I recognize you," he began, "you're Dybbuk of the fourth in command."

It took Dybbuk a few seconds to recognize him as well. It was Chargen, one of the Overlord's smallest, and dumbest, lesser drones ever hatched. It appeared that he was promoted to superior status, grew five feet taller, gained hundreds of pounds, and acquired more intellect in three short years, a feat uncommon among their breed.

"Chargen, it's been a long time. You have developed quicker than any of your kind."

He drew a deep breath, expanding his powerful chest. "I have. The Overlord has been very pleased with me. Each time that I complete a task for him, he improves me."

"Improves you? How so?"

"He gives me a special drink that I consume, then I become stronger and tougher."

"It's good to see you."

"Are you here to see the Overlord?"

"I am."

Chargen suddenly looked up at the castle as if someone caught his attention. "I have to go now," he said and walked past him.

After Chargen was gone, Dybbuk patiently waited for the first Superior Drone to return and was growing agitated with each passing minute. Just when he was about to proceed into the castle, and break their laws of audience, the drone emerged with Grasant in tow.

The imp walked slightly behind the drone as if he was the Overlord himself. When they finally reached him, Grasant stepped in front of the drone.

"Dybbuk," began the little scamp as his tail fluttered back and forth, "the Overlord will address you now." He smiled sarcastically at him.

Dybbuk's eyes narrowed, and his muscles tensed. "Lead the way."

Dybbuk was escorted down the pathway, behind Grasant and the Superior Drone, as if he was a commoner instead of a high-ranking demon. The drones along the span stood by, silently watching them, as they passed, and he could feel their stares rip through his very dark soul.

When they were less than twenty feet away from the mighty citadel, the doors carefully opened and several Void Tirips spewed out of the entryway, swirled toward them, then all around Dybbuk as if they were trying to gauge his intentions. Suddenly, Dybbuk recalled the last time the Overlord gave this kind of reception, and that was to dispose of Sabnock of the second in command. When the Tirips finished, they parted, and he was allowed into the castle. As they passed through the entranceway, Dybbuk pondered whether his fate would be the same as Sabnock.

Instead of taking the usual passageway into the great hall, Dybbuk was led to the right, into another hallway and down several flights of stairs. He'd never been to this part of the castle, and this only made him wonder what was going to happen to him. They eventually came to a large room with rows of chairs seated on a platform and doors on either side of the chairs. He knew this to be the room of judgment.

"Why am I in this room?" Dybbuk demanded.

"You'll find out soon enough," Grasant responded.

Dybbuk could hear the delight in his voice. "Tell me before I lose my temper, you deceitful imp."

The Superior Drone readied himself for the pending confrontation, but Grasant held up his hand to stay the mighty creature. "Now, now, Lord Dybbuk of the forth in command, there is no need to get angry. If you did nothing wrong in the place known as the Other, then you don't have anything to worry about." He chuckled lowly.

Dybbuk was about to say something when Grasant turned around and left with the drone. They closed and locked the doors behind them.

Patiently, he waited and waited, until finally, the door to the right opened and in walked eight greater demons. Each carried a scepter and donned black robes with the insignia of the Overlord inscribed on the front. They proudly walked into the room, stopped in front of their respective seats, and faced him. Dybbuk recognized most of them. A few did not care for him, but demon law dictated he must have a fair and just trial or they too could face judgment. The judges introduced themselves in turn, from left to right:

"I am Gravis of the first judge."

"I am Tam of the second judge."

"I am Stratus of the third judge."

"I am Denin of the fourth judge."

"I am Tribler of the fifth judge."

"I am Avalos of the sixth judge."

"I am Hrad of the seventh judge."

"I am Brolumore of the eighth judge."

After they were finished, the door on the left opened and in walked the Overlord. He wore black and red robes and clutched the Staff of

Influence. Dybbuk knew by his garments that he was on trial, and if he was found guilty, then he would die. After the Overlord took up his rightful position in front of the biggest seat, he looked around and sat. The other judges followed his lead. The Overlord rapped the staff several times on the ground.

A few seconds later, the double doors behind him opened and in walked six drone guards, accompanied by Chargen and Grasant. Chargen and the other drones surrounded Dybbuk, while Grasant walked over, stood beside the Overlord, produced a scroll from underneath his robes and began reading it.

"Dybbuk, who is fourth in command, will face the following charges: failing in his mission to rule the place known as the Other, and being accountable for Raum and Ailith ceasing to exist." Grasant rolled up and tucked the parchment back under his robes. "How do you plead, Dybbuk of the fourth in command?"

Dybbuk knew it was pointless to plead his case as to why he shouldn't be on trial, so he flatly told everyone that he was not guilty and scoffed in outright disdain at the accusations. Grasant walked off the stage, smiling.

"Dybbuk, tell us what occurred in the place known as the Other," the Overlord said, and the trial commenced.

Dybbuk looked at each judge in turn and began. "Thirty-six moons ago, Ailith and I were allocated by the Overlord to transgress the place known as the Other. Our mission was simple; we were to infiltrate the surrounding towns and gradually take their souls into our world, so that we could substitute their essence with ours and populate their world." Dybbuk paused.

"Go on," Avalos of the sixth judge encouraged.

"The portal placed us in a forest to begin our charge. It was decided that Ailith would secure the forest by using a barrier ward around the area, while I went to one of the nearby towns to assess their strengths and weaknesses. I left and returned two moons later and found she didn't erect the ward like she was supposed to, so I addressed the witch for her disobedience and found she'd laid a trap for me."

"A trap?" Stratus of the third judge asked.

"Yes. While I was questioning her, my arm was pierced by a dart, causing it to go numb, and then humans materialized, pointing blowguns and arrows in my direction. I was about to attack them when Ailith told me that their weapons were tainted with demonsbane and said for me to stand down, which I did. She then offered me two choices: I consent to her by turning over my Amulet of Status or die. The choice was easy. I decided to live, so I gave her the amulet and left the forest."

"Why didn't you strike her down?" Stratus of the third judge asked.

"Revenge can be taken at any time," Dybbuk responded flatly.

"You turned over the amulet and thus gave up your position in our world? No demon would ever do that. They would rather die than face the humiliation," Tribler of the fifth judge furiously interjected.

"I agree," Gravis of the first judge chimed in.

When the remainder of the judges began to stir, the Overlord abruptly barked, "ENOUGH!" and the chamber went silent. "Continue," he instructed Dybbuk.

"As I was saying," Dybbuk coldly started. "I left the forest under their watchful stares and took up residence in the town of Redden. Many moons later, a group of human would-be assassins tried to put an end to my life. What they didn't know was that I erected wards of protection, and as soon as they entered my sphere, it not only stopped them and sent them scurrying away, it also left their trail behind. I hunted them down and killed them one after another until there was only one left alive and, in true demon fashion, I influenced him into telling me everything. I quickly found out Ailith sent them to end my life, so I sent him back, telling her they vanquished me. After he left, I resolved to take my revenge sooner than expected, but before I could, I needed some sort of protection against the demonsbane and opted to do something she would never suspect." He paused for effect. "I injected myself with enough of the substance until I became so resistant to the venom, I could face her again without any fear from her little helpers."

"Where did you get the demonsbane?" Hrad of the seventh judge asked.

"The assassins carried several small vials of the toxin."

"How did you know that it wouldn't have killed you in the process?"

"I didn't. Actually, I almost perished several times." Dybbuk waited for more questions, then continued when there weren't any. "With each passing moon, my body became more resistant to the poison until I could ingest several doses at once and remain standing. At that point, I knew it was time to take my revenge on her. On a cold, dark, rainy night, I entered the forest and killed every outsider who stood in my way until eventually I cornered her and ripped her apart piece by piece."

"That's a lovely tale you weave, but what about your amulet that you so willingly gave up to spare your life? By rendering your mark, didn't you demote yourself? Furthermore, by doing so, that would've put you under her command, and for that, you are guilty, and this trial is over." Gravis of the first judge savored his finding and wanted to convict him in the worst way.

"Yes, it would." Dybbuk smiled.

Gravis grinned and looked at the other judges in delight.

"Gravis, you're a fool," the Overlord snapped. "For Dybbuk to renounce his status, Ailith would've had to crossover to our world and reveal the amulet to me. Since she didn't, whatever he did in the place known as the Other is irrelevant. When this trial is over, take your feeble form over to the Great Hall and read from the Book of Repute. There you will find what you openly question."

Embarrassed, Gravis elected not to further question the one who stood in judgment on this day.

"What befell of the remaining humans?" Denin of the fourth judge inquired.

"What do you think happened to them?" Dybbuk's eyes never left the judge.

"Dybbuk, we are now going to pass judgment on you," the Overlord stated.

In turn, the judges, with the exception of Stratus, said he was innocent.

The Overlord rose from his chair. "I agree, you're innocent. However, you must defeat the six drones before you can be forgiven for killing another ranking demon. Do you agree?"

"I do," Dybbuk said and straightened his form, took a deep breath, and expanded his chest in acceptance.

The Overlord sat down and struck his staff a few times on the ground.

The drones released their swords, one after another, and circled the demon who stood in judgment. Dybbuk shifted his eyes, watching their movements. When they were ready, the drone directly to his left howled and lunged at him. The greater demon waited until the very last second, then effortlessly sidestepped the attack, grasped his assailant's limb with his left hand, and dug his claws of his right into his left shoulder, tearing away his extremity. The drone's momentum sent him to the ground where he bled out and never rose again.

Two more drones moved in, swinging their weapons back and forth, trying to distract their foe so that they could easily strike at him. Dybbuk was far too skillful of a warrior to fall for such a tactic and aggressively blocked each strike until their midsections were exposed, then he squatted, plunging his claws simultaneously into their stomachs and removing their innards upon retraction. Both drones fell to their knees, wailing in extreme pain, and then toppled over dead.

The Overlord thought his maneuvers were both brutal and flawlessly executed, which excited him.

The remaining drones began their assault much more cautiously than the others and circled the demon several times before taking turns lunging at him. Dybbuk elusively moved out of the way of each attack until they were within range of his sharp talons, then he removed their heads one at a time. Before the last of his executioners hit the floor, Dybbuk knelt on one knee, before the council, in victory.

"Very impressive, Dybbuk, you are absolved of Ailith's murder," the Overlord said and tapped his staff several times on the floor, clearly indicating this portion of the trial was over. "Now tell us what occurred leading up to Raum's death." He rapped his staff only once to commence the trial again.

Dybbuk rose and began his tale. "After her death, the portal back to our world collapsed, and I was trapped in the place known as the Other, so I left the forest and traveled north to continue my charge. Along the way, I visited several towns and one, in particular, caught my attention. It was called Mirkin."

"Why that town?" Hrad of the seventh judge asked.

"From the onset, I felt a very weak flow of energy from our world existing somewhere from within the town, leading me to search for it until I finally discovered the source buried deep within an underground passage. After I erected a portal, I collected data about the town and was poised to begin my duty when Raum unexpectedly paid me a visit with a sealed writ from the Overlord."

"Did you know he was in the place known as the Other?" Gravis of the first judge inquired.

"Yes, but I didn't know where. However, looking back, I was surprised that I did not sense his presence when he entered the town beforehand."

"Indeed, that is strange. His essence should have alerted you to him. So what did the writ say?"

"It stated that I wasn't supposed to leave the world known as the Other until my mission was completed and Raum was supposed to lead the charge of bringing their world under demonic control. It also said failure to comply with the writ would result in my death upon my return to our realm. I scoffed at him and told him to leave. Raum simply said, in a tone that would normally invite death, orders were orders, and he would not leave until we were finished. So I reluctantly agreed."

"Dybbuk," all heads turned toward the Overlord, "Are you sure that was my writ?"

"It had your seal, my lord."

"Very well, continue."

He nodded. "We hid in the cave to discuss our plans until we finally agreed on a course of action. It was simple yet effective. We would take up the guise of a high-ranking, or influential figure and build a large structure on top of the portal so that we could easily transport our kind into their world without drawing too much attention.

"Our first step was to blend in and observe those pathetic humans. It didn't take us long to come to the conclusion that the person who gave us our best chance for success wasn't someone of great wealth or power, it was one of the poorest of them all. A priest named Abiathar. Not only did the poor and middle class follow him blindly, but also the wealthy. We became followers of his and studied his ways until we felt ready, then he met with a terrible accident." Dybbuk smiled, "Raum quickly assimilated his body, while I did the same to his most trusted acolyte.

"When we felt confident enough in our roles, we paid the mayor a visit and convinced him to build a new cathedral, one that would draw more people to our teachings and raise money for his town. He agreed, and the structure took well over ten moons to erect.

"During that time, we developed a following none had ever seen before. People from the lowest, to the highest ranking attended our poetic services day in and day out, with many coming from different regions just to hear our word. Everything was going as planned. Our temple was built, the portal was safely canceled, and we had a strong foothold in the town and were now ready to set our true plans into motion." He paused and then continued. "Two nights before the beginning of the end for the humans, I was ambushed by two Water Tirips as I passed a nearby brook." His tone turned from calm to angry. "The guardians sprung forth from the stream and directed three-foot waves which crashed into me with enough force to send me to the ground and almost causing me to lose consciousness. After struggling to regain my footing, I was struck several times by their deadly water balls and thrown at least a hundred feet away. As I lay motionless, trying to regain my thoughts, the Water Tirips closed in. They were no more than twenty-five feet away when I conjured a small Air Tirip to my defense. The Air Tirip swirled before them in defiance and absorbed stream after steam of water, allowing me enough time to regain my footing and reach the temple. Frantically, I tried opening the doors but found them sealed from the inside. I called out several times for Raum, and he never answered. However, my voice did draw the attention of the nearby guards who came rushing over to investigate and arrived just as my Tirip dissipated into nothingness and the Water Tirips raced toward me. When they were within range, they sent balls of water, and I quickly grabbed one of the guards and used him as a shield, while others were hit and killed. The remaining guards engaged the Tirips."

"What happened next?" Tribler of the fifth judge excitingly asked.

"After tossing aside the corpse, I escaped. There was no point in fighting the Tirips or trying the doors again."

"Are you going to believe this liar?" Tam of the second judge stood up, raising his voice.

Dybbuk gazed upon him with hatred. He knew Tam's student-teacher relationship with Raum.

"My lord, how can his story hold true? You mean to tell me he survived both full-strength attacks from the Tirips, had an adequate amount of power to conjure an Air Tirip, and then, as luck would have it, guards showed up and diverted the Tirips long enough for him to escape?" Tam turned his attention back to Dybbuk and continued his rant. "What happened to the Water Tirips? They would have surely tracked you down until their charge was finished. This trial is nonsense, and you should die."

"Hold your tongue, Tam of the second judge," said the Overlord firmly. "You seem to forget how resourceful and clever Dybbuk can be at times. Now return to your seat."

Tam did not like being stifled, not even by the Overlord. However, he knew better and sat down without saying another word.

"Tam, it appears your emotions are tied to Raum's death. Do not let them sway your decision during this trial or you will face judgment. Continue, Dybbuk," the Overlord added.

Dybbuk bowed slightly and continued. "With my life force diminishing, I sought refuge in the town of Redden where I took up the guise of a wealthy man and lived among the humans until I was whole again. I was pretty sure Raum was the one who tried to kill me, so when I—"

"Tell us how you came to that conclusion," Avalos of the sixth judge interrupted.

"You didn't allow me to finish," Dybbuk said, staring at him.

"I apologize. Please, go on."

"Three things that pointed to it being Raum: he was skilled enough to conjure the Water Tirips, the temple doors were sealed shut, and after I tried reentering Mirkin, there were wards that blocked my entry. Satisfied?"

Avalos nodded and told him to continue.

"I knew to deal with Raum I needed to disable his wards first, so I persuaded a young human to aid me."

"Did you use our way?" Tribler of the fifth judge asked?

"No."

"Why not? Don't they behave better when under the influence?"

"Yes, but Raum would've sensed it and my plan would've failed."

"Then what did you use?" Gravis of the first judge asked.

"All humans crave trinkets of power, so I gave him a shiny trinket that would give him a false sense of security." Dybbuk smiled and continued. "With detailed instructions, my pawn traveled to Mirkin and deactivated his wards, thus granting me access to his sanctuary, where I confronted and defeated him." Dybbuk left out most of the details regarding Torhan's travels and how he really didn't deactivate the wards.

Upon hearing of Raum's death, Tam's emotions finally got the better of him. He rose from his chair, stared at the one who stood in judgment, then walked toward the door. The Overlord, surprised and angered by his actions, nodded toward Chargen, who stepped in front of Tam, blocking his way. Tam halted his progress and turned around.

"I will not participate in this trial any longer."

The Overlord rose from his chair. "Tam, you have disrupted this trial enough and—"

"My lord," Dybbuk interrupted the Overlord in midsentence, catching everyone's attention. "This is the second time Tam has acted in a negative manner during this hearing. I demand retribution."

Dybbuk wanted to seize the opportunity before him so that his challenge would accomplish two things: he would reinforce his status among his kind and destroy another rival.

The Overlord pondered his request for several seconds and was about to answer when Tam said, "I accept his challenge. Raum was my mentor, my friend, and I can't continue living if this traitor is still alive. Let me avenge his death."

"Tam, I don't think you can best him, but if this is the path you choose, so let it be written." The Overlord struck his staff three times, acknowledging the challenge, and sat back down. "Now take your seat and let us pass judgment."

After Tam was seated, the Overlord spoke again.

"Dybbuk, we've heard enough and will now rule." The Overlord turned to the judges. "How do you rule?"

"Life," Gravis of the first judge ruled without hesitation.

Tam sat there staring blankly ahead.

Well, Tam?" the Overlord hissed at him.

Tam shook his head as if he had just woken up from a long sleep, then he narrowed his gaze upon Dybbuk as he voted for death, a decision that Raum would've wanted.

"Life," Stratus of the third judge continued.

"Death," said Denin of the fourth judge.

"Life," Tribler of the fifth judge said after hesitating.

Avalos of the sixth judge and Hrad of the seventh judge each voted for death, leaving the wisest and only one who sat in silence during the entire proceeding, Brolumore of the eighth judge.

The demon's gaze never left the one who stood on trial this day. He simply said, "Life."

"Dybbuk, the court has ruled, and since there is a split decision, I will decide your fate." The Overlord stood up. "You have been acquitted of Ailith's murder, and now I will rule on Raum's death." No one, not even Tam, made a noise as they eagerly awaited his decision. "Given Raum's motives, actions, and this mysterious writ that was clearly forged, I find you not guilty of his death by reason of betrayal, not only to you, but to our kind as well. However, you are guilty of failure to carry out my plan. The penalty for that crime is usually dismemberment of a limb, but, because of the two fools who are now rotting in the abyss, you will not suffer that fate either. However, you must pay some type of retribution for failure."

The Overlord sat down, beckoned to Grasant, and his servant quickly brought over a goblet filled with a strange liquid. The Overlord embraced the chalice, finished its contents in one swill, and continued. "Since there is a challenge made and accepted," he paused and looked over at Tam, then back at Dybbuk, "you have the option of embracing it at first light or defeating one of my Superior Drones."

Dybbuk grinned, exposing his bottom row of fangs. "Even though I welcome the opportunity to battle one of your Superior Drones, I'll take greater pleasure in extinguishing the pathetic life of Tam."

Tam's eyes burned with rage.

"Let it be recorded that the battle will take place tomorrow morning in the courtyard. Send out word to the regions. You are dismissed." The Overlord rapped his staff loudly several times, indicating the trial was officially over, then he stood up, adjusted his robes, and left through the door from which he arrived.

Shortly thereafter, everyone else followed, except for Chargen and Dybbuk.

The big drone walked over. "I was disappointed that you didn't pick me for your challenge. I wanted to test my skills," he said.

"I would've hated to kill you, my friend," Dybbuk replied and walked past the stunned demon. In all reality, he wasn't sure if he could've actually beaten him, but learned at an early age to bestow some sort of doubt in others.

Dybbuk arrived at his keep, ate, then prepared for his upcoming battle with Tam. He donned his most prized armor, which was not only crafted from the finest material throughout the plane, but was also enhanced with special oil that made it virtually impervious to weapons. Even without it, Tam didn't pose any real threat, because he wasn't as strong or skilled as his teacher. However, what he lacked in physical prowess, he made up for in astuteness, and that was what he needed to keep in mind. Dybbuk knew the key to victory for any battle was to know your opponent's strengths and weaknesses, and be prepared to adjust to the unexpected during the fight.

After he finished making his final adjustments to the armor, he opened the cabinet housing his weapons and carefully selected the ones he would use for his fight. The first weapon of choice was a unique, two-handed sword he called Organ Hunter. The blade was longer than most swords of that style by three feet, crafted from the strongest steel, sharp enough to slice through metal, and had hinged blades running up and down the main blade that were angled toward the foible. The tiny blades served a unique purpose;

after the sword entered the body, they changed direction toward the forte and latched onto the surrounding organs. When the sword was removed, the organs followed and death was certain. He strapped the weapon across his back and stared at the remaining cache of weapons in the cabinet.

Several seconds later, he found just what he was looking for. A pair of perfectly well-balanced axes that, when thrown, would be drawn to his opponent's body heat and often scored a direct hit.

Lastly, he selected a curved dagger. It was the weapon he employed when he was about to finish off his opponents. Pleased with his choices, he hooked the axes to his side and placed the dagger into his boot, then waited until dawn before leaving for the courtyard to face Tam.

"No, my lord, don't fight him. You're far too valuable to our cause," Masset pleaded with his master.

"Don't be afraid for me, Masset. I have something he'll never possess: courage and the heart of a champion. He's a coward and a disgrace, and he assassinated my mentor. I will have my revenge, and his head, by the light's end," Tam confidently said.

"I fear that he'll use something to change the course of the battle. He's done that before, my lord."

"Masset," Tam faced his most trusted servant, "I do this not only for myself but for my teacher. His spirit will guide me to victory. Now help me with my armor."

Masset was about to say something more when Tam held up his hand and stopped him from doing so.

It took a little over an hour for Tam to get ready. After placing his helmet on top of his head, he said, "I will prevail on this day and move up in rank, so for both of our sakes, don't interfere. Do you understand?"

Masset nodded in acknowledgment. Tam took hold of his mighty two-handed axe and left.

Masset watched his beloved master of seven years walk away. He wondered what would happen to him if Tam fell. Usually, if your master died, you had two choices: join him or serve another. He was too old for the latter, and when his fears finally got the better of him, he went to his room and grabbed his throwing blades, then stormed out of the keep after his master.

Under gloomy skies, the courtyard stands were packed with restless demons eagerly awaiting the fight between two high-ranking Demon Lords. It wasn't every day they witnessed a battle of such magnitude.

A short while later, the Overlord, dressed in royal robes, arrived. He was escorted by several Superior Drones and took up his rightful seat in the center of the courtyard. His appearance was followed by both warriors entering from opposite ends of the courtyard and walking over until they stood in front of the Overlord.

Thunder suddenly crackled overhead, which was followed by thick sheets of acidic rain falling from the sky. This excited the crowd, and they erupted into a series of cheers that didn't stop until the Overlord stood up and hushed them with a wave of his hand. After the crowd quieted down, he spoke.

"We are here to witness the battle between Dybbuk of the fourth command and Tam of the twentieth command for the right of innocence and ascension."

The crowd once again erupted into a frenzy of cheers and only calmed down after the Overlord waved his hand several times.

"Combatants, do you have any last words before we begin?" the Overlord asked.

Tam was the first to speak. "My master will be avenged on this day." His statement, simple in sentiment, brought a brief round of cheers from the crowd.

"And your death will bring me great satisfaction and prove to our kind that your life meant nothing." The crowd hissed and howled in response to Dybbuk's rebuttal.

The Overlord waited for the masses to be quiet before stomping his staff and telling them to begin.

Tam withdrew his axe, and Dybbuk unsheathed his mighty sword, then both demons circled each other. Tam, the larger of the two, howled in rage and attacked his opponent by swinging his axe repeatedly. Dybbuk raised his blade and deflected every attack Tam had to offer, then shoved him backward. Tam stumbled, regained his balance, and attacked again. Dybbuk successfully fended off his advances, then grabbed his arm and tossed him over his shoulder, where he landed hard onto the ground.

Dybbuk walked away from him. "You're too slow and will die soon," he taunted and angered his adversary further.

Tam got up and attacked again. This time, he used a style he thought Dybbuk didn't know. His adversary effortlessly avoided the onslaught while countering with a series of near misses, using them to analyze and effectively draw Tam off-guard. Unaware of the latter, Tam thought because he was avoiding his attacks, he was better than him and pressed forward, feeling confident. Dybbuk suddenly swung at the side of his head, causing Tam to raise his axe, then he changed direction to a low strike and sliced him across his right leg and midsection, cutting through his armor and stomach. Tam stumbled a few steps until his legs gave way and he fell to the ground. He wasn't sure how deep his stomach wound was until he saw thick blood turning his platemail crimson. He tried to rise again, but his leg weakened, and he fell back down to one knee. Confident the battle was nearly finished, Dybbuk slowly approached his wounded prey.

"Very soon, Tam, you'll be crossing over to the abyss to stand by your master. Like his, your techniques are flawed and did not serve you in the end," he said laughing and moved closer.

Tam waited for him to draw nearer, then found the strength to lunge forward, striking his left arm and nearly severing it. Dybbuk's arm went limp, and he dropped the sword and fell. Tam's sudden rush of adrenaline caused him to forget about his injured leg, and when he shifted his weight upon it, the leg faltered, and he missed Dybbuk's head. His following attacks were thwarted after Dybbuk produced an axe and deflected them, then moved out of range. Tam hobbled after the retreating demon. When he failed to gain ground, he called him a coward and beckoned him to fight. Dybbuk had enough of his mouth and hurled his axe with such velocity and accuracy that it struck Tam's left shoulder and sent him sprawling to the ground. Holding his last throwing axe, he waited for Tam to get to his feet, savoring his death.

Tam used his axe to stand and steady himself on his good leg.

"Tam, it's time for you to meet your maker," Dybbuk said.

Tam stood proud and raised his axe one final time. "Let's end this," he said.

The crowd cheered in response, sensing the fight was coming to an end. Dybbuk grinned as he approached Tam for the final time. Meanwhile, Tam knew he had to be patient if he wanted this fight to end favorably for him, so he waited for his adversary to move within range and then swung for his head. His attack surprised Dybbuk. If it wasn't for his deep wound, he would've hit him. Instead, his weapon went wide, exposing his right arm to Dybbuk's axe, which came crashing down upon the limb and severed it at the elbow. Tam wailed in pain, his axe fell away from his grasp, and he dropped to his knees. A hush fell over the crowd as Dybbuk positioned himself directly in front of him and grabbed his throat, lifting him upright.

"You're a disgrace to our kind," Dybbuk said and tightened his grip to begin crushing his windpipe.

Tam immediately felt dizzy, and his eyes began to bulge from their sockets as he struggled to breathe. Dybbuk smiled, gazed over at the Overlord, and loosened his grip, allowing Tam to inhale much-needed air.

"I offer his pathetic life to you, my lord," Dybbuk said.

The Overlord stood up and replied, "Dybbuk, you're absolved of your crimes. Now finish him."

Dybbuk looked into Tam's eyes and began choking his life away once more. The demon, that was twentieth in command, who failed to avenge his teacher, saw black stars dancing before his eyes.

Dybbuk was savoring his opponent's final moments when a welcoming death came sooner rather than later for Tam. From out of nowhere, a dagger pierced his left temple, killing him instantly.

Dybbuk, along with most of the courtyard, turned toward the

assassin and, to their shock, it was Masset. He did the unthinkable and stripped Dybbuk of his right to kill his opponent.

Chargen quickly raced over, grabbed the little servant by his neck, and brought him in front of the Overlord.

The Overlord glared down at him. "Why did you rob Dybbuk of his glory?"

"I did not want him to disgrace my master anymore."

"That was stupid, and now you will share Tam's fate."

The Overlord nodded to Chargen, who then flicked him high into the air with ease. Two female demons swooped down, took hold of his limbs, and lifted Masset higher above the courtyard. Masset struggled against their superior strength, and pain quickly coursed throughout his body as his limbs were being slowly pulled apart. Long agonizing seconds passed, allowing Masset to feel the pain and weight of his fate, before both demons flew in separate directions and ripped his limbs from his torso. The little demon fell freely, for what seemed like an eternity, until he slammed into the ground, shattering nearly every bone in his body. Barely alive, he looked over at his master one last time before closing his eyes to the darkness and hoping he would join him again in the abyss. After Masset's death, the Overlord dismissed Dybbuk, and he gathered his weapons and left the courtyard to a series of cheers.

Back at his keep, Dybbuk placed an item called Wrap of Regeneration on his wounded arm. The enhanced cloth would heal his injury as long as it was wrapped tightly around the wound for three uninterrupted days. Before turning in, he thought about Tam and smiled. He always hated him and was glad to end his life; because that was something he would have to do if he was going to be the Overlord someday.

When he awoke at dawn, he tested his arm. It felt tight and sore, so he knew the cloth was already working. He knew the Overlord would be expecting him, so he dressed and left his keep. As he approached his castle, he felt a sense of ease knowing that he wouldn't be on trial and that the accusations against him were finally put to rest. Another good indication everything was back to normal was that the bridge was lightly guarded, and the Void Tirips were nowhere to be found.

He was almost across the bridge when Chargen came walking in his direction. Dybbuk greeted the Superior Drone and was escorted the rest of the way into the Overlord's castle. Chargen led him down a dimly lit passageway until it ended at a large rectangular-shaped room. This was one of the Overlord's meeting rooms, Dybbuk knew. It was finely decorated with furniture, paintings, and plants throughout the room and was brightly lit by the many torches hanging on the walls. His escort motioned for him to sit at the square table in the center, then said what was on his mind since yesterday.

"I would like to test my skills in combat against yours."

Dybbuk smiled inwardly, knowing his comments from yesterday made an impact on the big drone. "You'll have your test when I return from the place known as the Other," he replied coolly. In reality, the only reason why he didn't accommodate the drone right now was due to his wounds.

"I'll look forward to it," Chargen said and left.

Dybbuk thought about the challenge and knew if he could best the drone he would gain his loyalty, thus achieving another foothold toward his ultimate goal of ruling their world.

An hour would pass before the Overlord entered the room and sat down across from his guest. Dybbuk remained seated because his rank of fourth in command meant that he was entitled to do so and not have to bow to the Overlord if they were alone. Servants entered the room, a few minutes later, carrying jugs of wine. They poured the sweet nectar into massive goblets and placed them in front of Dybbuk and the Overlord. The demons clanged their cups and took a few mighty swigs together.

"Now why don't you finish your tale about your time in the place known as the Other? And don't leave out the details."

Dybbuk leaned back in his chair and told him the information he suppressed from the court yesterday. Quietly, the Overlord listened and was impressed that a human could accomplish what he did. Dybbuk continued. As soon as the Overlord heard him mention that Ailith was still alive, he stopped him.

"You said that you killed her, so how is she still alive?" He asked.

Dybbuk smirked. "I did kill her, well, at least her physical form."

"So what proof do you have that she's still alive?"

"My pawn used an arrow that broke Raum's immunity to mortal weapons."

"Where did he get it?"

"The leaves on the shaft could only be found in the forest where I killed her physical form, and there was no way my pawn would have known about it. I questioned him further, and he confirmed my suspicions when he said there was a Tree Spirit in the forest that told him what to use."

"How do you think she escaped death?"

"I believe that prior to her death, she must have invoked the ancient Chant of Transformation and left her body before her life force faded."

"Hmm, you might be right," the Overlord stated.

"I will be rid of her once and for all soon enough."

"How do you plan on doing that?"

"I have released my pet into their world to find and destroy her new vessel." Dybbuk grinned.

"She definitely deserves it. So tell me why didn't you kill the mortal?" the Overlord asked, interrupting his brief celebration.

"Because he decided the outcome of the battle and helped me end Raum's life."

"Nonsense. You had no way of knowing that. Next time, stick to our ritual and kill all who know of us. Do you understand?" The Overlord was annoyed by his lack of tradition.

"Yes, my lord." Dybbuk nodded his head in acknowledgement, even though he didn't agree with him.

"What's next?" the Overlord asked just as Dybbuk raised his goblet to his mouth to enjoy the nectar he so eagerly wanted to taste.

"In two moon's time, I will emerge once again in the place known as the Other and travel to the forest to make sure my pet did as he was instructed. After that, I plan on continuing our campaign for total domination."

"Good, that's what I like to hear." The Overlord smiled for the first time.

"My lord, whatever became of the chosen one?" Dybbuk asked and took a swig.

"The lookalikes failed to assess her weaknesses, and she fell into what we call a lifeless rest. Although she is strong in some ways, she is weak in others, and her mind is one of them. They are working on bringing her out of it, and once they do, she will come to us." The Overlord sounded confident on the latter.

"And if they fail?"

"They'd better not, because there won't be a trial."

"Is there anything I can do to help?"

"No. You have your destiny, and they have theirs."

"What about Asherah of the fifth in command?"

"Asherah is making leeway in establishing a permanent way for us to travel back and forth among their plane. Once he has finished, then he will bring our kind with him, and together, we will rule their world."

When they were finished speaking, Dybbuk got up. "I have much to do, my lord, and must be going."

"Very well."

Dybbuk turned to leave.

"Don't disappoint me again, Dybbuk."

After he was gone, the Overlord refilled his goblet, took another swig, and began pondering his future. Would he live long enough to see his dream come to fruition or would time finally catch up to him and rob him of his glory? He glanced at his body and knew that it was nothing more than an illusion created by his staff. Outwardly, he looked like a young demon with the physique of a Superior Drone, but inside, his strength and endurance were that of an archaic demon. The staff was a blessing and a curse. It once bathed him in power, and now it was slowly robbing him of it. There was a time when he could defeat five demons at once, and, at the moment, he didn't think he could defeat a single low-ranking demon.

His thoughts suddenly shifted to what would become of his kingdom and who would rule after he passed into the abyss. He considered Boruta of the first in command. He was a great tactician, skilled fighter, led by example, intelligent, had a gifted ability to analyze an opponent's strengths and weaknesses, and was very competent and persuasive. However, he was stubborn, easily provoked, dishonest, and quick to judge.

Then there was Forneus of the second in command. He was task-driven, intelligent, and crafty. Conversely, he wasn't a true leader and was easily influenced by others.

Oso of the third in command was crafty, highly intelligent, and could outwit just about anyone. He was also a good leader and would be fair. Nevertheless, his fighting skills were far worse than the others, and he feared that, in the end, he would be overrun if a civil war started.

Finally, there was Dybbuk. He was clever, crafty, skilled in battle, charismatic, had proven that he could adapt to any situation and was intelligent.

But he was too much of a risk-taker and would change their laws, and if he did, it would most likely disrupt the harmony he'd created many decades ago.

Demon laws dictated that Boruta was next in line, but he knew that he couldn't be trusted to be fair and would rule with an iron claw. Forneus and Oso might be better suited, but they were not as skilled in the art of leadership as Boruta was. Dybbuk was the better choice over them, but for that to happen, he would have to eliminate Boruta, which wouldn't be easy, and the courts would have to agree with his selection as well.

Suddenly, Grasant entered the room with a satchel filled with important scrolls that needed his attention right away.

Dybbuk stayed in his stronghold over the next two moons, training his mind and body feverishly and studying with Darn, the greatest tactical lieutenant of their time. Together they analyzed various scenarios he could encounter in the place known as the Other. When he was satisfied with their new approach, he left his world to fulfill his destiny.

CHAPTER 7: A CHILD'S DREAM (PART I)

Daybreak ushered in more snow and chilling wind, causing Katara and Torhan to pack up their belongings rather quickly.

"Do you know how much further until we reach Snowdrift?" Torhan asked.

"I think we'll arrive within the next day if we hurry." She took off the Ring of Warmth and presented it to him. "It's a great ring. I was warm throughout the night."

Torhan smiled. "Why don't you hold onto it for a while?" He offered it, despite being cold.

Katara's eyes lit up as she placed the ring back on her finger.

"Just to let you know; the ring's ability does dissipate in time. It needs fire to recharge itself."

"I'll keep that in mind. If you get too cold let me know, and I'll give it back."

"Okay."

It was around mid-afternoon when they crested a hill and saw a large frozen pond. They carefully proceeded down the snowy hill and stopped when they reached the bottom.

"What do you think?" Torhan asked staring at the ice.

"It looks relatively solid, but we won't know until we start crossing. If we go around, it could take us until nightfall and with the weather," she gazed skyward, "I really don't want to be out here any longer than we have to. I plan on eating a hot meal and being in a nice warm bed tonight."

"I'll go first and let you know if the ice holds." Torhan offered and started walking out.

"Hold on." She said and rifled through her backpack until she found a length of rope. "Here tie this around your waist in case you fall in."

Torhan did as he was instructed.

"Do you want the ring?"

"It won't do any good if I fall in." Torhan said and started crossing the pond.

Katara held the rope firmly, listening for the warning sound of ice cracking while watching him intently.

On top of the hill and slightly to the west, a hunter watched the male walk on the ice. The white furs he wore blended him in with his surroundings so well you wouldn't notice him unless you were standing right in front of him.

"What do we have here?" He asked his wolves as if they could actually understand him.

"Should we have some fun or kill them outright?" He said to them, while he notched his bow, and pointed it at the male.

Torhan was fifteen feet across the pond when his scabbard began to glow causing him to stop abruptly.

"What's wrong is the ice cracking?" Katara shouted after seeing him pause.

Torhan held up his hand, as if, indicating it was. In the open, he knew they were quite vulnerable and realized that whatever was out there might not be close enough to stop him from getting back to the shore, unless of course, they were huntsmen with ranged weapons.

"The ice is cracking." He shouted, turned and ran as fast as he could back towards the shore.

Peering around the tree the hunter snickered and then looked over at his wolves.

"Look at that? That boy can run," he said.

The animals paid him no mind and continued to stare straight ahead awaiting their master's orders. The hunter pulled the drawstring and fired the arrow in an arcing manner. The arrow sailed through the air and stuck into the ice a few feet in front of Torhan causing him to stop dead in his tracks, knowing it was intended as a warning.

"That's far enough." The hunter shouted from atop the hill.

Katara turned around in surprise and then back at Torhan, who shook his head indicating for her to stay put. A few seconds later, a man of a medium build, with a patch over his right eye, descended down the hill along with two wolves. His short bow was notched with an arrow.

"We mean you no harm and only want to pass." Katara said after he finished his descent.

"Ya, well, I want to eat and who knows," he smiled, "maybe we can get warm together."

The hunter stopped ten feet away from Katara.

"You," he looked directly at Torhan, "drop to your knees, or I'll drop you." The hunter trained his bow at Torhan, and he did as he was told.

"Pretty one," he said without taking his eyes off of his target. "Place your mace on the ground."

Katara was in the process of doing so when two more men, dressed similar to the first hunter, came walking down the hill along with two more wolves. When they reached the bottom, both men leered at Katara. The hunter on the left smiled exposing his remaining tooth and the one on the right, with two long scars that crisscrossed on his face, winked at her. The lines made him look very disturbing and repulsive.

"Well, well, well what do we have here?" One Tooth said giving, Katara a look that could only mean one thing.

"I caught these two roaming freely on our land." The first hunter, eyes riveted on Torhan, replied.

"I was talking about the woman, she sure is pretty."

"Remove your friend's weapons and tie him up." The hunter with the scars said to Katara.

Torhan had a good idea what their captors were going to do them after he was tied up. They were going to have their way with Katara and possibly kill them both afterwards. The thought made his stomach churn and blood boil. He was about to do something foolish when Katara approached giving him a reassuring look not to. When she was close enough, she began chanting in a foreign language so low that no one, except for Torhan, heard her. By the time she finished removing his weapons and tying him up, she completed the chant and winked at him before turning around.

One Tooth grinned in delight. "Now bitch, on your knees." He said, clearly indicating he had some sick plans in store.

All at once, the four wolves began growling in the direction of the lake, drawing the hunters' attention towards them. "What is it?" One Tooth said to his friends.

"I don't know but something is exciting them." The hunter with the eye patch replied.

The ice slowly moaned and cracked. "I think there is something is out there." The scarred hunter added.

"Like wha…"

The ice suddenly burst apart sending shards of ice skywards. The wolves darted away, so did One Tooth and the first hunter. Katara dropped to her knees, extended both arms upwards, and on cue, a fifteen-foot high water column rose up from the depths, began moving in a circular motion, mesmerizing the scarred hunter and freezing him where he stood. Katara commanded the Water Tirip to attack, and it did by lashing out with three large balls of water at the hunter closest to them. For the hunter, time seemed to slow as the projectiles slammed into his body, knocking him off of his feet and sending him into a nearby tree, knocking him unconscious.

"Kill." Katara commanded.

The Water Tirip changed into a ten-foot wave and rolled up the hill towards the other two hunters.

"Nice work." Torhan commented.

"Call me bitch will they?" She smiled and then freed him from his bonds.

One Tooth knew he was going to die when he saw the water creature taking shape. He saw one once before, when he was much younger. He remembered the havoc it caused and the men who lost their lives. But still, despite that, he ran as fast as he could until he was pelted in the back by a ball of water that sent him sprawling to the ground. He lay on his stomach breathing heavily, waiting for the end. He was tired of his life, the cards he'd been dealt and missed his dead wife. When the Water Tirip rolled over his prone body, it filled his lungs filled with liquid, drowned the man and then moved on.

When the other hunter saw his friend go down in a burst of water, he never looked back again, despite his guilt. He ran faster and harder, changing direction often, hoping to lose the creature. Eventually, he became winded, was unable to run any further and sat down on a log to catch his breath. He smiled, thinking he gave the water creature the slip, but his smile faded when the wave abruptly appeared and moved in his direction. He cursed the guardian, notched an arrow, and fired it at the water, only to watch it pass through the mass with little resistance. He cursed it repeatedly until the Water Tirip came crashing down upon his head, drowning him within seconds.

****

Torhan was in the process of taking the unconscious hunter's furs off when Katara came walking over.

"You know he should die." She commented.

Torhan looked skywards. "There's a storm coming, so how long do you think he'll live without his furs?"

When he was finished removing his furs, they tied him to a tree and waited for the water guardian to return. When it did, Katara ordered the sentinel to guard the prisoner.

"Just in case he gets free." She said to Torhan with a sly look.

Now that the ice was broken, they had to walk around the pond and made camp shortly before nightfall. Katara created their shelter while Torhan gathered wood for a fire. Once situated together on a log, Torhan placed the Ring of Warmth next to the fire to recharge it, and they began eating. An hour later, the well anticipated storm, consisting of snow and ice, fell in heavy sheets, prompting them to huddle closer under the furs until they grew tired and went to sleep.

By morning, the storm dissipated into light flurries. They packed up their belongings, using a portion of the fur trappings to cover their booted feet to keep them warm and dry for their long trek ahead.

It was midmorning when they arrived at the town of Snowdrift. The quaint little town had a modest amount of people, strolling about doing their daily rituals, and a few patrolling guards keeping a watchful eye. Hungry, thirsty, and tired, they found the closest tavern and were promptly seated in the middle of the room next to a table with two elderly gentlemen in their sixties engaged in light conversation. Once food was ordered, Torhan turned and greeted them.

"Good day gentleman."

The balding man on the right grumbled in response because he interrupted them.

"Don't be like that." The man on the left with short white hair and a beard scoffed at his grumpy friend. "Good day stranger. I am Erea and this here is Kipt."

"I'm Torhan and this is Katara."

"Glad to meet you. Are you from around here?"

"No we're not. We're just passing through. Can you tell me about this town?"

"Well, this town is older than I can remember," Erea said and loosened his fur jacket. "We've both lived here since we were children and been friends for…" He rubbed his chin in a pondering manner.

"A long time." Kipt finished his friend's sentence and grinned.

"Ya, a really long time, in fact, too long." Erea said, and they laughed.

"What do you do around here?" Katara asked.

"Back in the day, I was a farmer and Kipt was a merchant and now, well; we just hang out here to get away from our nagging wives." They laughed again.

"I see they like to keep themselves amused." Katara whispered to Torhan.

"Can you tell me about the merchants here?" Torhan asked after they stopped giggling.

"Well, if you want weapons or armor you should go to the Sharp Edge. If you need healing stuff, the Herb of Life is the place to go. Both merchants are right in the middle of town. If you desire furs and outerwear, by all means go next door to the Tracker's Delight." Kipt paused to take a swig of ale.

Erea continued for his friend. "If you fancy strange items of the dark arts, then go see the Mystic Stone located at the end of the street, and this place here has the best-tasting food and ale in the town."

Just then the serving wench arrived with their food and ale, and Katara ordered tankards for the two men, who in turn were delighted and thanked them. Torhan and Katara began eating their stew and fresh-baked bread.

"The stew is very tasty." She commented.

"It sure is. I wonder what's in it."

"Tastes like boar meat."

"I think you're right."

They gobbled down the contents and ordered another bowl. When they were finished, Katara called the serving wench over and ordered several more ales for Kipt and Erea. They were pleasantly surprised and thanked them again. In between their third and fourth mug, Katara took it upon herself to inquire about Sybil.

"Excuse me," she said and waited for them to stop talking and look at her. "We're looking for a young girl named Sybil. Do you know where we could find her?"

They looked at each other and then back at her.

"Are you related?" Erea asked.

"The girl and her parents are close relatives of mine, and my mother asked me to look in on them. She hasn't heard from them in several months."

"When was the last time she did?" Kipt asked.

His tone was both curious and suspicious at the same time, and Torhan picked up on it right away and cut Katara off by saying,

"Has something happened to them?"

"You said that you haven't heard from them in several months and…" Kipt paused.

"And what?" Katara interrupted.

"That would be impossible because her parents died a year ago. Who are you?" Now Erea was suspicious as well.

"Okay, we're not family we were sent here to investigate Sybil's unusual condition."

"And what would that be? Did that uncle send you?" Kipt was clearly getting quite agitated and nervous.

"No. My Order did."

"Order? Which one?" Erea snapped.

"The Order of the Hallowed."

"Never heard of it. My advice to you is to leave this town and tell your Order that child is cursed and there's no help for her." Kipt stated firmly.

"Can you tell us where she is?"

"No. Now leave here or I'll tell the captain of the guard that you've been asking about the girl and trust me, you don't want that." Kipt's threatening tone angered Katara.

"Why? We didn't do anything. All we want to do is see the girl."

"So did her uncle and after he left she fell into a deep sleep, and that's when bad things happened."

"What sort of bad things?" Torhan pressed Kipt.

"Get out of here or I'll make good on my threat."

Torhan, knowing that he wouldn't get any further with them stood up. Katara did the same and they left the inn. A few tables away, a young woman overhearing the entire conversation followed them out the door.

"That didn't go the way I thought it would." Katara said as soon as they were outside.

"They seemed spooked. I wonder what Molech did."

"So Molech is her uncle?"

"Yes."

"To be honest with you, I think Grappin and Molech were working together and using you for some greater purpose other than Grappin's revenge on priest Abiathar."

"Like what?"

"Here are the facts and correct me if I am wrong. First, you meet Molech and he sends you to his friend's store and the one item you wanted, and couldn't afford, shows up in your room. Then the shop owner turns up dead and Molech was near the crime scene and just as the law was coming for you an assassin shows up and leads you to Grappin's house where he protects, and hides, you, and he helps you escape. When did Molech ask you to help his niece?"

"Grappin's underground tunnel leads to a warehouse and he was there."

"It all fits together; what are the chances of Molech being at the exact place you're escaping from? He even rescued you from the jail in Mirkin. Do you see what I mean?"

Torhan nodded.

"What is your reward for helping him?"

"He offered me another item just like the scabbard and a lot of money."

"Okay, how are you supposed to collect it?"

"He said to meet him in a cave a mile north of Snowdrift."

"What happens if you can't help his niece?"

"He didn't say."

"I wish you had some more of those arrows"

"Why?"

"Because he might be a demon too."

Suddenly, Katara caught a glimpse of a young woman standing nearby trying to listen to their conversation.

"Can we help you?" She asked her.

The woman, slightly older than Katara, wearing tattered formal clothes, came forth.

"I overheard you talking to those men about young Sybil," she paused and looked around before continuing. "If you come with me, I'll tell you where she is and what happened after her uncle left."

Katara and Torhan looked at each other and nodded.

They followed the woman to her house a few streets away. She was nervous the entire time and when they reached the front door, she paused looking left and right as if making sure no one was following them. She unlocked the door and they entered. The small house was just like the woman, dirty. It didn't surprise Torhan and Katara given the woman's personal appearance. Stairs leading to the second floor were directly in front of them. To their left, was the living room with a sofa and square table that saw better days, and a bookshelf full of old beat up novels. To their right was the eating area. In the center of the room was a square table with many dirty dishes scattered on top, and beyond the table, was a hearth. A fire burned inside and a kettle, hanging by a hooked arm, sat just above the flames.

"Please excuse the mess, I wasn't expecting any company." The woman said and led them to the table in the kitchen. After clearing the dirty crockery, she introduced herself as Clodovea and offered her guests tea and cheese, which they politely accepted and sat down. Once served, Torhan and Katara introduced themselves, and Clodovea began telling them about Sybil.

"Five years ago, a family named Lockington arrived in Snowdrift and purchased one of the biggest houses just outside of town. They were a cute family; mother, father who made his fortune after he discovered a platinum mine, a son named Rodle, who was the age of seven and a four-year-old little girl named Sybil. Shortly after they moved in, they hired me to care for their house and children. Over the years, I became very close with them, especially Sybil. She was such a doll. We would play games all the time, and she loved my scary bedtime stories." Clodovea paused as if she was remembering a pleasant thought and then her facial expressions changed somewhat to concern. "What was strange was that while Sybil played outside, different types of animals would just walk up to her and sit by her side as if they were protecting her. Small harmless ones at first like cats, dogs, squirrels, and birds. Then, as she got older, bigger ones like bears, wolves, and big cats. Even when she came inside, they remained out there for a very long time."

"When it first happened, did you tell her parents?" Katara asked.

"I did, but they told me it had been happening since she was one."

"That is very strange. I wonder what summoned them to her."

"It's like the child can commune with the animals." Torhan added.

"When Sybil was older, she said the animals did speak with her, but the parents said to ignore her because she's just a child and for her not to mention it to anyone else."

"Did you tell anyone?" Katara asked.

"I loved the job, the children, and the money, so I kept quiet." She looked towards the door and then back at them. "Would you like some more tea?"

They both nodded and she got up, grabbed the kettle, and refilled their cups.

"When did Molech come to Snowdrift?" Torhan asked Clodovea after she was seated again.

"A few years ago and I can tell you right now I did not like him from the moment I met him." She paused. "It was something in his eyes that I didn't like. Anyway, it was Sybil's sixth birthday, and he stayed for several days and nights. Before leaving, he gave her this beautiful nightgown and teddy bear that she absolutely loved." She paused to take a sip of tea then stared down at the table.

"What happened next?" Katara asked.

"Well everything was fine until a few nights later when Sybil went to bed. I was reading her a story, and normally she likes to interact, but this time she went silent halfway through. When I looked up, I noticed she was just staring at the ceiling. When I couldn't snap her out of it, I called her father, and he wasn't able to either. In a panic, Mr. Lockington rushed her over to the healers, they used all sorts of herbs and techniques, and her condition didn't change. Mrs. Lockington summoned priest Piersum, and he believed Sybil was either under some sort of spell or curse and left to research her condition."

"What did he find?" Torhan asked.

"He returned several nights later and declared she was under a curse and the only way to bring her out was to use an amulet called... it was strange sounding... Hmm... RIM, RUM..." She paused.

"Was it called REM?" Torhan said.

"Yes that's what it was called REM. How did you know?"

"Katara's Order knows about the amulet of REM as well. Please continue."

"Priest Piersum told them he believed the amulet was in a nearby crypt, and the parents took his advice and hired some people and went looking for it. That was the last time anyone ever saw them or the group, for that matter." Clodovea somberly said looking down.

"Whatever happened to Molech?" Katara asked.

"The townspeople hired a tracker to find him, but the tracker never returned either."

"Where is she now?"

"She is in the care of priest Piersum."

"Why didn't you look after her?"

"The parents wanted him to care for her while they were away."

"We're going to see the priest." Torhan said.

Clodovea gave them directions and Torhan gave her some money, which brought a smile to her weathered face.

It was around dusk when they finally left Clodovea's cottage and made their way to the far northern part of town. They walked along in silence and when they arrived at the Temple of the Saintly, they found the doors locked. Katara knocked a few times and when no one answered, they walked around back to the small house next to the temple.

"This must be where he stays." She stated, walked up to the door, and knocked.

An elderly man, wearing brown robes opened the door. He was of medium height with a stomach that gave off the impression that he hadn't missed a meal in very long time. The white rope trussed around his large stomach was cinched so tightly it looked like it could snap at any minute.

"Can I help you?" He asked.

"Are you the priest Piersum? Katara asked.

He nodded.

"Can we talk to you about Sybil?"

The priest looked at them for several long minutes before responding. "Who are you?"

"My name is Katara and this is Torhan. We hail from the town of Mirkin, and my Order has sent me to help."

"And what Order would that be?" The priest was growing a bit suspicious.

"I belong to the Order of the Hallowed."

"If that's where you're from, then answer me two things first, and I'll allow you entrance. Who leads your Order now?"

"Brother Pien."

"And before that?"

"Brother Migtra."

"Very good. Come on in." The priest opened the door and allowed them inside.

The building was outdated and somewhat poorly maintained; Katara noticed, as they were being led through several rooms until they arrived in the eating area. Priest Piersum asked them to sit down at the small round table.

"Now tell me why the Order of the Hallowed has an interest in helping this child out?"

Torhan and Katara looked at each other and then back at the priest. Katara chose her words carefully before speaking.

"A few weeks ago a man, wounded and half-crazed, appeared at my Order asking for our help." She began. "While we were working on his injuries, he kept rambling on that he was part of an expedition that went looking for an amulet called REM near the town of Snowdrift. Before losing consciousness, he pleaded with us to come to Snowdrift and help a girl named Sybil and not to let her parent's death be in vain."

"I see. So just like that they sent someone to investigate?"

"If a cause is just, then my Order rarely turns anyone away."

"Did you talk to him?" Piersum quickly injected trying to gauge if their story was truthful.

"Not directly. I heard that he succumbed to his wounds shortly thereafter."

"And what's your story?" The priest asked, looking directly at Torhan.

"Katara and I are childhood friends and when she told me that she was coming here I couldn't let her go alone."

"Childhood friends huh, where are you from?" Torhan wasn't sure where he was going with the question, so he plainly said.

"Mirkin."

"Mirkin you say? Who are you people?"

"What do you mean?" Katara interjected quickly.

"Torhan you say that you are from Mirkin, but your accent says you're from the southern region. In fact, you don't sound like you're from Mirkin either," he looked at Katara. The priest was becoming edgy as he gazed at them.

"Priest Piersum you're becoming paranoid," Katara said in a calming voice. "It is true we're not originally from Mirkin. We both grew up in the town of Wistful."

"Then why did you say you were?"

"I was living there studying under the tutelage of priest Abiathar when my Order sent me to investigate her condition. Torhan is my best friend and was staying with me. If you don't want us to help her just say the word, and we'll leave."

Priest Piersum realized the child's well-being was more important than his fears and relaxed a bit.

"I apologize for my doubt, but that uncle of hers is to blame for this mess."

"What uncle?" Torhan asked as if he didn't know.

Priest Piersum proceeded to tell them the story of how Molech suddenly showed up for her sixth birthday, gave her a silver and blue gown along with a black teddy bear as gifts, then after he left, she fell into a trance shortly thereafter.

He looked down and said. "I should have never told the parents about the amulet. I knew retrieving it was beyond their skills."

"You shouldn't feel guilty about them," Katara said when she noticed his face took on the appearance of guilt. "It's not your fault. Any parent would have done the exact same thing they did. Let us help, we're quite skillful and should be able to retrieve the relic."

The priest thought about it and then stood up, "Come with me." He said.

He led them upstairs to the room farthest in the back. Sleeping on a large bed was a little girl dressed in a white nightgown. Sybil's long, curly blonde hair was draped over her chest, moving in rhythm with each breath she took; she looked peacefully asleep.

"Here she is." The priest said.

"I thought she was in some sort of trance?"

"Sometimes she closes her eyes and sleeps."

Katara walked over to the bed and knelt down beside it. She

whispered into her ear, telling Sybil that she would do whatever it would take to bring her back. Surprisingly, Sybil stirred as if she'd actually heard her.

Katara smiled. "Sometimes the sleeping can hear you and need encouragement." She announced.

"Are they the gifts?" Torhan asked priest Piersum, pointing to the dresser with a blue gown and stuffed brown teddy bear on top.

The priest nodded. "We removed it a few days after she developed her condition, thinking they are what caused it."

Torhan picked up the garment and bear. The gown felt silky under his touch, and the bear appeared to be just a stuffed animal. He placed them down again.

They left the room and went back downstairs and sat at the table again.

"Where is the amulet located?" Torhan asked.

"I do not know where the amulet is, but I do know someone that does."

"Who?"

"A hermit named Tole. He used to serve at our temple several years back and often spoke of the amulet, but never revealed its location."

"What exactly does the amulet do?" Katara asked.

"He said it could grant the bearer the power to enter someone's mind while they're asleep."

"It sounds like a powerful item." Torhan added.

"It certainly is. Think about what someone could do to if they enter your dreams and place subliminal messages or worse kill you outright."

"How will the amulet save her?" Katara asked.

"I believe she's trapped inside of her mind. If someone, like myself, can use the amulet to get inside of her head and lead her out she will be cured."

"Can you do that?"

"I can."

"So once we get the amulet we'll bring it back here, and you'll save her right?"

Piersum nodded.

"Where can we find Tole?" Katara asked.

"He decided to take the life of solitude and lives in a large grove northwest of here. You can't miss it; it's the first one you come to after you clear the forest surrounding Snowdrift."

"We'll go see him in the morning."

They spoke for several more hours before leaving and getting a room at the inn.

The only room available was one with a single bed. Torhan offered to sleep on the chair, but Katara wouldn't have it. As long as they slept with their clothes on she said she would be fine. Once they were situated, Katara spoke in hushed tones.

"I wonder what Molech's intentions are? We heard the same story about him from two different people. Do you think the gifts put Sybil in the state she's in or was it merely coincidence?"

"I'm not sure. He seemed genuinely concerned when he asked me to bring her out of it. He had to know we'd find out about what people were saying."

"Maybe someone framed him by either drugging Sybil or giving him the cursed items to give to the child."

"I'm not sure it's a drug because the priest said he did everything he could to bring her out, and it would've left her system by now, right?"

"Yes. Unless the priest is a demon in disguise and is working with Clodovea to frame Molech."

"But why?" Torhan paused, "What can anyone gain by using a child who could commune with animals? It doesn't seem like it could be of any worth, I mean what are they going to do, use Sybil to summon a pack of wolves and terrorize a town?"

"It does sound a bit odd. Furthermore, Molech knows about the amulet, so why doesn't he get it himself?"

"He knows about it, but maybe he doesn't know where to find it and he can't come back to the town and ask anyone because he's a wanted person."

"There are so many unanswered questions." Katara stated.

"I agree it doesn't make much sense. So let's say what they are saying is true about Molech; what is he going to do with a child with her abilities?"

"Even if he's a demon what ties does a demon have with Sybil and why would he need her? What could she offer? Do her skills increase as she gets older? Does the gown enhance her abilities, so he can leverage her skills for his own needs?"

"I guess we'll find out when we bring her out of it and try to collect the reward from Molech."

"We'd better stay on our guard from him and priest Piersum once we get the amulet."

They remained lost in their thoughts until they fell asleep. When morning arrived, they dressed and left the inn. Outside the snow was falling heavily.

"Where do you think we should go first?" Torhan asked.

"Let's stock up on outerwear and see if the weather gets worse. If it does, we'll wait until tomorrow to visit Tole." Katara replied.

They entered the Tracker's Delight store. The store was filled with many items, including furs, hiking gear, pots and pans, rope, oversized backpacks, tinderboxes, and bundles of kindle. Mounted on the walls were the heads of different animals; some they recognized and some they didn't. The store was empty of people, so they took their time looking around. When they got near the front of the store, a plump man in his mid-years, , came walking out.

"Welcome to my store. I am Domin and if you have any questions, please feel free to ask me. If I can't answer them I'm sure the wall will."

"The wall?" Torhan replied.

"Yup the wall, I'm sure one of the heads has the answer you seek." Domin laughed loudly.

"I love that one." Katara said chuckling along with him.

"What do you have in furs?" Torhan asked after he was finished laughing.

"Let me ask the wall. Wall, what do we have?" Domin looked around, and Katara smiled. "The wall says for me to go look in the back." He said and left.

"Do you think the wall talks to him?" Torhan asked jokingly, and Katara nodded.

Their wait wasn't long before Domin came out holding many fur items, which he plopped down in front of them.

"What exactly are you looking for?"

"We'll need something warm that can offer protection against weapons." Torhan answered.

"How much?" Domin quickly asked.

"How much what?"

"How much protection do you want against weapons or the cold? Or do you want an equal amount of both?" Domin was quick to point out.

"What do you recommend?" Katara asked.

"Rule of thumb," he held up his left hand pointing to his thumb with the finger from his right. "More warmth means less mobility, more mobility means less warmth and protection against weapons and the weather. What I would do, given this time of year is buy the warmest boots and hats I sell. If you switch weapons to let's say a spear or halberd, then I would get one of my heaviest furs as well. You don't need much movement if you want to poky, poky someone, right?" Domin suddenly bent down and when he appeared again, he was holding up an oval oversized wooden shoe. "You should also think about buying this for your feet. I call it The Snowshoe."

"Isn't it too big for my feet?" Torhan asked, and Domin rolled his eyes in response then turned his attention towards the western wall. "Oh great wall he doesn't get it. The shoe is designed to be that way so that it can work by distributing the person's weight over a large area allowing you to move over deep snow as if you were floating on top." His eyes widened in excitement.

"Did you invent these?"

"I did, with the help of the wall of course?"

Torhan smiled. "We'll need a few minutes, please."

"Take your time, but hurry." Domin laughed and walked into the back of the store.

Torhan turned towards Katara. "Since you have the ring you should go light with the upper fur. I'll buy a spear and get the heavier coat."

"Those snowshoes might come in handy too." She added.

"I agree. Let's get some gloves and maybe a hat as well."

"What about your scabbard?"

"I'll wrap it around the furs."

"Do we have enough gold?"

Torhan drew forth the pouch, looked inside and then shook his head yes. "We're ready." He shouted towards the back.

Domin appeared instantly. "What will it be?"

Torhan purchased the fur jackets, pants, gloves, hats, and snowshoes, plus a few more furs to use as blankets and a score of arrows. Domin then tailored the furs to fit them as best as he could. When he was finished, they tested their mobility with what weapons they had and were very satisfied. Torhan paid him, bid Domin farewell, and left the store to brave the ever-growing snowstorm.

They stopped at the store called the Sharp Edge. Katara purchased a small metal shield, and Torhan bought a six-foot barbed spear, arrows, a dagger, and a belt large enough to fit around his furs. He tied his precious scabbard around his arm and placed the dagger in it.

"Pull on the scabbard." Torhan said, referencing the one on his arm.

Katara yanked on it really hard and it wouldn't budge. "How is that possible?

"I'm not sure. Grappin said it can only come off if I want it to. Where do you want to go?"

"Mystic Stone."

They arrived at the Mystic Stone and found the building lackluster in appearance from the outside, but the inside was another story. It was dark and gothic, with poor lighting and strange-looking gargoyle statues sitting on the shelves. Tables adorned the room with low burning candles and incense burning. Their smoky smell permeated throughout the store adding a calming and alluring effect. Several people milled about. Suddenly a young woman, with long black hair, dressed in red robes, came and greeted them.

"Good day strangers, welcome to the Mystic Stone. I am Mistress Lernie owner and fortune teller. Feel free to browse and if you want your future laid out before you, please come to one of my tables and have a listen."

Torhan nodded back to her, and they went about looking at the store's wares.

"What are you looking for, in particular?" Torhan asked Katara once they started strolling around.

"I've always wanted to try the darker arts because it might be fun, plus I found a scroll that had a recipe for Black Fire and I wanted to see if it works."

"Black Fire?"

"According to the scroll it enables the user to throw tiny balls of fire at its victims. Hopefully, her store will have the ingredients I need."

"What do you think about Mistress Lernie telling us about our future?"

"I don't buy into fortune tellers and found their messages to be very cryptic, but by all means talk to her, you never know."

Torhan decided that he would and asked Mistress Lernie to do so, while Katara continued shopping. After they were seated, Mistress Lernie asked his name.

"My name is Torhan."

"Torhan before we begin, know that the cards I place in front of you could mean a variety of things. Some you might recognize as events or people that have come to pass, while others will be vague, and you will not fully understand. Please do not hold me accountable for the outcome, by all means make your own assessment and try to heed their warnings. Do you understand?"

Torhan nodded.

"Let's begin." She placed three decks of cards in front of him. "Here are three decks of cards. The one on the left is named "Adventure." The one in the middle goes by the name of "Dreams," and the last one goes by the name "Life." Please choose only one deck."

Torhan stared at them for several long seconds. "I pick Adventure." He said.

Mistress Lernie removed the other decks and started splitting the cards face down into three piles, instructing Torhan to choose only one pile. After doing so, she dealt eight cards face down and into four separate piles consisting of two cards each. Mistress Lernie turned over the cards on Torhan's left. One card had a picture of a pair of hands clasped together, and the other one was a picture of an olive branch. She gazed down at them for several long seconds before speaking.

"The combination of these cards tells me that one of your childhood friends, who is very dear to you, is doing good deeds by helping others. I also feel that he is…" she paused, "is trying to help you in some way, but I do not know how."

Torhan immediately thought of Jacko and wondered how his

friend was actually trying to help him.

"Would you like to tell me what you're thinking?" Mistress Lernie asked.

Torhan shook his head no, and she flipped over the second set of cards. The first was a picture of a gravestone and the other was a picture of a scorched tree.

"These two cards represent a person who takes great pleasure in hurting others. Be warned he is very cunning and dangerous."

Grappin and Molech came to Torhan's mind. "I have met two people that could fit that description." He said.

"Remember, you might've met them already or are going to, so be on your guard." She warned and proceeded to flip over the third pile of cards. One card was of a mouth, and the other was a pair of eyes. "Strange," she began, "this set represents one of two things. Either the death of someone or life after death." She studied the cards further. "I feel they mean the latter and there will come a time when the dead will contact you."

Torhan was puzzled. "How?"

"I don't know how; all I can say is that they will. Shall we continue?"

He nodded, and she turned over the last pair of cards. One was of dark skies, and the other was of a rainstorm. Upon seeing them, her eyes went wide and she gasped.

"What is it?" Torhan asked after seeing her expression.

"In all of the time that I've told fortunes, I've had never turned over these two cards together. They represent pure evil and will cost you a great deal of pain, suffering and possible death if this evil comes in contact with you. Please be really careful." She warned emphatically.

"Can you tell me anything else about this evil?"

"I cannot."

Katara approached them with a basket full of items and asked if they were finished. Mistress Lernie looked at Torhan, and he nodded that they were. He got up and paid her ten copper coins for the reading. Katara purchased her wares, and even though she didn't find the components to create Black Fire, she was happy.

Outside, they were met by freezing rain. The sky was already turning dark, indicating they had spent too much time inside of the Mystic Stone. They decided to leave in the morning, no matter what the weather was like.

After they arrived at the inn, they placed their stuff in the room and came back down to eat. They sat off to the back of the room, at a private table, so that no one could listen to them. During the meal, they spoke about what Mistress Lernie had said. Katara offered her own insight about the meaning of the cards and warned him that he should take the Mistress' reading with a grain of salt. When they finished, they returned to their room and went to sleep.

Katara slept soundly. Torhan dreamed he was standing on a bluff overlooking an angry sea. The powerful waves pounded the rocky shoreline below. Behind him, he heard what sounded like a door opening, turned and saw a two-story stone cottage and a young girl, in her teens, emerging from the building.

She walked right up to him. "You are the reason why I do this." She proclaimed and walked to the edge of the bluff, outstretched her arms, and spoke in a foreign language.

When she was finished, she turned around and walked toward the cottage, all the while grinning wickedly at Torhan as she passed. He watched her disappear back inside the building and then heard a loud thundering noise erupt from the sea. Torhan wheeled about and came face-to-face with a very large Water Tirip. The creature swayed back and forth, paralyzing him with fear. The Tirip created a watery arm with an oversized fist, drew it back slowly and then slammed him against his head.

Torhan awoke, startled, sweaty and scared, until he realized that he was dreaming. He took several deep breaths to calm himself. Looking out of the window, he noticed dawn was still hours away, so he laid there pondering his dream and what it meant, until the sound of sleet gently hitting the windowpane lulled him back to sleep.

A few hours later, Katara woke to the sound of hail bouncing off of the window. She rolled over and noticed Torhan was already awake and staring up at the ceiling.

"I slept like a baby, how about you?" She asked.

"I didn't because I had the strangest dream involving a teenage girl…" he paused trying to recall the dream, "I was standing on a bluff, and the girl summoned what must have been a thirty-foot Water Tirip."

"You have some imagination, because they can only grow to six feet," Katara said. "Did you recognize the girl?"

"No, but in the dream, she said that I was the reason why she called forth the guardian."

"Well, I hope you don't anger anyone like that." Katara laughed. "Don't read too much into the dream, it's just your subconscious."

After preparing for their trek, they stepped out of the inn into a light hail and chilly wind. The furs were so insulated that if it wasn't for their faces being exposed, they would've never known it was cold out.

"I don't even feel the cold, do you?" Torhan asked.

"Only on my face. These furs are great."

"It looks like the snow is really deep over there." Torhan said, pointing towards the path they had to travel.

"I guess it's time that we find out if these shoes actually work."

Katara placed the snowshoes on. "If they don't I'm getting our money back." She said and began walking around.

Torhan put his on as well, went over to the deep snow, and walked around. At first, the shoes were a bit clumsy, but once he got used to it, he thought it was like walking on solid ground. Some of the parents and children, walking nearby, made comments about their strange-looking shoes, but Katara and Torhan ignored them and left when they were ready.

By mid-afternoon, they arrived at the small grove of trees that priest Piersum said Tole was supposed to live in, and stopped just short of entering.

"We should be really cautious." Torhan warned

"I agree. When we find Tole what's our plan?"

"I was thinking the direct approach about the amulet might be best."

"What do you mean the direct approach? Tell him about Sybil and how we want to use the amulet to free her? If he did kill her parents, don't you think he'll try to do the same to us?"

"Then what do you propose?" Torhan said and took out his waterskin for a long, refreshing swig.

Katara thought about it. "Maybe we should tell him we are relic seekers and offer him money if we find the amulet."

"That sounds like a good plan, but what if he gets suspicious?" He said and offered her the waterskin.

She grabbed it and took a sip of water. "Then we hit him over the head and force him to tell us."

Torhan chuckled. "That sounds like a better plan. It looks like the snow isn't as deep inside the grove." He said, and they removed their snowshoes and entered.

After walking for a while, Torhan began feeling as if they were being watched. The feeling grew to the point that he became uneasy and slowed his pace. He gazed at the scabbard, expecting the artifact to confirm his suspicions, but it didn't.

"Do you get the feeling we're being watched?" Katara asked.

"I do, but the scabbard isn't glowing."

"Does it always work?"

"It hasn't let me down yet. Let's keep moving." Torhan said and held his spear in a protective manner.

They walked until Katara thought she heard something somewhere off to her right, and signaled for her companion to stop. She equipped herself with her shield and her father's mace called Righteous. Gripping the weapon tightly, she carefully scanned the area, listening intently for several minutes, before motioning for them to continue.

Eventually, they came upon a part of the forest where fallen trees, thick shrubbery, and dense trails hindered their progress, slowing them considerably. Torhan was about to comment about the area when the scabbard glowed intensely. Alarmed, they stood defensively with their weapons in hand. In the next instant, they heard a horse galloping towards them. Torhan's dagger left the scabbard, flew off in that direction and was lost from sight. A few seconds later, the horse stopped abruptly and the sound of fighting ensued.

"We need to get out of here." Torhan said.

They were about to leave when a creature, covered in black-and-white fur and holding a large spear, jumped over a fallen tree and stopped directly in front of them. The monster's head, chest, and arms were that of a powerful ape, and the lower half was that of a horse. The half-ape, half-horse creature glared at them with hatred, raising its spear high into the air and licking its sharp protruding fangs. The creature reared up on its hind legs, and charged. Katara and Torhan rolled away from the thundering beast and were on their feet again rather quickly. The beast turned, stopped, and threw its spear at Torhan, missing him by a few feet.

The beast was about to charge them again when it was hit in the back by something, howled in agony, then turned around to engage a floating dagger. Torhan advanced on the creature. Katara was about to do the same when another ape-horse beast, with many wounds from a recent encounter with Torhan's dagger, came leaping into the clearing on her blind side, with a massive club poised and ready to strike. The creature tried taking her head off with the weapon as it passed, but at the very last second, Katara deflected the attack with her shield. However, the powerful blow sent her to the ground.

Torhan heard the commotion and turned around. When he saw Katara on the ground and the creature, he dropped his spear, grabbed his bow off of his shoulder, quickly notched an arrow and fired. Unfortunately, his aim wasn't true and he missed. The creature wheeled about and charged headlong towards Katara, who was still on the ground, intent on crushing her beneath its hooves.

Torhan fired another arrow, and this time, hit the monster in the shoulder, causing the beast to stop a few feet from Katara. Torhan quickly fired again and hit it the chest. The beast howled in anguish and pulled the arrows out. It was about to charge after Torhan, when Katara whacked it twice in its left hind leg, shattering its bone with a loud crack and sending the half-mare to the ground. The ape-horse tried standing several times but fell back down.

Katara was on her feet again and while she was positioning herself above its head, the beast grabbed her leg and yanked her off of her feet with a mighty pull. With a vice-like grip, the hybrid pulled her closer to his waiting mouth. Katara thrashed and kicked with her free leg until she connected with its nose and broke it. The beast let go of her leg and Katara unleashed hell, in the form of her mace, against his head. The first strike dazed the monster; the following ones cracked open its skull, spilling its brains onto the cold, snowy ground.

Across the way, while the Torhan's dagger was still fighting the other ape creature, he launched several arrows at the beast, with the last being a carefully well-placed shot that ended its life. The dagger stabbed the creature a few more times before returning to its home, until the scabbard stopped glowing altogether.

Torhan helped Katara up.

"What the hell are they?" She said, gazing at the beast.

"No idea, I just hope there isn't any more of them." He looked over at her fallen shield, which had a big dent right in the center. "Are you ok?" He asked.

"My arm hurts, but I should be alright. The shield took the brunt of the blow." She said and painfully removed her fur coat. "Inside of my pack there's a small, disk-shaped container. Can you get it for me?"

Torhan nodded and fished through her pack until he found it.

"Now I need you to help me out of the armor." She said. Gingerly, they took her wounded limb out of the chainmail shirt. Katara opened the container and rubbed a black, gooey ointment all over her forearm and shoulder.

"That feels better. I can feel it working already." She said.

After they placed her armor back on and retrieved Torhan's weapons, they left.

Snuggled deep inside of several bushes, the master of the grove watched with fascination as the two strangers killed his pets. It was not easy for him to do, but he knew it was necessary if he wanted to gauge their abilities. With a broad smile, he decided to continue his little game, by leading them around the forest for several more hours, before putting his plan into action.

"You know this area is starting to look vaguely familiar." Torhan said after another hour of walking.

"This isn't a grove; it's more like an endless maze. If we don't find him soon, we should go back and force Piersum to show us where he lives."

They pressed on until the area darkened, and they were exhausted.

After finding an appropriate place to camp, Torhan retrieved some dry wood and lit a small fire. They ate a meal of dried beef and nuts, then cleared an area on the ground for them to lay comfortably under their blankets. Katara fell asleep right away, while Torhan watched the dancing flames, deep in thought. He was thinking about demons in general, when a glass container shattered against a nearby tree and engulfed the area in a cloudy white smoke. The haze overwhelmed him quickly and he was ushered into a deep sleep.

Torhan was the first to wake from his slumber. He quickly realized that he was bound to a large tree by leather straps fastened to his wrist and wrapped several times around his torso and neck. He glanced over to his right and saw Katara tied the same exact way with her head down. He began working on his restraints when someone spoke.

"Stop struggling. It's of no use, you are not going anywhere." A cloaked, hooded figure said. He was using a walking stick for support as he emerged from around the tree.

"Untie us and let us go." Torhan demanded.

"In due time, but first you will answer my questions." The captor lowered his hood. He was older in years, small in stature, and frail looking, with short, cropped black hair.

"Are you Tole?" Torhan asked.

"Never mind who I am, I'm not the one tied up. Now what are you doing here?"

"We are looking for the hermit named Tole."

"Why would you be looking for him?"

"That's my business."

Katara stirred awake, drawing their captor's attention.

"Is it? I might need to ask your friend if you continue to have an attitude." He grinned and glanced at her and then back at Torhan.

"Touch her and you die."

The captor chuckled and called out in a strange language. In response, an ape-horse creature carrying a spear, galloped into view.

"I think my pet, Rime Lord, might have something to say about that," he paused, "although you did dispatch his brothers rather easily. But then again, you're now weaponless." He laughed like an insane person.

Torhan began using his newly acquired Slipknot skill by working on his restraints ever so slightly, while hiding his movements.

"Now I am going to ask you again." Their captor pulled out a dagger. "Why are you in my grove?"

"Tole," Katara shouted getting their captor's attention. "Priest Piersum sent us to find you; he said you can help us."

Tole turned around. "Why did he send you?" He responded.

"He said you can lead us to an item called the Amulet of REM. We need it in order to help a girl named Sybil."

"And why should I care? That ignorant fool sent me away."

"Whatever your feelings are towards him shouldn't matter. What matters is the girl and you can help her."

"I don't care. No one has done anything for me!"

Katara noticed Torhan working his restraints and needed to keep

Tole occupied for a little longer. "You need to let go of your anger. You're a man of the cloth right?"

"I was, but that life died a long time ago." Tole turned his attention back to Torhan. "How does your magic dagger work boy?" Tole waved the blade back and forth.

"Release me and I'll show you how."

His comment made Tole laughed insanely.

"Tole, if you help us maybe you can give up this life of solitude and return to the Order?" Katara offered.

Tole straightened his bent form. "Maybe we can work out a deal." He said rubbing his chin.

While Tole's attention was diverted, Torhan finished untying his left wrist and then freed his right a few seconds later, while loosening the bonds around his chest.

"What do you want us to do?" Katara asked.

"I need you to recover an amulet called Insight. Once you have done so, I'll help you find the one you seek called REM." He paused. "Her parents came looking for it a long time ago," he paused again, "you know I never did hear back from them." He laughed loudly.

"Hey!" Torhan shouted, and Tole turned his attention back toward him. "Tell your pet not to do anything aggressive towards us."

"Why?"

Torhan stood up, letting his restraints fall to the ground. "Because he will die."

The Rime Lord howled in anger and galloped toward Torhan. The scabbard glowed, the dagger ripped free from Tole's grip and engaged the Rime Lord. Torhan raced over and grabbed the hermit by the throat and tightened his hand enough for him to gag and flail about.

"Tell him to stand down, or he'll die." Torhan loosened his grip enough for him to speak. By now the Rime Lord was wounded in several places and breathing hard.

Tole said something in the Rime Lord's language and the creature ran off into the woods. The dagger returned to Torhan's scabbard after the threat was gone.

"Nice dagger." Tole said, in between coughs.

"Where are our weapons?" Torhan barked at him.

Tole pointed to a spot several feet away.

"Don't think about doing anything foolish." Torhan warned as he walked over and untied Katara.

Once she was freed, he retrieved their weapons.

"Now, what is it you want us to do?" Torhan asked Tole.

Tole was somewhat surprised that he asked him instead of forcing him to tell them where the amulet they sought was.

"If you retrieve the amulet of Insight, I'll tell you exactly where the amulet of REM is. Do we have a deal?"

"Alright, we'll get you the amulet. Describe it to us." Katara stepped forward.

"The amulet is circular in design and has five indentations set upon the surface. A unique stone will fit into each one.

"Where is it?" Torhan asked.

Tole Grinned. "To the north and set deep in the forest lays a mansion. The owner is a man named Fefantor and he has it."

"What does he look like?" Torhan asked.

"He's of medium build, middle aged, and wears his long black hair in a ponytail."

"If you know where it is, then why do you need us?" Katara asked.

"Simply because I'm not skillful like you are. Plus, he's crazy, and if he catches me anywhere near his house, he'll turn me into one of his creatures."

"Creatures?" Torhan interjected, raising an eyebrow.

"He robs graves at night and somehow creates a race of super monsters."

"Super monsters. How is that possible?"

"I don't know."

"Did you ever see one?"

"No."

"We're good fighters, so they shouldn't be too hard to kill." Katara added.

"And don't take them too lightly, because once I hired a very experienced fighter to retrieve the amulet and he never returned." Tole straightened his back and then he hunched it over again.

"Anything else?" Katara asked.

"Just be careful if you enter his house, I heard that it is full of traps. Here, take this." He handed them a steel set of lock picks. "They're stronger than any set you'll ever find. Good luck."

They bid the hermit farewell and left the grove.

CHAPTER 8: FINDING A LOST BROTHER

Konafar, Tonles, Erantel, Lud, Fleck, and Thessor with his kinsmen, entered the town of Wistful just as it was starting to snow. They proceeded to the healer and after arriving at the little cottage, an elderly woman in brown robes stepped out of the house. Her youthful appearance made her look much younger than her long silver locs indicated.

She gazed at the group then plainly said. "Wounded only, please."

Konafar dismounted, told the others that he would meet them at the inn, and bid them farewell. He turned and before he could take another step towards the house, the woman spoke.

"You'd better have enough coin, or else you'll lose your most treasured item." Her eyes rested on his crotch, he smiled at her, then stepped inside.

She led him down the dimly lit corridor, past a small waiting area, and into a large circular-shaped room with oil burning lamps scattered throughout. Exotic incenses filled his nostrils the moment he entered, leaving him feeling euphoric. A large table sat in the middle of the room, equipped with leather straps and several more tables lined the walls with herbs and different colored liquids in glass canisters. In the corner of the room was a small cauldron with something brewing inside.

Konafar laid down on the table, at the healer's request, and was strapped in. She walked over to another table, poured some sort of clear liquid onto a rag, and placed it over her patient's mouth. Konafar remained conscious for only a few seconds before succumbing to the sweet-smelling liquid.

Lud, Fleck, and Erantel went to the brothel in search of some female company, while Tonles and the two lizardmen took the horses over to the stables, and then went to the inn of the Slaughtered Fawn. As they approached the establishment, a group of men intercepted them and barred their path.

"What are they doing in this town and why are you with them?" Said a tall lanky fellow dressed in leather armor, with a short sword sheathed at his side.

"Ignorant fool," snapped Tonles. "Step aside or feel my axe."

"Hey big man, stand down, or you'll be dealing with me." Someone said from his right.

Tonles glanced at the speaker siting in a rocking chair. . "This is not your affair, but if you insist on sticking your nose where it shouldn't be, then it will be." Tonles stated firmly.

The man stood up from the rocker, stretched his arms ever so casually, and walked down the stairs. Tonles took note to his sheathed sword and chainmail armor.

"Tonlesss wesss can handlesss thessse men." Thessor hissed.

"I'll take care of this one. You handle the others if they get involved."

The man, taller than Tonles, stopped directly in front of him, gazing at him confidently. Tonles curled his right fist, grinned at him, and punched him in the stomach, knocking the wind out of him and doubling him over. Tonles then quickly removed the troublemaker's sword from his sheath and shoved him backwards onto the steps. As some of the others were reaching for their weapons, Thessor and his brothers raced over and grabbed them by the throats. Their claws dug in enough to get their point across that if they reached for their weapons further, they'd pay the price.

"APOLOGIZE TO MY FRIENDS!" Tonles barked at the men. They looked at each other and then one by one, did just that. "If I catch you disrespecting another friendly race again I'll be sure to cut you down where you stand." Tonles said in a much calmer voice and turned his attention back to the guy he'd punched, who was getting to his feet. The man reached for his weapon and found it missing.

"Are you looking for this?" Tonles held the sword outwardly. "It's mine now." He said waving his free hand back and forth like an adult would do to a child who was being scolded. "However, you could always try to take it from me?"

The man hesitated briefly and instead of reaching for his booted dagger, bowed his head in disappointment and walked away.

"Here keep this." Tonles handed the sword to Thessor's brother, who appraised its worth by the jewel-encrusted hilt and swapped it out for his own sword.

The two lizardmen exchanged words in their native tongue. "Tonlesss, mysss brother needsss to leavesss." Thessor said, and his kinsman left.

"Let's go inside, I need a drink." Tonles said, leading Thessor through the doors.

After Jacko and Woo parted company from the prisoners, they returned to their school; the Order of the Open Palm. Mao was still running a fever, and his shoulder looked pretty bad, so they dropped him off at the healers. Woo decided that Jacko should see the Master by himself and left.

As Jacko neared the entrance to the Master's chambers, two of his fellow students, both the rank of Gray Hawk, guarded the doors. He displayed a series of secret hand signals and was allowed to enter. He proceeded through the other rooms until he could go no further and knocked on the wooden doors. A few seconds later, an Elite Student named Wii Loo, answered.

"Jacko it's good to see you." He said.

Jacko bowed. "Can I see the master?"

Wii Loo returned his greeting with a nod and stepped aside, allowing him to enter. "I will tell him you are here. Please have a seat over at the table."

Wii Loo waited for him to be seated, before leaving through the door in the back.

A few minutes later, the Master entered the room, and Jacko immediately stood up and bowed.

"Back so soon? I'm surprised to see you." The Master said.

"There's a reason why. While I was on my way to Mirkin, we passed by Redden. Did you know that the city fell?"

"I heard it did. Have a seat."

After they were seated Jacko continued. "I was supposed to meet my friend Torhan in Redden and when I heard it fell; I needed to find out if he was somewhere inside.

"Just you, Mao, and Woo entered the city?"

"No. Before I left I hired several others to escort me to Mirkin. When they found out what had happened to Redden they agreed to help."

"Did you find him?"

Jacko shook his head. "We couldn't find him. We did rescue a dozen prisoners though."

"You did? I must say, I'm impressed to say the least, and it was very brave of you and the others. You went searching for one person, and saved twelve. Think about that. If you'd never entered the town, those people would be dead. Did anyone get hurt?"

"A lot of people got hurt."

"What about Mao and Woo?"

"Mao hurt his shoulder really bad, but Woo is fine." Jacko looked down. "I feel like it's my fault."

"Jacko, don't feel that way. People make decisions of their own free will. When it's someone's time, there's nothing you can do about it. For your bravery, you are entitled to additional training."

"But Master, that wasn't my intention. I was only looking for my friend."

"Maybe so, but you were a part of something special."

"What about Woo and Mao?"

"Woo will receive training as well and when Mao is well again; he will be promoted."

Jacko smiled.

"Now, tell me everything that happened and what you saw."

Jacko told him what transpired, how they rescued the prisoners, what type of army was there, and about the brave men and women who lost their lives.

The Master processed the information and then said. "I feel it's only a matter of time before they come here and attack our town."

"What should we do?" asked Jacko.

"I want you to go to Mirkin like you were supposed to and warn Ma's father." The Master took out a piece of parchment, scribed something onto it, folded it up, and then slid it into a wrapper and sealed it. "After that, I want you to go to our Order a few miles west of Mirkin and present this letter to Brother Lee Chee Wa." He handed him the sealed parchment.

"And leave you and the Order to fight?"

"Hopefully they'll leave us in peace, if not then we'll defend the town."

"But their army is so vast. There are giant folk, war beetles, and plenty of boarmen and goatmen. I'm afraid for you and my brothers."

"Don't worry I'll talk to the other Orders in town and try to sway them to stand with us."

"And if they choose not to?"

"Then we'll save as many people as we can and seek sanctuary in one of our other schools."

"Master, you're far too important to risk your life."

The Master grinned. "Jacko, if I should fall, Brother Chee Wa and Brother Tae Fu are more than capable of taking over."

"I'm staying." Jacko insisted.

"No you're not. Given your skills, you would serve the Order better by doing what I ask." The Master abruptly got up. "There's much to do, please see yourself out." He said and walked through the door in the back.

Shortly after leaving his chamber, Jacko sought Sun Chin and found him in the training area. He told him what happened in Redden, and he was proud of Jacko. Since Mao was wounded, he offered to escort him to Mirkin if the Master allowed it. Jacko couldn't be happier because Sun was not only a trusted friend, he was also carried the rank of Eagle, which was three levels higher than he was and would definitely be a valued asset. After Sun left to go speak with the Master, Jacko made his way over to the healers to check on Mao, and arrived just as Woo was leaving.

"How's he doing?" Jacko asked.

"He suffered a severe shoulder injury and may either lose the use of the limb or be severely hampered. That's the best they can do, the healers said."

"I wish that he didn't want to come along."

"Look, it's not your fault. He, and everyone else, knows the risk you take by leaving the school and going on missions. He'll be fine. What did the Master say?" Woo asked, trying to change the subject.

"He said we'll receive training, and Mao will be promoted for our part in the rescue."

"I didn't expect that."

"Me either. Will you still come to Mirkin with me?"

Woo rotated his sore arms back and forth several times. "Of course, the school will be fine without me."

"I feel guilty about leaving because the town may come under attack."

"If the Master told you to go to Mirkin, then do so."

"Let's meet tonight at the inn of the Slaughtered Fawn. Hopefully, the others will be there. I'll be in my room resting." Woo said and turned.

"By the way, Sun Chin will be coming with us if the Master allows it."

"Sun Chin? That's good, he's quite skillful." Woo said and left.

Jacko waited for Sun and when he saw him wearing his dark green traveling clothes, he smiled.

"Okay, the Master gave me his blessing and a new task in addition to going with you. He wants me to train you." A proud look was etched across Sun's face. "Maybe you'll learn a few things."

"Have you ever trained anyone before?" Jacko said jokingly.

"I've trained a few students, but none as pathetic as you."

"We'll see if I'm as bad as you say."

"Is Woo coming with us?"

"Yes. He said he'll meet us at the inn of the Slaughtered Fawn around supper time."

It was around dusk when Jacko and Sun entered the crowded tavern. Jacko saw Tonles, Thessor, and surprisingly Breen, sitting in the back. Her long blonde hair was tied in a ponytail, and she was wearing leather armor on her upper torso, looking the part of a warrior. Jacko led them to the table, introduced Sun to the others and then sat down.

"Where's Konafar?" Jacko asked after he was seated.

"He's at the healers getting fixed up." Tonles said.

"Is he hurt badly?" Breen asked.

"Unless he's six feet under it's never that bad, so he'll be along shortly." Tonles chuckled.

"Where's everyone else?" Jacko asked.

"Erantel, Lud, and Fleck decided to stay in town for a few more days before returning to our Order. They'll need to inform them about what befell our brothers and notify their next of kin. Are you still traveling to Mirkin?"

"Yes. Do you want to come along?"

The big man rubbed his beard. "I'm thinking about it. I need to speak with Konafar first.

Thessor how about you?"

"Sorry Jackosss, I needsss to returnsss to my peoplesss."

Jacko glanced at Breen and realized how pretty she was with her face cleaned up, also thinking she looked sexy dressed up as a warrior. "Breen you look like you're ready for a fight." He said, trying to hide his thoughts behind his smile.

"I'm ready for one now that Tonles gave me the coin for my gear. It feels good to be armed again. I swear…" she paused and looked away.

Sun noticed a tear trickling down her left cheek and felt for her. "Are you okay?"

"Those bastards; I'll never allow anyone to take me prisoner again. I'd rather die first." Her tone had anger behind it.

"Don't worry it will never happen again as long as I'm around. I promise." Tonles said trying to make her feel better.

"Thanks, it means a lot."

"Do you want to come with us?" Jacko asked.

"I think so."

"Breen do you have any formal training?" Sun asked.

"No. My father taught me everything because I wasn't allowed to join the Order in my town."

"He must have been very good with a blade. Sun I've seen her fight and she can handle a weapon." Jacko said.

"I agree, but you lack experience." Tonles added.

"Any time you want a lesson, let me know." Breen said to him, grinning.

"Sun why don't tell us about yourself and what skills you possess?" Tonles asked him.

While Sun was talking, Jacko began looking around for Aurora. When he didn't see her working, he excused himself and walked toward the innkeeper behind the bar.

"What's he doing?" Tonles asked Sun.

"I'm not sure. Maybe getting us drinks."

The elderly innkeeper was in the middle of pouring a tankard of ale when Jacko approached.

"Excuse me." Jacko said, catching the old man's attention. "Do you know where Aurora is?"

The innkeeper finished pouring the ale. "You just missed her. She finished her shift, and I think she said she was stopping at the market on her way home."

"Thanks. If I miss her tell her Jacko was looking for her."

Jacko returned to the table and said that he needed to go to the market to see a friend. Sun wanted to go, but Jacko waved him off and left.

"Why is he going to the market at this time of night?" Tonles asked

Sun once Jacko was out the door.

"I think he might be looking for his friend Aurora."

"Is it his girlfriend?" Breen asked smiling, because she loved hearing about people in love.

"I believe he has feelings for her." Sun replied.

Jacko navigated his way through the streets with haste until he arrived at the market. Through the semi-crowded streets, he saw Aurora right away. She was wearing a blue dress and looking very pretty with her long, curly black hair draped over her shoulders. He strolled over and touched her slender arm. She turned around and her eyes widened in surprise, then she gave him a big hug.

"Where have you been? You were supposed to have dinner with me a couple of days ago."

"I'm sorry about that. My Master needed me to do something. Can we talk privately?"

"Sure, let me pay for this first."

After she completed the sale, Jacko led her down one of the streets and stopped when he knew no one would hear them.

"Aurora, can you leave town for a few weeks?" He suddenly said.

"Why?" She looked confused by his question.

Jacko told her what had happened in Redden and his thoughts about the days ahead. Aurora had a newfound respect for him, especially after hearing how brave he was and what he did for the prisoners. She also thought it was really sweet how much he cared about her well-being.

"Where will I go?" She asked.

"Anywhere but Redden."

His look of concern touched her heart all over again.

"I can't?" Her eyes welled up.

"Why?"

"What will happen to my family if I do?"

Jacko didn't think of that.

"Where are you going?" She looked at him apprehensively.

"I have to go to Mirkin and take care of more pressing issues."

"My mother can't travel."

"Please listen to me. I've seen what they'll do if they take the town, and it's not pretty." Jacko spared her the gory details.

"Do you believe they'll attack us?"

"I don't know. My Master is staying behind and will talk to the other Orders to decide which course of action is best if they do." He paused looking into her eyes. "Come with me, it's safer."

She shook her head in protest and reiterated that she didn't want to leave her family.

"Do me a favor then," he placed his hand gently on the side of her face and brushed aside her hair. "If they do attack, hide and stay out of sight until I return."

"You're scaring me. Please stay with me."

As much as he wanted to, and saw the pleading look in her eyes, he knew that he couldn't. The Order always came first, so he told her the truth, hoping she would understand. "Remember my teacher who was killed?"

She nodded.

"His father is in grave danger and my Master needs me to warn him."

"Can't they send someone else?"

"No."

Will you be okay?" She asked.

"Yes. Sun Chin is coming with me and a few other people."

"You'd better be. You owe me a dinner."

The way she looked at that moment told him all he needed to know about how she felt. He pulled her close and kissed her. To his surprise and delight, she responded even more passionately. When they finally separated, he confessed his feelings for her, and she kissed him again.

"I need to go back to the inn. Remember, stay out of sight and seek sanctuary in my Order if the town comes under attack." He handed her a small trinket with the school emblem etched on it. "Take this charm and show it to the guards. Tell them you got it from me, and they'll allow you inside."

She nodded.

He kissed her once more and parted. She watched him walking away and her eyes welled up anew in sadness and fear that she would never see him again.

Jacko returned to the tavern and saw Woo and Konafar seated at the table. The mighty warrior smiled when he saw him walking over.

"Are you feeling better?" Jacko asked him.

"It's going to take more than a couple of giants to stop me." He flexed his wounded arm, and the bandage tightened. "Good as..." he abruptly coughed and his side hurt, "new."

Tonles chuckled. "Maybe you're not."

"Will you still come to Mirkin?"

"Yes and so is Tonles." Konafar tossed him a pouch full of coins.

"What's this for?"

"It's your money; I decided to go for free."

"Why?"

"Because of your bravery in Redden, plus I'm sure we'll find more of it along the way. There are always thieves to kill and monsters to slay." Konafar laughed. "How's Mao doing?"

"He's still recovering and won't be coming along."

"Too bad, I liked him."

"Well? How is she?" Sun suddenly asked Jacko.

"Who?" Jacko responded, knowing full well who he meant.

"You know who." Sun's expression sort of embarrassed him.

"I asked her to come with me, but she can't."

"It's better that she doesn't."

"And why not? I can protect her a lot better if she's with me." Jacko was clearly agitated.

"Because she doesn't have any fighting skills and might get hurt."

Jacko knew he was right and let the matter drop.

"When do you want to leave?" Woo added.

"We'll meet at the stables, first thing in the morning. I'm going to enjoy myself tonight because who knows when I'll get another opportunity." Tonles said.

They stayed in the inn for a few more hours before leaving. Jacko, Sun, and Woo went back to the Order to sleep and prepare for their trek. Thessor bid the others farewell, and Tonles, Konafar, and Breen went to their respective rooms.

Around dawn, snow was falling again as they met at the stables. Everyone was geared up and ready for their journey. Konafar was sporting tough hide leather leggings and boots, a thicker gambeson underneath a chainmail shirt, and sheathed across his back was Carnage. He wore a black cloth cape draped across his broad shoulders. Tonles wore similar garb and was carrying Ripper. The weapon looked even more menacing in the morning light, Jacko thought. Breen was dressed in her leather outfit underneath a green hooded cloak. She carried a small wooden shield, and sheathed on her side was a short sword. Her leather boots were lined with fur for added warmth.

Sun was wearing his traditional red and black traveling clothes, made of thick woolen cloth that was resistant to most sword slashes. The soft leather boots were insulated with fur. The studded leather gauntlets complemented his Iron Fist technique and would deliver extra damage if you ever got hit with them. Woo and Jacko wore the exact same outfits as Sun, except Woo's clothes were yellow and brown and Jacko's were green and black. They also wore dark cloaks and had small sacks slung over their shoulders, which held various items that they would need.

After paying the stable boy for the care of the horses, they left Wistful.

By midday, they entered a forest and found a place to rest. The horses were given water and oats while the others ate a light lunch of dried beef and berries. Around the seating area, they made small talk with Konafar and Tonles telling them about some of their most dangerous adventures. Whether their stories were real or not, they were still quite captivating and entertaining.

Breen mentioned that she was also a healer and proceeded to tell them about some of her own affairs. Her stories paled in comparison to them because she lacked the flair they had for telling tales of adventures. When she was finished, Konafar announced that she was a nice addition to the group and her skills, as a fighter and healer, would surely come in handy in the days ahead. Jacko wondered if he was being truthful or flirtatious. When they were finished resting, they left.

A couple of hours later, they came upon several large trees blocking their way. They were placed in a row and far too big to jump over them. Konafar knew they didn't fall by accident. They were about to go around them, when a group of giants emerged from the surrounding foliage. Konafar and Tonles recognized them as Woodland Giants. They looked almost identical, standing over seven feet tall, weighing a few hundred pounds, with long red unkempt hair and beards to match. They wore furs from different animals and carried really lengthy spears. They were neutral in alignment, and for the most part, kept to themselves.

Konafar dismounted. "Wait for my signal and then follow my lead." He said and approached the giants.

They looked at Tonles. "Eyes forward and don't say another word." He whispered.

Everyone did as they were told and watched Konafar approach the giants while speaking in their language. The giants gathered closer and conversed with him for a while. When he was finished, he walked back to the group.

"They require a fee to allow us to pass because they own this part of the forest. They are tired of allowing creatures to use it for free."

"They own this grove by whose right?" Woo said.

"Do you want to tell them differently?"

When Woo didn't respond he continued.

"Anyway their fee is useful items like furs, food, ale, large weapons and stuff like that."

"Maybe we should fight our way through." Woo said.

"Woo, in life it's not about fighting everything you encounter, and besides, they look very formable don't you think?" Tonles said and looked directly at him.

"Let's vote." Jacko said.

"Let's not." Konafar replied.

During the discussion, Breen noticed one of the giants had a large wound that appeared to be infected.

"One of them looks hurt. Ask them if I mend his wound will they let us pass." She said to Konafar.

"That might work." Konafar said and walked over to the giants.

After a brief discussion, they agreed to her terms. Breen dismounted, grabbed her small bag, and approached the injured giant.

"I was right about her proving to be useful. I just didn't think it would be this soon." Konafar said proudly while she was away.

Breen worked on his arm for a little more than an hour and when she was finished, the wound was stitched and bandaged. She gave them herbs and ointments and showed them how to use them. The grateful giants allowed them to pass.

Once they were clear of the forest, they couldn't help but turn their attention skywards and to the darkening skies ahead. They indicated a storm was on its way.

"I don't see shelter anywhere. What should we do about the storm?" Woo asked.

"Well we can't go back if that's what you mean." Tonles replied.

"Why not? We just helped them."

"Do you want to ask them if we can stay? I don't. Giants are unstable at best and can turn on you in an instant."

"He's right," Konafar added, "we should make our way over there and seek shelter." He pointed toward a cluster of trees with a rock face behind it.

"Do you think there's a cave in there or something?" Jacko asked.

"If not, the trees should be adequate enough."

The plains opened up for several miles, and despite the group riding hard across the flats, they were met by the storm. The torrential downpour came upon them swiftly, and within minutes, they were soaked to the bone. The terrain also became a slippery mess and almost toppled a few of the horses.

By the time they reached the trees, the rainstorm intensified and was now a mix of sleet and ice. Despite the thick canopy of leaves, the storm fell through with little resistance and everyone knew that lighting a fire was a foregone conclusion. They dismounted from the horses, split up, and began searching for somewhere dry.

Woo was over near the rock face, spotted a cave set deep within the cliffs and told the others. Once inside of the cave, Tonles hid the horses near the entrance, while Sun Chin and Woo explored the deeper parts of the cavern. Konafar lit a roaring fire using scattered timber Breen had found inside of the cave.

After the Green Knight left Redden, he marched his army north after he received reports of fresh horse tracks leading that way. By the time the storm came upon them, they were only a few hours away from the forest that the group of Woodland Giants called home. After they entered and were confronted by the giants, one of their cousins from the north ignored the

Green Knight's command for a peaceful resolution, and started a bloody fight. The Woodland Giants fought like a pack of wild animals and when the last of them fell, a good amount of his troops were killed.

Before moving on, the Green Knight killed the instigator, making an example of any who disobeyed his direct order.

****

Sun and Woo followed the sloping passageway downward into the darkness. The blackness was so dense that it threatened to eclipse the torch light and leave them in total darkness. After the ground leveled off and went straight ahead for an additional thirty feet, then came to a T-junction. Sun wanted to split up and take different directions, but after Woo objected adamantly, they agreed to go left.

After another forty feet or so, they found themselves at the entrance to a circular room. Across the way, they saw a medium-sized hole with blue-light emitting from within. Holding their torches aloft revealed a wooden treasure chest off to the right of the hole, with a skeleton lying on top.

"I wonder where the light is coming from." Woo said.

"Not sure."

"The skeleton on top of the chest is creepy."

Sun nodded and entered with Woo following closely behind. They were at the chest when a blast of cold air, mixed with water, hit them square in their bodies.

"It appears to be coming from the hole." Woo stated.

"I feel water in the air." Sun said. "I wonder what's causing that."

"I have no idea."

They moved closer and by the time they were a few feet away from the chest, a powerful burst of wet, freezing air shot out of the hole and extinguished the torches, leaving the blue hue as their only light source. While they were trying to light the torches, they heard movement coming from inside of the hole. Glancing below, they saw something moving. The creature's movements were fast enough to cause the light to flicker. Both men began backing up, and just as they were about to turn and run, a metal gate at the entrance to the room slammed down from the ceiling, trapping them inside to face whatever was coming.

"They should be back by now." Jacko said, looking at the far end of the cave.

"I'll go to have a look." Konafar said.

"I'll go with you." Tonles added, lighting a couple of torches and venturing into the darkness below.

When they reached the junction, they decided to split up, with Tonles going left and Konafar moving toward the right.

The corridor Konafar took eventually led him to a large circular room that felt warmer than the rest of the damp cave. To the back of the room, he saw a medium-sized hole emitting a reddish hue and many treasure chests, half of which were opened and scattered about. He also noticed several skeletons, dressed in ratty, decaying, armor lying near the chests.

Intrigued, he moved into the room, toward the wooden chests and what he imagined were riches beyond his dreams. The temperature steadily grew warmer the further in he walked, and by the time he reached the chests, he was sweating. Instead of playing on the side of caution, he slowly bent down to open one of the chests, and in the next instant, a gust of hot, searing air surged forth from the hole. The intense heat was too much to bear as it scorched his face and robbed his body of precious fluids. His muscles cramped and brought the big man to his knees in pain. A few seconds later, the sound of a metal gate slamming shut left him trapped inside the room.

Instead of moving toward the entrance, Sun and Woo stood to the side of the opening opposite each other and waited for whatever was coming their way. Sun was poised and ready to punch or kick the creature, while Woo curled his hands into the shape of a claw.

At the exact same time, a blast of cold air burst out of the hole and a blue and white creature slithered past them with blinding speed. They turned in unison to see a scaly snake with short arms and legs holding a small trident. The creature was in the center of the room staring at them.

Woo was about to advance, when Sun heard movement coming from the hole and told Woo to stay put and keep an eye on the creature in the center. Sun anticipated the arrival of the new threat by the length of his shadow and when he thought that it was in range, he threw a kick and hit the creature, sending it back down the hole.

What he didn't know was that he actually missed the initial snake-like creature and hit the second one because it was trailing to close to the first. Turning around, Sun saw two snakes in the center of the room, already up on their hind legs, waving small tridents defensively in front of their reptilian bodies. Puzzled as to why there were two, but with no time to figure it out, he ordered Woo to move away from the hole and each other.

The four-foot long creatures fell onto their stomachs and slithered towards them, emitting coldness as they approached. Sun charged the closest creature while Woo waited defensively for his.

Upon seeing its next meal moving in his direction, the creature stopped, reared up, and stabbed at Sun several times. Sun quickly blocked the attacks, slipped behind the creature and hit it in the back of the head with a roundhouse kick. The snake creature slumped forward from the impact and slithered away before Sun could hit it again.

Sun, thinking he'd hurt the creature, gave chase. He was right behind the creature when it suddenly turned around, emitting a cold aura that chilled Sun to the bone and drove him away defensively. The creature pressed forward and attacked with its spear, aiming for Sun's chest in a vicious attempt to kill him. Sun blocked the attacks while moving off to his left and then quickly shifting his stance to the right, leaving the creature exposed. With a precision punch that only a master could make, Sun struck the creature's arm directly on the muscle and caused it to drop its spear.

The snake instantly emitted another wave of cold, drawing more heat away from Sun's body and forcing him backwards. Sun's limbs were beginning to turn blue, become numb and were feeling heavy and slow.

The creature leapt onto Sun's back, then clamped down hard on his right shoulder with sharp teeth, piercing through his garments, and sinking its chilly bite deep into his flesh. Sun winced in pain, and despite the cold intense chill, he punched the creature in its face, driving two ridged studs from the gauntlet into the creature's eye socket. The beast released its maw and fell off of him, hissing in pain. Sun kicked the creature twice in its chest with enough force to stop its beating heart; killing the slithering monster.

While Sun was battling the snake monster, Woo was poised and ready to deploy the Eagle Claw technique, as the creature glided seamlessly across the cold damp earth towards him.

"One blow, that's all it will take." He thought and raised his hands, while tensing the first two fingers and thumb further into a claw.

The creature stopped in front of him, feigned rearing up, and then darted forward, stabbing him in the side. The ridged spear ripped through his clothes, into his flesh and was withdrawn a second later. Woo scampered backwards, avoiding another attack, and the creature followed. When it was close enough, Woo lunged forward and clawed the monster's throat with his right hand, then struck his chest with an open palm attack.

The impact hurt the snake creature and sent him slithering away. Woo advanced and was about to deliver a palm strike to the back of the creature's head, when the being emitted a cold aura that stifled him long enough for the creature to turn and stab him in the left leg. The creature pulled the weapon away, removing pieces of uniform and flesh with it. Woo bent down, more out of reaction than pain, and the creature struck him again, this time delivering a glancing blow to his right arm that tore cloth and fleshy tissue, as the ridged weapon passed his arm.

In obvious pain, Woo limped away fairly quickly until he hit the wall and couldn't back up any further. The creature, sensing its victim's demise, took its time and slithered closer, savoring the kill. The creature stopped directly in front of Woo, rose up to its full height and darted its forked tongue in and out of its mouth, as if tasting the air. Woo became enthralled by its tongue's movement and lowered his guard. The creature saw that he did, hissed and lunged forward, plunging its weapon into his exposed

Demon's Quest The Beginning of the End Vol II

stomach. Woo snapped out of his hypnotic trance screaming, and immediately grabbed the weapon with both hands, falling to his knees. The creature released the weapon and emitted another cold blast, freezing him to the bone and leaving him in excruciating pain.

****

Tonles saw a faint blue-light emitting from somewhere up ahead and when he heard someone scream; he ran. When he reached the gate, he saw his comrades battling two blue and white creatures, which he recognized at once as the dreaded Coldtilians. Sun was winning his fight, but Woo was on his knees with a trident jutting out of his stomach and a Coldtilian a few feet in front of him. He gripped the gate and lifted with every ounce of strength he had, and despite being stronger than most humans, he failed to lift it. Angered, he tried prying the bars apart.

As soon as Woo fell to the ground, the third Coldtilian emerged from the hole and slithered over biting him on the leg. Woo screamed as the razor-sharp teeth sunk deeply into his calf muscle. The other Coldtilian, thinking it was taking its meal, grabbed his arm, and began dragging him towards the hole. Sun had just killed his creature and when he heard Woo's cries. He turned and saw them dragging him towards the hole. Acting quickly, he ran over and leapt through the air with a side-kick, aiming for the back of the closest Coldtilian. The creature sensed him, dropped Woo's arm, and ducked under Sun's attack and then slithered after him.

The Coldtilian bit down harder on Woo's leg and began to enter the hole. By the time the creature's upper torso was the only part of its body outside of the hole, Woo realized that he wasn't going to fit through the hole in one piece and became horrified. With his left leg firmly in the creature's mouth, he placed his right foot on the side of the wall and began pushing, countering the creature's strength and stopping his descent. A fierce tug of war ensued with the creature pulling its morsel closer towards its children and the desperate man pushing in the opposite direction. Woo's adrenalin increased, and with it, his strength. He began pulling his left leg out of the hole along with the creature. The Coldtilian desperately moved its rear legs, trying to pull Woo's down into the hole, but Woo held fast and then suddenly, bent at the waist and raked the creature's face with his fingers. He wrapped the other hand around its throat and forced the Coldtilian to open its mouth and released his leg. Blinded, hurt, and gasping for air, the creature did the only thing it could and sent forth a wave of coldness that caused Woo to let go of it and allow it to slither down the hole. Woo fell back, exhausted, and fell unconscious shortly thereafter.

Sun and the last of the Coldtilians were locked in a fierce battle, and despite not having its trident, the Coldtilian was still a formidable foe with its claws and mouth. The creature bit and slashed Sun several times, tearing through his garments as if they were mere parchment. The martial artist was slowly losing the battle, and would have eventually done so, if he hadn't placed his head within reach of the creature's claws. The creature took the bait and when it swung at his head, Sun timed his move perfectly, ducked under the attack while punching it on both sides of its ribs, crushing bones and cartilage and sending it slithering away. The Coldtilian moved toward the hole in a desperate attempt to leave the room.

Sun gave chase to ensure it wouldn't take Woo down with it, and as he was falling on the creature, it blasted him with the last of its cold aura attacks directly in his face. The freezing effect enveloped his mind and body, causing him to lose his concentration and stumble away. The Coldtilian jumped on top of his shoulders and sank its fangs and claws into his shoulder, causing so much pain that it weakened his legs, and he dropped to his knees. Sun's strength was draining away and as he was about to fall over and succumb to the Coldtilian, the creature released its mouth and clawed its way around his back. The sudden movement snapped Sun out of his daze. As the Coldtilian reared its head back to bite his neck, Sun grabbed its claw with his left hand, dipped his right shoulder, and rolled forward until the creature was on its back staring up at him. Sun held him down and curled his left hand into a claw and grabbed the creature's throat. No matter how hard the Coldtilian flailed about, or dug its talons into his flesh, it couldn't break free from Sun's Dragon Claw technique. Sun tightened his grip until the creature stopped moving.

Sun looked over his shoulder, saw Woo lying motionless and got up and stumbled over. The first thing he noticed was the trident still lodged within his stomach, and his clothes soaked through with blood. He bent down, checking his neck for a pulse and was thankful when he found one, even though it was faint. Tonles stopped bending the bars and called for them. Sun was surprised and relieved to see him and dragged Woo over to the gate. He joined Tonles and together; they pried apart the rusty bars until there was enough room for them to squeeze through. Once they were out, Tonles came to the realization that Konafar might be facing a similar situation, scooped up Woo and ran off with Sun in tow.

****

Konafar construed that he was now facing some sort of trap and fought his way to his feet, taking up position next to the hole with his back towards the wall. He listened intently and heard the sound of something clawing its way toward the surface. It was faint at first and then grew louder. Just like the noise, the reddish hue and heat intensified as well. Squatting down and hefting Carnage into a high guard, he shifted his weight and shoulders further away from the hole and when his instincts told him something was there; he swung the sword as hard as he could.

The first red and black creature slithered under the attack, but the next two weren't as lucky as Carnage cut the first one in half and hurt its brother. In retaliation, the wounded creature emitted a heat aura, which felt like hot compressed air burning Konafar's face and arms, causing him to back away. Remembering the one he missed, Konafar turned his attention towards the center of the room, where a black and red snake creature, with arms and legs, grasped a small trident and was moving towards him. He recognized it at once as a Firetilian.

The Firetilian slithered to his left and moved forward in attack formation, with the weapon held firmly in front of him. Konafar met the creature, with his sword in the Pflug guard, and deflected several attacks while maneuvering his body in such a way that the ones he missed did little to penetrate his armor. The wounded Firetilian recovered and slithered out of the hole to join the fray.

Fighting both creatures at once kept Konafar on the defensive, and as he was growing tired and getting wounded, his curse triggered deep inside, which supplied his body with a surge of energy, making him fight like a possessed madman. Disregarding his safety, he shifted his body weight and brought Carnage down upon the wounded Firetilian's head, splitting the creature down the middle. The other Firetilian blasted him with its aura attack and instead of stopping the intruder, like expected, Konafar's curse enabled him to fight through the pain and intense heat. The creature continued to attack him until it found its mark and stabbed him in the side, through his armor and biting into his flesh.

The attack did little to slow him, and when he raised Carnage to end the reptilian's life, the Firetilian used the last of its heat aura attacks to bathe him in heat. Konafar brought Carnage down upon the creature's right shoulder and didn't stop until it exited through the Firetilian's left leg, slicing the creature diagonally in two. After the body fell away, Konafar stood erect for several seconds, breathing heavily, then toppled over exhausted, and overtaken briefly by sleep.

Tonles and Sun arrived shortly after Konafar's battle. They saw him lying motionless near the back of the room. Tonles placed Woo on the ground, and together they worked on the bars until they were wide enough to enter. He instructed Sun to get Breen, then climbed through the opening, rushing over to his friend. He was relieved to find him alive and did his best to comfort him until everyone else arrived.

Breen feared the worse when she saw Woo's pale face and the trident jutting from his stomach. Immediately, she went to work on him and removed the weapon by cutting around the injury with her dagger. After she was finished, she stitched his wound, applied an ointment, and made her way over to Konafar. She found it puzzling that he was wounded, but not severely enough to leave him unconscious.

Tonles told her about his condition and how he believed that when his energy was depleted, he would pass out. She never heard of his affliction and went about bandaging his wounds. When she was finished, she poured a bluish liquid down his throat that would rejuvenate his stamina. A few seconds later he opened his eyes. Konafar sat up, she handed him a few more vials of the blue liquid, told him what they were for and then tended to Woo. Meanwhile, Jacko guarded the hole until Tonles and Sun finished ripping the gate from the ceiling, using it to block the opening with the intention of discouraging, or at least slowing, any more Firetilians.

When they were through, Sun went to the entrance of the cave to stand guard, whereas Tonles revisited the other chamber. He went over to the dead reptilians, cut into the bellies and removed a tiny blue sack. He knew the small casing contained the crux of their cold ability. After rejoining the others, he showed them his prize.

"What are they?" Jacko asked.

"These, my boy," he dangled one of the sacks proudly in the air, "are what gives the Coldtilians their special cold powers."

"Their what?"

"Cold powers. When threatened, they can radiate cold."

"What do we do with them?"

"Smear the liquid inside the sack across your weapon. It will add a chilling effect that stuns their nervous system and gives them pause for a second or two."

"How do you know?"

"Some fool used it on me once, but before he could end my life, one of my brothers beheaded him. The red ones have them too, but theirs will burn like a branding iron. Hold these." He said, handed them to Jacko and then went about removing the sacks from the Firetilians.

By the time Tonles finished retrieving the rare items, Konafar was on his feet, and Breen was finished doing all she could for Woo. Tonles gave a red sack to Breen and Konafar, kept one for himself, and gave Jacko a blue one. He then explained how to coat their weapons without getting the liquid on their hands and said to use it sparingly. Just as he finishing with the instructions, Sun came running down.

"We've got trouble." He said.

"What is it?" Konafar asked.

"A small group of boarmen and goatmen are heading towards the cave."

"Do you think they're from Redden?" Breen asked.

"I don't know, but given their size; I think they're some sort of scouting party."

"Well let's give them a group welcome, shall we?" Konafar said and smiled.

"I don't think that's a good idea. If they are a scouting party and go missing, then the rest of them will come searching for them, and we'll be trapped down here." Breen added.

"Good point. Alright, let's stay down here and fight only if we have to. After they leave, I want someone to follow them and find out if they are from Redden. Are they close by?"

"Real close." Sun replied.

"How did you see them?"

"I went outside to check on the horses and heard them."

"Did you put out the fire?" Jacko asked him.

"I did, but it still smolders."

"We'll need someone to hide outside the cave in case they send for reinforcements." Breen stated.

"That sounds like a perfect job for me." Tonles answered before anyone else could offer.

"Make sure you count the heads of those who enter, and if there are less men when they leave, kill them all. Do you understand?"

Tonles chuckled. "My sentiments exactly. Here take this." He gave the last blue sack to Sun. "Jacko will explain." He said and then ran off.

Jacko explained how to use the liquid to Sun, while applying it to his finger knives.

Konafar and Breen moved Woo toward the back of the room, extinguished the torches, and joined the others by the passageway leading upwards.

Situated behind a large boulder with the mouth of the cave plainly in view, Tonles watched a group of fourteen Chatar, and Hurnol enter the cave. His knuckles turned white as he gripped the axe handle, and it took all of his reserve to stay the weapon from doing its job. After they were gone, he crept closer to the opening and hid behind a tree waiting with his only companion, the falling snow.

The scouting party entered the cave, and right away the captain, a big Chatar, sensed something was amiss. He walked over to the extinguished fire and bent down, while running his hand over the smoldering ashes.

"They're either still here or they left within the hour. I'm guessing they're below. You two," he snorted and pointed to two of the goatmen in the back, "go back and tell the others what we found. I want you four to wait here and guard the cave. The rest, you're with me." The boarman said, and led them below.

****

Tonles observed two goatmen leaving the cave and as fortune would have it, they were walking straight towards his tree. He lived for the rush of the kill and waited until they were parallel to where he was, before

Ripper sang the song of death and dismemberment, cleaving them both in half. Admiring his handiwork, he turned to a nearby tree.

"That was easy, don't you think." He said chuckling at his own humor. He quickly threw their body parts away and went back to watching the cave, hoping for and wanting, more fun.

At the bottom of the passageway, Konafar and Sun waited on the left while Jacko and Breen stayed poised on the right. They watched the eight silhouetted forms, with their weapons drawn, walking toward them. While Breen was thinking about her pending fight, sweat began dripping down the sides of her body.

"This was a good sign." She thought, because every time it happened before a battle, she fought bravely, more focused, and more determined to win.

When the enemy was halfway to the bottom, the lead goatman suddenly halted them, as if he was sensing something waiting for them below. Several seconds later, he threw his torch below, and it landed a few feet behind Jacko. Instead of continuing down further, or saying something, they started slowly retreating backwards.

Konafar thought they were discovered and rushed toward them from his hiding place. He was followed by the others. Before the enemy could react, Konafar caught up to them and brought Carnage upwards, from the tail guard, into the first boarman's groin. The creature gasped and didn't utter another sound as the weapon passed right through his body, exiting out of the top of his head. Then in one continuous motion, Konafar turned his blade downwards into the thigh of a goatman, cutting his limb in half and sending him rolling down the passageway screaming in pain.

Jacko saw a Chatar closing in on Konafar, and before he could reach help, Konafar turned at the last second and rammed his sword through his stomach, killing him instantly. Sun raced past them both and engaged a Hurnol who was moving down the slope. The goatman jabbed twice at Sun, before his spear was grabbed and he was kicked square in his knee cap, breaking the bone and sending him rolling away in pain.

Breen moved in front of a rather large boarman and deflected two of his attacks with her shield before the Chatar slammed into her shield with his and pressed forward, driving her downwards. After Jacko killed the Chatar, he engaged a goatman, defensively sidestepped him and blocked several attacks before grabbing his spear, jerking him closer and stabbing his arm with finger-knives. The fluid from the Coldtilian sack numbed the Hurnol's limb and caused him to drop his weapon. Jacko sliced his throat and killed him.

Sun charged after another boarman, blocked his sword and struck him in the face with the Dragon Claw, digging two of his fingers into his eyes and blinding him. The creature wailed in pain, Sun punched him in the throat, crushed his larynx and sent him rolling down the passageway. Unfortunately for the Chatar fighting Breen, his comrade rolled right into his legs and was distracted enough for Breen to slice open his belly, causing his innards to spill out onto the earth. The last goatman turned to try escaping, but Sun was quicker, grabbed him by the armor and pulled him backwards into the waiting pommel of Konafar's blade. The goatman was knocked out with a thud.

In the aftermath of the fight, Sun left to find Tonles; Breen checked on Woo, and Jacko searched for materials to make a carrier for his classmate.

When the remaining party members heard the screams from their comrades they became so frightened they ran from the cave. They never saw or even heard Tonles as he came out of hiding and sent them to the afterlife.

When Sun came out of the cave, he saw Tonles hunched over four dead bodies, searching them for anything of worth.

"Did any of them escape?" Sun asked.

"They tried." He grinned.

"None of us got hurt."

"Good. Help me hide the bodies and then we'll go back inside."

Breen finished her assessment of Woo and walked over to Konafar.

"I don't know if we can move him in his present condition." She said.

"We can't stay here, so we'll take him to Wistful and hope it's not too late." He replied.

Just then Tonles and Sun came down the passageway toward them.

"Did anyone get away?" Konafar asked, despite knowing that he didn't have to.

Tonles grinned proudly. "No."

"Nice work. We need to get Woo to a healer, so help Jacko look for something to carry him out of here.

Due to a lack of materials, they decided the gate was their best option to carry him out. As they were shaping it into a carrier, Breen did one final analysis on Woo and came over to them. By the look on her face, they knew what she was going to say before she uttered a word.

"Woo has passed." Her voice was sad.

Tonles took the heavy gate and threw it against the wall in frustration.

Jacko's heart sank for his classmate.

"Let's get out of here." Konafar said.

They left the cave and found a suitable place to bury him. When the last of the stones was placed on his body, Konafar looked at them then started speaking.

"I believe we owe our friend Woo some revenge." His voice sounded sinister and cold.

"We do." Jacko chimed in.

"Let's find out where the rest of them are hiding."

They followed the rocky wall eastward until they came upon a small passageway leading upwards. It was shortly before nightfall, and they figured it was the perfect time to discover anyone making camp for the evening. Tonles had really good eyesight at night and took the path alone. When he reached a part of the trail overlooking the entire area, he quickly discovered thick smoke rising above the trees just south, indicating he'd found what they were looking for. After returning, it was decided that Sun and Konafar would go investigate while Jacko, Tonles, and Breen stayed behind.

Sun and Konafar walked for an hour before coming upon the encampment and positioned themselves on a small bluff overlooking the enemy. A small number of boarmen and goatmen were either walking around or sitting by a fire drinking. Two giants were seated towards the west side of camp drinking, and by the look of the jars at their feet, Konafar thought they should be drunk by now. A large war beetle, chained to several trees, was about twenty feet away from camp. It looked like it was sleeping.

Sun's gaze fell upon the lone human wearing platemail on the other side of camp.

He was engaged in conversation with a lot of boarmen and goatmen. "That must be their leader." He said, drawing Konafar's attention to where he was looking. "That's quite a large group looking for us, don't you think?" He added.

Konafar didn't reply and continued to study the man in the armor. "It can't be?" he said.

"What?"

"He looks like my friend Runit."

"In the green armor?"

"Yes."

Sun focused on the man. "Why would your friend be there?"

"He must have been captured when we raided the town. The bigger question is, why is he helping them? Wait here, I need to find out." Konafar said and left before Sun could protest.

"He's going to get himself killed." Sun said quietly.

Konafar pulled his cloak tighter to help hide his features, walked down to the ground level and around the bluff without incident or detection. For a big man, he moved effortlessly throughout the camp. The ones who saw him paid him no heed, because they were too inebriated to comprehend that an enemy would actually breech their camp. He eventually took up position near Runit, using the thick underbrush to listen to him speak.

"Is there any news from the scouting party?" When they didn't have an answer, he became angry. "I want you to take some men and search for them. If you happen to find the ones we are looking for, kill everyone except for my two brothers. I want them to join us."

"What do they look like?" A goatman asked.

Runit went on to describe Tonles and Konafar in great detail, and it took all of Konafar's restraint to fight back the urge to attack, because even though he was sure he could; the others would fall on him, and he would die. After listening for several more minutes, he returned to Sun and left the area.

Konafar told them what they had discovered, the number of men, giants, and the war beetle they had with them.

Tonles was the first to speak. "Runit is leading the enemy?" His angry reaction didn't surprise anyone. "Why does he want us alive? He has to know we would never be taken."

"I don't know why he wants us. Maybe he wants us to join his cause."

"Join him? He knows we would never do that."

"I think he might be under the influence of something."

"Like a drug?" Breen offered. "But that will wear off eventually."

"They're going to send another scouting party to find the others. We should either kill them or attack the main group."

"Attack the main group, the five of us? Are you crazy?" Breen said.

"It doesn't look like they'll stop searching for us. If you don't want any part of this, then leave."

"He's right," said Tonles. "They'll continue to look for us until we're either captured or dead. Sun and Breen, they don't know you, so you could actually escape. Jacko, I'm afraid he knows you personally, so I don't know if he'll stop looking for you."

"I'm in. I don't feel like running and hiding for the rest of my life." Jacko responded bravely.

"I will help as well." Sun added.

"Breen, if you still want to leave, then I suggest you wait in the cave until morning." Konafar told her.

"Let me hear your plan first then I'll decide." She said.

"I was thinking we have a couple of options. We could continue to ambush the search parties and play cat and mouse with Runit's troops until they are depleted, and then attack. However, I don't think he'll fall for that if the next party goes missing. Or we could attack tonight, under the cover of darkness, after the other group leaves."

"And how many men do they have?" Breen asked.

"The last time they sent around ten, so we should expect another group of that size. I'm guessing they have around thirty. You've got the two giants, Runit, the beetle, and maybe twenty of the boarmen and goatmen. I know it's not the best circumstances, but I'd rather fight them while they are unprepared and drunk."

"Good point. Plus we'll have the element of surprise on our side." Sun added.

"I've been thinking; we'll need a distraction for this to work," Tonles began, "and the best way to do that is to let the war beetle loose. I'm sure if the creature was on the rampage, everyone would be so preoccupied with it that we could get close enough to kill Runit and the giants."

"What about the others and the scouting party?" Jacko interjected.

"Trust me. Once Runit and the giants are dead, the rest will be so frightened and disorganized they'll run away. We won't have to worry about the scouting party either. If they return before we leave, they will have no interest in us."

"How do you plan on getting the beetle free? Breen asked.

"Should we use fire to excite the creature?" Sun asked.

"That would be the logical thing to do, given the fact that fire is a beetle's weakness; however, that isn't what we want because it might burrow underground until its body cools off. We need to damage the creature by striking its eyes, legs, or mandible. Konafar, what are they using to hold the creature?"

"Chains."

"I'm pretty sure the bug can break its restraints once we rile it up, when that happens it will lash out at anything nearby, be it friend or foe. Once freed, I'm assuming the giants will try to settle the creature, and that's when we'll attack. No matter what, we can't allow any more than one of the giants to control the bug, or it could be disastrous for us."

"Runit has to be confronted during this time as well."

"Who will attack what?" Jacko asked.

"We'll decide that after we enter their camp." Konafar stated. "Breen, we really could use your help."

She thought about it and agreed. "When do we leave?"

"Now, while the other scouting party is away."

By the time they reached the bluff, activity within the camp was down to a minimum. Tonles and Konafar quickly assessed the whereabouts of the giants, whom hadn't moved from their original spot, and Runit, who they figured would be in the largest tent near the middle of camp. Konafar gathered them close and spoke in hushed tones.

"Since Tonles is the strongest, he's the best choice for agitating the beetle. After doing so, he'll move back into the forest and wait for the giants to make their move. As they approach, he and I will attack them. Sun, I need you to go after Runit." Sun nodded. "Jacko and Breen, I want you to intercept all others that may interfere. Our plan must be adaptable, so if something happens to Tonles, Jacko you're with me. Breen, keep to your assignment; we'll need all the time you can give us. Does everyone understand?" They nodded.

"Can you spare me some throwing knives? I'm pretty good with them." Breen said.

After giving her the knives, they left.

Quietly, they climbed down the bluff, and snuck around the perimeter until they were in their assigned positions. Tonles was near the beetle. Konafar and Jacko were positioned behind the drunken giants. Breen was somewhere in between them, and Sun was further north, ready to move when the time was right. Tonles waited within the shadows of the trees until all but a few of their enemies were awake, then crept slowly into the camp.

When he was on the side of the beetle, with his back towards the woods, he raised his axe and brought it down into the hard shell. What he didn't expect after the impact split the exterior, was being sprayed in his face and body with bug's hot, bloody ichor. It sent him backpedaling into the forest where he tripped over a fallen log and bumped his head on the rigid ground. When Breen saw him fall, she took a mental note of his location and then remained vigilant for anyone who might interfere with their plans.

When Tonles attacked the beetle, he set off a chain of events that went as followed. First, the beetle shrieked so loudly it woke the entire camp, second; it yanked on its restraints, easily broke them and began trampling on anyone nearby. Third, most of the boarmen and goatmen began running for their lives when they saw the beetle free, and finally; the bug got the attention of the giants who then ran over to restrain it. Sun ran across the camp, killed the distracted guards posted outside of Runit's tent, and entered.

Konafar advanced on the giants from their left, and the trailing giant didn't see him until it was too late, with Carnage in mid-strike. The blade sliced through bone and cartilage and amputated both legs at his knees, leaving the helpless giant rolling on the ground bleeding to death. After he screamed, the other giant turned around, and as he was about to advance on Konafar, the war beetle wrapped its mandibles snugly around his waist and carried his meal off into the woods. After the beetle disappeared from view, Jacko and Konafar ran toward the green knight's tent while cutting down anyone who got in their way.

****

"So you're Runit the traitor." Sun said to the Green Knight after he came through the flaps of his tent.

Runit stood up from behind his table. "I'm grateful that you've come here to die." He coldly replied.

"You have that wrong. Right now, your camp is in disarray, and your old classmates are here to send you to the seventh layer of hell."

"Maybe they will, but I can tell you; you won't. Do you really think you have anything that can penetrate my armor?" He tapped on it a few times. "In fact, even if you did, I don't think you can defeat me, so you might want to run along and wait for your turn to die." Runit smugly looked at Sun, who believed there was something very disturbing about his appearance. Maybe it was his pasty white complexion, or the fact that his left eye twitched every time he spoke.

"Well let's see if that tin suit of yours can withstand my attacks." Sun said.

The Green Knight laughed at him, closed the visor to his helm, unsheathed his two-handed sword, and moved out from behind his desk to attack.

Sun had defeated other armored warriors before with his powerful kicks and punches, so he felt confident he would win, He met the charging warrior with a series of kicks that passed through his defenses, hitting him several times in the chest and arms. Although the force of the blows moved Runit in different directions, they had little to no effect on his armor, except for the loud, resounding thud.

The green knight recovered and countered with several slashing swings before lunging forward. Sun maneuvered and twisted his torso out of the way. After sidestepping to the left, he connected with Runit, hitting him squarely in the chest. The hard metal studs from the glove, coupled with the Iron Fist technique, dented the re-enforced armor, but not enough to cause any damage.

Runit smiled inside of his helmet and then feinted once to the left, while letting go of the hilt with his right hand, and thrust the blade singlehandedly at Sun's leading leg. At the very last second, Sun saw the attack and stepped backwards, but not fast enough, and was grazed by the sharp steel as it sliced through his garments.

Runit advanced on him, and Sun deflected his next two attacks before jumping up and kicking him in his chest, denting the armor further, and sending him stumbling backwards. Sun pressed in and stopped when Runit recovered and started swinging his weapon repeatedly in front of his body. As he continued, Sun moved side-to-side, searching for an opening, while purposely leaving his leading leg exposed again. Runit fell for the decoy and when he brought the blade down, Sun stepped away, causing Runit to overextend his attack and become off balance.

Sun stepped closer and punched the left side of the helmet repeatedly, causing a reverberating sound deep inside the metal shell that temporarily stunned his opponent. He continued to pound on the steel helmet, thus dazing Runit further, and then flipped open the visor to deliver a devastating blow, one that could end his life.

However, before he could, Runit regained enough of his senses to whip the flat part of the blade into Sun's side, cracking a few of his ribs and sending him to the ground. Runit stepped away, shaking his head trying to clear the cobwebs, which gave Sun time to get to his feet while gripping his side. He thought about escaping, but the entrance was on the far side of the tent, and he would never make it in time. So he resolved himself to the fact that he must finish his fight with Runit if he wanted to live.

Instead of hiding and waiting to be rescued, Tonles crouched into a waiting position with Ripper at the ready. His blindness would not leave him defenseless; he knew, as he thought back to the training the Order had often put them through. They never wanted their warriors to be at a disadvantage due to unforeseen circumstances, and now that it had happened to him; he was grateful for their painful, blindfolded lessons.

Tonles concentrated on the sounds around him and when he heard the footfalls of someone approaching, he timed his attack perfectly and removed his legs at the knees. His follow-up attack silenced him for good. A few minutes later, more feet came running in his direction, and by the time he finished swinging his axe of death, three more met their end in a similar fashion as the first. After the noises faded, he stood up.

Trailing behind the other three, a goatman stopped abruptly when a human holding a large axe suddenly stood up amidst the tall grass. He was ten feet away and couldn't comprehend why he wasn't attacked by the human. His fears shifted to bravery when he noticed the human turning his head to the right as if he was listening. The goatman grinned thinking there must be something wrong with him and decided to end his life. He raised his spear, took aim, and just as he was about to slay the motionless target, something struck him in the side of his head, then everything went dark.

Breen was moving through the woods looking for Tonles when she spotted the goatman near him. Tonles wasn't doing anything about the Hurnol. She knew it was too late to warn Tonles, so when the Hurnol aimed his spear, she threw a dagger and hit him directly in the temple. She hit him with another knife for good measure, and then called for Tonles. The big man was relieved to hear a familiar voice and lowered his axe.

"Are you okay?" Breen asked while walking over.

"I can't see a damned thing. I'm blind."

"That explains why you didn't see the goatman ten feet away."

"I heard something hit the ground. I'm guessing that was because of you?"

"You might say that."

"Thanks. I guess I owe you?"

"You do." She chuckled. "So how did it happen?"

"I got sprayed in the eyes by the beetle's blood after I hit it. Where is everyone else?"

"I don't know. Let's get out of here." She said, and guided him out.

After Konafar and Jacko entered the tent, they saw Sun off to the side and Runit closing in, ready to attack.

"RUNIT!" Konafar shouted his name, catching his attention and giving him a reason to pause.

Runit backed up a few paces defensively and grinned when he recognized Konafar. "Konafar, I'm glad you're here. I was looking for you." He said.

"Why are you leading these creatures?" Konafar demanded.

"I want you to join my quest."

"Your quest?"

"Yes. I was given a rank of command and want you to join me. I'll even make you second in command. Is Tonles with you? I want him to join me as well."

"You're insane."

"No. I'm empowered." Runit grinned.

"I'm only going to ask you once more. Drop your weapon and surrender."

"I can't."

"What does that mean?"

"You'll see." Runit said and suddenly dashed forward, swinging his sword in a wide arcing manner, which caused Jacko and Sun dive out of the way so they wouldn't be hit.

Konafar met him in the middle of the tent and the two men began fighting like rabid animals. They each parried a few attacks, grappled the other's weapon away, and then began wrestling on the ground. Konafar was bigger and stronger, but Runit countered his strength by being quicker and more nimble, even though he wore heavier armor.

They moved around so often that it prevented Jacko and Sun from getting close enough to help Konafar. One moment Konafar was on top of him, then in the next Runit flipped him over and held the position and so on. The rolling around stalled when Runit produced a knife and was trying to drive it into Konafar's face. Konafar grabbed his wrist at the last second, pushed his arm out of the way, rolled him over at the same time and pinned his arm down. Runit almost got free, but Konafar held his arm firmly in place with his left hand, grabbed his throat with his right and began squeezing.

Runit's eyes bulged as his life was slowly draining away. Then something strange happened. His demeanor changed from a hard looking person to someone waking up from a trance.

"Konafar…help…me." He pleaded.

Konafar squeezed harder, then changed his mind about killing him and released his hold. He grunted in frustration and stood up, while Runit went through a coughing fit.

Jacko picked up Runit's weapons and Sun handed Carnage back to Konafar.

"Get up and tell me what this is about." Konafar demanded.

Runit got to his feet. "I really don't know. I—"

"What do you mean you don't know?" Konafar demanded.

"I thought that I was dreaming until you began choking me."

"I don't understand. You sounded like you knew who you were talking to when I entered the tent."

Runit removed his helmet. His thick, wavy, dark hair, that was once the talk of the Order of the Dragon, was gone and his scalp was full of deep ugly scars.

Konafar looked on with horror. "Who did this to you?" He asked.

Runit put his hand on his forehead for a few long seconds. "My memory is a bit fragmented, and I don't remember everything, so bear with me." He paused. "During our raid, I was captured and led before someone wearing red platemail armor. He asked me many questions. At first, I resisted, but then…" He paused again, "he began flaying my skin… tearing it right off of the bones…" He paused once more, his eyes shifting in different directions. "It was horrible. Every time he removed my skin from my arms or legs, they smeared green ointment on it to stop the bleeding, but it did little for the pain… oh the pain was so great." He cringed. "MY ARMS… MY LEGS…" He stated, as if realizing for the first time what had been done to him, and then he began unbuckling his armor. "Look at what they've done to me."

After the first piece fell away, they now knew what he was talking about. There was nothing left but bones and the straps that held them in place. It was a horrifying sight for Konafar, Jacko, and Sun.

"How are you even still alive?" Konafar asked.

"I'm not sure. All that I know is that after they transformed my body into this…MESS…the worst was yet to come. I was visited by this being. Not physically, even though I thought he stood by my side on many occasions, but mentally. He tortured me while I was awake and when I slept, until my will was broken. I was led to believe that this Red Knight was my salvation, and I had to follow him." Runit looked away and when he turned back, his eyes were full of tears. "Kill me." He pleaded.

"No, we'll take you to a healer." Konafar replied.

"It's too late for that. A healer could never make his voice go away." He said and gripped his head.

"Runit, let me help you."

"There's no other way brother." He said and pushed Konafar into Sun, then punched Jacko in the face with the metal gauntlet; dazing him. The Green Knight grabbed his weapon away from Jacko, and as he turned to stab his friend, Konafar thrust Carnage into his midsection and straight through to the other side of the armor. Runit dropped his sword and fell to his knees, while looking into Konafar's eyes.

"Thank you for freeing me." He said, smiling, then fell over dead.

"This Red Knight and whoever possessed his mind will die for what they did to him." He looked down at his friend again. "This I promise." He removed his sword.

After Jacko was on his feet again they left the tent. They saw Breen and Tonles, wearing a cloth around over eyes, coming toward them. Breen explained what had happened to him, and Konafar told them what befell Runit and how he didn't have a choice but to kill him.

Tonles was angry, not at Konafar, but that Runit had died. "We will make them pay." He said.

"Yes we will." He paused. "Are your eyes going to be okay?" Konafar asked.

"I washed them out, so I think they'll be okay. I won't know for sure until later when I have more time to work on them." Breen said.

"Let's get out of here."

After leaving the enemy's camp, they traveled on horseback for a few miles then stopped for the evening. They lit two fires, a smaller one for Tonles and a much bigger one for everyone else. Breen continued her treatment on Tonles' eyes and when she was through, she instructed him to lie down and rest for a while. Reluctantly, he did so and then she rejoined the others. Once she was seated on an adjoining log; she rubbed her cold hands near the flames.

"How is he?" Sun asked Breen.

"To be honest, I don't know if he'll regain his vision. I cleaned out his eyes again and applied an ointment. We'll know within a few hours. What did I miss?"

"Nothing much, we were discussing what's next. Konafar wants to hunt down the Red Knight, and then go after whoever tortured and turned Runit into that monster," said Jacko. "I, on the other hand, have to go to Mirkin and stop someone from getting murdered."

"You never mentioned that before." Konafar suddenly said.

"I was told not to tell anyone." He lied so that Konafar wouldn't be offended. He went on to explain what had happened to teacher Ma, his encounter with the fox, and Ma's last request.

"It appears that we now have two objectives. Jacko needs to go to Mirkin, and Konafar wants revenge." Sun stated after Jacko was finished. "Konafar, are you set on taking your revenge right away?"

Konafar thought about the question. "It depends on Tonles, if I need to get him help, then that will be my priority. If he's okay, then I still want to sleep on it."

"Fair enough." Sun replied and looked at Breen. "What about

you?"

"I'd rather come with you and Jacko if that's okay? I can't go back to that town right now."

Sun nodded his approval and was glad she chose to go with them.

They stayed together for another hour around the warmth of the fire before getting up. It was decided Konafar would take the first watch, followed by Breen, Jacko, then Sun. After Konafar left to walk around the perimeter, Breen checked on Tonles then went to sleep. Meanwhile Sun and Jacko made themselves comfortable then went to sleep.

Tonles awoke a few hours later, removed his bandage, and found his vision hazy and clouded at first. Then everything came into focus. He looked at the fire's flames flickering before his eyes. He sat up and peered around the camp. Konafar, Breen, and Jacko were sleeping by the fire, and Sun was walking the perimeter with a glow rock to help illuminate his way. He got up and walked over to him.

"How's your vision?" Sun asked when he saw him approaching without the bandages.

"I can see again. I have to thank her. She saved my ass when I couldn't see and now has worked a miracle."

"I'm so glad she came with us."

Sun informed him about Jacko and Konafar's intentions.

"I'll talk to Konafar in the morning and try to convince him to come to Mirkin. Revenge can wait." Tonles said.

"And if he won't?"

"I guess I'll go with him, and we'll raise an army to do battle with this Red Knight character."

"Do you really think you could get one large enough?"

"No, but if that doesn't work, then we'll…"

Sun held up his hand suddenly and motioned to Tonles to stop speaking. They listened intently to the silence for several minutes and when Sun was satisfied, he lowered his hand and whispered. "I thought that I heard something."

They listened again and when nothing else transpired, they decided to part ways and continue talking in the morning.

Tonles went back to his bedding while Sun continued walking around, but this time he kept the glow rock closer to his body to help conceal his presence further.

With the arrival of dawn came unusual warmer weather, which was rare for this time of the year, but welcomed by the group as they rose to eat. Before Tonles and Konafar ate they spoke privately and when they were finished, they joined the others.

"I have made a decision." Konafar began as he looked flatly at Jacko. "We have decided that you will need our help, so we will make sure you get just that."

The announcement brought a smile to everyone's face.

"Thanks, and when I'm through you can count on my help as well." Jacko responded.

"Were not that far from Mirkin, I think we'll be there in a few more days or so." Sun added, then continued eating the sweet red berries and nuts he'd gathered from the nearby trees.

When their bellies were full and the fire was extinguished, they galloped toward Mirkin and the looming forest that stood in their way.

CHAPTER 9: THE ANNIHILATION OF A RACE

By mid-afternoon Tonles and the others arrived at the forest.

"Mirkin is on the other side." Jacko said after everyone slowed their horses.

Breen's eyes were riveted on the forest. "How is that possible?" She said drawing, everyone's attention to her.

"How is what possible?" Tonles asked.

"The forest is bathed in fog. Usually, the temperature dictates when fog forms in an area. I've seen it happen after the weather turns from cold to warm."

"Fog? Who cares?" Konafar said.

"Maybe it was warm before we arrived." Sun added.

"Doubt it, because if that were true, then the fog would have dissipated already and not still clinging to the trees." Breen countered.

"Are you afraid little girl?" Konafar said jokingly.

"No just cautious." She snapped.

"Come on its only fog. It's not like there's a fire-breathing dragon."

"You're funny." She said looking at him.

"Plus, I don't feel like traveling for days to go around it, so I think we should go in."

"I don't like the feeling I'm getting from the forest." Breen sternly added.

Konafar moved his horse closer to hers. "Come on, I'll protect you."

"And who will protect you?" Tonles added and then laughed.

Sun continued studying the forest while the others were bantering back and forth. "This might sound strange, but I think the trees are shifting." He announced.

Tonles turned his attention toward the forest and looked at the trees for several seconds. "You're crazy. Trees can't move, maybe it's the wind blowing the branches back and forth."

"Can we just decide if we should go in or around? I don't want to be here all day." Jacko asked.

Tonles looked at Konafar, and they wanted to go in. Sun still wasn't sure if what he saw was true, but agreed to go anyway. Breen, still miffed about the fog and what Sun said about the trees, actually contemplated turning around and leaving, but eventually decided it was safer to stay with them, and agreed.

"I suggest we leave the horses behind." Konafar added.

"Why?" Jacko quickly responded.

"The forest is too dense, and they'll only slow us down."

They quickly agreed to set the horses free and entered.

Inside the forest, it grew darker and foggier the further in they walked. Most of the trees, whether fallen or standing upright, were covered with a thick black and yellow moss that ran from the base all the up to the tips of their branches.

"Has anyone ever seen this kind of moss?" Sun asked the group.

"I've studied different mosses and this one is unknown to me, so I suggest we stay clear of it." Breen said.

They took her advice and picked their way over and around the trees.

Shortly before nightfall, they stumbled onto an abandoned encampment.

Konafar knelt down before the remains of the campfire and studied the charred and blackened wood. "It appears that a small group made camp less than a few weeks ago. I think it will be safe for us to stay here for the night." He said.

After gathering enough wood for the evening, they lit a small fire, ate, and sat around enjoying the warmth of the fire. As the hours passed, the temperature grew colder, and a light rain began to fall through the thick canopy, causing everyone to don their cloaks to help ward off the chill. Within an hour, a steady rain began to fall.

"How is this possible? There is no way all this rain can pass through the trees." Tonles said looking upward and pulling his wet cloak tighter.

After another hour, the fog grew thicker and the rain increased to the point that their clothes were soaked through. The fire was consistently hissing in protest of being extinguished.

"Now what do we do? It's too late and foggy to go looking for a better place to camp." Breen said in disgust and stood up, acting like she wanted to leave.

"Are you thinking about leaving?" Jacko said to her.

"Look. I'm cold, tired, and wet." She replied.

"This is why I don't travel with women. They complain about everything." Konafar said.

Breen shot him a look that if looks could kill, he would have been a dead man. She made a motion, as if she was about to storm off, when Sun stood up, staring directly at Konafar and said.

"Stop giving her a hard time."

Konafar's smile faded, and the big man stood up to his full height. "You should watch your tongue."

"You're not helping the situation."

"No one speaks to me like that." Konafar said in a challenging tone and rested his hand on Carnage. He started feeling angry.

When Breen gripped her sword, Tonles knew where this was going. He stood up and looked at his friend. "He's right, leave her alone."

Konafar looked at him and then at Sun. "I need to get away from you people." He said and walked off.

Jacko got up and was about to go after him, when Tonles spoke. "Word of advice boy, let him cool down. He's not used to someone standing up to him."

Jacko nodded and sat down on the wet log.

"Sun, that was gallant, but very stupid. You really don't want to challenge him in any way, unless you expect a fight." Tonles said, then sat down with his back against a tree.

"He has to know when to stop."

"I'm tired." Tonles announced and closed his eyes, letting the matter drop.

Breen touched his arm in a way to get his attention and thanked him. He smiled back at her.

****

Konafar activated a glow rock and walked around the area trying to cope with what had just happened. He didn't know why he got so upset with Sun for coming to Breen's defense. He felt rage toward the man, and if it wasn't for Tonles' quick words, he might have attacked not only him, but anyone else that got involved.

A short time later, he heard something moving across the tree tops and then stopped somewhere overhead. He hid the light source, unsheathed Carnage, and listened. For many heart-pounding minutes, there was only silence. He looked upward, but the fog made it impossible to determine where this thing was.

After several minutes, he began moving quietly back to camp. After taking a few steps, the sound of claws scraping against bark clearly indicated that something was climbing down a nearby tree. He quickly grew fearful and hid behind the closest one and watched intently in the direction of the noise. Bathed in the moonlight and fog, he saw the outline of a very large creature, with horns about the length of a man's arm, climbing down the tree a few yards away. The creature slowly and methodically descended until it was a quarter of the way, then it flattened itself against the bark, and become one with the structure. The creature's ability to blend in with its environment was perfect, even though Konafar knew where it was.

A few seconds later he lost track of the beast altogether. Both he and the creature remained motionless for several long minutes, until suddenly the creature lifted his head, turned around with remarkable agility, scampered up the tree, then ran along the treetops in the opposite direction of their camp. Breathing a sigh of relief, he hurried back.

Back at the campsite, they were sitting around the fire when they heard something quickly running in their direction. They were on their feet instantly, with weapons drawn.

A few seconds later, Konafar came rushing in. "We need to leave this place right now!" He said breathing heavy.

"Why?" Sun asked.

"There's something in the woods, and from what I saw, it's big and can walk along the treetops."

"We can't leave, it's too dark." Breen said.

"I don't care. That thing can even camouflage itself to blend in perfectly with its surroundings."

"Does anyone know how far it is to the other side of the woods?" No one knew.

"Are you sure it's headed in our direction, because we didn't hear anything while you were gone." Sun asked.

"No. It ran towards the west, but that doesn't mean that it won't come this way."

"Can anyone track our way in the dark?" Tonles asked.

They shook their heads no.

"I think we'll be safer here with the fire instead of running aimlessly through the woods."

"If that thing comes back, we're going to have our hands full."

"We should be safer here by the fire if it's nocturnal." Tonles added.

"Why is that?" Breen asked.

"They usually hate fire."

"We should add more branches to the fire just in case and use them as weapons." Sun said.

After doing so, Sun and Konafar took first watch while the others slept.

Jacko dreamt he was standing in a meadow. Large fluffy clouds dotted the sky; water trickled from a nearby stream, creating a serene sound, and trees with their many-colored leaves, set the stage for a beautiful autumn day.

His attention was suddenly drawn to the large wooden table on his right. Seated there was his mother, father, sister, grandfather; Aurora covered in blood, Torhan, and a female made of wood. He walked over and sat down.

The wooden lady was speaking of troubled times ahead and pointed at Aurora on several occasions saying that she would die, which caused her to cry tears of blood. She turned to Torhan and said he was in grave danger from an unknown entity and would die if he didn't have help. After she was through talking, his mother also spoke of ill times to come and at one point, reached over and touched his hands, telling him everything would be okay.

Suddenly, the sky darkened and rain began to fall in thick sheets. Jacko could feel the wetness against his skin. The wooden lady looked directly at him.

"I'm here in these woods, and I have news about Torhan. My name is Ailith, seek me out." She said.

Jacko awoke a short time later and sat up. It was still dark out, and everything seemed peaceful. Sun, Tonles, and Konafar were sleeping nearby, but Breen was missing. Most likely, she was keeping guard. He laid back down, thinking about his dream and the meaning of it. He was about to write it off as just a dream when he heard a female's voice whisper gently over the light wind.

"Jacko, I'm here in the woods, seek me out."

At first he thought it was his imagination playing tricks on him when she spoke again.

"Look for the camp to the east and take the path leading south."

Frantically, he sat up and looked around. He thought about waking Sun, but when the voice didn't return, he decided not to.

"Good you're awake. It's your turn to keep watch." Breen said as she was walking over.

"What?" He turned his attention to her.

"Are you okay?"

"Yes, I just had a weird dream. What time is it?"

"Still have a few hours before dawn."

"Did everything go okay?"

"Nothing eventful happened. Come on, I need sleep." She said, wrapping her cloak around her.

After Jacko got to his feet, she laid down on his bedroll and was asleep within minutes.

When dawn finally arrived, the rain ceased, the fog lifted and everyone else rose and began gathering their equipment.

Jacko walked over to Sun. "I need to talk to you privately."

"Is everything alright?" Sun could tell something was troubling him.

"Sort of."

"What is it?"

"Let's talk away from the others."

Jacko told the others they needed to talk about something very personal and followed Sun deeper into the woods.

When he knew they were far enough away Sun stopped him.

"What is it?" He asked.

"I had a dream…"

"So did I." Sun interrupted and smiled.

"Let me finish. The dream involved my family, Torhan, Aurora, and a wooden lady who predicted ill times ahead for me. She also had information about Torhan."

"So? It was just a dream."

"I don't think so. The wooden lady told me to seek her out in these woods."

"It's just your subconscious jumbling events together."

"Normally, I would agree with you, but after I woke a voice said for me to travel east until I come to a camp, then take the path leading south."

"I think this place is playing tricks on you."

"Make me a deal then. If there is a camp to the west and a path leading south, we'll investigate."

Sun thought about it, then agreed. "What about the others?"

"If they don't want to come along, I'll go by myself."

"You won't have to as long as I'm with you, but we'll try to convince them anyway."

They walked back, grabbed their belongings, and left.

They proceeded eastward, with weapons drawn, and eyes constantly scanning for the creature Konafar had encountered. Breen noticed birds were no longer chirping or critters scurrying about, there was only stillness.

Around midday, they came to a part of the woods where the trees looked sickly and dead. Leaves that would normally be the colors of orange, yellow, or brown were a strange shade of gray. They were standing around accessing the area when a thick pungent smell of death wafted further westward catching their attention as it began to fill their nostrils. Tonles didn't want them to wait around longer than they had to, and led them in that direction.

After another mile or so later, they came to an area that appeared to be the beginning of someone's campground. Pots, pans, and plates were thrown everywhere, and an unrecognizable carcass still hung over a burnt-out fire. While they were walking through the knee-high grass, Breen tripped over something solid and fell to the ground. After regaining her footing, she discovered that it wasn't a log she tripped over, but an armless, headless corpse.

She gasped in horror. "There's a body over here." She said.

"That explains the smell." Konafar said.

"The smell is too strong for just one, there must be more." Sun added.

The area continued to reveal many more surprises; arms holding weapons, legs, feet, torsos, organs, and severed heads from a race of creatures that no one recognized. Further in, they came to the main camp and there was more of the same. The amount of carnage was so brutal that Konafar said he'd never seen such a scene before. From the state of decay that the bodies were in, Tonles surmised the fight had taken place only days ago.

"What could have done this to them?" Breen asked no one in particular.

"Let's not linger any longer then we should." Tonles warned.

They were passing through the camp when Jacko noticed a large path leading to the south. He showed it to Sun.

"Do you think that's it?"

"It has to be."

"Are you really sure you want to go?"

"I need to find out if this Ailith person is down there."

Sun nodded, and they walked over to Konafar.

"Konafar there's a path over there that I need to take." Jacko said.

"What path?" The big man glanced at him, and Jacko pointed to it. "Why?"

"Because I have to."

"What do you mean you have to? We need to leave this hellish place." Konafar snapped at him.

"I know, but I have to go there."

"Then explain yourself."

"I had a dream…"

"A dream?" Konafar interrupted. "You're going there because of a dream?"

"It's a long story."

"I'm not staying here another night."

"If I'm not back in an hour, then leave, and I'll meet you on the other side of the forest."

"You've got to be kidding me? You do remember the thing I told you about that still roams this forest?"

"I know, but I still need to go."

Tonles and Breen walked over.

"What's going on?" Breen asked.

"He says he needs to follow the path over there because he saw it in a dream."

"A dream!" Tonles said.

Jacko proceeded to tell them about his dream and the voice he heard while he was awake.

"So you are following a dream and a voice you think you heard?"

"I'm not asking you to come with me. Just wait here for an hour, and if I'm not back, I'll meet you on the other side of the forest."

"Do you want to go?" Tonles asked.

"This will be the last time we do something like this if it turns out to be a waste of time." Konafar added.

"Agreed." Jacko said.

Breen slung a short bow over her shoulder that she'd found a few minutes before.

"Where did you get that?" Konafar asked her.

"I found it over there near a corpse." She then secured a quiver full of arrows around her waist.

They followed the road through a series of twists and turns until they reached a huge pond with a small island in the middle and an uprooted tree lying on its side. The area, just like the camp, was once a place of beauty.

"There's nothing here but death and decay." Konafar stated.

"Jacko where is she?" Tonles asked looking around.

"I don't know. Maybe she'll show up." Jacko said.

"It's going to be dark soon, so we should get going."

Jacko was about to agree and leave, when he noticed a pair of booted footprints leading into the water.

"Let's go." Konafar nudged them again, turned around and began walking away.

Breen and Tonles did the same, hoping their actions would convince Jacko and Sun.

"They're right we shouldn't linger here much longer." Sun said and took a few steps away.

Jacko surveyed the area and was about to follow them when he heard a faint voice.

"Help me please." A female voice said from somewhere on the other side of the pond. "Please, I am dying." The voice begged.

"Where are you?" Jacko said aloud, causing the others to stop walking and turn around.

"I am on the island." The voice said to him, so low that only Jacko's ears could hear her. Jacko stared at the island and said.

"What is she?" Sun asked him.

Jacko ignored him. "I don't see you?"

"I'm the...tree... please..." The voice seemed to become weaker with every word.

Jacko looked at Sun. "I'm going across. Wait for me." He said, and entered the chilly pond.

"Now what? Has he gone mad?" Konafar asked.

"Why is he going across? There's nothing on that island but a dead tree." Tonles added.

Sun joined the others and sat down after Jacko climbed onto the island.

Jacko waded across the water and when he reached the small island, he found a strong foothold and pulled himself up. Leading up to the tree were the same size footprints that he'd seen on the other side and very large paw prints around the entire area.

Jacko approached the tree and could tell by the way it was positioned, that only a creature of substantial size could've actually toppled it. Claw marks marred the bark so much that sap flowed freely like they were wounds.

Taking it all in, he finally said. "Are you Ailith?"

"I'm glad you decided to come here." Her voice sounded weak and Jacko definitely knew it was coming from the tree.

"I'm here because you said you know Torhan. I'm not sure how you've come to know this information. Did you read my mind?"

"I can commune with the living if I know about them."

"What are you?"

"I am a Tree Spirit, and I need your help."

"Why should I help you?"

"Because I can give you information about Torhan that will save his life."

"Tell me what you want and then I'll decide."

"If you promise to avenge my death against the one that did this to me, then I will tell you."

"What information could you possibly have about Torhan? How did he end up here in this forest and in front of you?"

"Do you promise to help me?"

Jacko was hesitant to give his word, but given the fact that he'd never found Torhan in Redden, and it was possible that he had traveled this way; he agreed. "I can't promise that I'll be able to slay this monster, but I will do my best." He looked at the paw prints again thinking he might not be able to at all. "Alright?"

"Agreed. Torhan visited me a short time ago and is in grave danger," she began, "not by the creature that has wounded me beyond life, but by something far more powerful and is known to your kind as a demon."

"Impossible! Demons don't exist. You speak lies tree."

"They do exist and this one, in particular, is very powerful and will stop at nothing to achieve his goals."

"Nonsense." Jacko said in anger.

"Believe what you want."

"Then tell me why?"

"He made a deal with him to assassinate the priest in Mirkin."

"He would not willingly make a deal with anyone, be it man or demon. And he isn't an assassin, so he must have been tricked."

"Demons are very cunning, and yes; he was tricked by the demon because he appeared as a human and went by the name of Grappin."

"Let's say I do believe there are demons. Why is he in danger?"

"If he doesn't live up to his end of the bargain the demon will kill him."

"How did you meet Torhan?"

"Lord Sim sent him to me."

"Who?"

"Lord Sim, he leads a race of beings that inhabit these woods."

"Why did you help him?"

"I merely answered his questions and revealed the demon's true identity. I also told him how to defeat him."

"So how did you know Grappin was a demon?"

"We tree spirits know much, and demons, just like all creatures, give off signature vibrations that enable us to see through their disguises and..." Ailith's voice trailed off into silence.

While waiting patiently for her to speak again something scurried across the treetops toward his direction. Jacko knew at once that the creature coming his way was the same being Konafar had encountered. There was nowhere for him to go, so he quickly jumped into the water and hid along the side of the island.

"What's that?" Breen asked as soon as she heard something scurrying high above.

"I knew this was a bad idea. We need to hide; it's that creature from last night." Konafar barked.

"What about Jacko?" Sun asked.

"I saw him jump into the water." Breen answered.

"He'll need our help."

"If we want to have any chance of helping him, we'll need the element surprise."

"Why are we so scared? You've fought giants before." Breen asked him.

"Something tells me we should be really wary of this creature." Konafar said and ran off into the thicker part of the woods. The others followed.

****

The creature stopped directly over the island and then came crashing down on top of the tree with a thud, splintering wooden fragments in every direction. Jacko huddled closer to the island while carefully peering up. From where he was, he saw a very large, cat-like creature with horns that pointed backwards. The dark skinned beast was hairless, except for its big mane and was much more intimidating than Konafar had described it.

The cat remained as still as a statue for several minutes, then it arched its back and let out a horrifying roar that shook the forest. The creature's terrifying bellow scared Jacko as he drew closer to the island.

"Is that the creature you saw?" Eyes wide, Breen asked.

"That's it." Konafar answered.

"We need to do something. Jacko is going to get killed." Sun said.

"It hasn't seen him yet, because if it had, he'd be dead." Tonles added.

"What's it doing?"

"Just sitting there…wait…it's moving." Tonles said.

Slowly, and methodically, the creature sniffed the tree and then moved off of the log and did the same on the ground. Jacko glanced toward the shore, and his heart sank when he didn't see his companions there. He was terrified, alone, and escape was not an option. So he pushed aside his fears and equipped his finger-knives.

The sound of the creature sniffing drew closer to where he was, and after a few seconds, black and red horns emerged over the edge of the island. Jacko gripped a hanging root for support and was ready to strike the creature's throat when it appeared. The beast's head began to form, first the base of its horns, then the ears, and just as its large head was coming into view, it suddenly reared back, howling in pain and fell away from view.

Seconds later, he heard it jump into the pond and tread through the water. Jacko remained motionless until he heard screams coming from the shoreline. Fearing for his companions, he quickly peeled his eyes away looking at the shore. Instead of Sun and the others doing battle with the monster, he saw a group of well-equipped humanoids, covered in fur, engaging the beast.

The humanoids fought as a unit. They moved in, struck the monster and then quickly withdrew, allowing the others to do the same. The tactic confused and frustrated the big cat, but something was wrong with their weapons, because no matter how many wounds they inflicted; they never drew blood.

One of the defenders rammed his spear into the side of the creature, and as he tried to topple the brute, the cat reached out and ripped his head off with a quick swipe of its paw, then leapt onto two more defenders, tearing them apart with claws and teeth. Another humanoid tried to help his fallen comrades and was gored to death.

Jacko knew that if they failed to slay the monster, they would never leave this place alive, so he rushed across the water to help.

Upon seeing Jacko running for the shoreline and knowing what he was about to do; Konafar, Tonles, Sun, and Breen left their concealment to join the fray. When Jacko reached the shore, he took a running leap and jumped onto the cat's back, grabbing hold of its mane with one hand and stabbing it repeatedly with his finger-knives in the neck and head.

The monster, somewhat surprised by this, thrashed about trying to dislodge this pesky nuisance, but Jacko held fast until the creature jerked forward and threw him off and into the woods beyond.

After Jacko was gone, Breen took aim with the bow and shot the beast in the back. Her arrow, just like the rest of the weapons, failed to hurt the creature. Sun, Tonles, and Konafar engaged the cat. The latter was the first to land a blow to the creature's right leg, but instead of cleaving the limb off, Carnage stopped moving after it bit into its flesh. The creature whipped its head around and hit Konafar with the side of its horns, knocking the big man off balance and into Tonles, sending them both to the ground.

Sun punched the beast several times and was surprised when it had no effect. Another of Breen's arrows hit the creature's neck just as a defender, wearing a patch over his left eye, slammed his obsidian axe into the monster's torso. His weapon tore through flesh and bone, spraying everyone nearby with blood.

The beast reared back, jerking the weapon away from the bearer's hands, and howled a deafening scream, causing everyone to cover their ears and fall to their knees. The monster fell to the ground and violently convulsed.

Instead of falling over and dying, like everybody hoped, it grew several times larger. The weapon that was once lodged deeply into its chest was pushed out and fell to the ground. They watched in horror as the wound closed and the beast appeared to be unscathed again.

Several of the defenders rushed the cat, thinking they could now hurt it, but instead were rewarded with quick striking claws that mortally wounded them. Tonles was on his feet again and brought the full force of Ripper down upon the creature's back, and just like Carnage; it did little to no damage except for getting the creature's attention.

The monster whipped its body around with speed and agility. It was poised to claw Tonles, when an arrow flew by his head and pierced the creature's left eye, causing it to scurry backward, howling in pain. The one-eyed defender retrieved his weapon and swung his massive cleaver, hitting the creature's right leg and biting into his flesh and bone, sending the beast toppling away. More defenders closed in, and the cat jumped onto a nearby tree, scurrying upward until it disappeared from sight.

"Leave while you still have a chance." The one-eyed defender said to Tonles as he scanned the treetops.

Jacko came over holding his head.

"Who are you?" Tonles asked him.

"My name is Din. Now be quiet." Din listened for several minutes. "Human, take your people and leave. This is not your fight, and your weapons are…"

His words were cut short when the beast jumped out of the trees, landed on another of his kinsman and began tearing him to shreds within seconds. Tonles noticed the creature's leg was already healed, and he'd grown twice his normal size.

The monster roared with a new-found energy and leapt for Sun with his claws extended. The kung fu artist rolled out of the way and then had to use a series of maneuvers to evade the deadly attacks. Others tried to distract the beast with their weapons, but the cat ignored their feeble stabs and pressed Sun, keeping him on the defensive and driving him backwards until he tripped over a log and fell onto the ground. Konafar and Tonles rushed to his defense, but it was Din's quick action that saved Sun's life. He threw his two-handed axe, hitting the creature in the side. The beast yipped in agony and jumped high into one of the trees, disappearing from sight, along with the only weapon that actually hurt it.

"GO! We're finished." Din said to the humans.

"Come with us?" Tonles pleaded.

"No!" He snapped in response. "The beast will not stop hunting us until we are dead. You, on the other hand, have a chance to escape because it hasn't tasted your blood yet."

"It's not in my nature to leave a fight." Tonles said. Something deep inside of him drove the warrior and his need to help people against impossible odds. Maybe it was the bad taste left in his mouth when he failed to protect his friend from a group of thugs, or perhaps it was his chosen profession. Nevertheless, he wanted to help Din.

"It's pointless for you to die with us today. You do not even know us." Din sounded defeated.

"You don't have a chance either with your weapon gone." Breen told him.

Din smiled. "I still have this." He unsheathed a long silver stiletto and held it forth. The blade sparkled ever so slightly.

"What if I attack and…" Jacko was saying when the beast swooped down and attacked two more of Din's people, ripping one to shreds and cleaving off the head of the other.

Din screamed in rage and ran over. He was about to deliver an attack to the creature's neck, intent on cutting its throat when the beast turned around and gored him in midsection, piercing through his flesh and killing him instantly. With the death of Din, the rest of his countrymen broke off and ran in separate directions. The beast discarded Din's lifeless body with a twist of his neck, roared at Jacko and the others in warning, and then gave chase after the forest dwellers.

Din's clansmen ran north with the beast following closely behind, while the others ran eastward toward Mirkin. Sun led the group through the twisting, tangled, forest and shouted for them to run faster after they heard dying screams somewhere far away.

Exhaustion started over taking them a few miles later, and they were about to stop and catch their breath when they heard the familiar sound of something scurrying across the treetops.

"RUN!" Sun shouted.

"I'm getting tired of running." Tonles said, breathing heavily.

"We'll make our stand on the other side of the forest if we have to." Konafar said.

"Look there's an opening up ahead." Breen said when she saw a break through the trees and an open field beyond that.

When they were less than twenty feet away from the opening to the field, the beast landed on the ground and gave chase.

After clearing the trees, they turned around one-by-one to face the beast one final time. To their surprise, the creature stopped just inside of the forest and stared at them with hatred in its eyes. It growled and roared, but still didn't advance. It was as if there was some sort of force field erected and keeping him at bay. After several intense moments, the creature disappeared back inside of the forest.

"How can...that be...?" Breen said huffing and puffing.

"I don't care, let's get out of here." Tonles said.

"Let's head for those trees over there." Sun said.

They remained silent until they reached the small cluster of trees. After they were situated around the fire, Tonles spoke.

"In all my travels I've never seen a creature immune to weapons." He simply stated.

"It appears that silver and the axe Din was using hurt the creature." Sun added.

"But they didn't kill it either. Did you see that it could heal itself and double its size?" Jacko said.

"Now tell us why you needed to go to the pond? You almost got us all killed." Konafar said to Jacko, because he was still pretty mad at him.

"I'd like to know as well." Tonles added.

"The night before I had a strange dream that involved my family and a wood lady named Ailith."

Konafar was about to say something, but Tonles held up his hand signal to let Jacko finish.

"In my dream she mentioned my friend Torhan and the danger he was in."

"And that's what convinced you to go to the pond?" Konafar pressed.

"What convinced me to go to the pond happened after I woke from my dream. I heard a voice with almost the same exact message."

"Could it have been that creature that lured him down there?" Breen asked.

"No, because when I went to the island the tree actually spoke to me and told me about the danger Torhan was in."

"The tree had a mouth?" Konafar asked jokingly.

"No, it spoke using telepathy."

"Next time, involve us right away so we can at least be better prepared." Tonles said.

Jacko nodded.

"What did the tree say to you?" Breen asked.

"It, or shall I say, she, said he passed through the forest and was being pursued by a demon."

Tonles raised an eyebrow in surprise. "Demon? Here on earth? That's a child's bedtime story, there are no such things."

"Maybe so, but if he's not in Mirkin, then I need to go look for him."

"Does anyone think that creature could have been the demon she was referring to?" Breen asked.

"I don't think so, because she said that the demon was far more dangerous than the creature we fought."

"What's strange about this whole ordeal," said Sun, "was that if the creature always lived in the forest, then why did it take so long to go after Din and his people? And I wonder why it didn't pursue us after we stepped out of the forest. It had to sense that it was more than capable of killing us."

"Maybe it was bound to the forest somehow." Breen added.

"Maybe…or possibly it was told never to leave the forest. Therefore, that brings me back to my original thought. When did the creature appear? Din's people would've been killed off a long time ago."

"I guess there are questions we'll never have the answers to. The good news is that we should be inside of the city walls by tomorrow afternoon." Tonles said.

"Good. I need a hot bath and a hearty meal." Konafar said.

When morning arrived, they packed up their belongings and left.

CHAPTER 10: A DEMON'S RIGHT

Two moons after Jacko left the forest; Dybbuk passed through a portal and entered the place known as The Other. He found himself situated inside of a forest near the town of Mirkin. It was nighttime, the darkness did little against his keen sense of sight, and the smell of a nearby campfire didn't escape his senses either.

His first order of business was to take up the guise of a human and knowing them; he would most likely find some sleeping around the fire. Such easy targets relying on flames for warmth and protection, but on this night, it would lead to their deaths.

Smiling, he followed the aroma until it led him to a group of travelers camping for the evening. He counted four humans total. Three were sleeping in their blankets while one was sitting upright against a tree keeping guard. It was too easy for the demon as he made short work of them, but then again, it always was. Humans had inferior skills, and their weapons didn't pose any threat at all. The only thing they had going for them was their numbers, but eventually they wouldn't have that either.

He grabbed the closest corpse and removed his armor while being careful not to damage the material. What came next was savage by human standards as he ripped open the dead man's chest cavity and took hold of his intestine and tasted the organ. The bitter flavor disgusted him, but it was a necessary evil in order to transform him into an exact copy. When the transformation was completed and he looked exactly like the human, he stood erect and dressed in his armor, then strapped his two-handed sword across his back. He was now ready to embark on his journey to find out what had befallen his pet.

It took him several hours to find the woods where Darkener had entered. He was met by the sweet sound of silence. Birds did not chirp; animals didn't scurry about, and not even the bugs made a sound. The area felt dead, and that's the way he liked it.

The further in he traveled, the more he realized that he couldn't sense his pet's life force, which was strange and a little disturbing to him. A few hours later, he came upon a place where dead bodies decorated the area, all of which were either twisted or ripped to shreds in a horrifying fashion. Their deaths clearly indicated that Darkener had passed by at one time. Still not sensing his presence, he followed the trail of dead toward the south and arrived at a lake.

On an island in the middle of the lake was an uprooted tree laying on its side. A unique essence radiated from the tree, and he knew right away that he'd found the demon bitch. He crossed the lake, climbed onto the plateau and approached the broken and splintered tree.

"Well now. I didn't expect to find you here." Dybbuk said.

"Dybbuk, I am sorry." Ailith's voice was faint when she answered.

"SORRY!" He spat. "You've betrayed me and you're sorry? The only thing you're remorseful about is your pending death." He paused. "Did you really think you could've swayed my pawn into doing your bidding? You're nothing but a fool."

"Please help me back to our world and I will repent." She pleaded.

"The only help I will offer you is a quick passing into the abyss. However, I want you to take solace in knowing that your lover, and his underling Tam, are already waiting for you there. Now tell me where my pet is, and I'll send you on your way quickly."

Ailith knew that without his help with the passing, she would remain in these woods for many years, and that was a fate worse than the abyss. "He waits for you towards the east." She said.

Dybbuk unsheathed his sword, produced a small vial, and poured its contents all over the weapon. "Enjoy eternity." He said and drove the weapon into the trunk, twisting the blade back and forth until the wood split. The liquid did the rest and poisoned the root, cutting off the remaining life force.

A whimper echoed from within the tree and then all went silent.

Dybbuk left the area and headed eastward. Along the way, he encountered more mangled forms of Ailith's followers and only paused when he saw one, in particular. It was Lord Sim himself. His severed head rested beside what was left of his broken body. By the look on his face, Dybbuk could tell his last moments were ones of excruciating pain.

He knelt down and studied the ground. His sense of smell picked up his pet's scent somewhere southeast and he proceeded in that direction. His trail led him to a large circular clearing, and Dybbuk called out for his companion. Minutes later, the treetops towards the west rustled in response, and Dybbuk smiled with delight. As the noise drew closer, the joyful occasion quickly disappeared when he heard a loud thud somewhere nearby. Not the sound of his pet pouncing on the ground in a playful manner, but more like a fall.

Hurriedly, he moved toward the place and when he saw his pet laying down on the ground motionless, he ran over and knelt by his side. Darkener was sliced and stabbed in many places and covered in thick blood. The creature looked up at his master, took a few deep breaths, and died.

Dybbuk took his pet's head into his hands and stared into his lifeless eyes. The one thing he loved was dead and this angered the mighty demon immensely. He gripped his pet's head tighter and recited the ancient words of recall, thus entering Darkener's mind and began searching through his memories. Dybbuk saw everything from his entrance into the place known as The Other, to this forest. He saw the destruction of Ailith, the battle with Din and his people, the humans that escaped him and finally the epic battle between Lord Sim and Darkener.

Dybbuk was surprised that the aforementioned, like Din, had a weapon that could hurt his pet, so they battled back and forth, with each wounding the other several times. The dramatic conclusion came to an end when Lord Sim fatally stabbed Darkener in the chest, then his pet taking off his head in retaliation.

Dybbuk saw enough and stopped the chant. What puzzled him the most was why he allowed the strangers to escape and didn't kill them. Obviously, they were no match for him. A few seconds later, it finally dawned on him. He'd instructed his pet not to leave the forest until he returned.

The demon shook his head and said. "You were so loyal my pet. I will greatly miss you."

He spent the better part of the day gathering anything that could be used against his kind. After placing them neatly on top of Darkener's body, he said his final good-bye, lit a fire, and left the woods.

Chapter 11: A Dangerous Place

In the late-afternoon hours, Jacko and the others arrived at the city gates of Mirkin. Many armed guards were posted on top of the wall and several more stood at the front gates, stopping everyone who entered.

The line was long, and people were getting irritated waiting for what they thought was a waste of time. The sentries searched them, and weapons were handed over. If anyone didn't abide by their rules, and still wanted to enter, they were either turned away or beaten if they became too unruly.

Jacko spoke to some of the people in line and found out the town's beloved priest was murdered by a local girl and a stranger, and that was the reason for the heightened security.

Konafar became enraged when he heard the news. "If they think I'm handing over my weapon they have another thing coming." Konafar said, looking at the guards up ahead.

"What will you do if they insist?" Sun asked.

Konafar looked at him and grinned. "You'll see."

Sun shook his head, looking worried. He didn't want to go to jail or be turned away.

"Relax, he knows the captain of the guard." Tonles whispered to Sun.

"Carts and donkeys to the left, light sacks, backpacks, and people carrying weapons to the right." The guard ordered.

When it was finally their turn, they were told to step to the right.

"State your purpose and place your weapons in the cart over there. You may wear your armor, as long as there are no spikes attached to it."

"Why do I need to give you my weapon?" Konafar demanded.

"We're under lockdown for now, and it's our policy."

"What happened?" Sun asked.

The guard peered at him and said. "Weapons over there." He pointed to the cart on the left.

"I'm not giving up my blade." Konafar announced, getting the attention of several other guards.

"Then you can leave, or we'll escort you away." Another guard said as he walked over.

Konafar faced the man who was as large as he was. "You're going to escort me? That's a good one."

Several more guards were now approaching.

"What's going on?" A guard who looked much more official than the others said.

"He's refusing to give up his weapons, sir."

The official-looking guard looked at Konafar for several seconds, as if he was either trying to recognize him or size him up. "Step this way sir."

Konafar did as he was asked and after a brief exchange of words, they clasped arms and walked back.

"Let them pass, weapons and all." The officer said.

"What? That's against orders."

"Rin you don't know who this man is, do you?" Rin looked at Konafar and shook his head.

"He's Konafar."

"Never heard of him."

"This is the man who saved Captain Strom's life several years ago."

Rin felt foolish, because he must have heard the story at least a dozen times from the captain himself. "It's nice to meet you." He extended his arm.

Konafar laughed in the man's face and turned towards the higher-ranking officer. "Where is the good captain?"

"In his quarters relaxing, I'd imagine. I'll let him know you're here and to meet you at the Inn of the Wolf." The guard reached into his pocket and took out some badges. "Wear these so that no one will question why you are carrying weapons. "

Konafar and the others thanked him and left. After they were gone, a young man said something about Konafar and the others carrying weapons and how he didn't think it was right. The guards responded by beating him severely and sending him away. No one else said anything further.

The Inn of the Wolf was crowded when they arrived, with only a few empty tables toward the back. Konafar spotted one and led them through the cluster of tables. Some of the patrons stared at them suspiciously as they passed, but Konafar and the others ignored them.

Once they were seated, a very plump serving wench waddled over. The dingy white dress had seen better days, and her disheveled gray hair was up in a bun. Tonles thought that perhaps at one point in time she might've been pretty. The woman politely greeted them, took their drink order, and left.

After she was gone, Sun spoke. "Who is this, Captain Strom?"

Konafar smiled. "He's a good friend. Resourceful, loyal, takes pride in his job, and does whatever it takes to keep this community safe." He said proudly.

"How did you meet him?" Jacko asked.

"A few years ago, I was in this very tavern enjoying some fine ale and overheard two people talking about assassinating some guy named Rasin Strom. I pretended to be drunker than I was, so they didn't realize I was eavesdropping.

Normally, I don't get involved, but when they said he was running for Captain of the Guard it piqued my interest. So I pretended to stumble out of the inn and find this Strom character and let him know there was going to be an attempt on his life. He was very appreciative and asked me to help him take care of the assassins and uncover who was plotting to kill him. Since I had nothing better to do, and I needed the exercise, I figured why not?

To draw the assassins out, Rasin decided to make an official announcement that he was going to travel to Snowdrift on business, while I was going to leave the night before and hide a mile down the road. The assassins took the bait and when they passed where I was hiding, I made short work of them." The big man smiled.

Just then the drinks arrived. Konafar grinned and took a big swig.

"Did you find out who was behind the plot?" Breen asked.

"Before I killed the last assassin, he told me the name of the person who wanted him dead."

"What was his reason?"

"Something stupid. It had nothing to do with him running for Captain of the Guard."

"Then what?"

"The guy was still angry at Strom because he'd dated his wife a few years ago. Do you believe that?" Konafar raised his tankard and finished his ale in one long gulp.

Breen moved closer to Sun and whispered in his ear. "Can't wait to meet Strom, I bet he's like our friend over here."

Sun chuckled. "Something tells me you're right."

Over in the corner, a young lad, not more than fifteen, began tuning his lute for the night's festivities. The plucking of the strings caught Tonles' attention. He then got up and excused himself.

Breen watched Tonles exchange a few words with the boy, and he handed him another lute. Tonles spent a few minutes tightening the strings and when it was tuned to his liking, Tonles and the boy began playing. Their beautiful melody sounded so sweet and soothing that almost everyone started singing and dancing.

"Wow I didn't think he was the type to play an instrument." Breen said over the music.

"That's where his passion lies. There were many nights, he entertained our Order. He's quite good, don't you think?" Konafar asked.

The two musicians quickly became three then four, and the quartet played to everyone's delight for an hour. While they were playing, Captain Strom entered the tavern and was delighted to see people singing, dancing and enjoying themselves. He waited just inside the doorway until they finished their set and then walked over to Konafar's table.

"Strom it's good to see you." Konafar got up, and they clasped arms in greeting. Konafar introduced the others.

Rasin clasped arms with Jacko, Sun, and when it came to Breen, he kissed her hand. She blushed.

"Such a beauty, so why are you hanging with this guy?" Strom tilted his head toward Konafar.

"I have nothing better to do." Breen answered.

"Is it true Konafar saved your life?" Sun asked.

Captain Strom looked over at his friend. "Saved my life?" He smiled. "It's more like I saved his. I'll tell you how it really happened, but first, I need a drink."

No sooner did the words leave his mouth, than a tankard of ale suddenly appeared in front of him. The serving girl who anticipated his thirst was slender with long red hair, big heaving breasts, and a gorgeous face that could stop men in their tracks. Jacko thought she was one of the most beautiful women he'd ever seen, and the dumbfounded look on his face confirmed it to everyone seated there.

She sat down on the captain's lap and started rubbing his arms in affection. Breen hated women who threw themselves at men, but could see why they would with Captain Strom. He was tall and muscular like Konafar, but much more charming and handsome. His hair and beard were both well-trimmed and except for the scar on his left cheek, his face was flawless.

After she kissed him on the cheek and whispered something in his ear, she left.

The captain smiled. "You'll have to excuse her. We've been together for a while, and she can't seem to stop doing that in public. Now where was I? Oh yes, how Konafar saved my life. I'm sure he told you about the assassination attempt and how he heard about the plot in the tavern." Everyone nodded. "That part is true; however, did he mention that I saved him when we were fighting the assassins?"

"You lie; I killed them before you even got there." Konafar countered.

"You make me laugh my friend. When I arrived, you were getting your butt kicked, and if it wasn't for me, you'd be dead."

"I see your memory is fading with age." Konafar stated.

"It's nice to know you haven't changed one bit."

Just then, Tonles walked over and sat down. "I see you are bickering about who saved whom. Strom, how are you?"

Captain Strom reached over, clasped his arm, and then guzzled the last of his ale. "Is anyone hungry?" He asked after wiping his mouth on his sleeve. They nodded, and he ordered food and more ale.

While they were eating and drinking, Konafar, Tonles, and Rasin continued telling tales of adventure and heroics with each one trying to outdo the other. The drinks and laughter continued to flow until Sun brought up the death of the priest.

Captain Strom's facial expression turned serious. "Konafar I'm glad you're here. I need your help, and I am willing to pay you whatever you want."

Konafar's eyes lit up. "That's sounds good to me, so what happened?" He asked.

"About a week ago our priest was murdered along with his acolytes and some townsfolk."

"Do you know who did it?"

The captain nodded. "We arrested a stranger and placed him in jail, but somehow, he escaped and murdered several of my guards. People I respected and loved." Captain Strom's eyes welled up, and then he slammed his fist down on the table in anger. "I should have killed him when I had the chance."

"Do you think someone helped him escape?" Tonles asked.

"Yes, a local woman named Katara was involved. Whether she was forced to help or did this on her on accord, I'll never know." Captain Strom paused and they could tell he was still having a hard time dealing with the losses. "Anyway, after he escaped the jail, he went to the temple and murdered the priest and his acolytes."

"How did he get away?" Breen asked.

"We almost had him again. As my men were closing in on him in the cemetery, someone threw him a rope over the wall, and he climbed over it." Captain Strom decided to leave out the part of the story about his fight on the wall, because he was too embarrassed.

"Why would someone murder a holy man?" Breen asked.

"Only a devil of a man would." Tonles added.

"I want him dead and the woman brought back here to stand trial."

"Captain Strom, how did they leave town?" Sun asked.

"They left through the cellar of Katara's cottage. She had an escape tunnel underneath the city that no one knew about." He paused, looking down into his tankard and then continued. "Two of my men were also found dead in her tunnel. They were torn apart limb from limb, and their heads were severed. It really angers me that I could have prevented everyone's death if I had just killed him in the first place instead of arresting him."

"Such savage brutality; I wonder why they spent time killing them in that fashion if they were escaping?" Sun said.

"I don't think they did, because we found a wooden guardian. I think they are called Tirips. Konafar be careful of her, and you should also know that this stranger has a dagger that fights on its own."

"A what?"

"A dagger that fights on its own. I don't understand how it does."

"How are his fighting skills?" Konafar asked, wanting to understand exactly what he was up against.

"Pathetic. I beat him easily when I captured him the first time, even with his dagger."

Konafar sat back, mug in hand. "Easy enough. Get rid of his dagger, kill him, and capture the girl. Are you sure you don't want him alive?" He said and took a swig.

"If you can, do so, because I would take great pleasure in torturing him myself. Here take a look at this." Captain Strom produced a rolled-up parchment from his pouch, unraveled it, and placed it on the table.

Jacko's heart sank, because the man looked exactly like Torhan. Sun glanced over at him, and Jacko shook his head indicating to be quiet. Breen saw their silent exchange, but did not say anything.

After Tonles and Konafar finished studying the poster, Strom folded it back up and handed it to Konafar, who proudly announced that it would be his pleasure to capture or kill him. Jacko didn't like the sound of this at all.

"Excuse me Captain Strom, can you tell me where a person named Mui Shin lives?" Sun interrupted.

"Mui Shin? Do you know him?"

"Not directly, but I do know his son."

"He owns a store towards the west side of town. You can't miss it because there's a sign overhead with the word LENDER written on it."

"Lender?"

"Yes. People borrow money and pay him back with interest, and if they don't, he has friends who convince them otherwise."

"Sounds dangerous for both parties."

"How so?" Captain Strom was a bit puzzled by the statement.

"It's obvious how dangerous it would be for the borrower, but Mui Shin could eventually become a target for revenge or someone wanting the money without having to ask."

"The latter would be very hard to do because he has many men working for him. Besides the mayor, he's one of the most influential and richest people living here."

"Money and people can't buy you protection all of the time."

"What are you trying to say?" Strom's voice rose a bit, and he was becoming suspicious of Sun.

"Rasin, please calm down. Sun is a good and peaceful man," Konafar suddenly said. "I've known him for some time, and I can guarantee he won't cause you any trouble. You have my word on it."

Captain Strom's gaze never left Sun's eyes. "I'll need your weapons."

"Why?"

"Strom, I just said he's fine, plus I'll keep an eye on him." Konafar interjected.

"Look, you don't understand. After what's happened, the people are afraid to go out at night, and I promised the mayor there wouldn't be any trouble. Sun your weapons?"

"How about this, if something happens with someone in my party, then you can take me off to jail."

Captain Strom looked at Konafar. "I wouldn't want it to come to that."

"Here, take them." Sun handed him his daggers.

"I'll keep them safe until you leave. I need to get going now." The captain stood up, and Konafar did the same.

"Walk with me." Konafar said. Captain Strom nodded and said good-bye.

"That was getting tense." Breen said after they were out of the door.

"I'll say." Jacko added.

"Jacko, was he talking about your friend?" Tonles asked.

"No."

"Are you sure?"

"I said no." He answered flatly, and went back to drinking.

Konafar and Strom spoke while walking toward the guard house.

"Sorry about that I'm just nervous about strangers, and I don't want any trouble." Strom said.

"I understand. Enough about that. That girl was beautiful. I assume you're still cheating on Roga?"

"Roga passed away a year ago."

"I'm sorry for your loss."

Strom reflected and waited for several awkward seconds to pass before continuing. "She died one night of an unexplained sickness. No one could do anything to save her."

"How are the kids?"

"Getting big." He sounded down. "Sarae starts school soon. She fancies the healing arts. My boys are a chip off the block. Do you have time? I'd like to show you something."

Konafar nodded.

They arrived at the junior school of the blade a short time later. Outside of the building, students were sitting in a large circle watching two other students fight in the center with wooden wasters. The fight ended shortly after Konafar and Strom arrived, when one student whacked the other in the head, knocking him out cold.

The teacher tended to the fallen student until he woke and was helped out of the circle to the sound of applause from everyone watching. Two more students stood up, a young boy about the age of twelve and a bigger, slightly older one.

"There they are. Keller is my younger boy, and Kam is the elder." Strom announced proudly.

"They look just like you." Konafar said, bringing a big smile to his friend's face.

The kids marched over to the weapons rack, grabbed two staves, and then back to the center where they nodded to each other and began their fight. Slowly, they circled other until the older Strom went on the offensive by rushing his younger brother.

Keller quickly took one step back, lowered the staff so that it was level with his stomach, and rammed it into Kam's midsection, knocking the wind from his lungs and sending him to his knees gasping for air.

A few seconds later, Kam was on his feet, holding his stomach and eying his brother, looking for an opening. He repositioned the staff and attacked. This time he baited his brother into blocking two obvious attacks in order to move in closer. He then used his staff to manipulate Keller's out of the way, while placing his own behind his left leg and shoving him.

Keller lost his balance and fell to the ground. The younger boy got up and charged. Kam parried three times and then did the same move again and sent him back to the ground. Frustrated, Keller got up and attacked harder this time. Four blocks later by Kam and his brother was lying on his back.

The teacher, realizing the younger boy didn't know how to counter the move, stopped the fight and told the other students to start practicing their forms again.

"I taught Kam that one." Strom proudly said and called his boys over. "Keller, Kam, this is Konafar." Both boys nodded.

"That was very good." Konafar said.

"But I lost." Keller looked defeated.

"Keller you lost, but what did you learn?" His father asked him.

"That I need more training."

"You do, but you've also been shown that move before."

"Did you show him how to counter the attack?" Konafar asked.

"I did."

"I guess not well enough. Can I borrow your staff?" Konafar asked Keller.

The younger boy handed him his weapon. Konafar instructed Kam to do the same move and when he did, Konafar stepped back, whipped the backend of the staff up and stopped the weapon a few inches from his face.

"That's how you counter the move when someone wants to knock. You step out of the way." Konafar said.

"Can you show me more?" Keller asked.

"Rasin, do you care to assist?"

Captain Strom took Kam's staff and walked to the center of the ring. The other students stopped what they were doing to watch.

"I'll try not to embarrass you in front of your boys." Konafar taunted his friend and handed Carnage to Keller. "Hold this."

"That will be the day." Strom fired back jokingly.

When they were ready, the fight started with the sound of ash slamming against hickory, drawing the attention of many of the townsfolk walking by.

They fought back and forth with neither one gaining the advantage. Once they crossed weapons they began grappling.

Konafar was the first to drop his weapon and Strom shortly thereafter. They fell to the ground rolling around. Eventually, Strom mounted Konafar from behind, wrapped his arms around his neck and began choking him. Konafar struggled, but wouldn't give up and fought his way out of the hold. He turned Strom's strength against him by pushing his arm out of the way and then locking his arm under his own.

Just when everyone thought the captain was going to give up, he twisted his arm in an unusual fashion and escaped the hold, while rolling Konafar over, wrapping his legs around his stomach and his arms around his neck. Konafar knew what was coming and was helpless to do anything further as Strom pushed his arms and legs in separate directions while squeezing. It took a couple of minutes, but eventually Konafar grew tired and gave up. Both men stood up to the cheers and claps of everyone who was watching.

"Did you learn anything?" Konafar asked Keller.

"Not to mess with my dad."

Konafar and Strom chuckled.

"Dad, that was awesome." Kam said.

Rasin grinned from ear-to-ear.

"I have to get going. Remember one thing boys, never stop training and don't take your opponent lightly, or they might actually beat you." Konafar said. Keller handed him Carnage. "Strom I'll see you later."

Breen took a final swig of ale and stood up. "There's a potion store called Valor's, so that's where I'll be."

Jacko and Sun got up too. "We're going as well. We need to visit Mui Shin."

Tonles took the large drumstick away from his mouth. "Let's meet back here around dusk. I am going to the armory as soon as Konafar returns." He proceeded to take a big bite of meat.

Breen walked eastward through the busy streets until she arrived at Valor's Potions and entered. She was immediately greeted by smells of incense and scented oils that pleased to her senses. People milled about the dimly lit store looking for items, while others stood around engaged in conversation about daily events and the weather. She walked down the closest aisle and approached two men who were engaged in conversation. One looked like a merchant, and the other looked like a farmer.

"And I tell you, the only thing they found was the priest's skin." The merchant said.

"How can that be?" The other asked.

"That's what I heard."

"Nonsense."

"If you don't believe me, then go ask old lady Tronal."

"She's a hundred and two years old. What does she know?" The farmer scoffed.

"More than you."

"Excuse me." Breen said interrupting them.

"What is it?" The farmer responded while looking at her.

"You said they only found his skin? What happened to his body?"

"That's what I heard. There was nothing left of the body or the organs."

"When did the guards arrive?" Breen asked.

"About an hour later." The merchant answered.

"That's impossible. The killer would never have enough time to skin someone and get rid of the body."

"And I'm telling you that's all they found." He paused as if sizing her up. "And why are you talking to us? We don't even know you." The farmer said in disgust, walking away with the other following closely behind him.

Breen shook her head in annoyance and continued walking around the store picking up herbs and ointments. With her basket semi-full, she walked to the front of the store to pay for her items. When it was her turn, she unloaded the basket onto the counter.

"Will that be all?" The woman behind the counter asked.

"Do you have any recipes for sale?"

The lady reached under the counter and pulled out a box. She was about to open it when she noticed Breen's armband and paused looking at her suspiciously. "Are you an official?"

"What?"

"Your armband. Only officials wear them."

Breen didn't know how to respond, so she acted like she was one. "I am. What do you know about the murders?"

"Not much, just what I hear. Some say Priest Abiathar was sleeping in the temple, and two strangers broke in and murdered him and his acolytes. Others say an evil priest wanted to kill him. But the strangest story I've heard was that he was a demon, and a stranger conjured up another one to kill him."

"That last story does sound farfetched."

"You know how rumors start." The woman said, opened the box and began looking through the tiny parchments. "Now what recipes are you looking for?"

"Do you have any for advanced healing, removing nasty scars, or curing diseases?"

She thumbed through the papers for a few more seconds and said. "I have advanced healing and scar removal, but nothing for diseases. Hopefully, I have their components." She turned around and began looking at the shelves.

"Valor is a unique name for a woman." Breen commented.

"That was my father's name. My name is Ditora."

Ditora's eyes rested upon a small metal box. She grabbed it from the shelf and opened it. "Here they are." She took out several items.

"How much are they?"

"The recipe and components for healing are one hundred gold pieces, and scar removal will cost fifteen, but seeing you're an official; I'll give you both for seventy five."

"Thanks." Breen purchased them along with their components and left the store.

"Why did you lie to Tonles about Torhan?" Sun asked him as soon as they were away from the inn.

"Because we really don't know him and besides, if I did, and he told Konafar, then they might tell Captain Strom."

"You know they might figure it out."

"I want to try to prove his innocence."

"Okay, we'll investigate after we visit Mui and the Order. What are you going to do if you can't prove his innocence?"

"Try to convince Konafar not to pursue him." Jacko said knowing that was easier said than done.

"And if he won't?"

"We'll leave town without them and try to find Torhan first and worry about Konafar later."

Sun didn't like the sound of the latter and didn't know how they would ever stop Konafar, let alone Tonles.

Along the way, they noticed wanted posters placed randomly on the building walls. Underneath the picture in large letters was the reward. "Ten Thousand Gold Pieces DEAD and Twenty Thousand ALIVE."

"Did you see that?" Sun asked.

"It's the same picture Captain Strom has."

"Not that, the amount of money on their heads. That's going to bring every tracker and hunter within this region."

"Let's hope we find him first." Jacko said and then stopped a passerby and asked for directions to Mui Shin's house.

After arriving at Mui Shin's cottage, they found the house locked tight.

"I don't think there's anyone inside." Jacko said after peering through the front window. "Where to now?"

"Do you want to go to the armory or should we go to the Order?"

"It's getting late, so let's go to the Order tomorrow."

"Armory it is. We'll stop back here later." Sun said.

Konafar arrived shortly after Sun, Jacko, and Breen left the inn and sat down with his friend to have another drink.

"What happened to you?" Tonles asked after seeing Konafar's dirty clothes and redness around his throat.

"I was putting on a demonstration."

"With whom?"

"The good captain, he's a worthy opponent."

"He didn't look like one."

"Maybe not against Carnage, but with a staff, he's very good, plus he can grapple."

"I guess we'll need to work on that when we have time."

"You got that right." Konafar laughed loudly and picked up his goblet, swallowing its contents in one gulp. "Where's everyone?"

"Sun and Jacko went to visit that guy, Shin and Breen went shopping. I told them to meet us back here tonight. When we're finished, let's go to Wakefield Armory."

Five tankards later, they left the bar and stumbled their way over to the store.

Wakefield Armory was brightly lit and crowded with patrons who were walking about gazing at the armor stacked on tables. To the left of the room were racks of wooden and steel practice swords.

"This is ridiculous." Konafar exclaimed after picking up a single-handed short sword and running his finger over the edge. "This piece of crap couldn't cut anything."

"They're practice swords." Tonles said.

Konafar ignored him and walked to the front of the store, and pushed his way to the front of the line. "Where are the good weapons?" He slurred, annoying everyone in line, as well as the man behind the counter, who was in the middle of a transaction.

"Sir, I'll be right with you." The clerk replied.

Konafar was about to say something further when Tonles was by his side and guided him to the other side of the room.

"What does he mean I'll be right with you? Doesn't he know who I am?"

"Be calm my friend. Let's go look at the armor."

Tonles walked him around the store until he found something that he thought Konafar might like.

"Look at this?" Tonles showed him brigandine armor. "I like this better than plate. Do you?"

Konafar nodded and took the armor off of the table and put it on over his chainmail. It was thick, studded from top to bottom and his favorite color of deep purple. More importantly, it was the right size and allowed him to move his arms freely. Tonles was so impressed with the craftsmanship that he grabbed one for himself, but in black.

After Tonles found a suitable replacement for his shield, they proceed over to the counter and waited patiently for their turn.

The clerk looked at Konafar. "Oh it's you again!"

Konafar let his snide comment go. "I want to see your battle-ready weapons." Konafar said in a calm voice.

The skinny man looked at the sword strapped across his back and then at the armbands. "We're not allowed to sell sharp weapons until the mayor says so. The ones on display are for practice, and can only be purchased if you have a writ from Captain Strom himself."

"You do know you could still kill someone with those?" Tonles added.

"And you can kill someone with a fork." The clerk snapped.

Tonles felt like smacking the man.

"Now what can I get you. You're holding up the line."

"For one, we need our weapons sharpened." Konafar and Tonles placed their weapons on the counter. "We're also buying the armor, shield, and four sharpening stones."

The clerk started looking over the wares. "That will be five hundred gold pieces."

"Five hundred!" Tonles exclaimed.

"Yes, five hundred! Did I stutter?"

Tonles grabbed him by the tunic. "I have a good mind to slug you." He released him and grabbed their weapons. "Let's go, before I do something I might regret."

"Captain Strom is going to love this story." Konafar added chuckling.

They were about to walk away when the merchant said. "How about four hundred and fifty?"

Tonles grinned. "Because of your attitude, I think four hundred gold pieces is more appropriate."

The man agreed because he knew Captain Strom would pay him a visit and he didn't need the aggravation.

"How long will it take for our weapons?" Tonles asked.

"Give me two days. I'm a bit backed up."

After the coins were exchanged, Tonles and Konafar went back to the inn.

****

Jacko and Sun were approaching Killington's Armory just as a big guy dressed in an apron, was about to lock the door.

They stopped a few feet from him.

"Can we come in and see your wares?" Sun asked causing the big fellow to look over.

"Wait here, I need to ask my father." He said and walked back inside. A few minutes later he returned and allowed them to enter. "Welcome, my name is Mekel."

"Pleased to meet you, my name is Sun and this is Jacko."

A short, stocky, balding fellow walked over. "Glad to meet you, my name is Killington. Have a look around and please be quick. I need to close early because I have a date with Ms. Walfer." Killington smiled at the sound of her name.

"We will and thank you." Jacko said.

They walked around the store until Sun saw a suite of chainmail, colored black and gold, and stopped to examine it. He reached out and touched the links and thought they felt differently than any other he'd ever touched before. "The links are somewhat unusual."

"That it is." Killington said walking over. "It's made from a very rare material called Titanium, which is much stronger than typical chainmail links. A blacksmith named Yarn crafted this one for me. Look at how tightly the links are woven together. A spear can't even go through it."

"How much does it cost?" Jacko asked.

"It's not for sale. I'm holding it for someone, but I'm not sure if he'll return."

"Why is that?"

"He was the one accused of killing the priest, but I don't believe he did. He didn't seem the type and neither did the woman he was with." He paused and looked down. "She's a good person. A healer."

"Did you tell anyone what you thought of them?"

"No. I didn't even tell them he was here."

"Was his name Torhan?" Jacko asked.

"How did you know his name?"

"He's a friend of mine, and you're right, he's not a killer. We're trying to find him."

Killington started feeling nervous, because he didn't know these men. He looked around for Mekel and saw him enter the back room. Sun took notice to his son's movements as well and how Killington looked worried.

"Please listen, we mean you no harm, all we want to do is clear my friend's name."

A few seconds later, Mekel reemerged holding two loaded crossbows. He pointed one at Sun and the other at Jacko. "I think you should leave now." He threatened.

"Okay." Sun looked back at Killington. "If you feel like talking, we'll be at the Inn of the Wolf, please stop by. We'll pay you for your time and information."

They were about to leave when Killington stopped them. "Come with me." He said and led them to the back room.

Jacko and Sun sat across from Killington while Mekel moved to the corner of the room with the crossbows lowered.

"Why didn't you tell anyone about Torhan?" Sun asked Killington after they were situated.

"Before the priest was killed, I struck a deal with your friend. I asked him to locate Yarn's mine and as a reward, I would sell him the armor for what I paid for it. That's why I didn't say anything."

"What do you know about the murder and this girl named Katara?" Jacko asked.

"After your friend bought some supplies, my son was escorting him to see Katara and something very strange happened..." Killington paused. "Mekel, tell them what happened."

Mekel looked at his father who nodded for him to do so and then placed the crossbows down, but within reach. "While we were walking toward her house, something weird happened. One minute he was telling me that he wanted me to go with him to the town of Snowdrift and in the next instant he disappeared from my side. People were dead or dying in the streets."

"Wait a second. What do you mean he disappeared?" Jacko asked.

"It happened just like I said. We were talking one moment and the next he was gone."

"Are you sure he disappeared?" Sun asked.

"Are you calling me a liar?"

"Not at all, it just sounded strange. So what happened after that?"

"I left when the guards ran past me."

"Do you know what happened to Torhan?"

"I think he got arrested."

"You mentioned Snowdrift. Did he say why he wanted to go there?"

"He said he needed to help a little girl who fell into a deep sleep and find some amulet."

"Amulet?"

"He called it…" he paused. "I think it was called ROOM or RAME or something like that."

"Did he mention anything else?"

Mekel shook his head.

"Thanks Mekel. Killington, can you tell us everything you know about Katara?" Sun asked.

"I've known her since she was a little girl, and I can tell you that she'd never hurt anyone unless threatened."

"Did she have ties to the priest?"

"She did study under his tutelage a few years ago, and I don't know why she stopped. Maybe she outgrew his teachings, or perhaps; they had a falling out, but even if they did, I don't think she was the type to hold grudges; let along murder someone."

"Is there anything else?" Jacko asked

Killington shook his head.

"Thanks for your time and for not saying anything to the guards.

"Can you show us some of your wares?" Sun asked.

"Sure what do you need?"

"We'd like to see your clothes, throwing knives, and some flasks of oil. We'll also need to have our weapons sharpened."

"How did you get your weapons by the guards?"

"Our other friend knows Captain Strom."

"If I sell you throwing knives, you didn't get them from me. Got it?"

Jacko nodded and handed him the weapons that needed sharpening. After they purchased what they needed, they left.

After they were gone, Killington realized for the first time in a very long time that he was a business man above everything else, and he hated himself for being one. Looking back, maybe he should have helped the guards when they asked about Torhan, but if he did that would've interfered with his ultimate goal, and that was to know where Yarn's mine was, his dream of creating the best armor and weapons around and to become rich while doing so.

After they left the shop, Jacko stopped his friend. "Well what do think?" He asked.

"We're lucky he's a greedy old bastard."

"What about his son's story?"

"I'm not sure about that. How could Torhan just disappear and then people ended up dead?"

"Why didn't you challenge him further?"

"He would have shot at both of us." Sun said and grinned.

"Let's go see if Mui Shin returned and after that we'll meet the others."

"What about Torhan?"

"We'll go to Snowdrift after we visit the Order tomorrow."

"Tonight we should go to Katara's cottage and see if we can find anything that might clear his name."

They went to Mui Shin's house and waited for him on his porch when they found out he still wasn't home. It was nearing dusk when an aging man, wearing green and red robes, approached the house. His long gray hair was braided down his back, and his form was hunched over slightly. He was accompanied by four tough looking bodyguards, none of which carried weapons openly. When the old man saw the two strangers sitting on his porch, he stopped and the four ruffians walked past him.

"What do you want?" One of them asked.

Sun and Jacko stood up. "Are you Mui Shin?" Sun directed his question toward the elderly man.

"I'll ask you again. What do you want?" The same guard pressed.

"We're here to see Mui Shin, and you don't look like him, so if you don't mind, step aside." Sun's posture stiffened.

The bodyguard stepped closer and as he was reaching for Sun, he was kicked really hard in the stomach and doubled over in pain. The other three guards were about to join the fray when the old man told them to hold their position.

"Who are you?" The elderly man asked while stepping forward.

"I'm assuming you're Mui Shin?"

He nodded his head.

"We need to talk to you about your son Ma."

"Very well, but before we go inside tell me your names."

"My name is Sun Chin, and this here is Jacko."

Jacko bowed out of respect.

"We are friends of your son."

"Has something happened?"

"We'd better go inside and talk."

They were led into Mui Shin's house. The place was very traditional in style. Sun thought. There were statues of jade dragons, bonsai trees, rare flowers, and vases with ancient symbols carved into them. The table and chairs were constructed from bamboo. After they were seated and wine was poured, two of the four bodyguards left the room.

"Now what can you tell me about my son? And please be very direct." Mui asked, but his voice didn't sound too concerned.

"Ma has died," Jacko paused, "at the hands of a fox named Slyantom."

"Although tragic, what does this have to do with me?" His words didn't indicate worry, concern, or loss, just coldness.

"It has everything to do with you. He died for your sins."

"Nonsense, he most likely got himself involved with the wrong men or owed money to someone. You do know he had a gambling problem?"

"You're wrong. Slyantom and his men were sent by one of your former associates."

"Who?"

"A person named Thelmaer."

"Oh Thelmaer, that fool. He doesn't have the nerve to do something like that or oppose me."

"He did. Don't you care?"

"Care? I can handle him."

"No, care about your son?"

"Him? I gave up on my son a long time ago. He defied me and my way of business, saying it was immoral, wrong and wanted to find his inner light. What a joke." Mui scoffed. "He should have embraced my beliefs."

"Our school does not teach immoral businesses, and your son was a great man and teacher," said Sun. "You should be proud of him instead of thinking ill thoughts."

"It looks like we knew two different people."

"Thanks for your hospitality. I think we are done here." Sun stood up, and Jacko followed.

"For what it's worth, you should know that your son didn't have to fight. He could have escaped and left you to handle Slyantom by yourself." Jacko said.

"Then he should have, because he didn't do a good job anyway."

"Before he died, he wanted you to know that he forgave and loved you."

"If he'd chosen to work for me, then he would be alive." Mui countered.

"I'll leave you with this Mr. Shin. Slyantom is on his way here, and if I was you, I'd hire better bodyguards and lots more of them."

"Get the hell out of here." Mui yelled at them.

Sun grinned and left with Jacko.

"I hope he gets his someday." Jacko whispered to Sun as they were leaving.

"He will." On their way back to the inn, Sun asked a few people if they knew where Katara lived. Most of them were either agitated or annoyed with him for asking, while others ignored him altogether. One person was so mad about what happened to the priest, she almost started a fight with him. It took them awhile, but they finally found someone to give them directions to where she lived.

"Are you going to break in?" Jacko asked once the person was gone.

"Yes."

"When do you want to go?"

Sun stopped walking and looked at him. "I'm going alone."

"No you're not."

"No offense, but I am better equipped for such a task."

"Says who?" Jacko hated when someone said they were better at something then he was.

Sun placed a hand on his shoulder. "It's not that I am that much better at it than you. It's just that I'm more experienced and did this on more than one occasion. Plus, if you get caught, they might link you to Torhan, and you could end up in jail."

"Well if you get caught, they'll do the same thing to you."

"They're not going to catch me." Sun said seriously. "When we have time, I'll train you to be better at moving around silently."

"You will and don't forget you still owe me training."

"I know."

They entered the inn and joined Konafar and Tonles, who were seated toward the back, eating, drinking and joking with a couple of serving wenches.

"Do you guys do anything else besides drink?" Jacko asked.

"This is how we unwind." Tonles said, laughing.

"Have a drink and then squeeze this." Konafar said and helped the busty, fair looking wench, off of his lap. He turned her around so that they could see her plump derriere under her dress.

Jacko blushed.

"Awe look, he's blushing." The woman commented and walked over and squeezed Jacko's cheeks with her fingers, kissed him full on the lips and walked away.

Konafar, Tonles, Sun, and two other women at a nearby table laughed at his reddening complexion.

"More drinks!" Konafar yelled and banged on the table.

Wenches immediately came over with mugs of ale.

Sun took a swig and spoke in a serious tone. "We need to talk."

Tonles and Konafar gave him their full and undivided attention.

"What are you planning to do now that you've escorted us here?"

"We need to find this Red Knight and crush the living daylights out of him for what he did to Runit." Konafar answered.

"What about the murderer Captain Strom is looking for?"

"If we come across him, we'll kill him too."

Sun and Jacko were both relieved that Torhan wasn't their top priority.

"Did you find the Shun guy?" Tonles asked.

"You mean Shin. Yes, and he didn't seem to care about his son, or that he was in grave danger."

"What are you going to do now?"

"We still need to go to our Order and from there; Jacko wants to find Torhan."

"Speaking of which," Konafar suddenly said and Jacko knew what was coming next. "I've been thinking is it possible that the person wanted for the murder is, in fact, your friend?"

Jacko's heart sank.

"It is possible," Sun quickly said. "And if it is him, we'll find out why he did what he is accused of. My question to you is will you still kill him before hearing the facts?" Sun's tone was serious, and everyone knew it.

"I'll tell you this. If I do run into him, and out of respect to you and Jacko, I'll haul his ass back here to stand trial instead of killing him, unless you can prove his innocence."

Before Jacko could say something, Sun spoke again.

"What if we get you proof?"

"Konafar rubbed his chin. "If you get proof then save it for his trial."

"Do you really think it will be a fair one?"

"That's not my problem, but your friend should stand for his crimes." Konafar said sitting back.

"Know this," Jacko suddenly spoke up. "He's not a killer, and if he killed the priest and those other people, he must have had his reasons."

"Then you should have nothing to worry about after we haul him back here." Konafar raised his goblet mockingly and took a swig.

Breen suddenly appeared at their table. "Am I interrupting something?" She said after sensing tension around the table.

"It appears that the killer turned out to be Jacko's friend after all." Tonles said to her.

"Wait a second," Jacko was visibly and verbally upset, "you don't know that for sure. I'll prove his innocence, so back off."

Tonles liked his determination. "I'm sure you will."

"When are you leaving town?" Sun asked Tonles and Konafar.

"In a few days. Why?" Konafar responded.

"Give us until then and if we can't prove his innocence feel free to bring him back here."

"Sounds reasonable," said Tonles, "you have until then."

"Agreed." Sun stood up along with Jacko.

"Where are you going?" Breen asked them.

"We need to prove his innocence and drinking is a waste of time." Sun said and they left.

Breen knew that things had suddenly changed within the group as she watched them leave.

"What are you going to do now that we brought Jacko to Mirkin?" Tonles asked her.

"I don't know."

"You could always come with us."

"I'll know better in a few days." She stood up.

"You just got here, where are you going?"

"I've discovered a few things while I was out that might help them."

"Like what?" Konafar pressed.

"Just some strange stories."

"What did you hear?"

She looked around and then spoke. "Some said that when the guards arrived at the temple, that all that was left of the priest and his acolytes, were their skins."

"You mean they found their skins in one area and their bodies in another right?" Konafar said, placing his empty mug down.

"No, I mean their bones and organs were never found."

"So they killed the priest and his acolytes, skinned them, and took their innards?" Tonles said.

"He wouldn't have had enough time to do that. Think about it. The killer escaped from jail, butchered the priest and acolytes, and got rid of their bodies in under an hour."

"Well maybe the girl got a head start on killing the priest and his followers." Konafar said and shook his empty tankard back and forth, indicating that he wanted another to the serving wench as she passed by.

Breen was getting nowhere talking to these two. "I'll find you in a couple of days and let you know if I want to go with you." She said and left.

"It sounds like there is more to this story than meets the eye." Tonles said after she was gone.

"Well if he's innocent, or was forced to help her, then I hope they find proof." Konafar responded.

"Will you tell Strom about Torhan?"

"There's no need to. I just hope they can find what they need because I like Sun and Jacko, and I'd really hate to harm them if they try to stop us."

"Me too." Tonles said, just as the serving wenches walked over carrying more food and ale.

****

"Where do you want to go?" Jacko asked as they approached the market.

Sun paused. "There're still a couple of hours of daylight left, so after it gets dark, I'll enter her cottage and see what I can find."

"Where do you want me to wait?"

"Wherever you want, just meet me at the Inn of the Lion later. If I don't show up, you'll know I ran into a problem, so don't come looking for me."

"Where will you go?"

"I'll meet you at dawn outside of these walls."

As they were walking through the market, Breen came running up to them.

"Good, I found you...we need to talk." She said panting.

"What's wrong?" Jacko asked her.

"Let's go over there and talk." She nodded to a nearby alleyway.

After they were far enough away so that no one could hear them, Breen faced them both.

"How do you plan on proving Torhan's innocence?"

"I'd rather not tell you, in case we get caught." Sun said.

"Look. You saved me back in Redden, so I want to help."

"It's too dangerous."

"Don't shut me out. We've made it this far."

"It's not your affair." Jacko added.

"Let me decide what my affair is and what's not." She said sternly.

Sun looked at Jacko, and he nodded his approval.

"Okay. I'm planning on breaking into Katara's house and collecting anything that can prove their innocence."

"By yourself?"

He nodded.

"What are you going to do?" She asked Jacko.

"Wait for him at the inn."

"Are you sure you don't want help or a distraction?"

"Let me think about it?" Sun answered.

"When are you going?"

"After it gets dark."

They spoke for a few more minutes and then left. What they didn't know was that a dirty-faced vagabond, hidden behind a few baskets, was eavesdropping after they'd invaded the alleyway he called home. He heard almost the entire conversation and even took a few risky glances to see what they looked like and the clothes they wore. After they were gone, he found some guards in the market and told them what he heard and saw. They paid him a few gold coins and sent him on his way.

Shortly before nightfall, Breen and Jacko parted company from Sun and went to the Inn of the Lion. The place was dimly lit, less cheerful than the Inn of the Wolf, and the clientele appeared to be seedier. They were cautious about selecting a table where they couldn't be overheard. After they were seated and served ale, they kept a visual on their surrounding and spoke quietly. Breen decided she wanted to go with them if they wanted her to, and Jacko said yes.

They were on their third tankard of ale, when a few guards entered the inn, looked around until they spotted them and then came walking over.

"What's your business here in town?" One of them said.

Jacko was taken aback by his statement and simply said. "We're just passing through. Why?"

"Where's your friend?" The guard on the left asked.

"Which one?" Jacko answered.

"Don't get smart with me boy, or we'll throw you in prison." The guard's posture stiffened and the other two fanned out slightly as if they were expecting trouble. "The one you were with earlier, in the black and red traveling clothes."

"What's this about?" Breen asked.

The guard placed both gloved hands on the table. "We heard that you and your friend are thinking about breaking into that bitch of a healer's house. We're here to make sure you don't cause any trouble. Now, where's your friend?"

Before either one could answer, Sun entered the inn and walked over to the table.

"What's going on?" He said to the guards.

The guard on the right straightened and turned around to face him. "You're lucky you're here. Why are you asking about the priest and Katara?"

Sun did his best to look puzzled. "Just curious, that's all."

"Why?"

"After Captain Strom told us about what had happened to him, we became curious."

"Where did you get those armbands?" The guard on the right asked after noticing the one on Sun's arm.

"They were gifts."

"From who?"

"Captain Strom."

"How do you know the captain?"

"My friend Konafar is a personal acquaintance of his."

"I'm warning you don't get any bright ideas about snooping around her house or causing any trouble. You got that?" The guard said and then left the inn, along with the other two.

Sun sat down.

"What are you doing here?" Jacko asked him.

"As soon as we parted, I was followed by some guards, so I led them down a few streets, circled back, and came here to warn you that they are watching us. I guess I was late."

"I wonder how they knew about our plan," said Breen. "Do you think Konafar or Tonles said something?"

"No. I don't think they would, because they're not the type. I'm thinking someone might've overheard us."

"Now what?" Jacko asked.

"Let's wait here for a little and then go find Konafar and Tonles. Maybe they can help."

They arrived at the Inn of the Wolf and when they didn't see Konafar and Tonles sitting there drinking, they went up to their room and knocked repeatedly on the door. Several minutes later, they gave up and went back to their own room.

Once the door was closed, and they were seated, Sun spoke. "I've been thinking," he began. "I believe there will be guards at Katara's house, so I'll need you to create a distraction long enough for me to enter through the back. Do you think that you can do it?"

They nodded.

"I'm not sure whether the guards will be hiding or standing out in the open, so I want you to create one even if you don't see them."

"What kind of distraction did you want?" Breen asked.

"Just act like you're drunk and trying to enter the wrong house. That should work."

"What do you want us to do after that?"

"Return here and wait for me."

"Do you think guards will be hiding inside the house?" Jacko asked.

"Hopefully they won't be. We'll leave in a couple of hours, so get some rest."

When the night was at its darkest, Jacko and Breen arrived at Katara's cottage and saw that there was only one guard posted on her porch.

"Ready?" Breen whispered, and he nodded.

They stumbled around the walkway, crashing into a few bushes and flowerbeds, all the while laughing and apologizing to the shrubbery for their transgressions. When the guard saw the drunken pair stumbling towards the porch, he grabbed his spear and shouted for them to halt. Breen and Jacko didn't heed his warning and after the guard told them to halt again, Jacko tripped and fell to the ground. The guard raced down the steps to confront them.

"What are you doing here?" He said.

Breen was helping Jacko to his feet, and then she let go of his hand, allowing him to fall again. They started laughing. The guard grabbed Breen by the arm, she pulled away stumbling and then regained her footing.

"Hey." She said, slurring her words at the guard and swaying her body back and forth.

"What are you doing here?" He asked them again.

"We live here!" Jacko answered as he was rising to his feet and stumbling around.

This is not your house, and if you don't leave I'll throw the both of you in jail or do something I might regret. Now get out of here."

Breen stumbled over to Jacko, he grabbed her arm for support, and together they stumbled away.

Around the back of the house, Sun didn't find any guards waiting for him there, so he quietly opened the window and peered inside the house. Even in the darkness, he could tell the room was a mess with broken furniture all around. After picking an empty spot on the floor, he carefully entered. Activating a glow rock, he gazed around and saw that there were many personal items strewn about.

The only things of interest appeared to be a chest in the far corner of the room that had a smashed in lid, and a trapdoor partially covered by a rug. He figured that was how Torhan and Katara had escaped. The inside of the trunk contained a few personal items such as; copper coins, herbs, jewelry, and books.

He rummaged through the books and found most of them to be about healing, but two of them caught his attention. One was titled "Tirips", and another didn't have a title at all. At that moment, he thought that he heard someone trying to enter through the front door, placed the books into his bag and climbed out the window.

He returned to the inn and saw Jacko and Breen in the back, motioned to them that he was going upstairs and left. After entering the room, he lit a few candles, sat down at the table, and took out the untitled book. The initial page was titled "My time in Mirkin." He realized at once it must've been Katara's diary and began glancing through the pages until he came to the first passage that mentioned priest Abiathar, and then slowed his pace.

Day Thirty-Five

I met priest Abiathar for the first time shortly after his lecture. We talked for several hours and exchanged stories, teachings, and details about where I'm from. He seems like a nice fellow. I didn't ask him to take me under his tutelage yet, because he'll need more convincing of my skills before I can. However, I did mention brother Pien, and he was delighted that I knew his mentor.

Day Thirty-Seven

Today, priest Abiathar asked me to participate in his morning service. He must have been pleased, because he asked me to do it again tomorrow.

Day Thirty-Eight

Today, I assisted with the service again and this time, took lead over one of the acolytes named Kilder. Priest Abiathar was so impressed that he asked me to study under him. I'm very happy and can't wait for the lessons to begin.

Day Forty-Two

The first lesson was great. He taught me how to mend simple cuts and abrasions and how to treat minor sicknesses. Tomorrow's teaching will be much more intense he said. Brother Pien will be proud of me. I know it.

By the time he reached the fifty-ninth day, his eyes grew weary, and he felt tired from the day's events. He still didn't discover anything of relevance, but knew there were still a lot of pages to read through.

The door opened and Jacko entered. "What did you find?" He asked.

"I found her diary, which may shed some light on her time spent in Mirkin, and a few books for Breen."

"Did you start reading the diary?"

"I did a little, but it's going to take some time." Sun held up the journal to show him just how thick it was.

"Where's Breen?"

"In her room, she was tired."

"Did everything go alright?" Sun asked as he was preparing for bed.

"Yes. Breen did a great job."

"Good." Sun said and climbed beneath the covers.

Jacko did the same in his bed.

The sounds of the birds chirping outside of their window and a light cool breeze woke Jacko and Sun. They dressed, packed a few items, and went downstairs. The place was overly crowded with people, and if it wasn't for Breen, who was already seated, they wouldn't have found a place to sit. She smiled and called them over when saw them.

"Have you seen Konafar or Tonles?" Sun asked her.

"You just missed them; they were on their way to train. Did you find anything last night?"

"I did and I have a present for you upstairs."

Breen's eyes lit up because it had been a while since anyone had given her anything. "Can I go up there now?"

Sun handed her the key and whispered. "It's in a bag under the bed. Leave the diary alone."

She smiled and got up, because the excitement was too much.

"I meant to tell you. If you should ever come across a fox wearing an eye patch, avoid him at all costs. His name is Slyantom, and he's a killer." Jacko said to her.

"I will." She said and went up to his room.

Jacko and Sun ordered food and ale after she was gone.

Breen was delighted to find three books in the bag. Two were about healing and the third, much smaller than the rest, was titled "Tirips." She'd never heard of that word before and opened that one first. After scanning through several pages, she realized that it was a book of conjuration and given the complexity of the symbols and words, neither of which she understood, she found herself glancing over the pages. She was about to close the book when she came upon a page with two words written in a common tongue at the top of the page.

"Wood Tirips." She whispered.

The pictures were easy enough to follow, but the words to activate the creature was what she couldn't understand. She glanced over the next five pages which displayed pictures of the wooden creature, from the beginning stages until it was fully assembled. She paused and fantasized about owning one, then turned her attention back to the book and continued reading.

The next Tirip she came across was called Water and again, there were pictures and unrecognizable symbols. She was impressed and smiled at the thought of conjuring this one, because her cottage back home had a pond and it would be fun to use the creature to play tricks on the children as they walked by.

The remaining ten pages of the book went on to describe, but not conjure, five more Tirips and which one was better suited to battle the other. It appeared that even the most terrifying and deadly Tirip, called Vacuum, had an equal.

After closing the tome, she realized that she needed help to decipher their meanings and smiled at the prospect. She opened the healing manuals and began studying the material, which was easier to understand given her background. It was around midmorning when Breen grew weary of her studies and went back to her own room to rest.

Jacko and Sun finished eating and left the inn. Along the way, they saw Konafar and Tonles training some of the guards. Jacko nodded toward Tonles after he acknowledged their passing. Before they exited the city Konafar came up to them.

"Where are you going?" He asked.

"We're going to our Order." Jacko replied.

"Will you be back?" They nodded. "Good because I need to talk to you before you leave the town for good."

"Is it important?" Jacko asked.

"No."

"We should be back in a couple of days." Sun said.

"See you then." Konafar replied and left.

Jacko watched him walk away. "I really don't want to fight him, but I will if I have to." He stated.

"I feel the same way." Sun added.

They bid the guards farewell as they left the city.

About an hour later, they entered the forest towards the west and enjoyed the cooler temperature the trees provided.

"Have you ever been to this Order?" Jacko suddenly asked.

"Once. I delivered a message to Teacher Tae Fu, and he taught me a few things while I was there." He paused. "Speaking of which, I still owe you some training, so don't let me forget."

"I won't. Did you find anything else last night?"

"I saw a trapdoor that they must've used to escape."

"I've been thinking. Do you think the Master is alright? I hated the fact that we had to leave Wistful."

Sun stopped and faced his friend, placing a hand on his shoulder. "I think he's smart enough to know if the cause is worthy or not, so stop worrying, he'll be fine. Plus if we stayed, Torhan wouldn't have us to save him. I want to take a rest."

While they were doing so, Jacko ate some food while Sun took out the diary and began reading it again. He found the next thirty pages to be pretty much the same, with a little more detail about her training and daily activities.

He marked the last page and placed the book back in the bag and stood up. "Are you ready?"

"Did you find anything else out?"

"A little bit more. I'm not sure if she came to Mirkin of her own accord or was sent by someone named brother Pien. As far as I can tell, she spent her days training and nights to herself. I'll know better when I'm finished."

"Do you think it will be soon?"

"You saw how thick the diary is, right?"

"I don't mean to rush you, I'm just worried."

"I know you are."

By dusk, they had reached the Order and were greeted by several students walking around the perimeter, none of which were of higher rank then Sun. After some brief introductions, one of the students escorted them into the school, down a very long hallway, and into a small seating area with doors to the east and west.

"Please take a seat and someone will be with you shortly." Their escort said, bowed and left.

"Where do you think the doors go to?" Jacko asked.

"From what I remember, the one over there," Sun pointed to the western door, "goes to the upper student area and the other one is for us lower ranked students."

"Did they give you a tour the last time you were here?"

"Yes, but it was brief."

A few minutes later a student, dressed in a yellow and green uniform, entered the room from the eastern door. Sun and Jacko stood up, with Jacko bowing to the senior student and the student, in turn, acknowledged Sun's rank.

"My name is Kroy and my rank is Hawk. This way please."

He led them down to the dining room that had five large tables full of students and four doors scattered throughout.

"Are you hungry?" Kroy asked.

Jacko nodded.

"Good. Please have a seat. Tonight's dinner is a selection of roasted fowl and vegetables accompanied with an assortment of wines." Kroy said and then left.

Halfway through the meal, a student entered the room wearing a gray and black uniform indicating his rank of Red Falcon. Everyone stopped eating, stood up, and bowed.

The senior student walked right up to Sun and Jacko. "My name is Fen. Welcome to our school. The door to the north will take you to the training area, and the one beyond that will take you to the Master's greeting room. If you feel like training feel free, if not, let someone know and proceed to the greeting room. Teacher Lee Chee Wa will meet you there.

"Thank you brother." Sun said.

Fen bowed out of respect, Jacko and Sun returned the favor, and then sat down to finish their meal.

After they were done, Jacko and Sun went through the door and passed through the training area. The area was filled with students of various ranks practicing together, none higher than Griffin rank.

"It looks like this school has more students than ours." Jacko commented as they were passing the students.

"The school was built after ours, and Brother Lee Chee Wa decided to make it bigger and do things a little differently. He wanted students up to the rank of Yellow Sparrow to train together. I like that idea better because it exposes them to advanced techniques."

They proceeded through the door at the far end of the room, up the stairs and entered the greeting area. The room was very elaborate looking, from the designs carved into the floorboards, to the exotic plants and finally, the bamboo walls, ceiling, and furniture. The seating area towards the back was flanked by two ponds. After they were seated, they only had to wait a few minutes before the door to the side opened and in walked a man with a long white beard and ponytail. He wore a gray and green uniform and used a walking stick that was more for a show than assistance. Upon seeing him, Sun and Jacko stood up and bowed as he approached.

"Welcome, I am Brother Lee Chee Wa, master instructor of this school, and you are?"

"My name is Sun Chin, and this here is Jacko. We both hail from the school in Wistful and are honored to meet you."

"Well met Sun Chin. How's Master Shoo Sin Yan?"

"Health wise he's fine, but Jacko can tell you better what's going on in Wistful and why we are here."

Sun, Jacko, and Master Chee Wa then sat down.

"Jacko please tell me why you've traveled all his way to see me."

"I was sent here by Master Shoo for a couple of reasons." He began. "A few weeks ago I was granted a promotion and during my training, my teacher was murdered. I wanted to help him fight, but he sent me away in order to deliver his final message to his father, who lives in Mirkin."

"What was your teacher's name?"

"His name was Ma."

"Ma…" Chee Wa reflected for a moment. "I remember him. He was a gifted student and promising teacher. I will pray for his soul tonight. Do you know who killed him?"

"I do. The killer is a fox tracker named Slyantom, and he will most likely come after Ma's father."

"Did Ma say why Slyantom was after him?"

"He said Slyantom was sent by his boss. A guy named Repan, who has ties with his father and wanted revenge on him for something they were both involved in together."

"I see. Well, it appears Slyantom is just an extension of Repan's thirst for revenge. I'll send some students over to protect Ma's father and dispatch one of our highest ranking students to deal with Slyantom for his crimes. Where was Ma killed?"

"He died in a forest a few miles northwest of the town of Wistful."

Brother Lee Chee Wa handed a parchment and quill to Jacko and asked him to write down every detail he could remember about the fox. While he was writing, a young, low-rank student, walked through the door carrying a tray. He poured some teas for everyone. Brother Lee Chee Wa and Sun Chin spoke casually while Jacko continued to pen the rest of the details. When he finished, Jacko passed the parchment back to him.

"I also have this for you." Jacko said and handed him the note the master had given him.

Chee Wa opened it promptly and read the contents. "Master has granted you a promotion for your service, but since you had help, you're only entitled to advance halfway to your next rank. Sun, you are also getting the same promotion."

Jacko and Sun thanked him.

"Now, tell me what other news you have."

Jacko told him everything that had happened in Redden and what was about to take place in Wistful. He also informed him that both he and Brother Tae Fu were to take over the schools if anything were to happen to the Master. Brother Lee Chee Wa reflected on his words and then spoke.

"I will send some students along with Brother Tae Fu to assist the Master."

"Master said that if he couldn't convince the other the Orders in Wistful to fight, then he was going to seek sanctuary somewhere else." Jacko stated.

"I'll take that under advisement. Is there anything else?"

They shook their heads.

"Stay as long as you like." Brother Lee Chee Wa said and stood up.

Jacko and Sun got up and bowed to him.

"Come back and visit us whenever you like." Chee Wa smiled and left.

"What do you want to do?" Jacko asked.

"Let's get your training started, so that I can finish reading the diary." Jacko nodded in acceptance. "I can improve your blocking or teach you the Iron Feet or the Iron Fist."

Jacko reflected on the pain that he went through while learning to block, and decided on Iron Feet.

They returned to the training area with Sun leading Jacko to an area that had ropes attached to pulleys, four-inch brass rings, other stretching equipment, and a sandpit.

"Here's what we're going to do," Sun began. "Since we don't have a lot of time, I suggest that you concentrate on strengthening your legs and gaining greater flexibility. I can teach you the kicks anytime. Okay?"

Jacko nodded.

"Now watch me closely."

Sun walked over to a particular set of ropes and pulleys, placed his right foot inside one of the leather sleeves and pulled on the cord, lifting his leg until it was next to his head.

He looked at Jacko and said. "I want you to hold your legs in this position for thirty minutes."

He lowered his leg and sat down in front of another contraption, consisting of three upright logs with ropes and pulleys attached at the top.

After placing his feet into the harnesses and splitting his legs wide, he pulled down on the nearby rope, and his legs were pushed apart. When they couldn't go any further, he pulled harder on the rope until his legs were in a complete split.

"Hold this position for ten minutes and do this exercise three times." Sun instructed.

Sun released the rope, got up, and walked over to the sandpit. He stepped onto two metal plates and pushed his legs apart until he achieved a full-frontal split. He looked over at his friend.

"I want you to do this three times and hold this position for five minutes. Do you understand?"

"It looks painful."

"It is." Sun said getting up. "When you're done here, go over to the sandpit and put the rings around your ankles. Start with two on each leg and then begin kicking. I want you to do at least five-hundred kicks with each leg. Alright?"

"Yes."

"Good. I'll be over there if you have any questions."

Jacko began the exercises.

Sun opened the diary and continued reading once Jacko started. He did not find anything new or exciting until he read the excerpt from day one hundred and twenty.

Day One Hundred and Twenty:

We began our lesson like every other day and something very strange occurred while we were treating our sixth patient. Priest Abiathar chanted in a peculiar language and used symbols that I didn't recognize. The patient made a full recovery within minutes. I asked him how he managed to do this, and he didn't explain. I'll have to wait to see if this sort of behavior continues.

Day One Hundred and Twenty-One:

Today, priest Abiathar acted even more strangely. His attitude has been altered by becoming a little colder, and his skills appeared to be getting stronger. I've been around some skillful healers, but I have never witnessed their skills improving greatly in just two days. I'm sending a message to Brother Pien to get his point of view.

Day One Hundred and Twenty-Seven:

Today was even eerier. One of the female acolytes named Herat, who is always warm and friendly, was sort of cold and standoffish. Normally, that wouldn't bother me, but she, too, started doing things in the same manner as Abiathar. I hope Brother Pien responds to my request soon.

Sun glanced over the next ten pages because her writings were about how she was growing more suspicious of the priest, and that she is still waiting for Brother Pien to respond back, which he did on day one hundred and thirty-three.

Day One Hundred and Thirty-Three:

Today Brother Pien responded back telling me to keep an eye on priest Abiathar, and if there is indeed something strange going on, to let him know, and he will send help to deal with him. He thinks something evil has taken hold of his soul, and I need to expose this if it's true.

Day One Hundred and Thirty-Four:

Today, I spoke to priest Abiathar regarding my training. He said that I was ready for the next level of teaching he had to offer. When I asked him what that was, he said it was special and only for the ones who are truly worthy. Furthermore, there was something very strange in the way he said it and the look in his eyes. As I left, an acolyte by the name of Myrna pulled me aside and said she was scared and wanted to speak with me tonight in private. I told her I would.

Day One Hundred and Thirty-Four Continued:

Myrna just left my cottage and told me something strange was happening. Most of her fellow acolytes were acting differently, but she couldn't put her finger on what that was. I told her to leave the church until I can find out more. She said that she would as soon as she went back and got her belongings. I might have to get Captain Strom involved.

Day One Hundred and Thirty-Five:

Today was the strangest day yet. Priest Abiathar's healing methods changed entirely. At one point, I noticed he administered a different type of healing, one from the dark arts. I questioned his technique, and he said it was necessary in order to cure what ailed the woman.

As I was leaving, I saw Myrna, and she appeared to be relaxed. I asked her what she was still doing there and she acted like we never spoke then told me that I should join them. I have no idea what she means. Tomorrow I'll talk with Captain Strom.

Day One Hundred and Thirty-Six:

Today instead of my lessons, I talked to Captain Strom, and he said that I shouldn't go there anymore, and he would talk to priest Abiathar and get to the bottom of what he's doing.
Day One Hundred and Thirty-Seven:

Captain Strom just left, and he told me that Abiathar explained everything to him I wasn't allowed to go there any longer, and he will take me on as an apprentice. I asked Captain Strom to explain further, but he wouldn't elaborate. I'll send a message to Brother Pien.

Sun didn't find anything else of interest until he found the only entry regarding Torhan.

Day One Hundred and Sixty-Eight:

Guards entered my cottage and with them, they brought in a semi-conscious stranger for healing. While I was mending his wounds, he mumbled two names; priest Abiathar and Grappin.
After I finished working on him, I searched his pockets and found two letters. One was addressed to me from Brother Pien, which was odd, and the other was from this Grappin person. I read Brother Pien's note first, and he said the stranger's name was Torhan. Brother Pien also told me to find out what his intentions were, because he came to Mirkin to see priest Abiathar, and he didn't want Torhan to jeopardize my mission. The letter from Grappin mentioned that Torhan was involved in a murder and the theft of some items. Grappin also told him to come to Mirkin, take priest Abiathar's beads for proof that he was there, disable some wards, and return to Redden.
I tried to revive Torhan to question him further, but the guards took him away. One more thing; Grappin knows how to summon guardians, so he must be a priest of some sort. I'm going over to the temple to find out more.

He thumbed through the remaining pages and found them all to be blank. By now it was getting late. Jacko and a few other students were the only ones left practicing. Sun got up and told him to stop training for the evening, and that he should get some rest. Jacko limped over to him and Sun chuckled, knowing his training methods worked.

"Did you finish reading the diary?" Jacko asked.

"I did."

"Did he, do it?"

"Let's talk after we're in our room."

After they were shown to their room by another student, they sat down at the table to discuss the diary.

"I think Katara was originally sent to Mirkin to study with priest Abiathar, but things changed over time with him and his acolytes." Sun said.

"How so?"

"It doesn't really say. She only wrote of her suspicions and that she contacted someone named Brother Pien, who then told her to stay there and investigate."

"When did she meet Torhan?" Jacko interrupted.

"It seems like he has a history of getting into trouble with the authorities, because he was taken to her for healing."

"Look, he's normally not like this."

"Anyway, while Katara was working on him, she found two notes. One was from Brother Pien, and the other was from someone named Grappin. Has he ever mentioned either of those names to you before?"

Jacko shook his head.

"I wonder how he met Brother Pien and then ended up in Katara's care?"

"Maybe he was sent there by him and started a fight with the guards just to see her?"

"That's extreme because he eventually ended up in jail."

"What else did you find out?"

"You're not going to like this one. He's wanted for murder and theft in Redden."

"Is there anything in there that might clear him?"

"Not with Captain Strom."

"Did the diary mention why he was arrested?"

"No."

"I'm going to get to the bottom of this. He's not a killer or a thief." Jacko firmly stated.

"I believe you, but something is very odd. Maybe this Grappin fellow set him up in Redden."

"We need to find him."

"I agree. Let's get some rest; I'm tired."

****

Several hours earlier, Breen was getting some fresh air after her much-needed rest, and came upon a store called Bontinhammer's Unusual Items. Intrigued, she entered.

The place was old looking, disheveled, dimly lit, and smelled musty, but she pushed aside her disgust and began looking around.

The first floor didn't hold her interest, so she took the stairs on her left up to the second floor. While walking around, she passed many people milling about. Some of them were old, some were young, and a few were deformed and very odd looking.

"What a strange mix of individuals." She thought and walked down a few rows while scanning the shelves.

Preoccupied, she failed to notice the old man standing near her.

"Did you find the cure?" He asked.

"What?" Breen turned toward the speaker. "Excuse me?"

"Did you find the cure?"

In front of her was a person with a badly scarred face, wearing tattered clothes and no shoes. "What cure?"

"They say it's here somewhere. I just need to find it."

"What does it do?"

"It's supposed to make you younger and more beautiful. If you see it let me know." The old man said and left.

She shook her head and continued looking. The following aisle had glass display cases with tiny signs next to each one. The first one was of a small statue of an owl. The sign read: "Say the word 'Flight' and the statue will take shape, and you'll see far off into the distance." She thought back to the figurines Tonles had, and wondered if this one was part of a collection.

Next to the owl was an eyeball in another glass display case. The plaque read: "Remove your eye and place the Eyeball of Sight into your socket, and you will detect things that aren't there." She cringed at the thought of removing her eye and placing it in there.

The next item was a thin wooden finger with the inscription: "The master pick will open the most complicated locks, just like a master thief."

The rest of the row had even stranger objects such as a Head of Knowledge that would not only keep you company on lonely nights, but knew much just by speaking the word "Talk,"

Eyepieces of Understanding that allowed you to comprehend strange and foreign writings once they are placed over your eyeballs, and finally, the Rope of Intestine. Breen looked at the long, red, wrinkled organ and even though this one repulsed her, like no other, she still read the plaque anyway. It said: "The Rope of Intestine is as strong as steel and can be used to tie up the mightiest of foes, lift the heaviest of objects or pull several people up at once. Guaranteed to work."

The following row contained books, some of which caught her interest, namely the book of *Flame Arrow* that allowed the user to ignite arrows as they were launched from a bow. Another was titled *Poisonous Creatures*, which basically contained information about different types of animals that had toxic sacks, how to extract the venom, and use it on weapons without getting it on yourself. There were books of attributes and skills such as; strength, dexterity, health, archery, and acrobatics.

Breen continued down several more aisles until she came upon one with glass containers. Some she heard of and some he didn't. White Light that would blind your opponent; Searing Heat would burn your enemy to ashes; Dissolving, would melt the toughest of material, including limbs, and at the far, end was infamous Canister of Endless Drink, which allowed the owner never to thirst again.

Further down the row were oils and ointments. There was one called Oil of Elusiveness, which enabled the user to slip and slide out of any hold or bind. Oil of Protection toughened armor one grade higher. Oil of Taste, made simple food taste like a meal fit for a king. Ointment of Healing, mended severely broken bones and wounds within a day. Ointment of Relief allowed the relief of burns, whether they were from fire or cold.

By now, Breen was exhausted, and she went to the front of the store to ask the tall man behind the counter about prices. He frowned and handed her a parchment. Breen was shocked about how much things cost and after checking her funds, she purchased three flasks of Dissolving, one of Searing Heat, the Finger of Lock-picking, and lastly and the most expensive item on the list, the Eyepieces of Understanding. She hoped they would allow her to understand the book of Tirips.

It was nearing nightfall when she left the store, and despite being tired and hungry, she was eager to return to her room and use the eyepieces to see if they worked. Along the way, she saw Tonles, snuck up on him and tapped him on the shoulder. Almost immediately she regretted her actions, because the big man turned around and stopped just short of striking her in the face with a back fist.

"Girl, don't do that again. You're lucky that I recognized your pretty face in time." He barked at her.

"Sorry, I wasn't thinking. I was too caught up in my purchases."

Tonles relaxed a bit. "What did you buy?"

After showing him her wares, they went back to the inn.

They entered the tavern and joined Konafar, who was already sitting down and getting drunk.

"Have you seen Sun and Jacko?" Breen asked Konafar.

"They went back to their Order…" He answered and hiccupped several times and then burped.

Tonles ordered drinks for them as soon as the serving wench came over.

"Did they say when they were returning?"

Konafar swayed slightly to the left and then back to the right, looking at her blankly.

"Tonles did they tell you?"

Tonles didn't answer her because he was suddenly preoccupied.

"Tonles!"

"WHAT?" He snapped at her after hearing his name called for the second time.

"Did they say when they were returning?"

"They said in a couple of days." He turned his attention away.

She followed his gaze. "What's wrong?"

"That's the boy I played with yesterday and his lute is broken. I need to know what happened because it was the best sounding instrument I've ever heard."

Tonles got up and walked over to the boy. "What happened to your lute lad?" He asked.

The boy did not answer nor did he look up.

"Son, what happened?" Tonles asked again and this time the boy looked up.

His left eye was blackened, his lip was split and dried blood was still on the corner of his mouth. Torhan felt so bad for him because he was a good kid.

"They broke my lute and hit me."

"Who did?"

"The men sitting over there." The boy pointed to three men and four women sitting at the corner table.

"Let me have your instrument."

At first, the boy was hesitant and then handed it to him. Tonles, lute in hand, walked over to the table.

"What's he doing?" Breen asked Konafar.

Konafar turned his head toward Tonles and hiccupped. "Probabbbly going to administer some jussstice..." He slurred

"Should we help him?" Konafar squinted and said.

"Help who? The men at the table? There are only six of them."

"Six? You mean three."

"I see six."

"You're drunk." Breen shook her head.

"Oh there're only three then? That's it? That's child's play for him, watch what he ca..." Konafar's words faded as his head hit the table, and he passed out.

Tonles studied the three men as he walked over. The one on the left was almost comical in appearance. He was chubby and out of shape, his brown hair was in the shape of a bowl, and his nose looked like it was flattened with a board. The guy on the right was rail thin, balding, and didn't look like he could fight his way out of a paper sack. Both men posed no real threat; Tonles thought.

However, the man in the middle, wearing studded leather and built similar to himself looked like a grizzled veteran of many wars. He would have to be addressed first if things got out of hand, Tonles knew.

Tonles stopped in front of their table. "Which one of you broke the lute and hit the boy?" He held forth the instrument so they could see it.

No one responded. They continued drinking and carousing with the women. Tonles slammed the broken lute onto the table, knocking over several goblets of ale and getting their attention.

"Who are you?" The chubby man asked in a slightly effeminate voice.

"Now that I have your attention, who broke the boy's lute and hit him?" Tonles calmly asked.

"Tough words for someone with a weapon." The thin man stated.

"My axe?" Tonles smiled at him. "I don't need it to beat the crap out of you three." He unstrapped Ripper and tossed it aside. "Now this is the last time I'm going to ask. Which coward broke the boy's lute and hit him?"

The men and women seated at the table now had his full undivided attention, because they knew how serious he was by the tone of his voice.

"I broke the lute." The thin man answered and stood up.

"And I hit the boy." The middle-aged man in the center answered and stood up as well.

The women got up and moved away from the table just as the room got quiet.

"Why did you do that?" Tonles asked them.

"He didn't play anything we liked and when we asked him to play music from our hometown, he refused, thus insulting us in front of our ladies. The thin man responded.

"My words of advice are for you to replace the lute with something better, give him one hundred pieces of gold for his troubles, and go over and apologize. And don't forget to ask for forgiveness in front of everyone here."

"Is that all?" The chubby man said with an attitude and stood up.

"I'm not done. You will do this on your knees."

"And who's going to make us?" The grizzled veteran said, looking at his two other comrades.

Before he could turn his attention back towards Tonles, Tonles grabbed his right wrist, broke it with a mere twist and then wouldn't let it go. He screamed and fell to his knees. The thin man reached out to help his friend, but Tonles sensed his intentions and flung the injured man into him, knocking him to the floor.

The chubby man was about to do something when Tonles quickly grabbed him by the back of his head with his left hand, elbowed him with his right, and then slammed his head into the table, knocking him senseless.

The thin guy got to his feet, pulled a dagger from his boot and approached Tonles, waving the blade back and forth offensively. Tonles waited for him to attack and when he did, he stepped to the side and easily avoided several slashes. His attacker lunged at him, Tonles anticipated his move and stepped in, wrapped his arm over his, trapping his weapon and rendering it useless. The thin man struggled desperately to free his arm, but

Tonles held firm while punching him several times in the face, breaking his nose and jaw and knocking him out.

The grizzled vet got up and tried to run, but Tonles grabbed him by the armor and pulled him to the ground, then savagely stomped on his left knee three times.

Tonles dragged all three men over to the boy, woke up the ones that were unconscious and made them apologize, Then they handed him the one hundred gold pieces and another two hundred to replace the lute.

The boy went up to the man who gave him the black eye and punched him in the face. Tonles smiled at the boy and told him he would get him another lute in the morning. The boy thanked him. Tonles then allowed the troublemakers to leave.

He rejoined Breen and Konafar, who was somewhat coherent, and they drank for several hours before turning in for the night.

Around midmorning of the following day, Sun and Jacko walked down to the eatery to have their morning meal. They grabbed some food and sat off to the side.

"I slept like a baby." Jacko said and shoved a small tangyuan cake into his mouth. "These are delicious, have one?"

Sun took one from the plate. "After your training we should go back to Mirkin and show them the diary." He took a bite.

Jacko's smile faded. "Do you think it's a good idea we do?"

"Let's give Konafar the benefit of the doubt that he will allow us time to try to clear his name."

"And if he doesn't?"

"Then we'll leave right away."

"I don't want to fight him."

"I know, you mentioned that already. For now, worry about your training."

They finished eating, cleared their plates, and went to the training area. The room already had many students doing their morning routine.

"Today I want you to begin your training by doing the same exercises you did yesterday. After you're loosened up, do some light kicks. When you're finished, we'll move on to your next lesson."

Sun walked to the small bookshelf, picked up a manual, sat down in the corner, and began reading.

Jacko did as he was instructed and when he was finished, Sun led him to the far end of the room. In this area, there were five wooden pillars of different heights with metal jugs on top. To the left of them were seven rings dangling from ropes of various lengths. Next to the rings were ten bamboo frames with rice paper in the center. They were suspended from the ceiling. Finally, there was a gray wall that was six-feet wide and eight-feet high.

"Jacko," Sun began, "the four exercises in front of you each have a different purpose in order for you to master the Iron Feet technique. The jugs will help you develop reach, control, and power. The rings will help you improve your accuracy. The wooden frames will help you improve your speed and control, and finally; we have something called a soft wall." He walked over to it.

"The material is remarkable and will help you develop true power. Watch this."

Sun hit the wall with a side kick, and his foot went deeply into the wall. He kicked the wall harder and this time his foot didn't go in as deep. Jacko was puzzled. Sun's third kick was his hardest, and his foot barely made an imprint. He stopped and looked at Jacko.

"The material will adjust to your power, the more power you employ the less it sinks into the wall. It's quite remarkable. Now, watch me as I show you the others."

Sun demonstrated each exercise until Jacko said he had a full understanding; and then left the room to go talk to Brother Lee Chee Wa.

Jacko approached the rings and began his session with the one that was lower than his hips, figuring it should be fairly easy. His first kick missed the target, and the next few kicked the ring and caused it to move all over. After several more miserable attempts, he stopped the ring and tried again. This time was no different than the last, and it began to frustrate him that he couldn't put his foot through the middle like he was supposed to.

"Do you know what you are doing wrong?" The question came from a female who was behind him.

"If I did, then I would be able to put my foot through the hole." Jacko arrogantly responded, without even looking at her.

His next two attempts missed the ring entirely.

"Let me know when you want me to show you." She said.

Jacko tried a higher target and this time he put his foot through the ring by overextending his leg, but in doing so, he didn't have enough time to free it, and fell hard to the ground. While lying there, he heard snickers of laughter directly behind him and got up and turned around. Anger gave way to embarrassment as he looked upon, not one, but three young female students. They were very similar in stature; with slightly slanted eyes, they wore their black braided hair down their backs, and their skin tone was darker than his, indicating they were from the southern region. They were also ranked much higher than he was. He bowed to them, and they nodded back.

The highest ranking student smiled at him and spoke. "Are you ready for me to show you?"

Despite her young age, she was wearing a blue with red trim uniform, which indicated she was the rank of the Rock, which was four ranks higher than he was. The other two women wore solid blue uniforms, which indicated they were three ranks higher than he was.

Jacko nodded, and she walked over to the three rings, lifted her leg and kicked through them in succession, one after the other, with little trouble and then turned back toward him.

"Did you see how I did that?"

"I did, but I'm none the wiser."

"Watch my technique."

She did the exercise again, slower this time, and Jacko studied her movements.

"Now you try." She said.

Jacko took her place and as soon as he lifted his leg, she told him to stop.

"Look down at your leg."

He saw that his foot wasn't pointed toward the back, and that was stopping him from shifting his weight correctly. He did it again and this time he turned his foot all the way to the rear and kicked through the ring without hitting it. After several more attempts, he was doing the exercise correctly and stopped.

"Good, you have the basics."

"Thank you very much." He said clasping his hands together and bowed.

"Would you like me to show you the rest of the exercises?"

Jacko nodded.

"By the way, the way my name is Jia. Lin is on the left and May on the right."

Jacko introduced himself and bowed again.

Jia walked past him, over to the pillars and began the exercise. She kicked the first jug that was seven feet off of the ground, and given her stature, was quite impressive. The metal jug flew off of its perch and fell to the ground with a thud. She then jumped up and kicked another one, which was slightly higher than the last, and sent the jug sailing through the air, where it crashed against the wall.

"That felt good." She said and walked over to the bamboo frames. "You need to kick with all of your power and don't hit the paper."

Jia bent her knee, cocked her leg to the side, and did a roundhouse kick, stopping just short of the paper. She did this several more times to demonstrate her level of control, which was so impressive to Jacko.

"Now you try," she said.

He walked over, and his first kick went straight through the paper. He tried it again and had the same result. After the third time, she stopped him.

"You need to kick much slower."

Jacko raised his leg and did as he was instructed, and even though he stopped well short of the paper, he started to understand what he needed to do.

"Keep working at it, you'll get it. The wall is easy enough to understand. Good luck in your training and remember practice makes perfect, and do it often." She turned away.

"How many years did it take you to master the Iron Feet?"

She paused. "Years? Years are a number. You never really master the technique, just the knowledge."

"How so?"

She faced him again. "A title of Master indicates that you are fully understanding of the technique. Do you think you're a master if you are just proficient at it?"

"To me a master means you are the best at fighting and can't be beat."

She smirked. "Let's say you think you're a so-called master and beat everyone in our school and then one day you lose, are you not a master anymore?"

"That's a good question. I don't know."

"Take Master Shoo. He's very skilled in every technique, but I bet Brother Lee Chee Wa can best him in several of them. So you see, it's not about never losing, it's about wisdom. Do you understand?"

He nodded.

"It was nice meeting you Jacko; I must be going."

Jacko thanked her again and watched them leave. He returned to his training, and for some reason, kept thinking about Jia.

Sun returned a short time later, watched Jacko from afar and was impressed with how he was doing. After his friend, stopped to take a break he walked over.

"How's the training?"

"Good." Jacko said as he was wiping the sweat off of his face using a cloth.

"You really picked it up fast." Sun gave him a look and then chuckled.

"I see you ran into Jia." Jacko said.

"I did and she told me what she showed you."

"I should have paid better attention to your teachings."

"It's okay to take advice from your fellow students. Most of the higher-ranking ones are helpful, so don't be afraid to ask. We should be going soon."

"Give me a few more hours." Jacko said, then went back to training.

"I'll see you then."

Sun went to the dining hall to fill his belly.

After buying the boy one of the finest lutes the store had to offer and giving it to him, Tonles walked around town just to get some fresh air. He thought about what he'd done for the boy and it stirred up feelings about the family he'd always wanted, but never had. His profession didn't allow him time to settle down with any one woman long enough to start one, and now he wished he had.

He often fantasized about living on a farm, raising livestock, playing with his children, and living peacefully.

The smell of beef cooking over an open flame brought his attention back to the present, and he followed the scent until he arrived at the market square. Merchants and patrons stretched as far as the eye could see. Tonles quickly glanced about until he spotted white smoke emanating from one of the stands. He salivated, and his stomach grumbled several times, causing him to walk rather briskly in that direction.

Despite his best efforts, he was still slowed by the people milling about, and when he finally arrived, his eyes widened when he saw the slabs of beef and fowl roasting over an open pit. His mouth watered in anticipation as he purchased some beef and hunkered down eating until he had his fill. Sighing in satisfaction, he walked around the market shopping.

****

What Tonles didn't know was that three men were positioned on a rooftop waiting for the right opportunity to strike him down. The assassins were dressed in black from head to toe, and despite the ban on all weapons inside of the city walls, they managed to smuggle in crossbows and very sharp stiletto blades.

"Are we going to kill those idiots after we kill our target?" The assassin on the right asked the others.

"You know the drill. Kill the target, get the rest of the money, and then kill the people who hired us." The one in the middle responded.

"Ya, but one of them is my brother in-law."

"Doesn't matter, you know our creed. No one is allowed to live because they could identify us. Now spread out and get into position. Signal me when you're ready."

Tonles was in the middle of purchasing leather boots when the coordinated attacks took place. Heavy steel bolts, from three different locations, pierced through his chainmail shirt with ease, but only partially through his brigandine armor. He staggered due to the impact of the bolts piercing his flesh.

As he was seeking cover, he was struck by three more bolts. This time in his left leg, left shoulder, and one nicked his throat, missing the artery by a fraction of an inch. He grunted and fell to his right knee. People started screaming and scattered away from him. As he got up, another volley hit him, this time in the back, left shoulder, and left leg. He then fell to the ground.

A brave man ran over to help him, and as he was reaching for Tonles' hand, he was struck in the back of the head and fell on top of him. Thinking quickly, Tonles used his body as a shield and hid underneath just as more bolts rained down upon them.

On the roof, the lead assassin couldn't tell if their intended target was dead or alive, so after he ordered another round of bolts he then signaled his men to leave, because the guards were coming.

After they arrived, the guards searched frantically for the attackers, while a few others pulled the dead body off of Tonles and carried him off to the healers after they found him unconscious.

Konafar and Breen were eating when Captain Strom rushed into the inn and to their table. He was flushed and breathing heavy, indicating that something was wrong.

"Tonles was attacked by assassins." He said.

"WHAT! WHEN?" Konafar shouted and stood up.

"A few minutes ago down in the market square."

"Is he dead?"

"He's unconscious and my men took him to the healer. I'll take you there now."

They ran through the streets and entered the healer's house. There they found Tonles lying on a table, and the healers were in the process of removing the bolts.

"Is he alive?" Konafar asked.

"He is, but will he live is another story. We'll know better after we finish removing the bolts, so please wait over there." One of the healers pointed.

Captain Strom pulled them aside. "They're very good healers."

"Did you catch the killers?" Konafar snapped at him.

Strom shook his head.

"Can't your men do anything right? First, you lose the killers who killed the priest and now this."

Strom knew his friend didn't mean what he was saying. "We'll get them." He promised.

"You better or I will." Konafar was seething with hatred.

"You should know the attack wasn't random." Strom said trying to calm his friend.

"Tell me something I don't know."

"How so?" Breen interrupted.

"The attacks were too precise and there was only one other casualty. A bystander was struck down trying to help him. Let me ask you something. Does he have any enemies or had an argument with someone prior to the attack?"

"Last night there was an incident at the inn when Tonles beat up three men for picking on the minstrel boy." Breen said.

"Describe them to me." She described them in detail.

Captain Strom knew the men she described and after placing a reassurance hand on Konafar's shoulder, he told him that he would get them within the hour and left.

"Wait here." Konafar said moments later and followed after Strom.

"Don't do anything stupid." Breen's words fell on deaf ears as he left through the door.

She turned her attention back to the healers.

Within the hour, Captain Strom's men rounded up two out of the three men from the night before and found the third with his throat slit. After they were placed into separate rooms, Strom, Konafar, and a couple of guards went in to see the guy with the broken wrist.

"Why am I here?" He asked Strom as soon as they entered.

"Loist you're here because the man you had a run-in with last night was attacked today."

"Too bad for him, but I didn't do it. He must have had other enemies, and that wouldn't surprise me one bit. He started a fight with me, Cytep, and Posis for no reason. We were just minding our business drinking when…" Loist paused when he saw the angry look on Konafar's face.

"Go on." Strom urged him.

"Like I was saying that animal came up to our table accusing us of breaking some kid's lute and hitting him."

Konafar reached over and grabbed him by his tunic and lifted him off of his chair.

"You lie!" Konafar barked at the prisoner.

The guards tried to remove Konafar's hold on the prisoner, but they were unable to break his death grip.

"Please Konafar." Strom pleaded.

Konafar glanced over his shoulder at his friend and then threw the man down hard into his chair.

"I'm only going to ask you once," Captain Strom leaned in. "Did you hire the assassins?"

Loist glanced at Konafar and then back at Strom. "I'll answer if he leaves."

Strom nodded for Konafar to follow him out of the room. When they were safely out of earshot, Captain Strom stopped.

"We can't get information out of him if you keep acting the way you did. I know your emotions are high, but be patient and let us do our job." Strom said.

"What happened to you? You were always the one to administer the right amount of punishment in order to get the information you needed."

"I've learned that it is easier to get information this way than beating it out of them."

"This is useless." Konafar said in frustration.

"Let me show you how it's done."

Captain Strom reentered the room and questioned Loist for a long time, and then went to the other room. Cytep was a mess. His broken jaw and bandaged nose made his face look like it was run over by a wagon.

"Loist said you hired the assassins to kill the man who beat you up last night. Is it true?"

Cytep's eyes went wide with fear.

"Cytep if it is you'll stand trial for this alone."

"I did… no… such thing... We went… to the… healers and then back to our… rooms." His broken jaw made it difficult to speak.

"What?" Strom drew closer to understanding what he was saying.

"I didn't do… it. We went… to the healers… and then to our rooms."

"Are you sure that's what you did?"

Cytep nodded his head and Strom suddenly left the room, then waited for several minutes before returning. The man was sweating, and Strom continued to twist Loist's story around until Cytep finally broke down and told him everything.

"So you were embarrassed and humiliated, and that's the reason why you wanted him to die." Captain Strom said.

"Please Captain Strom, one of… the men was… Posis' brother in-law, and… if they killed him…" He looked down and then back again. "They'll kill us too." He was clearly growing nervous.

"Calm down and tell me how you met them."

Cytep gave Strom the location where they met the assassins. How many there were, the reason why they hired them, and how much they paid the assassins to kill Tonles. Strom reassured him that he was safe and left the room to talk to Konafar.

"I know what happened after their altercation last night. They wanted revenge on Tonles for embarrassing them."

Konafar made a motion to enter the room and Strom put his hand on his shoulder stopping him.

"I have an idea. We can kill two birds with one stone."

"How so?"

"Let's use either Loist or Cytep to draw the assassins out. After we kill them, I'll leave you alone with them to do whatever you want."

Konafar liked his idea. "So what's your plan?"

In another part of the town, the three assassins huddled together on top of a roof, drinking dark ale.

"One down, two to go."

"Nails that was my brother-in-law."

The assassin laughed at him. "So what, I didn't see you mourn for my cousin last year when I killed him, hence don't give me any crap Lope. Am I right Seiles?" Nails took a long swig.

"If you can't take what we do, then get out, but you know what would happen if you did." Seiles said, looking at him with cold, flat eyes.

Lope knew he was right, once you joined the Assassin's Order you were a member for life, and death was certain if you wanted to leave.

"I'd even kill my own mother if she hired me." Seiles chimed in, and both he and Nails laughed then clanged their wooden goblets together.

"You're not thinking of leaving are you?" Nails asked Lope directly.

He shook his head.

"Good, I'd hate to kill you."

"Ya, me too." Seiles said.

Lope looked at Seiles with disgust and then back at Nails and said. "I'll be fine. I just never killed someone close to me."

"The first one is always the toughest. Take Quick Shot, for instance; he had to kill his own sister after she hired him to assassinate that fellow who raped her." Nails said.

"Now that's tough." Seiles added.

"Where do you think my brother in-law's friends are?" Lope asked, changing the subject.

"I am sure we'll find them later getting drunk."

"Do you think we killed our target?"

"He couldn't have lived. We shot him like nine times and what does it matter? We have their money."

Nails reached over and grabbed Seiles by the throat. "Go make sure he's dead, and if he isn't, finish the job."

He shoved him away. Seiles got up and left.

"After we're finished here our next assignment is for us to go to Tinderrush and kill a high-ranking officer."

Lope nodded in acknowledgement, and they went back to drinking.

Back at the healer's house, Breen kept watch over Tonles, while the healers were eating in the other room. She was bored so she rummaged through her belongings until she found the Eyepieces of Understanding.

She held the case near the candle and looked at the tiny round objects inside. All at once, they changed colors right before her eyes, as if they were putting on a show for her. First, they were clear and then changed to blue, red, orange, purple, and finally back to the original. She smiled while opening the case and grabbed one to give it a gentle squeeze. The eyepiece was soft and flexible, and to further test its durability, she bent it in half and watched it spring back to its original shape.

She read the instructions and then wondered what would happen if she couldn't get them out, or worse, what if they were cursed, and they blinded her. Determination, and curiosity to understand the book of Tirips won the day, and she placed them into her eyes one at a time. Her first three attempts failed miserably, because every time she placed it onto her eyeball, her eyelid fluttered too fast. After several more attempts, she got frustrated and placed a firm grip on her eyelid, opened it as far as it would go, and forced the lens onto her eye. Instinctually, her eye watered and tears streamed down her face.

When the strange sensation of having a foreign object in her eye passed, she opened it and covered the other one without the lens. Right away, she could tell everything looked different on her left side. Things appeared clearer, and she could make out details on objects across the room.

Excited, she opened the book only to be disappointed when the words and symbols remained unchanged. She assumed that she might need the other eyepiece in her eye, but as she was about to reach for the other lens, she heard several a grunts followed by a thump of something hitting the floor, coming from the other room where the healers were.

Breen's gut feeling told her something was wrong, so she put the book and case back into her bag and hid behind the largest of the cabinets. Carefully, she watched the door and a few minutes later, a person carrying a long stiletto, dressed in black leather with his face covered so that only his eyes were visible, walked in. She knew right away what he or she wanted, unsheathed her dagger and reached into her sack without taking her eyes off the intruder.

The killer paused and scanned the room for any hidden danger and then proceeded towards Tonles. As soon as Breen grasped one of the flasks, it clanked against the others on its way out, causing the killer to stop and turn in her direction.

"Come out and I might let you live." He coldly said.

Breen didn't respond, and the assassin threw his blade in her direction, barely missing her face. In the next instance, he held forth another dagger.

"Last chance or you die where you stand." He said.

Breen's vision was skewed from the one eyepiece, so she told him she was coming out and left her dagger behind, while palming the flask to conceal it from the killer.

"Ah, a female healer dressed in leather and wearing a sword. Now isn't that an unusual manner of dress? You must be a friend of the soon to be deceased."

"What do you want?" She snapped.

"What do I want? Hmm let me think about it," he glanced at

Tonles and then back to her. "To kill him. Now down on your knees with your hands in the air."

As Breen was about to do what he requested, she threw the flask underhanded at the assassin. He tossed his dagger at her, scoring a direct hit in her chest, piercing through armor and flesh, and sending her sprawling to the ground coughing up blood.

Meanwhile, the flask missed the assassin's head by inches, hit the wall behind him and shattered, dousing everything within a three-foot radius, including the assassin's back, with the blackish liquid. The assassin's screams were frightening and loud as he fell to the ground, writhing pain. Before Breen passed out from the pain, she saw smoke rising from his body and smelled flesh and leather burning.

Standing outside of the Inn of the Lion, Captain Strom peered out from behind the door in the back and watched the room intently. Seated throughout the room were his most skilled guards, wearing common clothes and hiding long knives. Konafar was seated off to the left of the entrance, drinking with several patrons while keeping his hand on Carnage under the table.

The plan was to wait for the assassins to contact Loist and Cytep and either capture, or kill them outright. The serving wenches were instructed to keep serving Loist and Cytep ale to calm their nerves.

It was around dusk when an elderly man, hunched over, and carrying a walking stick entered the inn. He looked around and walked towards Loist and Cytep. Konafar lowered his tankard and watched the old man slowly making his way over, then exchanged some words with them and sat down. He wasn't sure if he was the assassin or not, but knew enough to know assassins were masters of disguises.

Captain Strom also watched things unfold but waited, because if they acted too hastily or were mistaken, then the assassin would get away. The old man began drinking with them, and both men didn't appear to be alarmed or indicate anything was wrong.

During the next hour, they continued drinking and everything appeared to be normal until Cytep's head hit the table, like he passed out, and then so did Loist's. The old man took one last swig, stood up, and threw several silver coins on the table. Captain Strom noticed something strange. The old man had lost his hunch, and that was enough for him to come into the room, shouting for him to stop.

The guards took that as the signal, grabbed their hidden weapons from underneath the table and stood up. Konafar grabbed Carnage and moved closer to the exit so that escape was impossible without going through him.

"You're under arrest." Strom said, short sword in hand.

The old man stopped and didn't say a word.

"Take him." Strom ordered his men.

As soon as they were close enough, the old man turned his walking stick around, gripped it with both hands, and shoved it into a nearby guard's chest. His eyes widened and blood spilled out of his mouth, He fell away, revealing a four-inch blade sticking out of the walking stick.

The other guards raced in, but the old man moved quicker and stabbed several more in the stomach, killing them instantly. The rest fearfully backed off.

Captain Strom had had enough and engaged the old man, parrying most of his attacks, but the assassin was quicker and stabbed him several times.

Konafar and the rest of the guards joined the fray. The assassin was an excellent fighter. He blocked and parried Konafar's attacks, wounded Strom severely and forced him to leave the fight, and killed the rest of the guards. Konafar was the only one left standing and backed away to catch his breath. All that stood between the old man and freedom was Konafar.

"Let me go." The assassin demanded.

"No, you tried to kill my friend." Konafar responded.

"Well if he didn't die from his wounds, then he's dead already."

"Is that so?"

"Yes, my associate should be joining me shortly with the good news." He smiled.

Konafar charged the assassin and he sidestepped the attack, and then stabbed him in his side, piercing through his armor and flesh, sending him headlong into a few tables gasping for air. The assassin made a motion to leave, and then turned around to face Konafar.

"You know what? I think I'll kill you and then kill the good captain." He laughed and began walking towards Konafar.

Meanwhile, Captain Strom found enough strength to attack the assassin's blind side, and as he was about to deliver a vicious blow to his neck, the assassin deflected the attack and then sliced him across the stomach, dropping the captain to his knees. The assassin was about to stab him in the throat, when Konafar charged him with Carnage in an overhead guard.

Out of the corner of his eye, the assassin saw him coming and waited until the last possible second before turning around and raising his stick over his head and at a slight angle. Konafar anticipated his block and changed the direction of his strike, bringing the two-handed sword upwards into his groin. The assassin screamed as Konafar moved Carnage back and forth in a sawing motion, until his guts spilled onto the floor. Exhausted, Konafar dropped to his knees gasping for air.

Outside, Nails arrived just as Lope's guts hit the floor. He thought about entering the inn and killing the captain and the man with the sword, but when he heard more guards rounding the corner, he made haste and went to the area where he was supposed to meet the other assassin, Seiles.

Breen regained consciousness and immediately felt her wound throbbing with pain. She took hold of the dagger and couldn't bring herself to remove the blade. Slowly, she climbed to her feet, staggered a few times to regain her balance, and then saw the body of the assassin, lying face down, near the door. His armor, back, and head looked like they had melted away. Apparently, she had thrown the flask of dissolving. The fluid did just that to him, some of the doorframe and most of the floorboards.

She stumbled over to Tonles and was relieved to find him alive. The pain from her wound suddenly became unbearable and she gripped the table, gasping in discomfort. She needed to remove the blade if she wanted any kind of relief. She wrapped her hand around the hilt and closed her eyes. She was about to yank the weapon free when a hand covered hers and stopped her from removing it. She opened her eyes and Tonles was staring back at her.

"You might die if you do it." He said. "What smells?"

Before she could answer, they heard people entering the cottage. A familiar voice called to them from the other room, and Tonles let them know they were in the back.

Feet shuffled into the mending room and in walked a few guards assisting Konafar and Captain Strom onto two other tables.

Captain Strom gritted in pain. "Go wake the healers from the House of the Blessed…" He winced. "Get them here right away. And get rid of the bodies." He ordered the guards.

Tonles got off of his table and helped Breen onto it, so she could lay down. He limped over to Konafar. "What happened to you?"

Konafar winced as he sat up. "We found out the men you beat up last night hired three assassins to kill you, so we laid a trap for them at the inn. Unfortunately, only one showed and we killed him."

"There's another one right there." Breen said.

"That leaves one more. Where are the men from last night; they'll know?" Tonles asked.

"They're dead." Strom added.

"Damn, we need to find the last assassin." He looked at Konafar's stomach and noticed blood seeping from his bandages. "Your wound looks deep; what kind of weapon did he use?"

"Nothing special, he fought with a walking stick that had a very sharp blade at one end."

Konafar turned his attention to the men dragging out the mangled body of the assassin. "What did you use on him?"

"It was a liquid that could melt just about anything." Breen said.

"Where did you get it?"

"At one of the stores in town."

"Which one?" Strom interjected.

"Bontinhammer's Unusual Items."

"I'll have to have a talk with him about what he is selling. Konafar, I want to thank you for what you did."

"Looks like you owe me again."

Just then, the healers entered the cottage, came right to the back room and began tending to the wounded. Two healers began stitching Konafar and Captain Strom, while another gave Breen a heavy sedative, then carefully removed the dagger from her chest. He commented, saying that she was lucky she didn't remove the weapon herself, because the pointy spikes down the shaft of the blade would have proven fatal if she had.

After wounds were sown and cleaned, the healers used the most potent herbs, potions, pastes, and salves to ensure that any infection would be killed off, and healing would happen at twice the normal pace. The healers left when they were through, so that the wounded would get some rest and many guards were posted outside.

A few blocks away from the healer's cottage, Nails hid on a rooftop waiting for Seiles to return. The assassin was already two hours late, so he figured he must've met a similar fate as Lope.

Down below, guards constantly patrolled the streets looking for him. He was sure that no one was allowed to enter or leave the city, so he'd have to wait a few days before making an attempt to escape. He thought about attacking Strom and the others in the healer's house, but when the rains began falling in heavy sheets, he decided to seek shelter instead of freezing to death.

"This is why I hate big towns," said Tonles. "You never know where an attack is coming from and by whom. Let's leave as soon as we're well enough, with or without Jacko and Sun."

"Sounds good, but let's wait outside of the gates for a couple of days." Konafar added.

Strom looked over at Breen, who was trying to put something into her eye. "What are you doing?" He asked her.

"I'm trying to put this lens into my eye."

The men looked at each other and then back at her. "And why?" Tonles asked.

Breen didn't answer, nor stop, until she placed it into her eye. "Got it." She said and closed her eyes, knowing they would water.

"What do they do?" Konafar asked.

"Hopefully they'll allow me to understand this book." Breen said, then reached into her bag, took out the Tirip book and opened it. For many minutes, the words remained unchanged, then suddenly they began to swirl together and changed into a language she could understand. However, the symbols remained unaltered.

"Did they work?" Konafar asked, after seeing a strange look upon her face.

"Sort of, I can understand the words but not the symbols."

"Maybe I can send one of our scholars to assist." Captain Strom offered.

The men fell asleep shortly thereafter, while Breen remained and awake riveted to the pages for a few more hours until sleep took her as well.

Earlier in the day, Jacko and Sun left the Order and headed back toward Mirkin. Their journey was quicker than expected, and they arrived at the city gates a few hours before nightfall. Several guards approached and told them no one was allowed to enter or leave the city anytime soon. When Jacko inquired why, the lead guard said that there was an incident, permission was only granted by the captain, and he wasn't available during this time. Jacko showed him the armband, and one of the guards remembered giving it to him and allowed them to enter.

Jacko asked about the incident again, but the guards told them they would have to find out on their own. Sun and Jacko eventually found out there were two attacks that day. One was a fight at the Inn of the Lion involving Captain Strom, several guards, and a big stranger with a mighty sword against an old man who was really an assassin in disguise. The other occurrence happened in the market square, but the details were sketchy.

"Do you think it was Konafar?" Jacko asked feeling sick in his stomach.

"We'd better go over to the healers' and find out."

They made haste and when they arrived, several guards blocked their way.

"This is as far as you can go." One of them said with his sword drawn and pointed at them.

"We need to know if our friend is inside." Jacko said.

The guard looked at them suspiciously, and more guards approached and began surrounding them in a semicircle.

"I'd advise you both to leave." Another guard said with his spear leveled.

Sun tugged Jacko's arm trying to get him to leave, but Jacko pulled his arm away.

"Can you at least tell me if someone named Konafar, Breen or Tonles is inside?"

The lead guard looked at them and then at the armband.

"What's your name?"

"Jacko and this is Sun."

"Wait here and don't leave." He said and walked into the cottage.

Several minutes later the guard came back out escorting Tonles, who was limping noticeably.

"I see you finally returned." Tonles said to them.

The guards relaxed and lowered their weapons.

"What happened to you?" Sun asked.

"Let's go inside, we have much to discuss."

Tonles led them to the back room. Breen was awake and reading her book. Konafar was lying down, and Captain Strom was still sleeping.

"We leave for one day, and all three of you almost get killed." Sun said.

Breen looked up and smiled when she saw them.

Konafar sat up. "Good to see you boys." He said.

"What happened?" Jacko asked.

"It's all Tonles' fault. He did one good deed and almost got killed yesterday." Breen said.

"And she was hurt protecting me." Tonles added.

"Are you okay?" Sun asked Breen when he saw the large bandage on her chest.

"Never mind her, take a look at my wounds." Konafar said showing them his many stitches.

"How did you get hurt? I thought you were tougher than that." Jacko said to him.

Konafar chuckled. "Let's just say Tonles pissed off a few people that knew some assassins."

"Is everyone going to be alright?"

"We'll be fine." Breen said. "We just need rest."

Sun studied the partially dissolved floorboards and door. "What did this to the room?" He asked.

"That was me. I bought something earlier that can dissolve anything it touches and used it on another assassin."

"So all the assassins are dead?"

"There's one more." Tonles paused. "We'll get him in a few days." He smirked.

"Did you find what you were looking for?" Konafar asked.

Sun made sure Strom was still asleep before answering. "Not enough to clear his name."

"Keep looking, I'm sure you will." Tonles said.

Sun and Jacko stayed for another hour or so before returning to their room. Along the way, Jacko contemplated telling the captain that Torhan was his friend, but under the advisement of Sun, he thought better of it. Before falling asleep, they agreed to tell the others they were leaving in the morning without them.

The morning came rather quickly; Jacko and Sun washed, dressed, ate breakfast, and then walked over to the healers' house. Tonles and Captain

Strom had already left; while Breen and Konafar were still waiting to have their wounds checked.

"We're leaving today." Sun said as soon as they entered.

"Why?" Breen asked.

"Because they need to find their friend before I do; that's why." Konafar answered for them.

"He's right we do, because he's in grave danger and I don't mean from you." Jacko said looking at Konafar.

"How so?" Breen asked.

Sun pulled the diary out of his backpack. "Read this when you get a chance." He handed it to her.

"What is it?"

"It's the girl's diary."

"Does it clear your friend?"

Sun shook his head. "Not really. I think there was something very strange going on with the priest before Torhan even arrived."

"How will you find Torhan?"

"They'll never tell you." Konafar smirked.

Sun looked at him. "You know we did think about leaving without saying good-bye to you, but instead we decided that we have nothing to hide and still believe that he's innocent." Sun paused. "He went toward the town of Snowdrift to help some child come out of a deep sleep. We don't know why, but I'm pretty sure all of this is tied together somehow."

"Can I go with you?" Breen asked.

"I'm afraid that we don't have time to wait for you to heal."

"I'm already on the mend." Breen tried rising, and her injury caused her enough pain to force her to sit back down again.

"Please tell Tonles we said good-bye." Jacko said to them.

"Will we ever see you again?" She asked.

"Meet us in Snowdrift if you like, and if we have to go somewhere else we'll leave word at the inn as to our whereabouts."

"Breen," Konafar began, "after Tonles and I, are better; we're going after the Red Knight, so if you don't want to come with us, then you should go with them or stay here in Mirkin."

Breen got up from the chair wincing all the while.

"What are you doing?" Jacko asked her.

"I'm not staying in this town and I really don't feel like going after that Red Knight character, so I am coming with you."

"Are you well enough to travel?"

"I'll manage."

"Good luck." Konafar sincerely said to them.

"And to you as well." Sun replied.

"No hard feelings."

Jacko and Sun took turns clasping arms with the big man and Breen kissed him on the cheek.

On their way out the door, the healers gave Breen some herbs to ingest daily until her wound was healed, and a knap sack full of healing supplies. She thanked them and donated fifty gold pieces to their Order. Before leaving town, they purchased horses and supplies for their journey ahead.

A few hours later Tonles returned.

"Where's Breen?" He asked when he noticed she wasn't sitting on her chair.

"She went with Jacko and Sun to Snowdrift."

"Snowdrift? Why?"

"That's where Jacko's friend went. They said for me to tell you good-bye."

"Did you want to go with them?"

"I was thinking we should go after the Red Knight and kill him for what he did to Runit." Konafar grinned.

"Just the two of us?"

Konafar nodded.

"I like those odds."

Both men laughed and then coughed due to their wounds.

"When do you want to leave?" Tonles asked.

"In a couple of days. I want to get drunk and fool around with some of those girls back at the inn. Did you find anything out about the assassins?"

Tonles smiled. "I went back to the marketplace and found the building the assassins used to attack me. While I was searching for clues on the rooftop, I came across a homeless person who happened to be hiding there the same day they attacked me and saw everything. He told me what they looked like, what they were wearing and their names"

"Did he say anything else?"

"Yes. After they attacked me, the bum got curious and followed them to their hideout."

"Did he show you where it was?"

"After I paid him a few coins."

"Do you think the assassin left town?"

"No. I think he'll wait until things cool down."

"Well let's go pay him a visit." Konafar said; smiling sinisterly.

A few nights later, in the worst part of town, Nails returned to his cramped, two-room dwelling, carrying a bag of loot from a recent robbery. On his way in through the window, the bag clanked against the windowpane, making enough noise to alert the two men waiting for the assassin.

Nails had grown sloppy over the last few days, mainly because he was growing impatient waiting for things to quiet down enough for him to leave. His assumption was right about Seiles. The assassin did die the same night as Lope, and it made him uneasy with no one around.

After lighting a candle and spilling the contents of the bag onto the table, he sat down and marveled at the wealth of diamonds, gems, platinum and gold rings, sapphire necklaces, and variety coins. He was in the middle of counting his good fortune, when he saw someone moving off to the right of the window. Nails slowly reached under the table and did not find his trusty crossbow.

"I guess you're looking for this?" The intruder said.

Silhouetted in the darkness, Nails could see the crossbow pointing at him. "What do you want?" He said in a calm voice.

"It's not what I want, it's what he wants."

From the bedroom Tonles walked into the room and Nails knew, without even turning around, who that person was.

"You know, for an assassin you're not very good at concealing your whereabouts or, for that matter, coming into the room quietly."

Nails reached for the dagger sheathed on his side and as soon as his fingers wrapped around the hilt, Tonles whacked his right collarbone with a wooden stick and shattered the bone. Nails screamed and fell off of the chair and onto the floor, reeling in pain.

"You bastards!" He yelled at them.

Konafar walked over and shot him with the crossbow in his left arm and then bent down close to his ear. "We're going to have a good time," he said.

"You should have finished the job when you had the chance." Tonles added.

"You kill me then." The assassin countered bravely.

"In time coward. In time."

Konafar grabbed his jaw, forced his mouth open, placed a very long knife into his mouth and skillfully removed the assassin's tongue. "We wouldn't want you to scream too loud now, would we?" He asked.

Tonles took on a sinister look, and both men went to work. They tied him securely to the chair and began removing his fingers by using two very dull knives. He silently screamed as the digits crunched under the weight of the blades until they eventually were removed. Konafar smiled and then tied rope around his arms and legs in various places, in anticipation of where they were going to chop next, so that he wouldn't bleed too quickly.

Tonles handed him a small axe, and together they began their fun. Nails' hands were chopped off followed by his arms in three different places and then his feet and legs.

Finally, when Nails was nothing more than a stump, they removed his eyes and proceeded to cut him down the middle of his chest and hack off his head. Covered in blood and gore, they gathered the stolen items and left the room.

Join me for the next installment of:
A Demon's Quest: The Beginning of the End (Vol III)

- Will Gilex successfully lead his men on their perilous journey to find the Circle of Demise? And what of the Book of Blood? Will it, as promised, release the Blood Knights from their eternal slumber?
- What does the Lord of the Mind have in store as he focuses his attention on the town of Redden?
- Now that Torhan helped Dybbuk overthrow Raum, will that be the end of their relationship or will the demon want something more after returning to the place known as the Other?
- Will Torhan and Katara succeed in saving Sybil from her condition or did they make a grave error by dealing with the mysterious hermit Tole?
- After Jacko's daring escape from Slyantom, will he be hunted down by the fox and share a similar fate as his teacher Ma?
- Will Norice succeed in ending his nightmares? And what about the mysterious entities known as Celthric and the Presence? What plans do they have for Norice?

The plot thickens; the journey will be memorable, and the fight scenes will be intense.

Stay tuned and enjoy the ride…

ABOUT THE AUTHOR

Charles Carfagno Jr. is a native of Pennsylvania. He's been writing since 2003 and currently writes on nights and weekends in addition to his successful day job in the IT field. He is really excited to share his writing with the world and would love to hear from and interact with other authors and readers

ADQ Series:
A Demon's Quest The Beginning of the End Volume 1
A Demon's Quest The Beginning of the End Volume 2
A Demon's Quest The Beginning of the End Volume 3
A Place Called the Other
The Awakening
The Dawn of the Chosen One
Lost Soul

Short Story:
The Wayward Knight

Standalone Novel:
Madness of My Dreams

Email:
cdcinkwell@gmail.com

Web Site:
https://demonsquest.com/

If you haven't signed up for my mailing list, you're missing out on exciting news, free stuff, and articles.

www.ingramcontent.com/pod-product-compliance
Lightning Source LLC
Chambersburg PA
CBHW071302170626
46809CB00001B/327